Praise for *The Bird King*

"A gorgeous, ambitious meditation on faith, platonic love, magic and even storytelling itself, with a trio of unforgettable personalities serving as its beating, endlessly vital heart. *The Bird King* is a triumph—immersive in historical detail and yet, in many ways, it could have happened yesterday. Wilson has once again proven that she's one of the best fantasy writers working today, with a book that's just waiting for readers to get happily lost in its pages."

—*BookPage*

"[A] head-spinning blend of realism, fantasy and history . . . deeply imaginative."   —*Washington Post*

"[*The Bird King*] thoughtfully contemplates the meaning of love, power, religion, and freedom. But even while exploring all of these heavy issues, this is a fun, immersive adventure that moves at a brisk pace through lush settings, across dangerous terrain, and eventually out to the open sea . . . [that] will appeal to readers of S. A. Chakraborty's *City of Brass*, Helene Wecker's *The Golem and the Jinni*, and Naomi Novik's fairy tale-esque *Uprooted*."

—*Booklist* (starred review)

"A metatextual bildungsroman about religion, war, and love . . . what good fantasy should do, after all: offer us alternative worlds that, no matter how fantastic, turn the mirror back on ourselves."

—*Los Angeles Review of Books*

"Teeming with secrets, violence, and magic, G. Willow Wilson's characters come alive in a backdrop of fifteenth century Spain that is at once sinister and lush. By turns humorous and heartbreaking, the world held me captive and I'm haunted by it still."

—Sabaa Tahir, author of *An Ember in the Ashes*

"[A] swashbuckling second novel amid an epic clash between cultures."
—*Publishers Weekly*

"A lovely fable set during the final days of the Reconquista . . . [*The Bird King* is] a thoughtful and beautiful balance between the real and the fantastic."   —*Kirkus Reviews* (starred review)

"*The Bird King* takes a time period that's passed into cliché and makes it new and strange again. In this novel, the real runs alongside the fantastic, one informing the other, G. Willow Wilson's eye for detail and her titanic imagination pumping together like pistons. She's incredible. *The Bird King* has big things to say about states and souls, and it's going to take you on a rollicking ride while it says them. I was fascinated and riveted and, by the end, deeply moved."   —Robin Sloan, author of *Sourdough*

"No summary, no quotes, no analysis of this book can communicate the all-encompassing pleasure of reading it, paragraph after paragraph, page after page. Read it, and treasure it."
—*Arts Fuse*

The Bird King

Also by G. Willow Wilson

The Bird King

G. Willow Wilson

Grove Press

New York

Printed in the United States of America

First Grove Atlantic hardcover edition: March 2019
First Grove Atlantic paperback edition: February 2020

Library of Congress Cataloging-in-Publication data is available for this title.

ISBN 978-0-8021-4829-2
eISBN 978-0-8021-4684-7

Grove Press
an imprint of Grove Atlantic
154 West 14th Street
New York, NY 10011

Distributed by Publishers Group West

groveatlantic.com

20 21 22 23   10 9 8 7 6 5 4 3 2 1

For my daughter Safeya, who fought and lived.

Though you have struggled, wandered, traveled far,
It is yourselves you see, and what you are.

—*Farid ud-Din Al Attar,*
The Conference of the Birds

Iberia
and the
Island of Qaf

Spain
and the
Island of Antillia

Antillia

Airá   Antuáb

Ansátli   Cón

Ansódi

Ansésseì

Ansólli

Qaf

Iberia

The Maghreb

Chapter I

29 August 1491 AD / 23 Shawwal 896 AH

Hassan was deep in prayer.

He was not on his knees, however, nor bowing toward the gold-painted medallion in the southeast corner of his workroom that marked the direction of Mecca: instead, he sat on a cushion in the sun with his legs crossed and a string of wooden prayer beads slack in his hand, his eyes focused on something Fatima could not see. She had no way of knowing how long he had been in this attitude when she slipped into his room from the shaded path she had taken through the Court of Myrtles. Sweat glowed on Hassan's brow where the sun struck it, and when she stepped on his shadow with her bare foot, the marble tiles beneath were cold. He might have been there for hours, so lost in God that he had trouble finding his way out again. His lips were parted as if he had gone silent in midconversation. A holy name had been upon them, but which?

"*Hayy,*" whispered Fatima, guessing. Yet that syllable fell on the wrong part of the palate.

"*Hu*," she guessed again.

There was a door in the western wall that hadn't been there on Fatima's last visit to Hassan's workroom. It stood innocently ajar in its frame of white plaster, a simple rectangle of wood dotted with iron fastenings, its edges cracked and dry, as if it had been there as long as the Alhambra itself. Fatima stood on one foot and leaned sideways to peek around the door, shielding her body behind its solid bulk to protect herself from whatever might lie beyond it.

Her worry proved needless. Through the doorway was the familiar lantern-shaped interior of the Mexuar. Fatima could see the outline of its low balcony and the wood-paneled ceiling above, the small dais at the end of the chamber where the sultan sat to hear lawyers argue and listen to the complaints of his viziers. It was empty now, though it still smelled of incense, as if the men who spent their days in its rich gloom had only just left.

It was certainly the Mexuar, yet the Mexuar was on the far side of the Court of Myrtles, in the opposite direction.

"It was convenient to have a door there."

Startled, Fatima turned and shut the door abruptly behind her. Hassan was alert now, smiling, his velvet brown eyes lucid and unperturbed, as though falling into trances and summoning passageways out of solid walls were ordinary late summer occupations.

"I got tired of walking back and forth across the courtyard in this heat," he continued, getting to his feet. "Why should the royal mapmaker burn to a crisp when all the other viziers and secretaries sit inside all day? Anyway, it doesn't matter. I can easily make another."

Fatima looked over her shoulder and saw only the chalky plaster wall she had seen a hundred times before, uninterrupted by passages of any kind.

"I didn't mean to close it," she said. "It's just that you startled me."

"I said it doesn't matter." Hassan, yawning, shuffled to the stone balustrade that ran the sunny length of his workroom. It looked out through a series of slender wooden arches onto the green hedgeways that gave the Court of Myrtles its name, separating Hassan's quarters from the courtyard in the briefest and most ceremonial way. Maps drawn on parchment and vellum and linen were piled along its length and weighted with stones, their edges curling in the heat while the ink upon them dried. Hassan teased one out from under a chunk of quartz and held it up critically. A grid of streets traversed its length, terminating in what to Fatima's eyes looked like a river.

Fatima went to her favorite spot along the balustrade, yawning herself as Hassan's indolence grew contagious. She pushed aside a pile of paper and sat on the sun-warmed stone, allowing herself, finally, to relax.

*   *   *

The golden hour bloomed around them, yellowing the myrtle hedge, the grass, the marble paths, the long reflecting pool that pointed through the courtyard toward the administrative wing of the palace. It was in this vaporous time of day, when Lady Aisha liked to doze, that Fatima would often slip away from her mistress, leaving the harem through an unguarded door used primarily by the washerwoman and the unfortunate pox-scarred girl whose job it was to empty the stool chamber. It led to a windowless corridor which was entirely dark when the doors at either end were closed, and emerged, by Hassan's benevolent wizardry, in the Court of Myrtles, allowing Fatima to come and go without being seen, provided she kept her wits.

"You're fond of that spot," said Hassan. He threw the map he was holding at his worktable, where it unrolled only a little, and picking up a small lead compass, began to clean his fingernails with the sharp end. "But you'd better get down from there before someone sees you."

"Why must I?" Fatima countered.

"You know very well why. You're not allowed to be here unchaperoned, let alone sprawled languidly across the railing of my terrace. The poor dear sultan looks weak enough as it is without you thwarting his authority as well. The Castilians and the Aragonese surround us on all sides, the Egyptians have abandoned us, and the Turks have swallowed all of Anatolia in one gulp. Our Abu Abdullah is master of an empire that no longer exists. His own mother overrules him when it suits her. Who is left to take him seriously if not his concubine? I pity the fellow."

Fatima sighed in irritation. She swung her legs over the edge of the balustrade and sat up, shaking the hem of her loose linen trousers to free the belled bracelets that lay in the hollows below her ankles.

Hassan chewed at a tuft of beard beneath his lower lip. His hair, another of his perversities, was reddish, the legacy of a Breton grandmother taken hostage in some war or other. Fatima was not sure he was handsome—his nose was too sharp, his eyes were too small, his complexion was too hectic, apt to turn red and blotchy on the frequent occasions when he was flustered. No, he was not handsome, yet he was the only man she had ever come across who did not desire her, and for that, she forgave him many things.

"Have you brought me anything?" he asked now, his voice boyish and pleading.

Fatima pointed to his worktable: in a handkerchief was a small, sticky pile of orange-scented sweets.

"Bless you," said Hassan fervently. He picked up the handkerchief and began to shovel its contents into his mouth.

"Slow down," said Fatima, laughing at the droplets of honey that clung to his beard. Hassan made a face at her.

"I forget you aren't starving," he said. "You live in the harem eating honey and playing the lute and mincing around in silk slippers all day, while the rest of us are chewing old shoe leather. You might at least have the grace to pretend to suffer. We're under siege, after all. The sultan will be forced to accept terms from King Ferdinand and Queen Isabella at any moment."

"Would you trade, then?" asked Fatima, her lip only a little curled. "I'll happily do your job and starve if you'd like to do mine and eat well. You can listen to Lady Aisha insult people all morning, mend dresses all afternoon, and then—" Here her voice caught in her throat. Hassan studied her with one ruddy eyebrow raised.

"And then lie with the sultan all night? I'd trade you in a flash, Fa, in an absolute instant. My God! Those melancholy lips. What? Don't you think he's handsome?"

Fatima thought nothing. Her body felt suddenly heavy and sluggish, like some unfamiliar borrowed thing growing damp in the heat. She hung above it in the air, tethered to it only loosely, and wondered whether she would find the sultan as handsome as Hassan did if she had a choice in the matter.

"Fa? I'm sorry, my love. Don't look like that. I didn't mean to upset you. Fa——" Hassan pressed an anxious kiss into her palm.

Fatima took a breath.

"Choose a bird," she said, changing the subject. It was the way all their conversations went now: the palace, rambling as it was, had grown cramped under siege, the air perpetually stale with the shut-up breath of a hundred half-starved mouths. Every conversation became an argument. It was safer to retreat into the games of their childhood, as they did more and more; into the stories of creatures that could fly away. Fatima returned to her patch of sun on the balustrade.

"A bird," she repeated.

Hassan chewed for a moment before answering.

"Red-crested pochard," he said triumphantly. Fatima laughed at him.

"That's not a real bird," she said. "You're just being an idiot."

"It is so a real bird! It's a sort of duck, a waterbird. We used to have them on my mother's land, near the lake. Hunters would come to trap them in the fall." In the course of their game, they had long ago run through all the ordinary birds, and had since moved on to more exotic ones.

"Very well," said Fatima. "The pochard, the pochard—since he has a bright crest, perhaps he was vain, and when the other birds sought him out to accompany them on their journey across the Dark Sea to the mountain of Qaf, he refused. Why should he leave his home, where everyone flattered him and he could spend all day preening? The people of Qaf might not appreciate his plumage as they ought to do. But the hoopoe—"

"Ah yes, the hoopoe is my favorite."

"The hoopoe, who also had a lovely red crest, scolded the pochard for his shallowness."

"And then?"

"I don't know." Fatima yawned. The effort of thinking too hard in bright sunlight had begun to tire her. "But surely something silly enough to be called a pochard wouldn't survive such a long journey. Make me a new map. I want a view."

"A view," muttered Hassan. "You've got lovely views already. Look at this view! Look at the fork-tailed swallows flying low across the reflecting pool! At night, you can see a second field of stars in the water. Enjoy it now, Fa, for soon it'll all belong to Castile."

Fatima had never seen the Court of Myrtles at night, when being caught anywhere outside the harem or the sultan's own rooms might have real consequences, but was in no mood for another argument.

"Will you make me a map or not?" she demanded.

"Yes, of course I will. A map. A view." Hassan wiped his hands on his coat and sat down at his worktable, a low, scuffed oak plank balanced on two stacks of books. Fatima knelt beside him. She liked to look at his face while he worked, to see it transformed by the fervent, vacant light that possessed him as his maps took shape. His lips would part in an eager smile, like a child's; there was a bliss about him when he worked and when he prayed that made Fatima wonder whether he knew what it felt like to have one's faith in the goodness of things removed. Fatima herself had never knelt upon a prayer mat except grudgingly. Obedience was demanded of her all day and on many nights; when she was asked to pray, she had no more left in her. Hassan was different. His obedience was always rewarded; whatever force he called upon in his silent moments always answered him, and though the maidservants might giggle and the undersecretaries scowl when he passed, he did not appear to notice.

Hassan was the only person she allowed herself to watch so openly. To look too long at anything male, the palace guards or the cook or the dozens of secretaries and lawyers who populated the Mexuar, was to commit impertinence; to look too often at the freewomen she served was to risk rebuke. Hassan was different. It gave her a stealthy joy to sit beside him and try to translate the lively conversation between his brows, and know he neither minded nor misread her. He saw her looking now and smiled absently, reaching out to stroke her jaw with one finger. He took out a charcoal pencil and whittled it with a small knife, removing a fragment of paper from one of the untidy stacks on his desk. His fingers—the length and suppleness of which almost redeemed his awkward features— moved quickly across the page, defining the right angles of a short hallway, the nautilus-shell progression of a flight of stairs.

"This is the way you came," said Hassan. His pencil rasped and shed black ash. "This is a door. It leads off the small antechamber in the harem where the washerwoman keeps her baskets and soap. That is the door you want."

Fatima teased the map from beneath his fingers and slipped it into the embroidered V at the front of her tunic, against her skin. Hassan watched her and sighed.

"You're wasted on me," he said. "God's names, look at you." He took her hands in his and turned her to face the sun. "Look."

Fatima smiled. She was not above admiring herself. Her eyes were so black and unflawed that they swallowed the afternoon light without reflecting anything, like a night without stars. They floated in a face whose pallor might make another girl look sickly. There was no high color in her lips or cheeks of the kind the poets praised: her beauty was something too remote for poetry, a tilting symmetry of jaw and cheekbone and dark brow. Only her hair seemed to be made of anything earthly: it billowed over her shoulders in a mass of dense sable curls that snapped the teeth of every comb Lady Aisha had ever taken to them.

The effect of it all was singular. Whenever Fatima encountered newcomers walking the halls with her mistress, they would invariably stop in their tracks, put one hand on Lady Aisha's arm, and ask, *Where did you get her?* And Lady Aisha would say, *She is Circassian.* And whoever it was would raise one eyebrow and say, *Ah.* It was always the same: *Ah.* Much was contained in that single syllable. *Ah!* All are equal before God, but some are meant to be bought and sold.

Yet Fatima was the only Circassian slave left in the Alhambra, the others all freed or sold off to pay debts, dispersing across the Strait to safety as the armies of Castile and Aragon pressed down from the north. There was no one left to praise her in the language of her mother, whose face she could barely remember and whose homeland she had never seen. She was the last reminder of a time of prosperity, when pretty girls could be had from Italian slave merchants for unearthly sums; there had been no money and no victories since. The Nasrid sultans, heirs to the empire of

Al Andalus, to the foothold of Islam in Europe, seemed to have few talents beyond losing the territories won by their forefathers. They preferred beauty to war: they had built the Alhambra, every brightly tiled inch of which represented the lifework of some master craftsman. That was all Al Andalus was now: an empire indoors. A palace, and inside it a garden, and inside that, a beautiful girl.

"Men would risk their fortunes for an hour in bed with you," said Hassan, letting her arms drop. "Other men."

"You risk your fortune for my company," said Fatima. "I love you better than I would love those other men."

Hassan leaned back in his chair and rubbed his eyes with charcoal-blackened fingers.

"You're a good friend to me, Fa. Friends are rare these days. But you've got to be more careful. Laughter carries in the Court of Myrtles, and a woman's laughter most of all. It may carry all the way to the sultan's quarters—and then what?"

Fatima shrugged. "The sultan knows what you are."

"Still, I'm not allowed to speak to you alone. It doesn't look proper. And there is a vizier coming in half an hour who wants a map of the Castilian military encampment at Rejana. So." He pressed a kiss into the palm of her hand. "Go look at your view."

Fatima touched the map beneath her shirt: it crackled under her fingers.

"What kind of view is it?" she asked. "Is it very pretty? Is it possible to see the sea from there?"

Hassan was bent over his work again.

"The sea is miles and miles to the south, across the mountains," he muttered. "Not even I can give you a view like that."

*　*　*

Fatima left the way she had come. There were no guards posted in the Court of Myrtles, situated as it was near the heart of the palace, away from the bustle and heat of the Mexuar, where the sultan heard petitions with his viziers and lawyers and secretaries. Yet it was summer, and the black-green bushes for which the courtyard was named were in full bloom, attracting a throng of beardless students set loose from their daily lessons. Fatima could see their skullcaps bobbing above the flowery hedge. She pressed herself against a pillar in the arched colonnade that framed the veranda and held her breath. There was a volley of laughter from among the myrtles. One of the students began to recite his lesson, half singing a few rhymed verses of the *aqeeda* in an unsteady tenor. Other voices joined his, growing softer as the students drifted away toward the shade of the interior rooms.

Fatima pressed her cheek against the tepid stone and forced herself to relax. The door by which she had entered the courtyard stood nearby: it was not quite closed, so that she would make no noise when she returned. She passed through it on light feet and shut it behind her. The hall was plunged into darkness. She felt her way by memory, breathing the austere reek of dust and disuse, until she came to a meager strip of light on the ground that signaled the door to the harem's antechamber. Here she paused. No noise came from beyond it, no footfall interrupted the light beneath it. Fatima found the latch with her hands and pushed the door open.

The antechamber was just as Hassan had described it, though Fatima had trouble imagining why he had ever set foot there himself:

buckets and rags were piled in one whitewashed corner along with stoppered jugs of vinegar and a tub of congealed soap. An arched passage tiled in blue and gold led to the common room of the harem itself. All these things were familiar. The small door set in the right-hand wall was not.

The door was half of Fatima's height and whitewashed, like the walls; a crossbeam cut across it diagonally, giving the impression of a cupboard or closet. She opened it, expecting stacks of bed linen. Instead she saw a flight of narrow stone stairs. Grinning to herself, Fatima ducked through the door, ascending the steps two at a time, pleased by the soft scuffing noise her feet made on the flecked stone. The edge of each step was worn to a fine polish, as if the staircase had been traversed by hundreds of pairs of feet, yet there was no sound save from her own movements, no hint that anyone else was near. There was strong light coming from somewhere; squinting upward, Fatima thought she saw a window or perhaps an empty arch. She put one hand on the wall—wide blocks of red-brown stone, in all respects a proper old wall like all the proper walls of the old palace—and crept along, stepping gingerly on each unknown surface until she reached the top. Her last step was only a half step: there were an odd number of stairs, which pleased her. They ended in a sort of parapet, a small, square tower room with a narrow window in each wall. Fatima picked one and stuck her head out.

She was greeted by a blast of wind. It smelled of dry hay and cold water: the summer heat would not last much longer. Fatima took several deep breaths, enjoying her own dizziness, blinking in the sharp-shadowed afternoon as the objects below her resolved themselves. She was in a southeast corner of the palace. Her window overlooked the low roof of the Mexuar and the wide lawn beyond, burned yellow now as it always was by summer's end. The hill spilled away beneath it, cloaked in dark elms, tapering off at the smoke-clad medina in the valley below. There were the red-tiled roofs of villas; the cramped knot of houses that formed the Juderia. She could see tiny green squares of garden in innumerable courtyards; below these, in the lap of the valley, the shallow river that supplied them.

In the distance, where the ground flattened out, there was the wide plain of the Vega de Granada, smudged here and there with plumes of smoke and dotted with the skeletal remains of siege engines. Beyond these human outworks were the shoulders of the mountains that receded south in a humid haze, as ambivalent toward their Catholic rulers as they had been toward their Muslim ones, their pelt of pines and grasses unfurling toward a pale and factionless sky. They ended in nothing, for Fatima's knowledge of the world did not extend as far as the sea. Yet standing there, she thought she detected the faint, damp scent of salt carried on the wind from the south. Hassan had tried his best.

Fatima pulled her head back inside with a feeling of regret. Lady Aisha had undoubtedly awoken by now and gone to bathe; her bondswoman's absence would be noted. She turned away from the window and hurried down the echoless stairs, her footfall landing strangely in her ears, emphatic, like a kind of speech. At the bottom, she lifted the latch on the little unassuming door and passed through, shutting it behind her as softly as she could.

She stood on tiptoe in the antechamber with Hassan's map in her hands. If she misplaced it, she would forget: the location of the door would grow indistinct in her memory, and she would confuse it with other doors that led to other rooms. She had, on occasion, attempted to find her way back to the places Hassan marked for her without a map, and inevitably got herself turned around or found familiar rooms rendered suddenly alien. It was unpleasant to be lost in your own house. She did not intend to repeat the experience.

Fatima folded the map and tore it along the crease, then folded it and tore it again, until she was left with a pile of tiny fragments. These she let flutter to the ground. Straightening, she smoothed her tunic and trousers, setting off down the tiled hallway that led into the harem itself. She did not look back: she knew well enough what she would see. The wall would fold up without a sound, as if it was made of ether, and the door would vanish, leaving no trace of itself but motes of dust suspended in the light.

*　*　*

The hall leading off the antechamber ended in a modest courtyard. It was ragged now with the remains of summer roses, their hips gone bulbous and discolored for want of pruning. When Fatima passed, Lady Nessma, the sultan's half sister, was sitting on a pile of cushions in a shaded annex, strumming a lute that was slightly out of tune. Her hair was loose, spooling on the cushions like a crumpled skein of black silk. It was her great vanity. She was surrounded by a gaggle of cousins from the countryside whose families had deposited them at the palace, siege notwithstanding, to procure husbands. They had been talking when Fatima approached, but hushed when they saw her, averting their eyes and stifling giggles.

"Girl! Where have you been?" demanded Nessma. She rose, her plump, pretty form snug against the green silk robe that confined it, and handed her lute to the air. It was snatched with dogged promptness by an overdressed girl sitting at her feet. "My stepmother went to the baths alone, cursing you the entire way."

"I was in the antechamber," said Fatima truthfully. "There was a stain on my tunic, and I went looking for some soap."

Nessma pursed her lips. Fatima knew she was weighing the satisfaction of demanding to see the treated stain against the risk that Fatima would complain to the sultan in bed.

"You shouldn't be so careless about your things," said Nessma finally, having decided upon a line of attack. "You think that because you've ensnared my brother, you can walk around with your nose in the air like a lady and dirty the clothes we give you, but if you ruin your tunic, I will see to it that you don't get another. We're at war, in case you haven't noticed. We can't afford to keep idle slaves in silk."

Fatima wondered whom Nessma was trying to impress. She lifted her chin. She had discovered that by walking softly and deliberately and keeping her eyes fixed on the person to whom she was speaking, she could inspire an odd kind of terror in whomever she chose. It came, she supposed, from her own ambiguity: she was something the sultan owned, not dissimilar from the weary-looking pair of trained cheetahs that had come home with him from Genoa, along with Fatima's mother, when Fatima was still a secret tucked inside her mother's womb. Yet Fatima too might be carrying a secret, as far as anyone knew. If that secret were viable and male, it would catapult her over all the other women of the palace and place her on a par with her own mistress, the sultan's mother. She could be despised, but not dismissed.

"Do you have anything else to say?" she asked Nessma. Nessma flushed a little brighter. Her lower lip, pink and slick with whatever she had been eating, quivered slightly. Fatima reached out and wiped it clean with her thumb. She almost wished they would come to blows, giving her an excuse to rake her nails across the exposed column of the smaller girl's neck. It seemed more honest. But Nessma only gritted her pearly teeth and trembled. Satisfied, Fatima turned on her heel and walked across the courtyard, through the weedy roses.

"Her heart is as black as her eyes," came Nessma's voice in her wake, much too loudly. "She will never learn obedience, poor thing—she hasn't got enough wits to know what's good for her."

Fatima forced herself not to pause or give any sign that she had heard. She walked on stiff legs through the common room on the far side of the courtyard, where the flyblown remnants of lunch were waiting for the last of the harem's serving women to clear them away. Here she steadied her breathing. A glossy, neglected dish of olive oil caught her eye: it was startlingly green, the first pressing of the season, and so heady with the scents of fruit and sap that it perfumed the room. A fly had succumbed to its temptations and was slowly drowning, wheeling in frantic half circles with its swamped wings. Fatima picked up the dish. It was glazed in contrasting shades of blue, which merged with the green of the oil and lent it a subterranean aspect, like a mountain spring she could hold in her hand. She plucked out the drowning fly by one wing.

"Sorry, little fellow," she said, flicking it away. "You've got to fight or flee like the rest of us."

The fly landed on the tiles at her feet and hobbled onward. Fatima stepped over it and made for the baths.

✳   ✳   ✳

Lady Aisha was soaking in a hip-deep stone tub when Fatima arrived. Her white hair, still thick, was gathered into a knot at the top of her head; her eyes were closed, as though she had fallen asleep. Fatima's eyes lingered on the knobs of bone that protruded from her mistress's shoulder and spine, demarcating the flesh that hung upon them, giving her body a weightless, fragile appearance. It would be easy enough to lean on that shoulder, or to wrap her hand in the ample white hair and watch the bathwater close over it. A scant minute would suffice, for how long could an old woman hold her breath? A far more cynical kind of violence had been waged to procure Fatima's mother, whose parents had sold her, screaming and wailing, to a Genoese man when starvation loomed, yet the thought of such a brisk, tidy end to Lady Aisha's life filled Fatima with sudden exhaustion. She could not act in the way she had been acted upon, and wondered, as the steam escaped from a star-shaped skylight overhead, whether this made her nobler than her keepers, or simply less decisive.

"Sit," came Lady Aisha's voice, still clear and deep. She patted the edge of the tub without opening her eyes. Fatima sat, avoiding the wet spot left by her mistress's hand.

"Lady Nessma says you came in here cursing me," she said. Lady Aisha clucked her tongue.

"Nessma exaggerates as usual. I may have cursed you once, but not continually."

Fatima rolled up her trousers and put her feet in the steaming water. It was strewn with lavender buds and dried linden, which clung in sticky clumps to the flesh of her calves. The task of cleaning the tub was, thankfully, not hers.

"You went to see our cartographer friend," observed Lady Aisha. Fatima no longer wondered how she knew these things. Lady Aisha had eyes everywhere, though how this was achieved remained a mystery.

"I like Hassan," said Fatima. "He isn't afraid of me."

"He ought to be." Lady Aisha opened one veiny brown eye to scrutinize her bondswoman. "If you like him, you shouldn't compromise his reputation—or your own, for that matter—by lurking about his rooms. A man of his peculiar gifts and inclinations can't afford scandal."

Fatima sighed and beat her head lightly against the flank of the stone arch behind her.

"I don't see why it should be a scandal," she muttered. "Everyone knows he doesn't like girls."

"You miss the point. For the sake of his dignity, we all assume he does like girls. That way, no one need make a fuss when men come and go from his quarters. But there must be a fuss if my son's own concubine visits him alone. It ruins the symmetry of the arrangement."

Fatima thought of arguing, then remembered where she was. The bathing room was built entirely of white stone and shaped so that a whisper carried all the way across it; secrets were exchanged elsewhere. She slumped, letting her legs slide farther into the water. For several minutes, neither spoke.

"How old am I?" Fatima asked, breaking the silence.

"Seventeen, my love. No—eighteen. No, I was right the first time. Your mother gave birth when the full moon of Ramadan fell on the first of May. That I remember distinctly."

"How old was she when she had me?"

Lady Aisha shifted in the bath, considering the question. A lock of white hair had come loose from the knot atop her head and trailed damply across her breasts, flattened by age and a succession of children.

"She must have been a bit older than you are now. Poor thing, what a muddle that was—solemn as the rain from the moment she arrived, and didn't tell anyone she was pregnant until it was obvious. Never spoke a word about your father. I imagine he was the Italian merchant who bought her in the first place. Though who knows? Perhaps she secretly took some handsome soldier for a lover on the journey between Sochi and Genoa. You must get your height and your temper from somewhere. Whoever he was, he was long gone by the time she arrived at the Alhambra." Lady Aisha frowned up at Fatima. "Why all these questions now, sweeting? Are you pregnant? Is that what this is about?"

"No!" Fatima clutched the edge of the tub reflexively. "No."

"That's a shame," sighed Lady Aisha, closing her eyes again. "I hope you'll conceive before that silly cow Hurriya does. She's desperate for a boy. Imagine her horror if her future glory was displaced by the son of a slave girl. Second wives, my dear! Second wives need keeping down."

Fatima kicked one foot restlessly. She wanted to reply that she desired no children, that the line between her own childhood and the role she occupied now was still unclear to her, but she knew better than to adopt this line of reasoning with her mistress. Still less could she admit to the little packet of herbs she had stolen from the apothecary and swallowed, in the dead of night, after she had failed to bleed during one particular moon, or to the upheaval that had come afterward, and the drying-up that had come after that. Instead, she kicked again.

"Don't, please, you're splashing me. Be a sweet thing and scrub my back."

Leaning across the tub, Fatima retrieved a sponge from a copper dish and squeezed it in the milky water.

"I hear rumors from the North," murmured Lady Aisha, pillowing her head on Fatima's knee.

"What rumors, Lady?"

"King Ferdinand and Queen Isabella have begun to expel the Jews of Seville and Córdoba and their other reconquered territories. They say there are priests riding about the countryside, lurking at the windows of those Jews and Muslims who converted to Catholicism in order to save their lands and fortunes."

Fatima rubbed Lady Aisha's shoulders with the sponge, careful not to chafe her delicate skin. Her mistress had aged rapidly in recent years. She was still slim and straight, her waist enviable, but a yellow pallor had settled on her face, and much of the anger had gone out of her.

"Why lurking?" Fatima asked, doing her duty to the conversation.

"To catch them in a lie, of course," said Lady Aisha. She gestured damply with one hand. "The priests wait for the poor fools to refuse a dish of pork or a glass of wine or to keep the wrong sort of sabbath. And then they burn them as heretics, leaving their lands and fortunes most conveniently unattended. They're calling it an inquisition, though I'm told the new pope looks very unfavorably upon the whole enterprise. It does no good to fake a conversion of faith. Remember that, my love. The people who want to burn you alive will find a reason to do it, whether you pretend to agree with them or not."

Though it was warm and stifling in the bathing room, Fatima felt a stealthy chill. The sponge in her hand was still on Lady Aisha's shoulder, dripping perfumed water into the pool below drop by drop.

"What's troubling you?" Lady Aisha asked in a voice that was almost kindly. "You came in here like a thundercloud and you've been frowning ever since. You'll get lines between your brows at this rate, and then where will you be?"

Fatima hesitated. Lady Aisha often invited confidences, but it was not always wise to indulge her. She thought of relaying Nessma's insults, but to Lady Aisha, who had never known how it felt to occupy a body that could be priced and sold like that of a goat or a tame leopard, it might look like whining. She thought of telling her mistress the truth, of attempting to describe the feeling that sent her to Hassan and his maps every day. Yet she didn't trust her own vocabulary. Whenever she tried to be poetic or philosophical, she ended up saying exactly what she meant in the plainest possible language.

"Hmm?" Lady Aisha was waiting for an answer, her eyebrows raised half-mockingly.

"I don't want to be a slave anymore," said Fatima. The plainest possible language. She cursed herself silently.

Lady Aisha gave an undignified snort.

"How modern that sounds," she chortled. "This is what happens when you let a concubine read Ibn Arabi and Plato and sneak about with cartographers. What on earth would you do with your freedom, if it were granted? A small house, a bad-tempered husband, a child every year—what happiness could that bring you? Here you are clad and shod in silk, taught to recite poetry and to do sums and figures. You listen to music and wait upon great ladies. What does the world offer you that you don't have here?"

Fatima looked around helplessly. The serving woman came in to light a clot of incense in a brazier. Its scent wafted up and mingled with the steam to form a dense, sickly smell, like flowers left too long in a bowl of water and gone to rot.

"Air, my lady," said Fatima.

Lady Aisha did not pretend to misunderstand her. She peered up at her bondswoman and pursed her thinning lips.

"Interesting," she said.

Chapter 2

The sultan called for her that evening. Fatima was sitting in the doorway of Lady Aisha's private room leafing through an illuminated volume of Hafez when his messenger arrived—a boy of eight or nine, young enough to act as liaison between the world of women and the world of men. The book was written in Persian, a language that Fatima did not know but which shared enough vocabulary with Arabic to be intriguing. She sounded out the foreign words, encountering a term here or there that was familiar, so that the poems became abstract impressions of themselves: love, seeking, oneness, restraint, prayer. It was a pleasant way to spend an idle evening, especially one as fine as this: through the open door she could see the courtyard, lit now by innumerable little oil lamps, and the cicadas, which had been riotous in early summer, had subsided to a pleasant hum. The interruption of the boy annoyed her.

"Mistress Fatima," he panted. "His majesty is asking for you. Now, or sooner."

Fatima clapped the book shut. The child was currying favor; she was no one's mistress, not even her own.

"Call me girl," she muttered, standing up. "Everyone else does."

"Girl Fatima," said the boy obediently, "his majesty—"

"Yes, fine, all right. I'll follow in a minute."

The boy disappeared. Fatima padded into Lady Aisha's room and returned her book to the carved wooden case where it lived with a dozen others: the Ibn Arabi and Plato for which Lady Aisha had mocked her, but also several volumes of *jahili* poetry, and a large, odd-smelling book of folktales called *Alf Yeom wa Yeom*. Tucked beside them was an unbound folio of yellowed paper, the first pages of *The Conference of the Birds*.

She ran one finger over the untidy leaves, pressed indifferently between two ledgers of receipts to keep them upright. They had been bought, at great cost, from one of the only booksellers the palace had seen in recent years: a man so elderly that the Castilians had not seen fit to embargo him as he passed through their siege lines. So elderly, in fact, that he had been allowed into the harem itself to spread his wares at Lady Aisha's feet. It was a paltry offering. There had been a few books of *fiqh* by lesser scholars, an illuminated French *chanson* or two. There were even, as Fatima remembered, shipping manuals and fat lists of tariffs, the source or interest of which remained unclear. *The Conference of the Birds*, though incomplete, was the only thing in which Lady Aisha had seen any value.

She bought it with a melancholy she did not bother to disguise. Fatima read the first pages to her mistress so many times that she had committed them to memory. But the story stopped just as it began to get interesting. It unfolded in the time before Adam, when the animals could still speak. The birds, forever quarreling with each other, had long been without a ruler, and gathered together in their meeting place to decide what must be done. The hoopoe, wisest among them, urged the rest to put aside their differences, and rallying the hawks and owls and sparrows and ravens, they set off to the land of Qaf to find their lost king. Yet there was no hint of what befell them next. The folio ended in midverse with the birds in flight over the Dark Sea. There were no teachers left in the palace, aside from a sheikh or two to instruct the sons of bureaucrats. If anyone knew the rest of the poem, no one was telling.

Unsatisfied, Fatima brought the folio to Hassan, who could make anything funny. He had not disappointed her. That was the beginning of their game: they chose a bird, gave it a story, and sent it off, like a child's paper sparrow, into the air. They had not, as yet, bothered with an ending.

Fatima smoothed the loose pages of the folio so that they were even with the edge of the bookcase. She couldn't stall much longer. Lady Aisha was lying on her divan with one arm thrown over her face, as if even the feeble light of the oil lamp above her was too much for her eyes. Fatima touched her foot.

"I'm going," she said.

Lady Aisha turned on her side with a sigh.

"This is a reminder," she said to Fatima, reaching out to stroke the papers she had just arranged. "This is what it looks like to live at the end of history. There was a time when the most flea-ridden dervish could recite the entirety of *The Conference* from memory. Now, like the birds, we've forgotten more than lesser peoples have ever remembered."

Fatima waited for the moment to pass.

"Wear something pretty," murmured Lady Aisha.

Fatima was already pulling her tunic over her head, scanning the fat wooden wardrobe that stood against one wall for something suitable. She selected a robe made from sheer, gauzy fabric, embroidered with thread-of-gold stars.

"There's no point," she said, wriggling into it. "It's just going to come off in five minutes, and it's nearly too dark to see."

"It'll give you confidence," said Lady Aisha. "He favors you more and more, my dear. My son is not a profligate man—unlike some other sultans one could name. He beds his two wives. Not even that—he beds one wife, as Lady Maryam has seen fit to shut herself away from the world since her children were taken. He beds you. And maybe, once in a while, he beds that blonde Provençal war captive who refuses to learn Arabic *or* Castilian—but she's not important. The point is: freedom is well enough, but influence is better, and if you wanted it, you could have influence aplenty."

Fatima softened at the thought that her mistress had listened and understood. She did not want influence but didn't say so; instead she bent to kiss Lady Aisha's slender hand.

"Tell him to come and visit his old mother," said Lady Aisha, nestling into her divan. "He hasn't been to see me in a week." She sighed again, but she was smiling now. Fatima blew out the lamp and left.

*　*　*

The corridor that led to the sultan's private quarters was dark as Fatima walked along it; someone had forgotten to light the torch in the wall sconce midway. But there was a moon, and eddies of silver penetrated the latticed windows overhead, creating a feeble glow that kept Fatima from blundering into anything. She dragged one hand along the wall at hip level to steady herself. Her fingers accumulated the dusty residue of whitewash as she went, but then encountered something warm and sleek: the pelt of an animal. She clung to the wall and bit back a shriek.

"Dog," she gasped.

A shadow detached itself from the wall and came toward her, panting, its yellow eyes hanging in the dark like drops of molten glass.

"What are you doing here?" Fatima demanded, still in a whisper. She reached out her hand: the dog breathed on it happily. "How many times do the guards have to throw you out? They'll poison you next."

The dog shook itself and farted, as if to demonstrate its bravado. Fatima stuffed her hand into her mouth to keep from laughing. In the daylight, the dog was a mangy, jackal-like thing: head too large, limbs too long, giving it a strange, loping gait, like that of a crouching man. How the creature continually made its way into the harem was the cause of spirited debate. Nessma and her ladies pretended to be afraid of it, claiming it was the daytime shape of some ungodly thing, a jinn perhaps, who entered and left the harem by turning sideways into the realm of the unseen. Lady Aisha was perpetually offering to kill it herself with her own eating knife, but this was an empty threat: the dog adored her, and would sit at her feet with its eyes closed, just like a real courtier, when she played the lute.

"You have to go," whispered Fatima, tugging on the scruff of the dog's neck. "The sultan can't see you here."

The dog snapped at her hands. It smelled of sulfur and warm iron. "I'm not joking," said Fatima. "Go. I have things to do."

The dog groaned and ambled into the dark, its nails clicking rhythmically on the stone floor. Fatima waited until she couldn't hear it anymore before wiping her hands on her tunic and continuing down the hall.

The door to the sultan's rooms was slightly ajar when she reached it. Fatima cleared her throat to announce herself. It opened wider to reveal Abu Abdullah himself, clad for sleep in a white *izar* tied at his hips, falling in pleats to his ankles. Fatima studied his bare torso ruefully. He was handsome enough, and still young—young enough to sire many more children—but there was already gray at his temples, and his face, always a little too round for a sultan's, had acquired a permanently stunned expression.

"Good, you're here," he said, grazing her forehead with a kiss. "Come in."

Fatima slipped past him into the room. Abu Abdullah's sleeping chamber was modest, as he was: a cotton mattress on a low dais at the center of the room, the skin of a large buck he had hunted as a youth growing ratty on the floor. Fatima had long thought that if Abu Abdullah had been born a commoner, he would have been perfectly content as one of the farmers who lived outside his walls: florid, hardworking men with smallholdings and large families. Kingship did not suit him. He had no taste for fine clothes or complicated dinners. When, in her rare bouts of enthusiasm, Fatima called him by his name instead of his title, he did not reprimand her.

"I've taken you away from your books," he said now, his voice amused and sad. "I can always tell when you've been reading. You come in with this unmistakable look of irritation."

Alarmed, Fatima ducked her head and smiled through her lashes in her best imitation of modesty.

"Never, my lord," she said promptly. The sultan laughed.

"There's no use denying it," he said. "I know you too well for that."

Fatima wondered whether this was true. She looked away, not daring to meet his eyes, and her gaze fell upon a map on the far wall. It was one of Hassan's early efforts, the size of his signature betraying the self-confidence of a very young man. It was large: ten handspans tall and at least as many across. Sketched along its mottled vellum perimeter was the outline of the Iberian Peninsula; below that, the crown of Africa curved up to meet it at the Strait of Jebel Tareq. To the southeast was the Middle Sea, called *mediterranean* by the Catholics; to the northwest, the Dark Sea, represented by an expanse of nothing. The nothing was inhabited by a sea serpent. It drifted in the featureless ocean with an expression of inky melancholy, treading water at the edge of the world. Fatima often found herself staring at it on nights when she would rather have been somewhere else, imagining what it might be like to be the only figure in the blank space at the end of the map: solitary but free.

East of the lonely serpent, the Iberian Peninsula was shaded green to show the extent of the Empire of Al Andalus. Beginning at the feet of the Pyrenees, it swept south, shying away from the kingdoms of León, Castile, and Pamplona, curving west to encompass

Lisbon, and dipping south again to Toledo, Córdoba, Seville, and Granada. It was a good size. There were ports marked in blue and high roads in red, which, taken together, gave the impression of unassailable prosperity. The Catholic kingdoms to the north were small and divided. They posed no threat.

The map was four hundred years out of date.

"You often stare at that map," came the sultan's voice, breaking her reverie. "Why do you like it so much?"

"Why do you keep it?" countered Fatima.

"I suppose to remind myself of what I might have ruled," said Abu Abdullah, kicking off the scuffed leather slippers he wore. "To give myself a reason to rise from bed in the morning. I tell myself that Al Andalus is still here, even if it extends no farther than the walls of this city. And then I can sit on my divan in the Mexuar with a straight face."

His candor alarmed Fatima. She scanned the room for something else to talk about, thinking of all the poems she'd read about other concubines; tender, jeweled, unfailingly loyal women who lived in a golden era receding ever farther into the past, and whom Fatima would never resemble. Her eyes were drawn to a small table pulled up next to the bed, stacked with papers and waxy scrolls: he had brought his work back with him from the Mexuar, as he so often did now. Fatima clucked her tongue and knelt next to the table, tidying the heap of petitions.

"You know you're not supposed to bring all this to bed with you," she said. "Your physicians have said over and over that it disturbs your sleep and your appetite. How many of these couldn't wait until tomorrow?"

"Considering the centuries of mismanagement that brought us to our current apocalypse—all of them," said the sultan drily, throwing himself onto his bed. He still moved like a boy. Fatima had found it charming once, but lately it had begun to unnerve her.

"Have you eaten?" she asked, scrutinizing his ribs. Abu Abdullah rolled onto his back with a groan.

"Now you're just nagging. Good God! Even my slaves nag me now. What a farce." He caught her by the waist, pinching her in a particularly ticklish spot. Fatima shrieked and doubled over and let him pull her laughingly down beside him.

"My dress," she gasped. The thread-of-gold was heavy and sharp and dug into her shoulders.

"Is there no end to these small humiliations? Here." Abu Abdullah helped her pull the offending garment over her head. It ended up in a crumpled heap on the floor. Fatima put her face up to be kissed. His mouth was fragrant and bitter with the mastic powder he used to clean his teeth. The taste of it never failed to remind Fatima of the first time she had been presented to him, on a night two years ago when Lady Aisha had declared her old enough to share a bed: he had been affectionate but impersonal, handling her as deftly as he would a horse on a hunt. She had left him on sore legs, bewildered and imagining herself in love, imagining, in fact, many things that would never come to pass: confiding in him, advising him on matters of state, giving and receiving impassioned letters hidden in flowers, as lovers did in poems. But whatever desire she felt had faded when she realized he was still her king. She could neither initiate their lovemaking nor reject it: it was a transaction in which her desire played no part.

Now, as he pulled her beneath him, Fatima found herself staring at the oil lamp on the table nearby and calculating how long it would be before she could return to her poems. But Abu Abdullah did not touch her in the usual way: instead, he pressed his face against her neck and tucked the wool coverlet around them both.

"Will you stay here?" he murmured. "Sleep here, I mean."

"Of course," said Fatima warily, wondering whether this was some trick. "If that's what you want."

"Good. I'd like company just now."

Fatima traced a scar that wandered down his right arm, a legacy of his ill-fated battles in Castile, and felt uneasy.

"What's wrong?" she asked.

For a moment, he didn't answer her. There was kohl smudged in the creases beneath his eyes; his hair, which he wore long, hung in lank strands across his pillow. Fatima imagined him in a farmer's unbleached linen shirt, his head shaved and his golden skin dark from long hours working under the sun. He would have been happier, and not much poorer than he was now.

"There is no money left," he said softly. "And no grain. The shipment of wheat from Egypt that was meant for us was stopped at the port in Rejana by the Castilian blockade. I had a courier this morning. You won't be spared this time, you and the other women. We will not last the winter."

Fatima was silent. All her life, meals had appeared at their appointed times, made by unseen hands and unseen means. She knew, or rather sensed, that the rest of the palace had been hungry for some time—perhaps even the sultan himself had missed meals, if the hollows between his ribs were any hint. Certainly Hassan was always eager for whatever she brought him. But the harem had remained apart, supplied in all seasons with bread and oranges and meat, even if there were fewer and fewer maids to serve it.

"We'll be fine," she said with more confidence than she felt. "Every year your viziers wring their hands and say it's the end of the world, but it never is. Granada is still here. We're still here. We'll be all right, surely."

She felt him shake his head.

"Not this time," he said. "Not anymore."

Fatima had never heard him speak so quietly. She felt a sudden pity for the man beside her. In other circumstances, circumstances in which she could say yes or no to the nights they spent together, she might well have loved him. The feeling was so analogous to desire that she pulled him toward her, sinking her teeth gently into the flesh of his shoulder. He caught his breath.

"Fatima."

"My lord."

He kissed her neck, pulling her upright, lifting her onto his lap. There was a frantic series of knocks at the outer door of the dressing room behind them. Fatima wanted to cry.

"Whoever you are, I'm going to have you executed," shouted Abu Abdullah.

The knocking continued. Cursing, Abu Abdullah rose, hopping awkwardly on one foot as he retied his *izar* around his waist. Fatima pulled the wool coverlet over her shoulders and followed him, hiding herself behind a large wooden wardrobe in the gloom of his unlit dressing room. Abu Abdullah yanked open the outer door.

"You are a dead man," he informed the trembling herald who stood in the hall.

"I'm sorry, my lord," the herald stammered. He was not quite a man—not old enough to have grown into a rather large nose—and he was so terrified that Fatima worried he might wet himself. "A Castilian delegation has just crossed through the Gate of Granada under a flag of truce. They're coming up the hill now."

"Coming *here*?"

"Yes, my lord. Half a dozen nobles, it looks like, and their outriders, and a baggage cart. And two women."

"What nonsense is this?" The sultan pounded one fist against the doorframe, causing it to rattle. "You, boy—"

"Rajab, my lord."

"Rajab. Wake up my pages. Wake the chief vizier, my private secretary—and get Hassan the Mapmaker, who is surely not asleep. I want to know where the rest of this *delegation* is hiding."

The hall was suddenly full of noise. The herald ran away, screaming orders, and was succeeded by the sound of doors opening and closing. Abu Abdullah slammed his own door, cursing again.

"Fatima!" he called.

Fatima presented herself.

"I need you to do something for me," said Abu Abdullah, cupping her face in his hands. "There's a party of Castilians at our doorstep, and for reasons that surpass my understanding, they've brought women with them—we'll have to put them up in the harem. They won't like it, but we have no other quarters for highborn ladies here. I want you to look after them. And keep an eye on my mother. She'll flay them alive if you're not careful. Can you do all that?"

"Yes, my lord," said Fatima, clenching and unclenching her hands. Abu Abdullah bent to kiss her.

"So young, and already so brave," he said. He looked as though he wanted to say something else, but hesitated and then turned away.

"Go down to the kitchens first and find out whether we have anything to feed them," he instructed her, grabbing her robe off the floor and tossing it to her. "Take my door, it's faster. We're not clinging to tradition tonight."

Fatima pulled on the wrinkled garment and set off into the hall. Men and boys in various states of dress were hurrying back and forth, knocking into each other and shouting accusations. None of them bumped into her, however, or even looked at her after the first startled glance of recognition. Fatima squared her shoulders and tried to appear nonchalant. She picked her way around a hastily discarded cup rolling about underfoot, its sticky green contents—emetic herbs, by the smell—congealing rapidly in a series of male footprints.

"Hsst! Fa!"

Hassan was billowing toward her like a wayward bonfire, his curly hair standing on end above a suspiciously pink face. Fatima felt herself flush.

"You're out of your senses," she hissed, pulling him into an alcove. "You can't just wave me down like a peasant. Didn't you tell me to be more careful just this afternoon?"

Hassan only grinned, watching the commotion in the hall with almost hysterical glee.

"Are you *drunk?*" asked Fatima.

"As a bandit," snickered Hassan.

"You're a madman. You know there are sheikhs at court dying for an excuse to have you flogged."

"I don't care," said Hassan. "It was very, very good wine."

Fatima rubbed her eyes. She thought with longing of the sleeping mat waiting for her at the foot of Lady Aisha's divan.

"And the boy who served it to me—you know what I'm saying, Fa, you're such a clever girl—his name was Rajab, and he left and came back, and when he came back, he told me the most extraordinary thing. There are real live Castilians at our gates. I mean, they've been at our gates for decades, but now they're *inside* our gates, and the sultan wants me to come and show him where the rest of them are. But I need pencil and paper to show him that. It's not as if I *see* things. I'm not one of these unwashed mystics. My brain is in my fingers. That's all. In my fingers." He waved his hands to demonstrate.

"You need to get sober," said Fatima.

"When did you become no fun whatsoever? And what the hell are you wearing?"

Fatima looked down. The outline of her breasts was visible, in exquisite detail, through the sheer fabric of her robe. She clapped one arm over her chest.

"Get sober," she repeated, then hurried toward the kitchens, dodging page boys who balanced shoes and basins of rose water in their arms, and prepared herself for the sort of night that ran headlong into morning.

Chapter 3

The delegation arrived well after midnight, in a limp hour that was neither very late nor very early. Fatima waited for them in the Court of Lions with her mistress and the other palace women, all scented and dressed as if for a wedding: the freewomen veiled in pale silk, Fatima and the other slaves bareheaded. Lady Aisha had demanded that Nessma surrender her second-best robe for Fatima to wear. There had been an argument and tears, and now Fatima was balancing a copper platter of bread and olive oil in both hands, wearing a beaded azure gown that was too short at the hem and too big around the bust and hips. She could hear Nessma sniffling some distance behind her.

"No one is to bow," instructed Lady Aisha, her face inscrutable beneath a layer of saffron-colored gauze. "It's not our way. The men might bow to you, but you are not to bow in return. Do not look them in the eyes, even though they will stare at you without shame. They may stink, my dears, for northerners are not fond of bathing, but you are not to remark on the smell."

Someone giggled.

"And do not speak to the men, now or ever," said Lady Aisha sharply. "The men are not our concern. We are here to receive their ladies, whoever they may be. Nothing more."

Fatima shifted on her aching feet. The weight of the platter seemed immense, though it was only a little bread—so little, in fact, that the cook had artfully arranged it with sprigs of flowers to disguise its meagerness. Fatima craned her neck to stare at the torchlit colonnade at the far end of the courtyard.

"How much longer?" she asked.

"Hush, impudence," said Lady Aisha, poking her in the ribs with a bony finger. "What will the foreigners think if we can't even manage our girl slaves? Pretend to be meek and obedient for once in your life. It will be good practice."

A moment later, there were voices approaching, punctuated by the ringing clatter of armored feet. Abu Abdullah entered the courtyard in a fresh turban and an embroidered coat, his bodyguards following a discreet distance behind, carrying pikes. The sultan's head was bent toward the man walking beside him. He was short, the man was: square, perhaps forty, with a full head of sun-blanched brown hair and a trim beard. He was dressed in ceremonial armor, his half helm tucked beneath one arm. Other men, similarly dressed, followed behind him, and behind them their own guards, one of whom carried the colorless flag of peace.

"Ah." Abu Abdullah stopped when he saw Fatima and the others arrayed in front of the lion-headed fountain, as if he was surprised to see them there. "Of course, forgive me—these are the honored women of my house, who are eager to play host to your own."

"Ladies," said the square man beside the sultan, sweeping back his free hand and corresponding foot in an elaborate bow. Fatima willed herself not to laugh.

"May I address them?" asked the man, rising again, his face somewhat flushed.

"You may," said the sultan drily, "though I hope you will not be offended if they do not address you. These are my wives, the ladies Maryam and Hurriya. My half sister Nessma. And my mother, the lady Aisha. Also their companions and attendants."

"Of course," said the man, bowing again. "The lady Aisha's wisdom and—and shrewd diplomacy, let's say—are known to us in the North. We all remember who really brokered peace after the battle of Loja."

Fatima watched Lady Aisha out of the corner of her eye. Aisha inclined her head ever so slightly.

"My dear ladies," said the man, tugging nervously at the buckle of his breastplate, "I am General Gonzalo Marquez, and I come as an emissary of peace from their most Catholic majesties, Ferdinand and Isabella of Spain."

"Your masters are unknown to me," said Lady Aisha. Fatima looked up at her with alarm. Her eyes were steady and dark, unwavering. "I know a Ferdinand of Aragon and an Isabella of Castile, but not a Ferdinand and Isabella of *Spain*. There is no such country."

Abu Abdullah's face had gone rigid. Fatima had a fleeting, sui-cidal impulse to set down her tray and go to him, but rocked back on her heels instead, pressing the flesh of her bare feet into the flagstones.

"My beloved mother," said Abu Abdullah in a chill voice. "It's very late, and you're overtired. No one would think less of you if you went to bed."

"It's perfectly all right," said General Gonzalo with a smile that did not quite reach his eyes. "The lady is half correct. There was no such country. Once we were Castile and Aragon and León, and we fought each other instead of our enemies. But our kingdoms have put aside the sin of fratricide and united under the banner of faith, with the blessing of His Holiness the pope. So now, you see, there is such a country. It extends from the Pyrenees in the north to the Strait of Jebel Tareq in the south. You are standing in it."

One of the sultan's guards shifted on his feet, palming the leather grip of his pike. Abu Abdullah held up a hand in warning.

"I am standing in the Emirate of Granada," said Lady Aisha in a voice that was almost pitying. "Seat of the Red Palace, greatest of the kingdoms of Al Andalus. You can't frighten me by changing a few names on a map. For centuries you have harassed us, yet here we are—the last emirate of Muslim Iberia."

General Gonzalo laughed. There was no amusement in the sound of it, only a well-tended anger.

"If you were not a woman, I might be surprised to hear such naive talk in a city surrounded on all sides and starving," he said. "But since you are a woman, your loyalty to your son and your people does you credit. Nevertheless, you're wrong. This war might have started on a battlefield, my lady, but it will end on a map."

Fatima was close enough to Lady Aisha to feel a tremor go through her body, transmitted through the thin flesh of her shoulder where it brushed Fatima's own. Her outrage was carried with it, and Fatima felt herself tense. This was what it amounted to, all their prodigious honor: even as great a woman as Lady Aisha was easily silenced, and she, Fatima, carrier of platters and bather of backs, was never welcome to speak at all.

"This is no way to begin," said Abu Abdullah. His voice was thin and tired. "We'll speak in private tomorrow. For now, please—rest and eat." He gestured toward Fatima's farcical arrangement of bread.

Fatima looked from the sultan to the general and back again. She could not tell why she felt the sudden urge to defend her master against this foreigner, why she should interpret the insult against him as an insult against herself, yet she did, and desired to punish the general for it. She set her platter on the bare ground. Straightening, she pulled the hem of Nessma's gown up to her calf and pushed the platter toward the general with the ball of her foot.

There was a collective sound of disbelief, a half cry. Fatima thought she heard Nessma shriek, though it might have been someone else; she did not turn to look. The general went red from his neck to his scalp. Something quivered in the thick slab of his jaw.

"We came here under a flag of truce," he said in a low voice. "We came prepared for your Moorish perversities, but not to be insulted like this—to eat from a tray some whore of a slave girl has touched with her filthy foot—"

"No—please, let's not start a fight with the white flag hanging over our heads. It's blasphemous. Here—" It was a woman's voice, high and musical. It came from a dark blonde head that was moving between the shoulders of the men, who shifted aside to let it pass. A woman—a girl, perhaps, though she was dressed in a plain velvet gown of widow's black and her hair was gathered at her neck beneath a matronly white coif—emerged from the throng of armored Castilians and hurried toward the platter of bread. As she bent to pick it up, she looked into Fatima's face and smiled. Fatima stared at her, startled.

"I would have done the same in your place," the woman whispered. Her face was long but delicate, her eyes strikingly pale against the rosiness of her skin and the brassy gold of her hair. She might have been twenty or twice that; the strange composite of her features made her age unguessable. Smiling again, she took the platter and presented it to General Gonzalo. Fatima was looking at his feet, trying to appear chastened, but she could feel him staring at her. He dipped a hunk of bread into the olive oil with an air of funerary calm.

"My lord and ladies," he said in a voice that matched his demeanor, "this is la Baronesa Luz Maria Martines de Almazan, one of Queen Isabella's closest advisers, who is here at her majesty's personal request."

"Just Luz," said the woman, inclining her head. "I gave up my title when I entered the order of Santo Domingo. Catalina! Come here and hold this for the general, please. I'd like to greet our hosts properly."

A pillowy maidservant extracted herself from the crowd and panted toward her mistress, accepting the platter of bread with a sigh. Luz crossed the courtyard in her wide black dress, its hem stiff and faded with dust, and sank in a curtsey at Lady Aisha's feet.

"I've been waiting to meet you, senora," she said. "And my own mistress is eager to meet you as well. She asked me to tell you so."

"Please get up," said Lady Aisha drily. "We heathens bow only to God."

Luz rose, her expression unwounded. She grinned at Fatima.

"And who is she? So beautiful, and such a temper. Does she always frown like this?"

Fatima attempted to adopt an air of serenity.

"This is my bondswoman, Fatima," said Lady Aisha. "Please forgive her in advance for the many offenses she is preparing to commit. I have never punished her for anything. There's no point."

"Fatima," said Luz, as if the name were an incantation. Fatima met her eyes. They were pale, yes, but not blue or green; rather some indeterminate color, like wintery air.

"I thought you always named your slaves after flowers and precious stones," said Luz. "Coral and Amber and Jasmine. I've never heard of a slave with a holy name."

"I named her," said Lady Aisha. "She needed something sturdy, as it was clear her mother would not last. I thought the name Fatima would make her pious and gentle, like the blessed daughter of the Prophet. I was incorrect."

"She ought to have been a Hind," mused Luz. "Or a Zeinab or a Khawla, or some other warrior woman."

"You know our history," said Lady Aisha. She sounded surprised.

"I do," said Luz, inclining her head again. "But forgive us, Fatima—we're talking about you as if you're not here."

"Everyone does," said Fatima. This was true.

"Well." Luz put her arm through Fatima's. "We'll stop anyway. It's late—maybe we should leave the men to be offended elsewhere. Are we really going to sleep in the harem? Will Catalina and I be the first Catholics ever to see it?"

"Hardly," said Lady Aisha in a blithe voice, turning away and clapping her hands to startle the other women to attention. "We've taken plenty of Catholic ladies hostage over the years. Perhaps you can talk some sense into the one we've got now. She's pretty enough but as stupid as a sack of rabbits. Girls! Wake up. Let's show our guest to her room."

They began to move toward the colonnade. The maidservant, Catalina, shouldered a leather traveling trunk and two smaller sacks with impressive dexterity, huffing to herself as she trundled along under their weight. Fatima tried to catch her eye. She was in some way analogous to this doughy freewoman, if there were such analogies; perhaps, if Fatima were kind to her, she would confide the kinds of things that only servants know about their masters. But Catalina was staring fixedly at the ground, her gaze blank and indifferent, and seemed, as the sweat stood out on her brow, no freer than Fatima herself.

The moon, as Fatima shook out the bedding in the blue guest room, was peeping through the latticework over the window, reddening as it sank toward the harem walls. It would be dawn soon. Luz was sitting on a pillow, unpinning her coif. She looked as though she had been born to a life without chairs, though Fatima knew, or rather heard, that northerners sat at high tables to eat and work and dress. Their clothes reflected this uprightness and pinched them around the waist; Luz's own gown was not made for sitting on the floor, and bunched up unflatteringly. She did not seem to notice or to mind.

"This is a lovely room," she said, handing her coif and pins to Catalina and combing her bright hair with her fingers. "Such woodwork! Even the ceiling is painted. And these little brass lamps you use for light—so ingenious. Our candles stink—they're tallow, mostly, and burning sheep fat is not the most pleasant smell."

"You don't seem to like your own lands very much," observed Fatima, tucking a bedsheet around its stuffed cotton mattress. Luz laughed a little abruptly; Fatima had succeeded in annoying her.

"Do I give that impression? No, I love Castile. Mostly it's not as mountainous as Andalusia, but it has its own charm. Fields that go green during the rains and then smell sweet when the sun is on them. The town I come from has a wonderful crumbly old castle in it."

"Is that where you live?"

"Oh no. I live in a manor. Or I did—after my husband died, I gave it up and took vows with the Dominican sisters at Santa Maria Dolorosa. I live in an abbey now."

Catalina was holding a bone fine-tooth comb. Fatima took it from her with a smirk and began to run it through Luz's hair, starting at the ends as she did for Lady Aisha. Catalina pursed her lips.

"Are you a nun, then?" asked Fatima. "I thought all nuns wore habits."

"I'm a lay sister," said Luz. "That's halfway to a nun, I suppose. I took vows of poverty, but not of seclusion—I can leave the abbey and work in the world."

"As what?"

Luz only smiled. "What about you?" she asked. "Where are your people from? You're no Berber."

Fatima divided Luz's heavy hair into three parts and began to plait them together.

"My mother was an Abzakh tribeswoman," she said. "From the mountains that border the Black Sea."

Luz looked blank.

"I'm Circassian," said Fatima.

"Ah! Of course you are. A real Circassian concubine! You're a very long way from your homeland."

"I've never been there. I was born here, in the palace. My mother was pregnant when she was sold to the sultan. That's what they tell me, anyway."

"Born into concubinage," said Luz, tilting her head back like a cat. "In the North, we have a hundred naughty songs about women like you. You're supposed to be a naked, immoral, ignorant creature, yet here I find you speaking three languages and completely clothed. And a little spoiled, if you don't mind me teasing you about it."

Fatima did mind. "An immoral, ignorant creature would be a poor match for a sultan," she said, and then paused with Luz's hair between her fingers. "But I was naked enough just before you arrived."

Luz burst into laughter, her face an improbable shade of red. Fatima didn't see what was so funny. It was a statement of fact.

"Shut up—you shut your mouth." Catalina was suddenly talkative. Her voice was sonorous and fat. "Don't you have any shame at all? How dare you speak about your sin with her own lovely hair in your hands?"

Fatima was on her feet before she knew it, brandishing the comb. Luz caught her by the arm.

"Quiet, Catalina," she said sharply. "Keep your own mouth shut if you can't say anything useful. She doesn't know any better. Sit, please, Fatima—please. I apologize for Catalina. She knows nothing about your ways." She let go of Fatima's arm.

The anger that welled up in Fatima had nowhere to go; she stood for a moment longer, forcing herself to ease her grip on the comb, the teeth of which dug into her flesh like thorns.

"He's my king," she said when she trusted herself to speak. "Why should I be ashamed to serve my king?"

"You're not married to him," muttered Catalina. She began unpacking the leather traveling trunk with great energy. "That's a sin, is all I'm saying."

"Do you think your king goes to bed every night with his own wife?" snapped Fatima.

"That's enough," said Luz. Her voice was gentle, but there was a chilly authority in it. "Everyone is tired. It's time to sleep."

Fatima set the comb on the hammered brass tray near the bed that served as a nightstand. Once upon a time, the nightstand of a lady guest would be crammed with ivory-handled brushes and silver kohl pots and stoppered bottles of perfume, but these had all been sold off or appropriated by the palace women as their own supplies grew scarce. The serving woman had strewn the empty tray with dried rose petals instead. It seemed everyone thought they could disguise the palace's insolvency with handfuls of flowers.

Soon enough, they would all be naked and pathetic, just as in Luz's naughty songs, and then they would need nosegays as big as washing buckets to satisfy their offended honor.

"Is there anything else you need?" Fatima asked. "Before I return to my sin?"

Luz had been knotting her braided hair with a leather thong, and now she shook her head and sighed.

"No," she said, "only come here and kiss me before you go. I won't sleep if we part with bad feelings."

"I'm only a slave," said Fatima. "You don't need to kiss me goodnight."

Luz gave her a measuring look.

"I'm not sure how to treat you," she admitted. "Slave means something different among your people from what it does among mine. You're more like a beloved mistress, or a trusted lady-in-waiting, than what we would call a slave in my own country."

Fatima leaned against the doorframe, communing with the dying moon as it fell beyond the walls of the harem. She knew little about the laws in the North, but Lady Aisha had once told her that when it came to the rights of slaves, the prophet of the Catholics had been silent.

"You should go to Egypt," she said. "The sultan there is a slave, and so are all his viziers and generals. The state could sell them, but they are the state, so they are both slaves and masters. My own master hates them—they're your allies, or they might as well be. They just sent us a shipment of grain, but it was really meant for you, wasn't it? They must have known it would be stopped at the blockade. This siege is all anyone ever talks about."

She had said more than she meant to say. Anger had made the temptation too great. The first and greatest lesson Lady Aisha had ever taught her was never to disclose what the sultan might confide in bed. She worried for a moment that her slip might lead to real trouble, but Luz had a canny look about her, one that promised conspiratorial silence.

"You're quite a puzzle, Fatima of Alhambra," was all she said. "Quite a puzzle."

It was a dismissal. Fatima touched her lips and her forehead in the gesture of peace and slipped out of the room, crossing the darkened, empty courtyard toward Lady Aisha's room. The air was fresh: dew would fall soon, beading up on the yellow rose hips in the garden, the low bushes and little trees, the sun-faded cushions scattered on the ground. A few more weeks would bring the light frosts that presaged winter. Fatima paused at the threshold of Lady Aisha's room, unbalanced by the sudden silence. She was alone in a borrowed dress after a long evening: for Nessma, in better years, such a moment would be the end of some triumph, a wedding in which she had shone to perfection, a feast for a large party of guests she had hosted impeccably. For Fatima, it signified nothing. No one had gone to bed wondering where she was, giddily waiting to discuss the night's events with her. She had practiced being alone, and she had grown adept.

Fatima tugged irritably at the cuff of the dress, resisting the urge to pull it off, ball it up, and throw it into a corner. She hissed when her nail grazed the underside of her wrist, leaving a stinging line. Did she also want to strip off her skin? When she was a child, everyone in the palace wanted to touch her, from cooks to kings: they all marveled at the profound color of her eyes, the evenness of her complexion, yet they joked with each other about taming her hair and her temper. It rendered all their praise suspect: even compliments were infuriating. When Fatima caught sight of herself in the polished brass of a lantern or the still water of the reflecting pool in the Court of Myrtles, her beauty was indivisible from her anger. Fatima raised her wrist to her mouth and sucked on the scratch until the sting subsided. She would change nothing about herself. It was lucky, she thought, lucky she had learned so early that there was no solid ground.

A soft cry of surprise came from the far side of the courtyard, breaking the silence. Fatima squinted across the garden. Luz stood at the threshold of her room in a loose linen nightdress, her feet bare. She was staring at something dark and boxy a short distance away. It was the dog. It was standing perfectly still, looking up at Luz with its unblinking sulfuric eyes. Fatima caught her breath in alarm. The animal was not precisely tame, and might even be dangerous to someone unfamiliar—for all Fatima knew, it had scabies, or the spittle sickness, or the plague. Yet she didn't dare call out, worried that any sudden sound would frighten the dog into lunging or snapping.

Luz did not seem afraid. She drew up one foot. It was milk-white on top and rosy underneath; the foot of a saint from a sacked altarpiece. Sneering, she delivered two savage kicks, one after the other, to the dog's ribs.

The dog wailed once, sprawling on its side, feet scrabbling against the ground. Luz said something to it that Fatima could not hear:

it sounded like Latin, though she could not be sure. She stood frozen outside Lady Aisha's chamber, unsure of what to do or what to feel. Luz, white-robed and silent, retreated into her room. For a moment there was no sound. Then Fatima heard a series of stuttering gasps, like someone crying silently. Making up her mind, she slipped through the garden, pausing briefly behind a convenient pot of rosemary until she was sure Luz was not coming back. The dog, when she reached it, was attempting to stand, favoring one leg as it tried to make do with the other three. Ugly as it was, Fatima felt a stab of real pity: it was a happy creature and had done no one any harm.

"Sh-sh," she soothed, squatting down in front of it. "Be quiet and I'll help you."

The dog immediately ceased its odd little gasps and looked at her expectantly. Fatima hooked one arm under its chest and another around its hindquarters and braced herself, prepared for the thing to be heavy. It was not. She lifted it so fast that she almost fell over, clamping her mouth shut to keep from shrieking in surprise. The dog was as hot as a fever and just as intangible.

"You must be starving," she whispered to it, carrying it across the courtyard. "You weigh nothing at all."

The dog only grunted. Warmth and snoring issued from Lady Aisha's room: Fatima hesitated in the doorway.

"You have to be very quiet," she said. "Otherwise, I'll be in a lot of trouble."

The dog put its chin on her shoulder. Fatima maneuvered awkwardly to her sleeping mat and set it down. She was so tired that she threw herself beside the dog with a thump, and without bothering to change out of Nessma's dress, though she knew this would be a source of mild hysteria in the morning. She didn't care: the heat radiating from the dog's body lulled her heavy limbs into a stupor. She was dreaming before she even shut her eyes.

Chapter 4

She awoke to strong sunlight. Her hair was damp with perspiration, her dress—Nessma's dress—clinging to her torso like a silk noose. The heat was unbearable and suggested a very late hour of the morning; so late, in fact, that it might well be afternoon. Fatima sat up and ground the heels of her palms against her eyelids. Why hadn't anyone woken her? Lady Aisha's divan was awash in rumpled coverlets but otherwise empty. The dog, too, had disappeared.

Fatima struggled to her feet. Her head was pounding; she needed a tincture of willow bark. She peeled Nessma's dress over her head and draped it across Lady Aisha's divan to dry. There was a basin of rose-scented washing water and a towel, only slightly damp, on the floor near the foot of the divan; availing herself of these, Fatima washed her face and her hands and underneath her arms and between her legs. She yanked a plain tunic and trousers from the dressing pole and hurriedly pulled them on.

Laughter came from the garden. Shuffling out, shielding her face from the sun with one hand, Fatima saw Luz seated next to Nessma on a pile of cushions, plucking experimentally at a lute. She had forsaken her widow's gown for Andalusian dress: a light chemise beneath a long tunic like the one Fatima herself was wearing, the same loose trousers gathered at the ankle. She was even barefoot. Nessma was leaning toward her like an old friend, pointing at this lute string and that one, praising Luz's efforts.

"Just so," she chirruped. "Give me another two weeks, and you'll be playing ghazals."

"You're an excellent teacher," said Luz, laughing. "But I'm a very clumsy student."

Nessma's ladies tittered politely around her. A short distance away, in a safe patch of shade, Lady Aisha was reclining on a sheepskin with a book, ignoring her guest in a way that suggested there had already been an argument. Fatima padded toward her and lay down, setting her head in her mistress's lap.

"You got dressed without me," she yawned.

"I'm not yet incapable," said Lady Aisha, stroking her hair. "You were so fast asleep that I took pity on you. And I was somewhat alarmed to see that scrofulous *canine* in my very own bedchamber, as relaxed as if he was lord of the—"

Fatima sat bolt upright and looked Lady Aisha in the eye, pleading silently. She tilted her head toward Luz. Lady Aisha paused, eyes narrowed, and nodded.

"You'll tell me later," she said in a quieter voice.

Fatima's back was suddenly cool; a shadow had fallen over it.

"There you are," said Luz with a smile, standing above her. "I'm freshly amazed to see you in the sunlight. You know, Lady Aisha, I think you've managed to acquire the most beautiful girl since Helen laid eyes on Troy. Such cheekbones, such eyes—"

"Her cheekbones and her eyes are regularly praised," said Lady Aisha, leafing through her book. "If she hears it too often, it'll go to her head. Praise her good sense, if you must praise anything. It will serve her much better than her cheekbones will."

"You're absolutely right." Luz pulled up a cushion and sat down with a happy sigh. "My abbess would agree with you. She always says that beauty is a test, a temptation to the sin of pride. The nuns cut off all their hair when they take holy orders, and never touch a pot of rouge or white lead ever again. Yet they radiate beauty of another kind. Their faces are always full of light."

"You didn't become a nun," said Fatima, feeling suddenly shy. Her own face was not full of light.

"No," said Luz, eyes flickering a little. "Only a lay sister. I'm too restless to spend my days in a cloister, though the other vows came easily enough. That's my great failing. I need to move, to have many tasks and many uses. We are all made for different things— sometimes not the things we want."

Discomfited, Fatima studied the pattern of tiles on the ground. A small beetle was making its way toward her, its carapace iridescent in the sun. It hesitated when it reached the sole of her foot. Fatima laid her hand flat against her heel and coaxed the beetle onto it, then held it up close to her face. What was she made for? The beetle's carapace split apart to reveal ash-gray wings: it unfolded these and was gone in a moment, possessing no answers.

"What would you like to do today, Baronesa?" asked Lady Aisha. She clapped her book shut with an air of finality, as if the silence had become onerous. "How do you intend to spend your time with us? You'll forgive me for being blunt, but I'm still not certain why you're here. Whatever terms Ferdinand and Isabella have to offer us will surely be discussed by the general and my son, for I'm in no position to negotiate independently."

"Please call me by my given name," pleaded Luz. "I'm no more a baronesa than Fatima is. We're both servants who own nothing—I serve Our Savior as she serves your house."

"Very well. Luz." Lady Aisha's voice was getting dangerous. Fatima cast about herself for something to do or say. "I'm relying on your honesty."

Luz considered Lady Aisha's face for a moment, her own expression inscrutable. "I'm here on behalf of Queen Isabella, just as the general told you," she said finally. "She wanted to send you a personal emissary, queen to queen, mother to mother, as a show of good faith. I hope you'll consider me your advocate, even your friend. You will need friends in the weeks ahead, if you'll forgive my candor."

Lady Aisha threw her book at the ground. Fatima seized her arm.

"Would you like to see the rest of the palace?" she asked Luz, her voice louder than she had intended. "It's very large, and you should see it while the light is good."

Luz hesitated only a moment. "Of course," she said brightly. "If Lady Aisha will allow it. Are you permitted to leave the harem, then?"

"She may, and often does, provided she is chaperoned and guarded," said Lady Aisha, disengaging her arm. "I will trust you to chaperone her—as for the guards, they are just outside the doors, probably sleeping. Only the oldest and most lethargic soldiers are assigned to the harem. We like to avoid unrequited love stories when possible."

Luz took Fatima's hand.

"Do we have to bring guards?" she asked. "How likely is an assassination attempt in the next hour and a half? It's so hard to appreciate a view when there's a man with a pike standing behind you."

Lady Aisha pursed her lips.

"Take her to see the pretty gardens and the fountains and the baths," she said to Fatima in Arabic. "But keep her away from the Mexuar. Keep her away from my son."

*　*　*

The heat of the day intensified. Fatima longed for one of Hassan's maps, so she could take Luz somewhere unseen, preferably with good shade and scenery that would keep her occupied. She felt pensive, and when she was pensive she was silent; Luz seemed to understand this and did not press her for conversation. Fatima led her through one set of corridors and then another, and then a portico, making for the tower they called the Captive, where, according to legend, a particularly possessive sultan had marooned his favorite wife.

On the way, they passed the private rooms of those high func-
tionaries and royal cousins lucky enough to be quartered in the
palace itself and not down the hill in the city. Knots of men con-
gregated in the shade, fanning themselves with the ends of their tur-
bans, their quilted outer coats discarded beside them. Their voices
were low and tense. Here and there was evidence of a distressed
bureaucracy: papers carrying official seals lay in shredded heaps on
the ground or burned in braziers, the smoke jutting up toward the
cloudless sky in plumes. Conversation ceased when Fatima and Luz
passed, and some men, the obsequious ones, pressed their hands
to their hearts and bowed their heads.

"They treat you with a great deal of respect," Luz observed
quietly.

"They treat me with caution," said Fatima. "I might be carrying
the sultan's child, in which case I'm very important, especially if
it turns out to be a boy. Or the sultan might sell me tomorrow, in
which case I'm not important at all. They hedge their bets."

"He wouldn't really sell you, surely."

"No, he wouldn't. But he could." Fatima shouldered open a
brass-studded door at the far side of the portico. "This way."

The Captive loomed above them, square and unsympathetic.
No one lived in it now. Fatima had played in the shabby rooms
near the top as a child, watching the swallows that roosted in the
eaves shed dander and droppings on stacks of discarded furniture
from grander eras. She could hear them now, the males trilling in
their nervous way, the chicks that had fledged in the spring darting
up and down through the air, preparing to abandon their parents.

"What place is this?" asked Luz.

"The nicest prison in Al Andalus," replied Fatima. "But it's empty now. I'm not sure why I brought you here, to be honest. I used to play at the window where those swallows are diving. Sometimes the princes would come too—Ahmed and Yusef. They were only a few years younger than I am." She sniffed and rubbed her nose with the back of one hand. "You have them now, of course. As hostages."

"They're quite well," said Luz gently. "They and little Aisha. I saw all three of them at court just before I left. They want for nothing—you can tell their father that."

"He loves his children," said Fatima, feeling suddenly hostile. "He wants to see them, not hear about them from me."

"It is within his power to bring them home," said Luz, looking up at the Captive's empty-eyed windows. "You can tell him that as well."

Fatima, unprepared to enter into a negotiation, kept silent. The tower before her exhaled its peculiar fragrance of dust and lost time, communicating nothing.

"Show me something else," said Luz abruptly. "Show me your favorite place."

Fatima chewed her lip and tried to decide whether it was wise to take this request literally. There were plenty of charming porticoes and courtyards, though many of them had accrued a permanent veneer of dirt in recent months. And there would be men in all of them, lawyers and secretaries and clerks, possibly burning more papers, or removing valuables, or doing any of the other things men do when faced with the end of an empire. Perhaps after all it was safer to do as Luz asked.

"This way," said Fatima, turning back the way they had come. She slipped through the open door, past the pyres of burning deeds and letters, and led Luz toward the Court of Myrtles.

✻ ✻ ✻

Hassan was dozing when they arrived at his workroom. He lay draped on a mound of cushions with his tunic open and a wedge of charcoal dangling from his fingers, as if he had fallen asleep in midsentence. Fatima rapped on the wall to wake him. He jerked upright, his eyes wide and red, and looked from Fatima to Luz with dazed incomprehension.

"I wasn't asleep," he said.

"Of course not," said Fatima, coming into the room. She sat on the balustrade and drew her feet up beneath her. "I've brought you someone. She doesn't speak Arabic, so far as I can tell."

Hassan stared hard at Luz, blinking, as if trying to determine whether she was real.

"What have you been speaking to her?" he asked finally.

"Castilian," said Fatima. "We should probably behave ourselves. She's almost a nun."

"Then why is she dressed like an Arab courtesan? What's going on? Who are you? Where are we?"

"Fatima tells me you're the court mapmaker," said Luz, pulling out a cushion and sitting down. The sound of her voice made Hassan sufficiently serious. He crossed his legs, gesturing with a hospitable smile at the cushion to which Luz had already helped herself.

"Please sit," he said. "Welcome to Granada. I hope Fatima hasn't promised you anything grand—I could tell you my workroom isn't usually such a mess, but I would be lying."

"You have a superb view," said Luz, her eyes sliding charitably past the heaps of paper and sooty pencil cases. "The Alhambra lives up to its reputation. But how does a mapmaker come by such a large and well-situated room in a palace like this?"

Hassan shot Fatima a nervous glance. She shifted on the balustrade, unsure of what to say. She had not expected Luz to ask a real question.

"I'm very good at what I do," said Hassan. He tilted sideways, as if making a joke.

"You must be," laughed Luz. "The royal mapmaker at Toledo works in a closet, I think. So! You're Fatima's friend. I didn't know that was allowed."

"It's not," said Hassan, glancing again at Fatima. "Not since Fatima came of age, anyway. We met when we were children. Ten years ago, it must have been—I was fourteen when I was sent here to begin my apprenticeship. Fa was still only a tiny thing."

"I used to steal Hassan's charcoals," supplied Fatima. "To draw."

"The master cartographer—he's dead now—would have absolute fits. But he couldn't go into the harem, so all little Fa had to do was run there and hide in Lady Aisha's skirts. She got away with everything. Still does."

Luz laughed again, tilting her head back to expose a white throat delicately crisscrossed in blue. Fatima wondered for a moment whether she was flirting with Hassan. Hassan seemed to be wondering the same thing, for he became very interested in a stray thread clinging to the sleeve of his tunic, picking at it with his thumb and forefinger.

"Was she as beautiful a child as she is a woman?" coaxed Luz.

"Who? Fatima?" Hassan looked up again. "Not that I noticed."

"Are you saying I was plain?" demanded Fatima, throwing a wad of paper at him.

"She was a skinny little tyrant," Hassan said with a grin. "Always alone, or if not alone, then bossing the princes around. 'You! Ahmed! Fetch the milk.' That sort of thing. Never playing with the other girl children, or not that I ever saw, anyway. And then one day, it seemed, there was this siren swaying down the hall, who had grown half a foot overnight and could stop men in their tracks just by looking melancholy. And that was the end of the raids on my charcoal."

A silence fell that was not entirely comfortable. Fatima tapped her foot to make her anklets jingle.

"It's sad," said Luz. Fatima tensed, guessing what might come next. She was not prepared to accept another woman's pity.

"What's sad?" asked Hassan, oblivious.

"This," said Luz, gesturing with her hand. "All this is going to vanish in the next few weeks. The last summer of the empire of Al Andalus. I don't mind admitting to you—you've all been so kind—that I will mourn it when it falls. I wasn't expecting to be so taken with this place, or the people in it."

"We're not going away," said Hassan with a forced laugh. "Right? Your masters don't intend to put us all to the sword, do they? They could've done that at any time in these past ten years, since they conquered the last of our territories, but they haven't."

"No, of course not," Luz assured him. "My masters are hoping to avoid further bloodshed. That's why they sent the general—and me. Everyone would like to see a just end to this awful war."

"Then why—" Hassan tugged at his collar, looking pale. Fatima tried in vain to catch his eye. "Why should you mourn anything? What will be so different? Power will change hands—the key to the city will hang on one neck instead of another. But the rest of us will go about our lives as we have been—only we will pay taxes to someone else, with different coins. The era of sacks and sieges and slaughter is over. Yes?"

Deep, sympathetic lines had appeared on Luz's forehead.

"I wish it were that simple," she said. "Truly I do."

Fatima thought it best to put the conversation out of its misery.

"Come," she said, sliding off the balustrade. "They'll be serving lunch in the harem any minute, though it's likely to be bread and olive oil again."

Luz smiled, regaining her good humor, and reached for Fatima's hand. "You're in for a surprise, then," she said. "We brought a wagonful of cured mutton and apples and wheels of cheese."

Hassan's eyes went wide.

"Is there any for mapmakers?" he asked. "Or is it just for insolent concubines?"

"I'll have some sent here especially," promised Luz. She shook the dust from her clothes and turned away. As she did, the hem of her tunic caught one of the leaves of paper hanging over the worktable and pulled it free, sending it fluttering to the ground like a flag of surrender. In a moment, as if snatched from a dream, Fatima saw precisely what was about to happen.

"I'll get that," said Hassan, bolting up. But Luz had already bent to retrieve it. She held it in her fingers a moment too long.

"What is this?" she asked. Her voice was so different—lower, coarser, as if she had descended several rungs in rank and breeding—that Fatima felt a physical thrill of alarm. She reached for the map, but Luz held it away.

"What is this?" she asked again.

"It's a map of Zahara," Hassan said quietly. "In Cádiz."

"I can see that," said Luz. "But what are these?" She pointed to several snaking lines near the map's perimeter. Hassan gave Fatima a desperate look.

"Let's go," said Fatima, tugging on Luz's arm. Luz didn't budge.

"They're tunnels," said Hassan.

"Tunnels."

"Yes."

"Under the streets."

"Yes."

"Have you ever been to Zahara, Master Hassan? You're clearly no soldier, and you would have been almost a child when—during that awful battle to reclaim it. I would like to understand how you could possibly know what you know. Please illuminate me."

Hassan rubbed his eyes. "Why did you bring her here, Fa?" he said in Arabic. "You know how terrible I am at keeping secrets. Especially my own."

Fatima began to comprehend the enormity of her mistake. In keeping Luz away from the sultan and the viziers and their burning papers, she had inadvertently taken her somewhere yet more tender. There was nowhere safe. Perhaps that was the point.

"Please," said Luz. Her voice was gentle again, pained. "My late husband was at Zahara. We never knew how you—it was thought, we all thought, that the Moorish forces couldn't possibly prevail, and yet—"

"I make maps," said Hassan. Fatima watched him, her breath fast in her throat.

"I know," said Luz with a terse smile. "That much is clear." When Hassan said nothing more, she leaned forward and touched his knee with her fingers, her eyes like river stones, the weight of her gaze heavy.

"You can tell me," she said in a half whisper. "The more I know, the more I can help. I do so want to help. Aren't we all on the same side now that peace is inevitable?"

"You make peace sound like a threat," said Hassan with a fluttery laugh. Luz laughed too.

"Only for the very wicked," she said. "Let me be of use to you, Hassan. If I don't know what you're hiding, I can't intercede for you."

"Intercede with who?" Hassan asked, his voice trailing off. But Luz didn't answer. Instead she waited, and Fatima saw in Hassan's expression a fatal innocence. He never had his guard up; he had no guard at all.

"I make maps of things I've never seen," he said. "And sometimes of things that don't quite exist, except when I need them to. That's what I do."

Luz licked her lips. She set the map back on the worktable and smoothed its edges with her fingers.

"It's funny," she said. "For years, we wondered how Granada managed to survive while cut off from absolutely everywhere—to find new supply routes, to slip communications past our forces. We assumed you had an army of excellent spies. It never occurred to us that you might be using more arcane methods." She laughed. It was a merry laugh, a forgiving laugh. Fatima dared to hope that things could still be all right.

"How did you come by this talent?" asked Luz, riffling the uneven stacks of paper on Hassan's desk into neat piles. She wasn't looking at him; her voice was light, as if they were all friends. "If talent is the right word."

Hassan began to chew vigorously on his beard.

"It's all right," said Luz with a little smile.

"I don't know," said Hassan. "I've never been lost, and I've always liked to draw. That's as much as I understand. It's just something I do, something that happens."

"And the sultan has been protecting you."

"I don't know what that means. As long as I'm accurate, he leaves me alone."

Luz sighed and straightened, her face cheerful again.

"Please don't look so frightened," she said. "Secrets don't matter now—the war is over, or will be very soon. You caught me by surprise, that's all. I don't know what to think or whether I should be frightened."

"We all learned to get used to it," murmured Fatima. "To Hassan being Hassan. You might try that."

Luz took her arm.

"So practical," she said, following Fatima out of the room. "Not an ounce of romance in you."

* * *

Fatima led Luz back to the harem without speaking. Either some-thing terrible had happened or nothing had happened at all; she couldn't decide. What Hassan did had never seemed strange to her. She couldn't remember a time when he had not inhabited that room, scribbling away with his eternally darkened fingers. People in the palace understood him in their own particular ways: the sheikhs understood that his abilities were too valuable to be blasphemous, the servants that he was uncanny and a little high-strung. He was needed, and that made him familiar.

Yet Luz's silence worried her. She was uncanny herself: Fatima felt as if she had known Luz for years, long enough to make such silences feel like intimacy, yet they had been together for less than a day. She had an odd impulse to kiss the woman walking next to her, to thank her for handling the shock so gracefully. Perhaps, after all, Luz was telling the truth: perhaps she was here to help. Perhaps Lady Aisha ought to have been kinder to her.

Fatima leaned over and brushed Luz's cheek with her lips. Luz put her golden head against Fatima's shoulder. The maidservant, Catalina, ample and sweating, appeared in the doorway of Luz's room as they approached, observing their intertwined forms with an air of disapproval. The scent of boiling mutton perfumed the breeze and the sound of giddy laughter came from the courtyard; someone close by was playing a feast-day song on the lute. Fatima allowed herself to relax.

"You've been asked for, senora," said Catalina to her mistress. "By the lady Nessma."

"I'll be there in a moment," said Luz. She looked tired, as if the morning's exertions were too much for her. "I think I want my coif—it's so hot that I can barely stand to have my hair against my neck like this."

"I'll get it for you," said Fatima, "if you tell me where to look." She was rewarded with a beaming smile.

"Thank you, sweeting," said Luz. "It's in my trunk—it should be near the top." Twisting up her hair in one hand, she followed Catalina across the courtyard toward the sound of voices. Fatima ducked into the shuttered cool of her room. Catalina had unpacked Luz's dresses—all black and plain, some with ornamental lace along the sleeves—and hung them in the wardrobe, tucking the leather trunk neatly into one corner of the room. Fatima knelt and opened it. There was a clever tray fitted into the top for smaller items: pins for hair and brooches for cloaks, a gold wedding band in need of polish. Her coif was folded up on one side. Fatima lifted it out and held it up to her face: it smelled of Luz's hair. She folded it again and tucked it into her sleeve.

As Fatima closed the trunk, her eye fell on a square of paper with a red wax seal that had been concealed beneath the coif. It was emblazoned with a crest she didn't recognize: a cross flanked by a leafy branch and a sword. Underneath it was written a phrase in Latin letters:

TRIBVINAL DEL SANTO OFICIO

Fatima sounded out the words beneath her breath. She could speak Sabir and Castilian well enough, but reading them was tedious. Lady Aisha was constantly imploring her to improve her comprehension, but since the Andalusian translation schools had long since rendered all the great Hellenic works into Arabic, Fatima had never seen the need. Now, in the grip of a powerful curiosity, she regretted it.

The serving woman was calling everyone to lunch. Fatima rose and left the room, wincing as the tiles underfoot went from cool to hot. She tiptoed across the courtyard in order not to scald herself. Lady Aisha and the other women were sitting in the common room beyond, leaning on cushions and rugs, a great brass platter of cooked meat and rice between them. Fatima felt her mouth water. She slipped in and sat down beside her mistress.

"How was she?" asked Lady Aisha in a low voice, handing Fatima a bowl of food.

"Fine," said Fatima. "She was fine. Only—"

"What?"

"She knows about Hassan."

Lady Aisha popped a piece of mutton into her mouth and chewed with noisy relish.

"That's unfortunate," she said. "But possibly inevitable. Did she speak to anyone else? A clerk, one of the secretaries?"

"No."

"Good." Lady Aisha wiped her mouth with a handkerchief. "We may be all right, then."

Fatima scooped up a mouthful of rice with her fingers. It was redolent of sheep fat and sea salt. She licked each finger clean. She wanted to tell Lady Aisha that Luz had behaved well, that she had been nothing but eager and kind, but thought better of it.

"What's a *tribunal del santo oficio*?" she asked instead. Lady Aisha froze with a piece of bread halfway to her mouth.

"Where did you hear that?" she demanded.

"I read it," answered Fatima, startled. "It was on a letter in Luz's trunk."

Lady Aisha said nothing for several moments. She set down her bowl and began to clean her fingers.

"Tribunal of the Holy Office," she said lightly, dipping her hands in a dish of rose water nearby.

"What's that?"

Lady Aisha picked up her bowl and set it down again, as if she couldn't decide whether or not she was hungry.

"I never used to underestimate people," she said. "I must be older than I think I am. She's very clever, this Queen Isabella of *Spain*—or if she isn't, there are very clever people advising her. I assumed the general was their hawk—that they sent their military man to bully our military men. But they know us better than we know ourselves, it seems. They know my son does not love his viziers or his generals. The people he loves are here, in the harem. They sent their dove to the men. The hawk, they have sent to us."

Fatima was not often afraid. She had never known a time without war; when it was not outside on the battlefield, it was inside on the birthing bed, or in the winters when the very young and the very old and the very ill died in their sleep without a sound. Yet now she had a sick feeling, as though she were looking off the edge of a tower. She swallowed to keep from gagging.

"I don't understand," she said. "What does that letter mean? What does it mean about Luz?"

Lady Aisha resumed her lunch, scooping up a quivering mass of mutton fat with a fragment of bread.

"It means that Luz was sent by the Inquisition," she said.

Chapter 5

The moon rose early that night. It lay fat and red in the clear sky, a solitary blemish unattended by stars. Fatima found Luz in the courtyard staring up at it. The garden was softened by lamplight, its straggling roses and withered palms rendered less offensive than they seemed in daylight hours, when the neglect was palpable. Fatima felt a strange, dislocated ache. Even the things with which she had grown impatient—this courtyard, this garden, the many restless hours she had spent there—seemed precious now that she knew she would lose them. The back of Luz's golden head, made pale by the dim evening, mocked her. No kindness was ever freely given: each followed from its own secret ambition. Fatima knew this, yet somehow Luz, who was so unlike Nessma and the others, had caught her off guard. There was a chill in the garden, a finality, as if the diminutive figure in black had drawn all the warmth from it, and all the memory of warmth. Fatima felt her lip tremble. No one was coming to save them. No one was coming to save them.

Luz's hair was plaited for the evening. She played with the frayed end of her braid, looking so like a little girl that Fatima hesitated, biting back the furious speech she had prepared in her mind.

"What do you call the game you play with Hassan?" Luz asked, as if continuing a conversation she had begun in her head. She held out her hand for Fatima. "The one with the naming of birds."

"It's not a real game," said Fatima after a baffled silence. "It started as a joke. There's a long poem by Al Attar about a party of birds who go on a journey to find their lost king. Lady Aisha bought the first few pages. We could never find the rest. So we've been making it up as we go."

"A shame," said Luz, half to herself. "It's always helpful to know how things end." She looked over her shoulder with a puzzled frown. "Why are you standing so far away?"

To her horror, Fatima felt tears prick her eyes.

"You're an inquisitor," she said.

Luz looked back at the moon. "Only priests can be inquisitors," she murmured. "I have no title."

"But you're still . . ." Fatima had begun to shake. She wrapped her arms around herself to keep it from showing. "You said we should think of you as a friend. An advocate. Those were the words you used. You were lying."

Luz turned, wide-eyed, and crossed the courtyard to Fatima. Gently, she unclasped Fatima's hands and took them in her own, rubbing them as if to make them warm.

"I am your friend," she said. "That wasn't a lie. It's because I'm your friend that I want—more than anything in the world—for you to accept your Savior, the Son of God. I can't bear the thought of you in hell, Fatima. I would do anything to prevent it."

Fatima had no adequate response.

"What are you going to do to us?" she asked. "When the city falls?"

"Nothing," said Luz firmly. "A forced conversion is unworthy of Our Lord. I only want to remove certain bad influences—certain people who might stand between you and salvation. There are those who, through no fault but their own human weakness, have fallen under the sway of the Enemy, and they must be dealt with. Delicately, if possible."

"You torture people."

Luz released her hands and shrugged, as if the suggestion was tiresome.

"With heresy so widespread, unfortunate methods have become necessary," she said. "Even according to your own faith, the student of religion—a *talib*, I think you call him?—has a duty to spread his knowledge to those who have gone astray. And that's what we are. Yes? Simple *talub*."

Fatima shook her head. She couldn't think; there seemed no rational thing to say, no retort, for Luz's argument depended on its own impenetrable logic. Luz held out her hand again. She was smiling now: an upturned slash of sympathy as fixed as a corpse's. It made the fine hairs on Fatima's arms stand up.

"Don't touch me," said Fatima. "Never touch me again."

The smile faltered. Fatima felt a pang of guilt and no notion of how to relieve it. What could she say? She could not envision a God who demanded such particularity of belief, whose mercy and forgiveness were confined to such a precise segment of humankind. Nor, if it came to that, could she fathom hell, which seemed a somewhat contradictory place: you could be sent there for behaving in the right way but believing in the wrong God, or for believing in the right God but behaving in the wrong way. And that, in turn, threw heaven into disarray, since those who both believed and behaved rightly were invited to indulge in the very pleasures for which those who behaved wrongly had been sent to hell. If Luz was right, she would be punished for failing to acknowledge that God had a son; if the imam who grumbled from the minbar in the royal mosque was right, she would be punished for even considering such a proposition. Belief never seemed to enter into anything: it was simply a matter of selecting the correct system of enticements.

"Please say something," said Luz. "I don't want this to be the last conversation we ever have."

Fatima considered her words carefully.

"If you love someone, you don't think of them in hell," she said. "If you can imagine someone in hell, it means you hate them."

Luz shook her head.

"No," she said softly. "Hate and love aren't like that. Hate is a false feeling. You can stop someone from hating something. Love is much more dangerous."

The air was smoky: this was the time when each household banked its cooking fire for the night. The entire city would exhale in one great acrid breath, making the darkest hours thick and cold and heavy on the tongue. Fatima wanted to crawl into bed beside Lady Aisha as she had done when she was a small child; to feel, if not safe, then at least protected by someone whose orders were always obeyed. Yet it was not to be: the sultan's little messenger had appeared in the lamplight at the edge of the courtyard, putting an end to the conversation.

"Mistress Fatima," he piped. "The sultan—"

"Fine, all right," said Fatima, feeling her cheeks go hot. She didn't want Luz to witness this particular interaction, this blunt prelude to the nights she spent with her master. She stole a glance at the silent inquisitor and found her looking back, her face ashen in the dark.

"You could be free of this," said Luz with a pleading lilt in her voice. "Say the word and I will make you free. My masters are more powerful than your sultan will ever be."

Though the night air had only just begun to cool, Fatima's teeth were chattering.

"Are you free?" she asked. "You can't even call yourself what you are because you're not a man. You have masters, you just said so. How can you make me free if you're not free yourself?"

Luz didn't answer. The sultan's boy was fidgeting in the colonnade, struggling, no doubt, to understand what they were saying.

"I have to go," said Fatima, turning toward him. "Good night."

"I didn't want to be your enemy," said Luz to her back. "Things are going to happen very fast, and when they do, remember that."

*   *   *

Abu Abdullah was still dressed in his court clothes when Fatima arrived at his quarters. He had removed his turban, however, and the weight of it had left an unflattering crease in his hair, like the nipped ring of a monk's tonsure. Though he had called for her, he barely registered her presence, absorbed in a long document that hung from his fingers and was written, or so it seemed, in Latin.

"What is that?" Fatima asked uneasily after a full minute of silence. Abu Abdullah looked up at her in surprise, as if she were unknown to him.

"The Castilians have laid out their terms," he said when he recovered. "This was delivered less than an hour ago."

"Terms of surrender?"

"Yes." Abu Abdullah threw the paper at his night table, where it landed with a loud clack. "Terms of surrender." He looked at her with the eyes of a lost thing. "I am going to be the last sultan of Granada, Fatima. Last and least. Ridiculous poems will be written about me and my reign. I'll become some awful metaphor. They want me to kiss their hands, these Spanish monarchs. It's right there. Kiss their hands! They know we don't bow, yet—" He ran a hand through his hair, doing nothing to correct the crease. "It seems I am to be humiliated."

Fatima plucked the treaty from the night table and examined it. It was a useless gesture; such a thing would take her hours to translate, and only with the help of someone fluent. A lump formed in her throat.

"Why do they hate us so much?" she asked.

"I'll tell you," said Abu Abdullah, pulling off his long coat. "It's our fault. We've given everyone too much freedom. Our poets write odes to their male lovers. My mother spent half her fortune on a university for heretics and alchemists. Muslims and Jews and Christians mingle and live alongside each other, and here we are—weak and indulgent, just as the Castilians say. And they see you—" Here he crossed the room and cupped Fatima's face in both his hands. "The most beautiful woman in all of Europe, and I keep you openly, and you are not my wife. They hate me because I do in the daylight what their own kings are ashamed to do in the dark. They have concubines, just as I do, but in their religion these women are adulteresses damned to hell, their children bastards. That's not our way. Our sons will be princes, our daughters will marry into the finest families, and none of them will be bastards, because there is no shame in what we do. And for that, they call me a libertine."

Fatima pulled away, declining to point out that the freedoms of which Abu Abdullah spoke did not extend as far as the woman in front of him.

"Maybe they don't hate us for our freedoms," she muttered. "Maybe they hate us because we've been harrying their lands for decades."

Abu Abdullah's mouth hardened. He took the paper from her hands and began rolling it up.

"It doesn't matter," he said. "Listen—I asked you here because they want something that will upset you, and I wanted you to hear it from me first, so that you would be prepared."

Fatima was baffled. She sat down on Abu Abdullah's bed, twisting her hands in the hem of her tunic.

"All right," she said. "Tell me."

"Hassan. It's Hassan."

Fatima had to repeat the name silently in her head before she was convinced she had heard what she had heard.

"I don't understand. What do they want with Hassan? What is he to them?"

"A sorcerer." Abu Abdullah smiled without humor and began to pace. "Presumably they've discovered his talents—and perhaps his weakness for dark-eyed young men, though if that's what appalls them, I could provide them with twenty more such, starting with my own vizier. As I understand it, they intend to hand him over to the Inquisition for questioning." He laughed helplessly. "Hassan, a sorcerer! The man couldn't make soup out of an onion and a pot of water. What do they imagine they'll get from him on the rack?"

The sting of this caught Fatima in a place she could not locate: when she thought of her head, her head hurt, and when she thought of her heart, her heart hurt too. She had delivered her friend to Luz like an offering. She could see him being led away, could imagine the look of bewildered panic on his face, and because she loved him, she could feel them break his beautiful hands as clearly as if her own had been shattered. Fatima covered her eyes and whimpered. How could the poets write about love so lightly, as if it was something pleasant? Love was terror and loss. Love was appalling.

"I'll slit her throat," she whispered. "That smiling bitch."

"What?"

Fatima looked up and into Abu Abdullah's face without blinking.

"You won't let them take him," she said firmly. "Of course."

"I don't think you understand, Fatima. It's already been agreed. They'll come for him tonight, quietly, before the treaty is announced and the date for the transfer of power is set."

The tiles on the floor seemed to swim, rearranging themselves into shimmering patterns that Fatima could not read.

"You can't do this," she croaked, her mouth dry. "They'll kill him. Don't you see? He doesn't know anything—he can't tell them what they want to hear, because he doesn't know. He doesn't know why he can do what he does. They'll *kill* him. Master—"

Abu Abdullah stopped pacing and put his head in his hands.

"You're not the only one who cares about Hassan." His words were muffled in his palms. "He's been here since he was a boy—since *I* was a boy. The only reason we have survived this long is thanks to his damned maps. But I have no choice, Fatima, surely you can see that. His life will save thousands of others." He looked up from his hands and met her gaze, his eyes bleak and wild. "They'll give me back my children, Fatima. My sons, my little daughter—my God, she's probably forgotten me by now. When you have your own, you'll understand. All your grand ideas about justice and fairness die when your children are born. There is no life so precious that you would not sacrifice it for theirs."

Fatima wanted to strike him and to weep with him and could not tell which impulse was the greater.

"It's not right," she said, suppressing an urge to stamp her foot as well. "You know it isn't. Ask them to spare Hassan. There's still time. You should never have agreed in the first place."

This was the wrong thing to say. Abu Abdullah raised himself to his full height, which was considerable. "You have no right to question my judgment," he said quietly. "I am the master here, not you. You've overstepped yourself once too often. Go back to the harem until I send for you."

Fatima clenched and unclenched her fists. Then she remembered that she, too, was tall, and pulled herself up, lifting her chin. When she stood straight, without bowing her head, she was only a finger-breadth shorter than her master. She knew she ought to apologize, to lower her head again and murmur some excuse, but she did not.

"I'll go now," she said. "Since you have no use for me."

Abu Abdullah stepped back, his face lined with sudden grief.

"You're always so angry," he said. "I don't understand. You have pretty clothes, entertainments, food when others go hungry. You have the love of a sultan. What else could you possibly want?"

Fatima licked the dry, taut line of her lips.

"To be sultan," she said.

He was suddenly someone else. Fatima flinched before she could stop herself, wondering if this would be the moment he raised his hand to her and undid whatever uneasy affection existed between them, as was his right by law. But he did not. Instead, he turned his back on her, fading into the umber shadows of his room.

"Get out," he said.

☆   ☆   ☆

The palace was quiet as Fatima skittered from one dark corridor to the next. Her feet would not take her back to the harem: she knew where she must go instead. She was so heady with the thrill of disobedience that she lost her way once, turning right when she should have turned left, and was forced to retrace her steps. Everything she did felt too slow. She had no way of knowing when the Castilians might come for Hassan, whether each minute she fumbled might bring a rap on his door, toward which he would stumble, possibly drunk, unaware of what waited for him. She wanted to run but was wary of making too much noise: there were muffled voices on the second-floor loggia above her head, and they were not speaking Arabic. Instead she danced along on tiptoe, racing through the intersections of hallways until she was out of breath and the strong green scent of the Court of Myrtles enveloped her.

Fatima crossed the grassy court, skirting the reflecting pool, leaving a muted trail through the newly fallen dew. Hassan's work-room was dark, but the door to his sleeping chamber was lined with firelight. Fatima jogged up the stone steps and past Hassan's mess of papers and pounded on it, hoping belatedly that he was alone.

The door swung open. Hassan squinted out at her, adjusting to the dark.

"*Fatima?*" His voice was an incredulous rasp. "What the hell are you doing here at this hour?"

"We have to go," said Fatima, slipping past him and shutting the door behind her. "Now, now, now." A canvas sack, such as tradesmen and itinerant clerks carried from city to city, lay sprawled at the foot of his bed: she opened it and began to grab robes and hose and sashes from the bright piles heaped on the floor.

"What are you talking about? Go where? I'm exhausted and famished! Before you turned up, I was debating whether I was too hungry to sleep, or too sleepy to nip down to the kitchen for some bread."

"Hassan." Fatima plopped down on the floor and looked up at him, pleading. "Listen to what I'm saying. The Castilians want to take you away. They're going to give you to the—anyway, you're part of the peace treaty. They're coming for you—*now*—and no one is going to stop them, because the sultan has already said yes."

Hassan's blotchy, unassuming face was drained of color. He sat down and looked at his hands as if to accuse them of something.

"I was going to perform the late prayer," he said. "In the courtyard, since the stars are out. I like to. Can we wait that long?"

"Wait?" Fatima twisted her lip. "The Inquisition is looking for you, and you want to sit outside to do the late prayer? The *late* prayer. It's not even one of the mandatory ones."

Hassan's eyes widened.

"Did you say the *Inquisition*?"

"It's my fault," said Fatima, trying not to cry. "It was Luz. She smiled and simpered and made us all like her, and I thought—" Here she was forced to admit something that she did not like. "I thought I was smarter than she is. But I'm not."

Hassan was quiet for several minutes as Fatima stuffed the canvas sack with clothing.

"Oh, Fa," he said at last, his voice very small. "Where are we going to go?"

"I don't know," said Fatima, wiping her wet eyes angrily with the back of one hand. "Away."

Hassan rose. He opened a small cupboard and began to remove sheaves of paper, charcoals, gum arabic, brushes, ink. These he arranged, with more care than Fatima had ever seen him put into anything, in a buckled case of boiled leather with a carry-strap sewn from end to end, which he looped over one shoulder.

"You don't have to come with me," he said. "Stay here, where it's safe. They'll give the sultan a snug estate somewhere, or he'll cross the Strait to Morocco. Go with him."

Fatima shook her head.

"They'll know I helped you get away," she said. "It won't be any safer for me here than it is for you."

"But sweeting"—he knelt next to her and plucked at her tunic, like a child seeking attention—"you don't own a pair of shoes."

Fatima looked down at her naked feet. It had not occurred to her that one might need things outside the palace that one did not need inside it. A sense of profound, infuriating helplessness overcame her, and she began to sob in earnest.

"Lend me some," she sputtered. Hassan leaped to his feet and began to rummage through a wooden chest, pulling out various small items and rejecting them, until, with a cry of triumph, he produced a pair of much-worn leather boots. Kneeling, he slipped them onto Fatima's feet with melancholy tenderness, tightening the drawstrings around her calves.

"There," he said. "Your first pair of shoes. May you live to wear a hundred nicer ones."

Sniffling, Fatima stuck out one foot and wiggled it experimentally. The boots were too big, far heavier and clammier than the quilted silk slippers that kept her feet warm in winter or the wooden clogs she wore to and from the stool chamber. Yet the weathering of the heels and the bend at the ball of the foot suggested they had carried Hassan many miles, and might do the same for her. That, at least, was something.

"Here!" Hassan was up again, clattering in a corner of the room, and turned around with a pair of daggers in steel-studded leather sheaths, which he held up, one in each quivering hand, like an improbable assassin. "Defensive measures! The captain of the infantry gave me these after the battle of Zahara—which I helped win, you know, even though I wasn't actually there—and I just chucked them into the corner. Whoever thought I'd need them? Here, take this one and put it in your sash."

Fatima pulled the weapon from its sheath. It was lighter than she expected and shone like cloudy glass in the firelight. She had no notion of how to wield a knife that was not meant for cutting up salted meat, but she sheathed it again and tucked it into her sash anyway. The feeling of the dagger against her hip, straight and cold in its swaddling of embroidered silk, sent a stab of anticipation through her body. She felt oddly alert, light-footed in her heavy boots, as though her bones had gone as hollow as a bird's.

Hassan shouldered the canvas bag that Fatima had packed. The weight of it seemed to press all the giddiness out of him, and his face fell.

"For a second, I forgot," he said, attempting to smile. "I told myself we're going on a little adventure, and I forgot that we're not coming back."

Fatima stroked the wall nearest her. It was warm from the heat of the brazier, and the glowing coals had gilded it red-gold. It seemed strange that she should mourn a place in which friendships had been so few and so tenuous, yet she did mourn. The palace was her home and home was not a matter of loving or hating; to leave it was to do violence to the past.

"Did you hear that?" Hassan was suddenly rigid. Fatima held her breath and listened. There were voices in the workroom beyond the door, growing louder as they approached. The clack and rattle of metal suggested men in armor. Fatima pulled her hand away from the wall and felt her heart thud against her ribs.

"We've waited too long," she whispered.

Fists pounded on the door. Fatima backed away, groping at the dagger in her sash, and nearly tripped over the clutter on the floor in her big boots. There was no way out of the room besides a narrow window in the outer wall. It was little better than an arrow slit—this was, in fact, its original purpose—and led to a long drop on the other side, where the ground sloped away. Fatima stared at Hassan in alarm.

"Wait," he whispered. "Wait." He grabbed a scrap of paper from a pigeonhole and fished a charcoal from the pocket of his robe. Pressing the paper against the wall, he began to sketch. The door latch flapped up and down as the men on the other side tried to pry it open.

Fatima was seized by a fury as irresistible as hunger.

"Go to hell!" she shouted. The door began to shake.

"You're a madwoman," said Hassan incredulously. He pressed the scrap of paper into her hand. Fatima looked at it: there was the four-walled room in black lines, the door and window reduced to neat squares, the bed to a rectangle along one side. Yet something else had been added: a square on the floor with a half circle at the center. Fatima dropped to her knees. She began shoving books and plates and piles of clothes out of her way, clearing the floor near the bed. Underneath the clutter, as trim and unobtrusive as she could have wished, was a trapdoor with a great iron ring in the middle.

"Go," whispered Hassan. Fatima gripped the iron ring and pulled with all her strength. The trapdoor grated open, exhaling clammy air and the scent of earth. Below it was darkness. Fatima hesitated.

"Go," Hassan said again, looking over his shoulder. "I'll pull the door shut behind us."

Fatima sat on the lip of the door and dangled her feet into the dark. Swallowing and closing her eyes, she pushed off and fell.

It was over in a moment. She landed in loamy dirt, illuminated weakly by the light of the brazier in the room above. Her hands flailing in front of her, she stumbled out of the way. She could see Hassan's feet hanging down, his robe hitched up to his knees, the exposed shins pale and covered in whorls of reddish-brown hair. With a cry of terrified hilarity, he landed beside her, the trapdoor slamming shut in his wake. The passage went black. Fatima could hear herself breathing in high panicked gasps, the sound amplified by unseen walls. The darkness was so complete that it felt like going blind. She reached out and smacked Hassan on the back with her hand. He yelped. Footsteps shuddered overhead.

"The map," hissed Hassan. "Tear it up, quick."

Fatima uncurled her hand. The map was damp with sweat. Shaking, she tore it in half and threw the pieces away. The footsteps overhead paused. Voices came as if heard from underwater, reduced to murmurs of incredulity and confusion. The footsteps resumed again, scraping against the stone above, kicking at objects that protested dully. Wood smashed, followed by the unmistakable clang of the iron brazier hitting a wall. The voices retreated, replaced by silence.

Fatima fought to quiet her breathing. She reached out again, groping for Hassan's hand. He felt her touch and interlaced his fingers with hers.

"Where are we?" she whispered.

"I have no idea," said Hassan. His voice shook so much that Fatima could barely understand him. "I haven't thought that far ahead."

"What do you mean?" Fatima's voice rose and collided with some invisible barrier. "You're the one who brought us here. What do you mean you have no idea?"

"I panicked, Fa! I was only thinking about a door, any door." Hassan moaned faintly. "I could try to make a proper map, but I'd need some light."

Fatima had not thought to pack flint or tinder. She reached out with her free hand, feeling in the dark for something to guide them. There was only undifferentiated gloom. Gripping Hassan's fingers, she took another step, hand before her face, and then another, and was finally rewarded by a flat plane of packed earth that might have been the wall of a tunnel.

"You've never been lost in your life," she said, trying to sound confident. "We'll just follow this until we can see something."

"All right," quavered Hassan. He squeezed her hand. Fatima groped along the wall, testing the ground with her foot before putting her weight on it. She pulled Hassan with her, inch by inch, pausing more briefly between steps as she grew surer of herself. The quiet was almost more unnerving than the dark: darkness might be infinitely large, but the heady sound of their breathing suggested a very small passage. Fatima didn't dare let go of the wall to test this theory. Instead, she told herself the tunnel had been made by someone, and thus must lead somewhere. She imagined a sultan in ancient chain mail and a pointed helm hurrying his troops through this passage to surprise the enemy; or perhaps a wise, ebony-eyed princess holding a torch aloft, quieting her ladies and children with a whisper as they escaped past the siege lines overhead. The thought that others might have passed this way before and lived—there were no skeletons littering the ground, anyway—comforted her.

"Heron," said Hassan in a pleading voice, breaking the silence. It took Fatima a moment to understand what he was asking for.

"Now?" she said with an exasperated laugh. "You want me to tell you a story?"

"Oh God, yes. Please. I never realized how afraid I am of small, airless, pitch-black tunnels without any sign of an exit. Tell me a story."

Fatima tried to think. "Heron," she repeated, attempting to clear her mind. "I'm sure we've done this one before. You always pick waterbirds, Hassan."

"I grew up with them, is all. They come to mind."

"Heron, heron. The heron is a hunter. A stealthy hunter who keeps very still and waits for his prey to come to him."

"Like Luz."

Fatima curled her lip. "Luz isn't a bird. She doesn't deserve to be a bird. Luz is some awful thing, like a—a weevil or a worm, burrowing into perfectly good food."

"Does the heron make it?" Hassan's breathing was shallow, rushed. "Does he make it across the Dark Sea with the others, to the realm of the Bird King?"

"Of course he does," said Fatima. Her own voice sounded unfamiliar. "It's the heron who feeds all the other birds along the way, diving into the waves for fish. Nobody likes him at first because he doesn't flock like the others, and spends so much time by himself, but they come to see how loyal and brave he is, in his own way. Not everybody has to be friendly in order to be good."

"That's nice," said Hassan, still quavery voiced. "I like it when the odd ones get a happy ending."

Fatima turned her head to respond and collided with a wall. Her nose filled with a plume of dust and a bitter, fungal scent. She sneezed violently, cursed, and sneezed again.

"Are you all right?" came Hassan's anxious voice.

"I'm fine," muttered Fatima, wiping her streaming nose with the back of one hand. "There's a turn here, apparently."

"Which way, which way?"

"I don't know," Fatima snapped. "Give me a minute to figure it out." She felt along the wall, which curved away from her in an odd fashion, as if it was sloping downward, yet when she put out her foot, the ground sloped up. She blundered forward, crouching, and encountered another wall.

"I think we're stuck in a corner," she panted. "Hold on to my sash—I need my other hand, please."

Obediently, Hassan relinquished her hand and fumbled until he found her sash, which he gripped unsteadily, as if he was unsure of his footing.

"All right?" asked Fatima.

"All right."

Keeping one hand on the wall, Fatima reached out with the other. The other wall, if there was one, was too far away to touch. Steeling herself, she let go of the wall entirely and reached out in front of her with both hands. She took one step and then another, and then set her foot on empty air.

Fatima shrieked. Hassan yanked backward on her sash, toppling them both into the dirt.

"You were falling," he panted.

"I don't know what happened," said Fatima. She was shaking so emphatically that her teeth chattered. "I don't know which way to go."

Hassan began to laugh.

"I've never been lost!" he shouted at the black, listening air. "I've never not known where I am or which way to go next. I had one talent, and now it's useless. I should never have come to Granada all those years ago. I should've stayed at home and minded my mother. I'm sorry, Fa."

"It's all right," lied Fatima. "Let's sit here for a minute. Let's just sit."

Hassan went silent, except for an occasional sniff. Fatima stared into the malignant darkness, straining her eyes, hoping, somehow, that they would adjust, allowing her to make out some helpful land-mark. She stared until she saw spots, light sparked by the internal pressures of her own body, weak splotches of yellow and white and blue. They failed to illuminate anything of substance. Yet she focused on them anyway—on two in particular, a pair of yellow specks as bright as lamplight, which bobbed and jerked when she examined them too closely. They persisted after the other lights had faded, dipping and weaving across her field of vision. She had to stare at them for another long minute before she could accept that they were eyes.

"Hassan," she forced herself to whisper. "Something's coming."

The sound of Hassan's breathing ceased. Fatima heard the dry rasp of metal against leather and realized he had drawn his knife. She hurried to do the same. Her dagger slid free of its sheath with the readiness of a well-made weapon. It was a prompt she did not know how to follow, except to grip the hilt as tightly as she could and point the blade away from herself.

The lights paused. Out of the dark came a volley of laughter.

"Little children," said a man's voice, as low and merry as a jackal's. "Little children have sprouted little teeth. What exactly do you plan to do with those pretty knives? Shave?"

Fatima couldn't move. She had a terrible feeling she was about to wet herself and clamped her legs shut. The lights drew closer and resolved themselves, shedding a pale, cold light on the familiar shape of the palace dog.

"Hello, young Fatima," it said. "What are you doing so far from the harem?"

Fatima fainted. She had never fainted before, so the order of things that came next was unclear: she was awake, then not, then there was screaming—not hers—and the face of a man hovering over her, his lean, handsome features marred by an expression of contempt.

"Oh, get up," he was saying. He had many teeth. "There are worse things than me down here, and you'll meet some of them presently if you keep shrieking and falling over."

"Nessma was right," slurred Fatima, half-conscious. "I used to think she was just being an idiot. You're a demon."

"I'm not a demon," said the dog-man. Invisible hands pulled her upright. "But I'm not far off, either. On your feet, little sister."

Fatima struggled to stand. Somewhere behind her, Hassan gave an angry yelp and slashed about in the air with his dagger.

"Put that knife away before you cut your own necessities off," said the dog-man. "There's a good child."

"Who are you?" demanded Hassan.

"Who are you, it asks," laughed the dog-man. He shook himself, and for a moment, Fatima saw a dark pelt and a pair of clawed feet. "It has a little spirit after all. You know who I am, Hassan. You've passed me in the halls of the palace any number of times these past ten years. A better question would be, 'Where am I?' for on that point you are clearly ignorant. Look here. Look where you two almost stepped." He turned away and the light from his eyes seemed to brighten, illuminating the faint edges of the tunnel around them. Inches from where Fatima stood, the ground stopped, falling away so sharply that the hole it created appeared like a flat blot of emptiness even darker than what surrounded it. The tunnel continued on the far side, a bit farther than Fatima could jump.

"I nearly just died." She felt no fear, only a wild solemnity.

"Life is a series of near misses," said the dog-man, slipping his talons beneath her elbow to guide her away. "Death happens only once. This way."

Fatima felt Hassan wrap one hand around her sash again. They padded behind their guide, whose molten eyes cast enough light to let them see a few feet of the path ahead, but no more. He led them along a ledge that wound around the sudden drop, hugging the far side of the passage. Fatima clutched at the wall as they went, digging her fingers into the pliant earth until her nails were so packed with dirt that they pained her.

"The roads that lead to hell are cold," said the dog-man to himself, half singing. "The fires of hell are colder still, and darker than the hour before dawn. Light, light, let's have a little light."

Fatima did not try to make sense of this. The path widened and narrowed at her feet, seemingly at random. She didn't dare look up from it at the creature loping beside her, whose scent alone—hot metal, glass pulled from a forge fire, the smell of something that was neither alive nor safe—alarmed her. Nevertheless, they had walked a long way without coming across any promising landmark, and her fear began to give way to curiosity. "What is this place?" she asked after what seemed like a prudent interval. "It feels less and less like something built on purpose."

"Ah." The dog-man turned and looked at her. The light from his eyes illuminated a predatory smile. "Finally a little sense. This isn't rightly a place anymore, only a crossroads between places. Some old and very nervous sultan tunneled under the Alhambra years ago, and a few of his cruelest descendants kept prisoners down here to die in the dark. But not for many decades now—or is it centuries? Now things that like the dark live here instead and have made little improvements of their own. That oubliette you nearly walked into is one of them."

Fatima felt gooseflesh break out on her arms.

"What things?" she asked. "Jinn? Ghouls, effrit, marid, corpse-eaters, and all the rest? What things?"

"Shut up." The dog-man halted so suddenly that Fatima stumbled into his coarsely furred back. An eddy of cold air seeped past her neck. The darkness before her remained inscrutable, but the timbre of the silence had changed, muffling her footfalls with a hollow sound, a half echo. The noise was so slight that Fatima could barely hear it, yet it filled her with terror.

"Something's there," she whispered.

Shut up, repeated the dog-man from somewhere between her ears. *Say nothing, do nothing. I'm going on ahead. Stay right here and keep your high-strung friend quiet.*

The warmth before her withdrew. Fatima could see two dim halos of light weave back and forth in time with the dog-man's strange gait, growing fainter as he moved away. A clammy hand groped in the dark for her own: she took it, wrapping Hassan's arm around herself, pressing her back against his chest. He was gasping oddly, as if trying to stifle the sound of his breathing.

"I might throw up," he stammered. Fatima squeezed his hand and said nothing.

A growl rumbled through the dank air. The halos of light had stopped and hovered, suddenly still, at the height of a tall man. They illuminated so little that at first Fatima saw only more darkness. She began to imagine she had invented the dog-man: she was asleep after the lamps had been put out, there was no moon, and she would wake presently at the foot of Lady Aisha's divan to begin the day as she had always done. She populated the darkness with ordinary artifacts, withdrawing her foot to avoid kicking over the copper bowl of washing water that always stood near her mistress's bed, expecting to encounter the prickle of her own woolen blanket.

The effect was so vivid that she did not, at first, realize the dark was moving. It uncoiled, arranging its myriad scales, the light from the dog-man's eyes gilding the lazy, variegated pattern of its hide. As it moved, Fatima saw the outline of muscle and sinew under skin: a limb she could not identify; a leg, or perhaps something else entirely, an assemblage of flesh from another way of being, from a place where nothing walked or swam or flew. The two spots of light did not waver. Fatima found herself pining for the dog-man with a sort of tenderness: he was surely just a jinn, dangerous but ordinary, the sort of creature that slipped into one's house when one forgot to invoke the name of God before entering. This other creature was drawn from forces Fatima's imagination could not touch.

She thought again of Lady Aisha's divan. She could smell the costly resins rubbed into the wood to make it glow and to perfume the air around it: sandalwood and oud, myrrh and aloe.

Get out of the harem, came the dog-man's voice in her head. *And tell your friend to leave the fishpond at the bottom of his mother's garden. Memory will not save you.*

Fatima began to back away.

Damn you for a fool, snapped the dog-man. *If you run from this thing, you'll set it loose. It will lodge in your bloodstream like a splinter and you'll carry it all your days.*

It's too big for that, thought Fatima, half to herself.

It's small, said the dog-man. *It's very small. It began as a mote in the eye of the Deceiver. Keep your back straight and don't look away.*

Fatima searched herself for the wherewithal to do as he asked. Every sense she possessed told her to run: a scream was already pressing at the back of her throat, waiting for her to open her mouth. Behind her, Hassan stumbled and whimpered, his voice so altered by terror that it was almost unrecognizable. The dark, the air, the childlike sound of Hassan's distress gathered into a knot in Fatima's gut.

"Stop it," she shouted, turning on Hassan. "Stop, stop, stop mewling like a baby and get up. What's wrong with you? Why can't you stand up?"

There was a sudden roar. Fatima felt the breath knocked from her lungs and tumbled onto her side, rolling once before coming to a stop against a hot rasp of fur that could only be the dog-man. She felt in front of her face for the ground, which was not where she expected it to be, and pushed herself onto her knees, gasping.

"I hope you brainless piss-stains are satisfied," snarled the dog-man. "It's gone, it's fled. You've let it out. I kept it off you, not that you'll thank me for it, and now it'll doubtless go and find someone else equally brainless to feed upon. Your left-hand angels will wear out their wrists scribbling all of this in the book of your sins! Get up, you idiots." The yellow eyes bobbed away through the dark.

Fatima groped in the dark behind her for Hassan. His silence was beginning to alarm her. Her own sudden rage had burned itself out, as it always did, and weariness had replaced it, as always happened. She felt cocooned within it, separated from the world, and even from the darkness, by layers of heavy gauze. She needed things she could not name. When her hand brushed Hassan's, he pulled away and got to his feet.

"Say something," Fatima pleaded. "I'm sorry."

"I don't want your sorry," came Hassan's voice, curtly. "I want to get out of here." She heard the unsteady scrabble of his feet as he made his way after the dog-man. Fatima rose and followed him. They walked in a line, guided by the dog-man's eyes and their own breathing, until it seemed, to Fatima at least, that the darkness had grown less profound.

"What was that . . . animal?" Fatima asked as soon as she dared.

"Knowing would only terrify you," said the dog-man from somewhere ahead of her. "You already know enough, and this flame-haired fellow"—here one claw gestured at Hassan—"knows more than any human should, with his clever hands and bits of paper."

"I don't know anything," protested Hassan.

"You are magnificently stupid," agreed the dog-man. "Neverthe-less, you have a rare and perplexing gift. You must have been born under a very lewd alignment of stars."

"I was born in August," said Hassan indignantly. "Under the sign of the virgin, like any respectable person."

Fatima grinned in spite of herself.

"A Virgo," mused the dog-man, as if this was a perfectly reason-able explanation. "Yes, they do have relentless, systematic little minds. But that doesn't explain everything. No matter. Watch your step, we're nearly there."

A faint light, emanating from a source Fatima could not discern, revealed the edges of the tunnel and the ground beneath their feet, outlining them in pale gold. The dog-man was suddenly a visible thing, solid and almost ordinary from the navel upward: tallish, cleanly muscled, neither fair nor dark, with an uncombed net of black hair as long as a woman's. He did not appear to be wearing clothes. Fatima found herself staring at his flank, which swam co-quettishly in front of her eyes: one moment it was the curve of a rather pleasing buttock, the next the hairy extremity of something meant to go on four legs.

"What are you staring at?" snapped the dog-man.

"You," admitted Fatima, too disturbed to be anything but honest. The dog-man looked at her for another moment and then burst into laughter.

"A truth-teller," he sang, loping toward the evanescing light. "Ever since it was a child. What steel it has beneath those pretty silks! I'll happily rut with you, if that's what you're after, though this is a somewhat uncomfortable place for it."

"No thank you," said Fatima, freshly alarmed. If he was offended, the dog-man gave no sign, but hummed to himself again, leaping over a mound of earth and rubble and landing on all fours. The light had taken on a piercing quality, filling the passage ahead of them. Fatima's eyes began to water. The dog-man rose and became a silhouette, the shadow of a beast standing upright.

"I've found them, my lady," he called to the flickering brightness. "They were lost in the borderlands of the Empty Quarter. Here they are, safe and sound."

"Good boy," came a familiar voice. Fatima put up a hand to shield her eyes. The light shifted. It was a torch, Fatima realized, held up by a slim figure in a robe and a saffron-colored veil.

"Well, Fatima," said Lady Aisha, lowering the light and pulling her veil down to reveal a wry smile. "Did you really think you could run away in the dead of night without saying good-bye?"

Chapter 6

Fatima stood dazed in the torchlight with her hands hanging limply at her sides. Her mistress was, in some strange way, a greater surprise than the dog-man had been: Fatima could count on one hand the number of times Lady Aisha had left the palace in her recollection, so to see her there in the darkness, with the bluish light of false dawn rising behind her in the rocky mouth of the tunnel, was an eventuality for which Fatima had not prepared. She was used to thinking of her mistress as indolent: rising late, sleeping often, spending hours at the baths. But this was—or rather, must be—an illusion, a sort of camouflage, like a mountain cat blending into the rocks, cultivated to outwit anyone who might be sizing her up.

"I'm hurt," she said now. "I don't mind saying so. I think I've been very good to you. I've certainly taught you much more than any concubine needs to know. I preferred you above my own freeborn daughters-in-law, my own stepdaughter. Yes! I've been an excellent mistress. Yet here we are."

"I couldn't let them have Hassan," said Fatima. Her voice had shrunk somehow and came out high and timid.

"My lady," said Hassan, stepping forward. "Forgive Fatima—you know what she's like, impetuous and so forth, and very loyal, which is a credit to you, my lady, if you'll forgive me for speaking, but she's still just a girl if we're being honest, so if—"

"No, stop. It's too early in the day for so much talking. There is only one question that needs to be answered: now that we're all together again, why shouldn't we go quietly back to our own rooms and have a little breakfast? No one need know about this misadventure."

Fatima looked at Hassan. There was an animal grief in his earth-colored eyes, a terror of death which he was trying valiantly to conceal. He met her gaze and managed a smile.

Fatima lifted her chin.

"You don't think it's right either," she said to Lady Aisha. "Let us go. You know Hassan isn't a sorcerer."

"Of course I know that," snapped Lady Aisha, tossing her torch to the ground. It whuffed hot air in protest. "That's not the point. These treaties are made for polities, not people. Lives are ground up beneath the wheels of peace. Why should Hassan live when so many others have died? And why should I lose you into the bargain?"

Fatima wondered whether Lady Aisha wanted an answer. She didn't understand why someone like Hassan, who had no power over anything save his maps, should be expected to make such a sacrifice for those who had plenty.

"There is another solution." The dog-man slipped forward, slinking along the ground to sit at Lady Aisha's feet. "If this fellow can blunder into the outskirts of the Empty Quarter just by scribbling on a piece of paper, he is a liability to my people. If the black-cloaks put him on the rack and he squeals, he ceases to be a liability and becomes a threat." Before Fatima could react, the dog-man was on his feet with his face an inch from Hassan's throat. "Let me take care of him here, now. You can have what's left over. The black-cloaks won't care if he's been chewed up a little, as long as they can still put his head on a spike."

Hassan began to laugh uncontrollably. The dog-man laughed too, then kicked Hassan's feet out from under him and sat down on his chest.

"Don't," he said as Hassan struggled. "One little slit and you won't feel a thing."

The dog-man had his back to Fatima. She grabbed a handful of his inky hair and yanked as hard as she could. With a yelp, the creature tumbled over. But Fatima could not keep her grip: the tangled mane in her fist turned to shadow, a flattened image of what it had been. The dog-man loomed over her in a dark plume and seized her throat.

"I like you, little sister," he said. "You've been kind to me and I haven't forgotten it. But I only like you a little more than I would like to eat you. Remember that."

"Enough," snapped Lady Aisha. "Put her down, Vikram, and let poor Hassan go before he dies of fright. Good God! You're getting theatrical as you age."

Fatima felt the claws around her neck relax. She tore away, rubbing her throat and gasping for air.

"You're disgusting," she snarled at him. "You're a monster."

"Yes," said the creature. Settling on the ground with a sigh, he lay on his back, stretching out the toes of one taloned foot, and began to hum again.

Hassan, meanwhile, was laughing in a way that Fatima found alarming.

"You're Vikram the Vampire," he crowed. "The master cartographer used to frighten us with stories about you after the fires were put out at night. You're not real."

"People keep saying that, yet it's never been true," said Vikram bitterly. "I'm as real as you are. More so, even, for I've certainly lived longer."

"No," Hassan insisted. He raised one hand as if to banish the dog-man like a conjurer's illusion. "You're a tale to scare children into behaving themselves. That's not the same as something real."

"Fear can make anything real," said Vikram. "The black-cloaks are afraid you're a sorcerer. If they condemn you as a sorcerer and burn you for it, then you are, for all practical purposes, a sorcerer, whether you began as one or not. Fear doesn't need to make sense in order to have consequences." He rolled over and eyed Hassan's stricken face. "The difference between us is that I am Vikram whether you fear me or not."

Fatima felt light-headed and wondered if she might faint again. She walked toward the mouth of the tunnel, taking deep, greedy breaths of the chill air. The light on the horizon had brightened in earnest. In the bluish dawn, she began to recognize where they were: the tunnel ended in a modest rock ledge downhill from the palace, whose outline abutted the sky above their heads. Below them, the shallow Genil River slid eastward, its banks lined with scrub and river rock. To the west, the medina was waking up: she could see rushlights winking in the windows of white plaster houses and shops. Milk cows were lowing quietly in their sheds, the sound carried up the hill by a wild little breeze. Before her, at the foot of the hill, was the Vega de Granada, flat and silent, stretching south toward the rim of the valley.

"I will go," came Hassan's voice gravely. Fatima turned to gape at him.

"You will not!" she declared. But Hassan held up his hand.

"It's all right, Fa," he said. "There was never much chance of me surviving this anyway. One of us might as well live." His eyes were watery and reddened. Fatima wanted to go to him, to put her arms around his neck, but with Lady Aisha and the dog-man watching, she did not dare.

"Then it's settled," said Lady Aisha. "Hassan will go to the Castilians. In exchange, Fatima will not be punished for treason. Everything will fall back into its rightful place. We will have peace."

Fatima studied her mistress. She looked calmly back through her bloodshot brown eyes, her face still except for a tiny tremor in her mouth, which told Fatima all she needed to know.

"No," said Fatima.

"*No?*"

"No."

Lady Aisha began to pace across the mouth of the tunnel.

"You are so eager to leave me," she said in a caustic voice. "I can't do without you, Fatima. I'm old. I am losing my home and my country. My son weeps like a woman for what he could not defend as a man. And now this little rebellion." She gripped an outcropping of rock at the mouth of the cave and lowered herself to the ground. Fatima, unthinking, ran to help her, putting her shoulder beneath her mistress's fragile arm. They sat on the cold earth, breathing the same air.

"You want me to love you," said Fatima. Her mistress's scent filled her senses, an admixture of myrrh and wool and the faint, unsettling smell of age. "But I'm a thing you own, and property can't love. I want to love you. Let us go and I will. If this is peace, then I hate peace. Peace is unfair."

Lady Aisha chuckled. Her gaze became unfocused and almost sad, as if she was in the grip of some profound memory.

"You're very young, my dear," she said. "Let me tell you something important. The real struggle on this earth is not between those who want peace and those who want war. It's between those who want peace and those who want justice. If justice is what you want, then you may often be right, but you will rarely be happy." She squinted at the brightening sunlight. "If anyone asks me what you've done, I'm going to tell the truth—I won't risk what little I have left, not even for you. But if you leave now and walk very briskly, there is a chance you may outrun the Inquisition. A small chance."

For a moment, Fatima didn't understand.

"I'm setting you free," said Lady Aisha gently. "You're no longer a thing I own, since that's how you put it. Go, make your escape."

Fatima let her head sink against Lady Aisha's shoulder. She kissed the exposed sweep of collarbone, thinly clad in skin the color of the elms on the hill above.

"Thank you," she whispered.

There was a sound above their heads, the sharp clatter of talons on rock. Vikram dropped to the ground beside them.

"There are dogs out on the hill," he said. "And silent men. You have minutes before they pick up your scent. It's time to leave, one way or another."

Lady Aisha got to her feet. Hassan, who had been sitting in a daze with his knees pulled up, did likewise, clutching his leather case to his chest with the fervor of a lover.

"What do we do?" he asked.

Lady Aisha sighed and surveyed the hillside.

"You'll never outrun dogs in this terrain," she said. "You'll have to cross the Vega. There's no help for it."

"The Vega?" Fatima looked out over the smoky plain and felt a stab of fear. "It's so open—it's just an empty field that goes on and on. There's nowhere to hide, no trees, no hills, not for miles."

"Then I suppose I must lose you as well," said Lady Aisha to Vikram. She stroked his head. "After all these long years."

"If you want these little palace-bred children to live, yes," said Vikram. He caught her hand and pressed a kiss into it. "For your sake, I will help them cross the Vega."

Lady Aisha withdrew her hand and twisted a ring off her finger, wiggling it over the bony protrusion of her knuckle. Fatima recognized it: it was set with a dark ruby encircled by tiny pearls, a gift from her husband while he still lived. Lady Aisha dropped it into Fatima's palm.

"When you reach the edge of the valley, follow the harbor road south," she said. "Stay off the road itself, if you can, but follow it, for there are few paths through those mountains and autumn is nearly upon us. When you reach the sea, this should buy you both passage on a ship, with a little left over if the captain is fair. Where you go then is your own business."

Fatima slipped the ring onto her own finger. It was heavy and still warm. She wanted to say thank you, but before she could open her mouth, she heard the faint baying of a hound, intent and anguished, echoing over the hillside.

"They're coming," said Vikram, leaping down the rocks. "Follow me."

Lady Aisha turned away.

"Go," she said, pulling up her veil. "Let's not spoil things with promises none of us can keep."

Fatima felt Hassan tug her hand. Stumbling, she followed him, feeling as though something needful had been left unsaid; longing, with a force that startled her, for the silk-shrouded figure that diminished in her wake. The palace above them had begun to cast its shadow over the medina, its red towers square and sharp, an extension of the hill on which they sat. They had stood for centuries and might stand for centuries more, but as she looked back, Fatima knew, though she could not say how, that she would never lay eyes on them again.

Chapter 7

Humming and picking at his ears, Vikram led them down the face of a sandstone cliff. The slope, all descending angles of umber and red, was so nearly vertical that Fatima's guts heaved each time she forced herself to take a step. Too soon, she began to wonder whether she had made a grave mistake.

"Your left foot goes there," called Vikram, pointing. "Then your right, here. You've got four limbs: as long as you only move one at a time, the other three will save you."

"This is insane," shrieked Hassan, who clung to a slanting boulder like a redheaded bat, his leather satchel swinging in the air below one shoulder. "We're all going to die."

"Not if you follow directions," sang Vikram, flinging himself into the air and landing silently on a largish rock below. "The hounds won't come this way. You need free will to do something this mad. We're nearly to the bottom. The hard part begins then."

Fatima wedged her left foot in the crack to which Vikram had pointed, uncurling one hand to shift her weight. She saw with dispassion that the skin of her thumb and forefinger had split open, leaving angry vertical tears. She was also profoundly hungry. None of it was pain, exactly—she was too alert for that, too focused to feel anything acute. Yet it was a hindrance. A small part of her quaked silently, convinced that she was ill-equipped for any purpose beyond that for which she had been raised.

"Tougher hands," she murmured. "A smaller stomach. Better shoes. Skill with a knife."

"Are you making a list for the greengrocer?" asked Vikram. He was standing below her on solid ground, looking up: Fatima had reached the bottom of the ledge.

"What do I do now?" she asked, craning her neck.

"Let go," said Vikram. "I'll catch you."

"I'm not sure I want to do that."

"There are other options," conceded Vikram, scanning the mounds of tufted grass that led down to the Genil, and beyond that, to the treeless expanse of the Vega. "You could fall and break your legs and I could leave you here for the black-cloaks, though the crows might make a pass at you first."

"All right, all right," snapped Fatima, sucking on her split fingers. "But if you cup something you shouldn't, I'll hit you."

"I will cup nothing," promised Vikram with a grin. Fatima held her breath and let go of the ledge. The world tipped. There was a rush of air and a squeak that was probably hers, and then Vikram was setting her on the ground beside him, laughing.

"You're next," he called up to Hassan, who was visible as a hemisphere of ballooning green wool overhead, one foot scrambling for purchase on a lichen-covered rock. With a wild yelp, the apparition tumbled down. Vikram caught him as deftly as he had Fatima.

"A shame you don't have more meat on you," the creature observed. "You'll be skin and bone before we're out of the wilderness. I hope you like rabbit, for there's very little else to eat between us and the sea at this time of year."

"I like rabbit fine," muttered Hassan. He lingered a moment too long before putting his feet down. As Vikram loped ahead, Fatima pinched Hassan's arm.

"You're attracted to him," she hissed accusingly.

"I can't help it!" whispered Hassan. "He's very well-formed for a jinn and he isn't wearing a thread of clothing."

"Come, children," called Vikram, without turning. "We must cross the river as swiftly as possible. If you put your feet in clever places, the dogs may lose your scent for a time. Every hour counts now." He bent down, hunching his shoulders, and ran along on all fours, his feet and hands falling soundlessly on the dry grass. Fatima stumbled after him in her big boots. She felt herself begin to tire. Behind her, Hassan's breathing was a labored staccato punctuated by the sound of his satchel as it thumped against his shoulder.

"Can't we slow down?" he complained between huffs.

"Do you want to live or not?" asked Vikram, turning and snapping his teeth at them. "If we don't cross the Genil, there's no point to any of this."

Fatima wiped sweat from her brow with the back of one hand. It hung in droplets from her lashes and the tip of her nose, and she became aware of a smell, not pleasant, emanating from the curdling silk of her tunic where it clung to her body beneath her arms and below her breasts. She pulled at the hem angrily and heard it rip.

"Already rending your garments?" Vikram danced on his toes and cackled.

"I'm too hot," snapped Fatima. "And I can't run properly in these ridiculous boots, and I'm so hungry I might faint where I stand."

"We're barely out of sight of the palace! What exactly did you think the rest of the world was like, little sister? Cool and clean and well-fed, with songbirds twittering in harmony and merry farm beasts shitting flowers?"

Fatima bent to pick up a pebble and hurled it at Vikram's head. He ducked and cackled again. The ground rose and then dipped and brought the river into view: milky green and smelling fecund, lined with gorse and thorny scrub alive with the trilling of cicadas. Fatima pushed past Vikram and made her way through the scrub toward the water. It was very low, as was often the case in late summer: a shoal of well-worn rock was visible in midstream and the exposed banks on either side were bone-dry, their skin of mud turned to pale dust.

"Don't go down to the water," called Vikram. "You'll leave a trail through that dust as plain as an invitation."

Fatima stopped where she was. The green water murmured restlessly to itself, cutting westward across the parched valley. A grid of fields left fallow by war undulated toward the feet of the mountains that surrounded the Vega on three sides, yellow-brown with the remains of untended olive groves and winter wheat choked with weeds. The sky that had been so blue at dawn was growing overcast, hinting at the first of the autumn rains. It reminded Fatima that she was thirsty. She clenched her jaw and felt granules of dust between her teeth.

"Here, little sister." Vikram bounded up to her, his hands cupped and dripping. "Drink."

Fatima put her lips against the edge of his palm. The river water was sweet and cold and smelled faintly ripe. She gulped it down in needy mouthfuls, swallowing so fast that she was left gasping.

"Better?"

Fatima nodded, wiping her mouth on the back of one sleeve. Before she could protest, Vikram had thrown her over his shoulder and bounded into the current, depositing her in the knee-deep water with a splash. Fatima shrieked as her feet slid out from underneath her. As soon as she stood up, she collided with Hassan and went down again.

"What was that for?" Hassan sputtered, his hair and beard streaming water. He floated on his back in the current, kicking up his pale feet in an attempt to right himself. Vikram danced on the far bank with Hassan's satchel and the canvas sack of clothing Fatima had packed, holding each up like a trophy.

"Wash," he sang. "Scrub off all the sweat and the dirt and yesterday's perfume. Perhaps we can convince the hounds you smell like a river, at least for a while."

Fatima dragged herself to her feet. Her boots were waterlogged and her silk tunic clung to her torso in one ruined sheet, the water drizzling from its hem tinted with purple dye.

"Take off the wet things," instructed Vikram. "Put on the dry ones in this clever sack of yours. Vikram will take the wet clothes a little way off and leave them on a rock to lead the hunters astray."

Fatima wanted to smash something.

"Stop telling me what to do," she spat. "No one is going to order me to take off my clothes, ever again."

The haughty lines on Vikram's face softened. He set down their bags in the dust of the riverbank and leaped into the water, landing on all fours at Fatima's feet.

"As you said yourself, I'm a monster," he told her, his mouth twitching upward wryly. "But I'm not that sort of monster."

"Why should I believe you?" Fatima rubbed her arms, her teeth chattering.

"I never lie," said the dog-man. "Lies are for those who are afraid or ashamed of what they are, and I am neither."

"I think we should do as he says," called Hassan, hopping on one foot as he pulled off a dripping shoe. "Let's not die today. It would be such an embarrassment if we barely even got away before we were captured again. If we're going to die, let's do it tomorrow at the very earliest."

Fatima looked closely at the hawkish face staring up at her. It was not as spiteful as it had first appeared, and the yellow eyes, though they reflected nothing, had a feral wisdom in them.

"Don't look at me while I change," she said.

"I won't," promised Vikram. He turned away and loped back toward the shore. Hesitating a moment longer, Fatima peeled her tunic over her head. The air that had been warm when she was dry felt very cold now that she was wet. She wriggled out of her trousers as quickly as the sodden fabric would allow, then tossed the bundle of wet clothes toward Vikram's back, as a sort of test, and was only half pleased when he caught it with one hand.

Fatima waded into the shallows on the far side of the river and stepped out onto an embankment of rubble on the far side, squatting to rummage in Hassan's pack. Hassan himself was splashing contentedly in midstream, cursing and woofing under his breath at the cold and the rocks underfoot. Fatima stole a glance at his bare form. His back was as pale as a northerner's and his ribs were visible; freckles dappled his shoulders. In this light, shivering and naked in the river, he seemed unremarkable, his genius invisible, yet he was alive, and her hope lived with him.

"You're judging me," declared Hassan, standing up and spitting water. "I can feel your eyes boring into the back of my skull."

"I'm not," protested Fatima, turning away with a grin.

"Yes you are. We can't all be as lovely and formidable as certain people. Some of us have flaws. Some of us even *like* flaws. If you were a man, I'd be afraid to flirt with you, no matter how much I might want to. You'd fix me with that knowing little smirk when I was in some terribly vulnerable state, and that would be the end of me."

"Am I really that bad?" asked Fatima, unsettled.

"Yes," said Hassan, clambering out of the river with his clothing piled on his head. "But it's all right. I love you nonetheless."

Fatima flushed and turned her attention back to the wad of clothing she had stuffed into Hassan's pack. It was all wrinkled now and smelled of canvas on the verge of mildewing. She pulled out the plainest robe she could find: it was a light felted wool dyed blue with indigo and embroidered with red yarn along the hem and cuffs. It was cut for a man, but she and Hassan were roughly the same height, and when she pulled it on, it fell where it should. Vikram took the two bundles of wet clothes in his arms and stood on a rock.

"Your daggers," he said, flinging them into the dirt at their feet. "Don't forget those. You will almost certainly need them."

Fatima dug out a dry sash and wrapped it around her waist, securing the dagger at her hip.

"That's better," said Vikram, eyeing her critically. "You don't quite look like a peasant, but you look much less like a royal concubine who has run away. Time to go, children! There are miles between you and a safe place to sleep." He climbed up the riverbank and into the scrub, passing through it as soundlessly as a shadow. Fatima hurried to follow him. Her feet squeaked in the wet boots, but on the whole she felt well enough: the water had refreshed her, Hassan's robe was less confining than her own had been, and though the afternoon threatened rain, the prospect of walking in a straight line, without corners or walls or doors in the way, was new enough to feel full of promise.

* * *

Vikram led them south, following the pebbly foothills of the Sierra Nevada. To their right, the Vega stretched westward, as flat as the palm of a hand, curving up at the horizon to meet the more forgiving hills that defined its farthest reaches. The farmland was empty now. Fatima could see the white remains of houses and stone walls that had once marked the perimeters of fields, like chalk lines dividing up the landscape. Years of siege had made them into roosts for crows, the roof tiles looted or smashed, the walls quarried for other uses. The little streams and tributaries that watered the Vega were at their summer ebb and in some places had run completely dry: they reached out into the silent plain like fingers of gray mud, withdrawing moisture rather than replenishing it.

Fatima watched Vikram as they walked. He seemed to know where he was going, for he rarely raised his head: instead he grumbled without cease, though in a voice almost too quiet to make out, and in languages Fatima could not decipher.

"You know Lady Aisha," she hazarded at one point, desiring to make conversation. Vikram looked over his shoulder, one elegant brow arched with scorn.

"Such powers of perception it has. Of course I know Lady Aisha. How many hours have we spent together in the courtyard while she played the lute and you moped about in corners, pretending to mend the linen?"

"I mean you know her particularly," said Fatima, exasperated. "You aren't just a dog, and she wasn't just playing the lute. You must have met her somehow."

"Ah." Vikram smiled. "Well. That is a good story. Once upon a time, when Lady Aisha was simply Aisha, not yet the wife of one sultan and mother to the next, I stole a pair of jeweled slippers from her."

"Why?"

"I wanted her to run away with me."

"Run away with Lady Aisha?" Fatima laughed. "Why would you want that, and why would you steal her slippers if you did?"

"She was bewitching as a girl," said Vikram defensively. "She still is. Not pretty in the profound sense that Fatima is pretty, but compelling and sly and maddeningly aloof, like Scheherazade or Cleopatra. Everyone was dying of love for her. She would have none of it, of course. She wanted the most powerful man in Granada, and by God, she got him. It was he who gave her the slippers as an engagement gift. I thought that if I stole them and she was found to be without them, there would be a scandal, and the engagement would be called off."

"That's not a very nice thing to do to someone you love," muttered Hassan, shifting his bags from one shoulder to the other.

"I'm not nice, as it happens. And anyway, this was not precisely love. Jinn don't love very often, or very much. We are prone to mild obsessions, however, which is what this was."

"What happened? I can't imagine Lady Aisha in a torrid love triangle with a jinn. She's always seemed so remote and forbidding to me. This is entirely new information."

"There was no torrid love triangle, so you're excused from imagining it. No, Aisha didn't care for me in the least, and told me so frequently. A day came when her betrothed—presently to become your master's father, Fatima—visited her in her father's villa, expecting to see her wearing his costly gift. She appeared before him barefoot, which was a shockingly intimate thing to do with a man to whom she wasn't yet married. She told him she'd given the slippers to a beggar who had no shoes in exchange for his blessing upon their marriage. Her fiancé left even more pleased with her than when he'd arrived, and the wedding was pushed forward by a month. Thus ended my pursuit."

"What did you do with the slippers?" asked Fatima.

"I gave them to my sister in the Empty Quarter. I've spent much of the last four decades paying off my debt. Which is why we are all here together. What a happy coincidence." With that, Vikram put his head down and trotted onward on all fours, resuming his private monologue. Fatima and Hassan struggled after him and lapsed into silence.

They walked until midday without seeing any sign of life. The foothills to their left turned white and shimmered in the heat, exhaling some internal luminescence. When the sun was highest, a lone falcon began to circle above their heads. It cried piteously and without cease, as if pleading for some response.

"That thing is eerie," Hassan said, stopping and huffing to catch his breath. Walking over the uneven ground had made his cheeks as florid as his hair. "Why is it making such a racket? Could it be a Castilian spy?"

Vikram looked up at the bird and knit his brows.

"You joke, but you may be more right than you realize," he murmured, climbing a rise to get a better view. "Falcons are curious birds. They'll follow anything that interests them. As long as it trails us, anyone hunting you will know there is movement here in the foothills."

"Can't we make it go away?" asked Fatima, peering up at it. The bird crossed in front of the hazy sun; she closed her eyes and saw its double.

"I don't speak with birds," said Vikram, jumping down into the dry streambed in which they had been walking. "Birds can walk and swim and fly and augur the future, so they're more like my kind than they are like yours. There's a certain mutual suspicion."

Fatima looked back up at the falcon. It floated in the thick air, tracing a series of oblong shapes against the clouds. Several times as they walked, Fatima had thought she heard the muffled howl of a dog, sometimes far off and sometimes nearer, though the hills to their left and the rise and fall of the ground made it difficult to tell where the sound was coming from. Vikram, for his part, never gave any sign of alarm. He trotted along on all fours across the broken terrain and growled like a madman, absorbed in his own opaque thoughts. Fatima told herself that if he was unafraid, she had no reason to be otherwise, and fought the upswells of anxiety when they came. But the falcon was different: it was neither pursuer nor friend, and the ambiguity made Fatima uneasy.

"Maybe we can distract it with something," she said. "Don't birds like baubles and shiny things?"

"Good idea," laughed Hassan. "What a shame we've left our diamond cuffs, golden necklets, and ropes of pearls in the Alhambra. They would be so handy just now."

Fatima glanced down at her wrists. She had, in fact, possessed a pair of gold cuffs, a gift from the sultan when they started sharing a bed. They were beautiful, beaten into a thousand facets and polished so that they caught the light. But Lady Maryam had seen her wearing them in the courtyard one day—it was before she had retired to her own room and stopped receiving anyone—and appraised her silently for a moment that went on far too long. Fatima put the cuffs away in a box. She wore no jewelry now except for her anklets.

"Wait," she said, coming to a halt. "Wait, wait. I do have something." Bending down, she unlaced her damp boots and withdrew one foot. The anklet clung to her flesh, its double row of tiny silver bells silent. She unclasped it and peeled it off, holding it up triumphantly for Hassan and Vikram to see.

"How resourceful it is," said Vikram with a toothy grin. "Well, well. Throw your pretty bells away, as hard and as high as you can, and we'll see whether they make any difference."

Fatima hurled the anklet toward the yellow flank of the hill alongside which they had been walking. The bells twinkled for a moment before vanishing into the scrub, landing with a merry sound. The falcon folded its wings and dived after them.

"Well done," said Hassan, clapping Fatima on the back. "All that shrieking was driving me mad. What would you bet that's a tame bird? Some wealthy merchant probably set it loose before fleeing across the Strait. It's lonely and hungry, poor thing—just like us."

Fatima said nothing, regretting the loss of her anklet. She could hear it jingling in the scrub as the falcon pecked at the bells.

"Can we get it back?" she asked. "After the bird has gone?"

Vikram laughed at her.

"It wants its pretty things back. Be glad, Fatima! Better the bird should make noise and draw the dogs and you walk a little lighter in your boots."

"Don't laugh at me," muttered Fatima, scuffing the dust with one foot. "I only own three things, and that's counting the ring Lady Aisha gave me. That bird is half as rich as I am now."

"You have many things more valuable than those bells, or even the borrowed ruby on your finger," sang Vikram, loping onward down the shallow crater of the streambed. "Youth, intelligence, health, strength of will, surpassing beauty, and now, freedom. Your anger, too, would be a gift, if you would only decide to harness it. There are many men in this world who have bells aplenty, yet are not half as rich as Fatima."

Fatima set her jaw, formulating a response. She did not have the opportunity to try it, however, for a moment later there came the baying of not one but several hounds, very close by. The sound echoed off the barren hillside and landed in Fatima's ears with a loud crack.

"How silly we've been," whispered Hassan, his face as white as the bleached stones under their feet. "Standing here making all this noise."

Vikram said something in a language Fatima had never heard before, a pair of harsh syllables like a cross between a growl and a log splitting open in a fire.

"Come," he murmured, taking one of their hands in each of his. "Stay close."

Fatima felt a tug on her wrist. Dazed, she stumbled to follow, breaking out into a run when the pressure increased, taking longer and longer steps until it seemed her feet barely touched the earth. The banks of the streambed blurred around her, becoming a tangle of stone and scrub and stunted trees tinted yellow where the sun struck them and blue where the shadows of the hills fell. Her lungs ached. Beside her, Hassan was a blot of red hair and green felt and heavy breathing. Fatima felt unconsciousness pressing out from behind her eyes. She struggled against it until the banks of the stream began to go dark, as if night were falling.

If you faint, I will get angry, came a voice in her head. *If you faint I will have to leave you behind, and then you will die, and I will have broken my promise.*

Fatima forced herself to breathe more deeply. She counted each breath in Arabic and in Sabir and in Castilian and in Latin. She counted until she ran out of numbers.

"Stop," she begged, her voice ragged.

The world began to slow. The pressure on Fatima's wrist relaxed. Gasping, she fell to her knees and pressed her forehead against the earth. A bitter tang rose up in the back of her throat. She tensed, retching.

"That's right," came Vikram's voice, tinged with amusement. A clawed hand thumped her across the shoulders. "Get it all up."

"It" was water and bile, for there was nothing else in Fatima's stomach. She coughed and sputtered and rolled onto her back. Images came into focus around her. Above, the sky was golden, the morning mist burned away. They had left the streambed behind and passed into open country. There was dry grass beneath her; beside her, the humming of cicadas in a lone willow. Hassan passed in front of her eyes, his hair a windblown halo about his face.

"Let's never do that again," he muttered.

Fatima attempted to sit. The ground tilted at a nauseating angle. Moaning, she lay down again and dug her fingers into the earth. The sweet tang of grass and dust pooled in her nose and the back of her throat and soothed her.

"Look at the horizon," instructed Vikram. "It will help."

Fatima blinked to bring the distance into focus. The Sierra Nevada began at her head and ended somewhere past her feet, pulling back in the middle as if out of modesty, like a lady drawing her veil across her shoulders. At this distance, the mountains were profoundly blue, succeeded at the tree line by an icy color as the snows that lay on the highest peaks surged upward toward their birthplace in the sky.

Between Fatima and the mountains, the ground was flat. Great squares of it were furrowed in preparation for crops that had never been sown. The willow tree under which she lay was the only upright thing in sight, aside from a charred, boxy shape a little way off that might be the ruins of a farmhouse. A path of packed earth led up to it before trailing away toward some long-disused high road. Everything was empty: the plain, the fields, the path, the skeletal house. It was vicious, somehow, the emptiness, as if the Vega was waiting to strike at them for the war that had left it fallow and burned.

Fatima grasped at the knobby trunk of the willow and pulled herself up.

"Why did you bring us here?" she asked, her voice feeble. "A baby could spot us from miles away."

"I had very little choice," said Vikram. He launched himself at the trunk of the tree and scuttled up into its thicket of branches. "The Vega bends eastward here and must be crossed in the open. The is no more shelter in the foothills, and anyway, the black-cloaks will be looking for you there. They too must come this way, for they have horses and dogs to water and rest, but with any luck they will not be here before dawn, and by then we will have moved on. Tomorrow we cross the Dúrcal River and make for the pass through the southern mountains."

"Keck to all that," muttered Hassan, throwing himself down at the foot of the willow. "When do I get to sleep in a bed? That's all I want to know."

"A bed?" Vikram sounded amused. "Forget your beds. You'll be sleeping on rocks and roots for days yet."

"A fire, then," said Hassan with a pleading lilt in his voice. "Or I will begin to value my life very lightly."

"It wants a fire," snorted Vikram, shaking the branches as he dropped down from the canopy. "A lone fire on the Vega would be visible for leagues and leagues. You might as well use yourself as tinder. But don't worry. Your old uncle Vikram will keep you warm."

"Are you *flirting* with me?"

"Maybe a little. Children! Listen closely. I am going away to fetch your dinner. Do not leave the shadow of this tree while I'm gone. Nod your head if you understand."

Fatima rolled her eyes. Apparently satisfied, Vikram cantered away across the tilled earth, leaving no footprints. Fatima watched him for as long as she could. He became a dot, and then a shimmer of air, and then nothing, leaving behind the uncomfortable impression that he had never existed to begin with. Shivering, Fatima pressed herself into a hollow between two of the willow tree's sloping roots. The ground at its base was littered with oblong yellow leaves that curled in the heat like tiny rolls of parchment. Fatima withdrew her feet from her boots and pushed the leaves around in the dust, enjoying the familiar sensation of air and earth against her toes. The haze had vanished and the sky was the deep cloudless color of late afternoon. Pulling her hands inside the sleeves of her robe, Fatima closed her eyes.

"Do you really think we're going to make it?" came Hassan's voice, heavy with fatigue. "I mean honestly. You can tell the truth now that it's—he's—gone."

"Of course we're going to make it," murmured Fatima. She was too tired to offer anything but platitudes.

"By all means, you sleep," said Hassan flatly, when it was clear no more encouragement was forthcoming. "I'll keep watch." She heard him shift his weight and lift himself to his feet with a groan. Fatima curled her knees against her chest and did as he suggested, falling asleep so fast that slumber came like a physical blow.

* * *

She dreamed of footfalls. Lady Aisha was moving about the room in her soft way, unspeaking, as she had done when Fatima was a small child and slept in her mistress's bed. Lady Aisha had always been careful not to wake her. She had strong opinions about uninterrupted sleep. She was sewing, or so it seemed to Fatima, who did not feel inclined to open her eyes: she could hear her mistress's bone needle rasping back and forth through a piece of raw silk. The mending was Fatima's responsibility now that she was grown. Lady Aisha was silent, but later she would purse her lips and drop the finished work into Fatima's lap as a reprimand. She should wake, then, wake and finish the work herself to avoid an ugly scene.

Her fingers twitched in the grass and reminded her she was somewhere else. There would be no more mending; no one in the harem save Lady Aisha was mourning her absence now. The other girls were probably gossiping, tittering to each other, spreading the

124

news in whispers until it reached the serving woman, who would tell the washerwoman, who would bring the juicy tidbit down the hill into the city itself along with her sacks of dirty linen: the sultan's concubine has run away. Nessma was probably comforting her brother even now, massaging his shoulders as she bent to whisper in his ear: *That girl was no good. I always said so. So haughty, so ungrateful—she never loved you. She never loved any of us.*

And the sultan? Try as she might, Fatima couldn't imagine his reaction to her flight. It was not his way to shout and break things. He might have one or two of the harem guards flogged, but only for form's sake; it must be immediately known that any lapse in duty would be punished. Would he send for the blonde Provençal war captive and console himself with her? Perhaps not. Perhaps he would finally cross the courtyard of the harem to knock on Lady Maryam's door, and stand before her, and talk, haltingly, about their children.

The rasping sound began again. Fatima opened her eyes. Twilight had fallen over the Vega: the sky was dark overhead and pale on the soft hills that formed the western horizon. Beside her, Hassan was asleep sitting up, his head lolling against the trunk of the willow, his mouth slightly open. The soft steps, the quiet rustling sounds, came from a man crouched on the far side of the tree, rifling through their bags.

Fatima screamed. The man looked up at her with a startled, savage expression, his eyes milky in the dark. He was wearing a black wool doublet over a shirt that might once have been red; his face, too, was sun-reddened, stubble running riot over lopsided features. They stared at one another for a moment. Then the man lunged.

Fatima's head knocked against a root and for a moment she could see nothing but bursts of light. There was a great weight on her chest. She struggled to free herself, to scream again, but a dirt-perfumed hand clapped over her mouth and pressed her head back against the bony foot of the tree. The pain in her skull was so great that Fatima thought it might crack open, that this sorry, furtive wriggling was what death felt like.

Hassan was awake now and scrambling to his feet: she heard a cry of dismay and then a grunt as he kicked the man hard in the ribs. The pressure on her mouth relented for a moment. Gasping, Fatima squeezed her hand down along her side, drew her knife, and pointed it up.

Hot liquid gushed over her knife hand. The man made a choked, frightened sound and rolled away. Hands wrapped themselves beneath her shoulders and pulled her upright, and then she was in Hassan's shaking arms.

"Are you all right?" he panted. "Is any of that yours?"

Fatima looked down: the front of her robe was soaked in blood.

"I don't think so," she said. Her feet went out from under her; Hassan tightened his grip.

"Are you sure?" he pressed. "Your face is this awful color that I can't quite explain. Say something, Fa, for God's sake."

"I haven't cut her." The man was lying on his back, his own face an awful color, one fist stuffed against the spreading wet spot on his doublet. He was speaking Castilian. "Though the little bitch has cut me pretty well."

Fatima was still holding her knife. She felt no desire to let it go. She held it up in front of her, though the man at her feet was hardly in a position to rise again. There seemed to be no connection between the things that she saw: the knife, the blood, the labored breathing of her assailant. Something else must have happened, something benign; there had been a terrible misunderstanding.

"Do you know what this is?" The fingers of the Castilian's free hand twitched, gesturing at his sopping doublet. "This is a gut wound. It takes a long time. Hours."

Fatima did not understand. She looked from her bloody knife to the man and back again.

"Do the right thing," he snapped, phlegm rattling in his throat. "The soldierly thing, since you've got a soldier's knife."

Fatima's knife hand began to shake.

"You want me to kill you?" Her Castilian came out blunt and accented. The man gave a horrible laugh.

"You've already done that," he said. "I'm asking you for mercy. Mercy is a virtue, yes? Even for an infidel like you."

"I can't." Fatima let the knife slip from her hand. "I can't. I'm sorry." To her horror, she felt herself begin to cry. "I'm very sorry."

There was a rush of air at her back. Vikram boiled up beside her, snarling. He tossed a brace of freshly gutted rabbits at the roots of the tree.

"What is this?" he barked. "Can't I leave you alone for an hour without coming back to a mess?"

The Castilian stared up at Vikram in horror.

"*Ave Maria,*" he wheezed, "*gratia plena, Dominus tecum, benedicta tu in mulierib—*"

Vikram fell on the man's throat with his teeth bared. The world around Fatima grew dim with screaming; she smelled blood, and then something worse than blood, and then the man went abruptly silent. Fatima could hear her own breathing. It came in high, whistling gasps she could not control, as if some exterior force was pushing air into her lungs and just as quickly withdrawing it, leaving her desperate for more.

The calls of insects returned to fill the quiet. Their trills were punctuated every now and then by the stony crunch of teeth through bone and another more unspeakable sound, the slip and hiss of viscera being separated from itself. Vikram ate methodically. His long hair, matted with gore, obscured his face; his arms and legs were pulled beneath him, bent at angles no human limbs could form.

When he looked up again, his face was painted crimson, a color that was almost beautiful, the same shade as the dark ruby adorning Fatima's finger. She stared at him and saw the gardens and baths and orderly days of her former life grow faint and irrelevant, something that only imitated what was real, a simulacrum tiled in blue and white. Vikram saw her watching and gave a smile that was almost sad.

"You should have done it," he said. He picked Fatima's dagger out of the dirt and began to clean his talons with it. "Then the poor idiot's last vision of this world would have been the face of a lovely girl, not a nightmare like me."

Fatima wanted to sit down. The Castilian's blood was stiffening on her hand; she wiped it on her robe, futilely, and succeeded only in smearing her forearm with more of the tacky substance. There seemed nothing left to do but cry and let the ground hold her up.

"Give me my knife back, please," she said to Vikram between sniffles, holding out one hand.

"Ha!" Vikram wiped the blade clean on his own shadowy pelt and handed it back to her, hilt first. "Of all the things you could have said, that was the most impressive. Here, take your weapon. Little murderess! My God, what a day." He squatted beside what remained of the Castilian, prodding the shredded arm of his doublet.

"Was that necessary?" quavered Hassan, leaning against the tree, his face waxy. His own knife was out, Fatima noticed, balanced between his long fingers like a very sharp quill. "Was that fair? Did you have to—did you have to—"

"Thank you, Vikram, for saving me from the brigand who would have killed me where I slept," the dog-man suggested with a leer. "That's what you meant to say."

"But did you have to *eat him*?"

Vikram pretended not to hear. He began to wipe his face with his hair, removing the crimson paint, returning himself to his usual late-afternoon color.

"Did you know that lions once lived in the Vega?" he asked. "Many, many centuries ago. The *banu adam* hunted the last one in the days of your long-ago grandfathers. They were big, these lions, with short, pale manes. They ruled over this whole plain, from foothill to foothill. But even the noblest predator must die, and when he does, he becomes food for the jackal." Vikram finished his toilette and shook himself, ruffling out his coat, looking suddenly like a dog again. Watching him was like looking at a robe of translucent silk: opaque in some lights, yet quick to reveal the body underneath when the sun struck it. "I'm the jackal. I get hungry too."

Hassan could marshal no counterargument and lapsed into dazed silence. Fatima stared at the Castilian's feet, the only part of him that had escaped their encounter unscathed: ordinary feet in ordinary shoes of soft-soled leather, crowned by bloodless ankles. Perhaps, after all this bother, life was only a choice between two kinds of brutality: the wretched sort that lay on the ground before her, and the civilized sort she had left behind.

"Who was he?" came Hassan's voice, cautiously. Vikram made a purring noise and peeled back the blood-reddened collar of the Castilian's doublet. Sewn inside was a crest embroidered on a piece of linen: a cross flanked by a palm frond and a sword.

"I've seen that before," said Fatima, wiping her brow with her unbloodied hand. "It was on a letter in Luz's trunk."

"The crest of the Holy Office," said Vikram. He let the Castilian's collar drop. "This man was a scout. They travel fast, your hunters—very fast." He rocked back on his furred heels and frowned. "Too fast."

"What does that mean?" Hassan pressed.

"I'm not sure," said Vikram. "For now, it means we must move on."

"Move on? Now? No—Fa has had a terrible shock. She needs rest. We both do. Our feet will fall off. We haven't had a real sleep. Or a meal. Some of us aren't made of fire or shadow or whatever it is you are."

"Do you have another solution?" snapped Vikram, clacking his teeth. "If this man has reached us, more will follow. There is only bare earth between us and the southern pass, unless you can coax a well-fortified castle out of the ground with your little talents."

Hassan, inclined to be literal, bit his lip and surveyed the landscape.

"No," he said finally. "There's not enough here. I can make little shortcuts—little rearrangements. Not whole houses or hills. The last time I tried that, there was a real—" His lip twitched. "A real mess."

Fatima knew what he meant, though she looked away and pretended she did not. It had been a day in midwinter, the year the princes and little Aisha had gone into Castile and not come back. Fatima had been carrying water from the kitchen to the harem. Her fingers were rigid from the chill and the weight of the buckets suspended from her hands. She had been furious. The serving women—there had been several back then, before the siege—usually performed these menial tasks, but now that the princes were gone, they looked at Fatima and saw a slave instead of a royal playmate.

As she hefted the buckets—water sloshing on her slippers, on the hem of her trousers—she rehearsed the impassioned complaint she planned to make to Lady Aisha as soon as her task was finished. The injustice of it filled her so completely that she set the buckets down again in order to better arrange her thoughts. In the silence, she heard Hassan sobbing brokenly somewhere nearby.

He was still a beardless apprentice then and had not yet grown into his large hands. He was sitting in the entryway of the sultan's private quarters, quite alone except for the sultan himself. The sight of her master made Fatima stop and hold her breath. The sultan was almost a boy that winter, though already several years a husband and father; he was also, Fatima remembered somewhat wistfully, at the height of his pale-lipped, dark-eyed beauty, though she had been too young to understand what this meant. Instead, she had ducked behind a pillar, filled with the kind of anxiety that comes from witnessing something one is not meant to see.

"Make it work," the sultan was saying to Hassan in a low voice. "Try. Try, Hassan, for your king's sake."

"I can't." Hassan was bent over a lap desk. Fatima could hear his charcoal scraping across a sheet of paper. "Please don't ask me. There are so many walls, so many miles—it doesn't work this way."

"How does it work?"

"I don't know, I don't know. I'm not a magician, sire. I can't simply open a portal. It's too far. It's two hundred miles, more than two hundred miles. Sire—"

"I need my children." The sultan's voice was shaking. "My wife is half dead with weeping. Make a map. Close the distance. Do something, or I will run mad."

There was a scuffle. Fatima could not see exactly what was happening, but as far as she could guess, the sultan had seized Hassan's hand, or perhaps his arm, as if to direct the strokes of his pencil. Hassan made a wild, despairing sound. It was then that the corridor in which Fatima stood, water pooling at her feet and bloating her slippers, went dark. She turned around and around in dismay. The windows had vanished. They had been swallowed by the walls, or so it seemed; there was only stone where there had once been wooden latticework and open air. The door at the end of the corridor had also disappeared. Fatima was standing in a long stone tomb that was sealed at both ends. She heard terrified screaming leaching up from the floors and through the walls.

It had lasted only a minute. Through the wall, Fatima could hear the sultan's muffled voice shouting orders. Hassan had become hysterical. She would never know what passed between them, but it had the desired effect: after an instant of pressure, a rapid condensation of air, the windows and doors were there again. The sultan walked back into his quarters with a curse. Hassan was left alone, bawling over his lap desk. Fatima did not go to comfort him. She was too frightened of the sound of grief.

✳ ✳ ✳

"Never mind," said Vikram. He slapped Fatima on the shoulder, startling her. "Your thoughts are naked enough. I understand what you are afraid of. Here is what we'll do: I will drag this dead fellow away for the crows to play with. If we're lucky, the main force following behind him will find the body and realize you are not as defenseless as you may have seemed. You will rest up here in the boughs of the tree—it's so thick near the crown that you will be invisible to human eyes, though not, unfortunately, to a dog's nose. Do your eating and sleeping. I will walk around and see how close the hunters are. We'll move out in the dark hour before dawn, unless I need to wake you earlier."

Hassan gave a sigh that was almost happy. Vikram pressed a rabbit into his hands and gave him an encouraging pat on the bottom.

"Up you go," he said. "Vikram will give you a boost."

"Am I supposed to eat this raw?" asked Hassan, waving the rabbit.

"Up," said Vikram. "As high as you can." He put his hands out for Hassan to step on and half threw him into the lowest branches of the tree, where Hassan landed with a shriek, clinging to the wide trunk with both arms.

133

"You next," said Vikram to Fatima. "Have a rabbit. It's perfectly clean and tender. You must eat the heart and the liver. You're a predator now."

Fatima did not see fit to respond. She took the rabbit with as much dignity as she could muster and climbed into the fat lower branches of the willow tree. She could hear Hassan shaking the limbs above her, his awkward half leaps raining ashy bits of bark down on her head.

"Up here," came his voice. "There's a sort of V where we can sit without falling off, or at least I hope so."

After a moment's hesitation, Fatima held her rabbit between her teeth and hauled herself farther into the crown of the tree. Hassan sat with his legs draped over one of its uppermost branches. The long, whip-thin fingers of the willow splayed out around them in a pungent wreath, obscuring the world outside. The only identifiable object was the young moon, which was cut into pieces just beyond Fatima's head. She settled onto the branch next to Hassan's, which did indeed grow outward at a convenient angle, allowing her to wedge herself next to him as a kind of counterweight.

Hassan was tearing the flesh off his rabbit with his teeth, separating muscle from bone with a wet, adhesive sound. Fatima was suddenly ravenous and began to do the same. The meat of the rabbit was soft and not at all bloody; the taste was like grass and iron and earth. She finished off the little ribs and flanks, and when she was done, fished in the expertly gutted cavity of the creature's chest with one finger to remove its heart, which she popped into her mouth, eyes shut, the single, metallic burst of sweetness flooding over her tongue like dark honey.

Chapter 8

Vikram returned when the moon was high. Fatima did not wake when he arrived but rather saw him in her sleep: a dark mass of fur and teeth and eyes that ascended the tree in darting motions and settled across her knees like a grotesque lapdog. Being asleep, however, Fatima was not afraid, only grateful for the feverish warmth that radiated from the creature's body.

"Are we safe?" she asked.

Vikram was silent for a time.

"They know things they shouldn't know," he said finally. "Your pursuers. That woman. And I'm not sure how, or why."

"Should I be worried?"

"Yes. But don't wake up. There's very little you can do about it, at least for now. Sleep is the best medicine for you." Vikram sighed and rolled on his back, closing his own eyes.

"Tell me a story," begged Fatima.

"What kind of story?" muttered Vikram.

"A nice one. Without dead things in it."

"All stories have dead things in them eventually, assuming they start out with live ones. But very well. Choose a bird."

Fatima smiled without waking.

"You know about our game," she said.

"I was present for your birth, little sister. I know most things about you. So choose."

"Falcon," said Fatima automatically. Vikram snorted.

"You're predictable in your sleep. I sometimes forget that dreams are where you *banu adam* sort out your waking lives. Very well, I'll sort it for you. Once upon a time, all the birds of the world gathered at a secret meeting place for a great moot."

"I know this part," said Fatima.

"Shut up and listen. For many years, they had been without a king. They were beginning to forget the ancient paths through the air and water and could no longer understand the First Speech of the angels and the jinn. Times had grown desperate. As the wren and the crow quarreled over seating arrangements and the peacock insisted he must speak first, the hoopoe, with her striped crest and sacred words carved into her beak, stepped forward. 'My friends!' she said. 'I have good news. The Bird King lives. He is hidden beneath an ancient mountain called Qaf, which sits on an island far across the Dark Sea. If we marshal all our strength, we may yet find him and restore our race to greatness.' Many of the birds scoffed at her, but they all died of cowardice long ago, so they aren't important. A smaller band, thirty birds in all, believed the hoopoe, and pledged to follow her. And so the party set off toward the sea, following the red crest of the hoopoe, who flew ahead. The autumn mists were gathering. The birds were uneasy, but the hoopoe led them on, following her secret sense.

"They had been flying for several days when the falcon grew restless. Why did the king have to live so far away? It seemed a very unreasonable distance to travel. Spotting something glimmering in the grass below, the falcon veered away from the party and swept down to investigate. There, wedged between the rocks and tufts of dry reeds, was a bracelet of beaten gold.

"'Oh,' cried the falcon. 'Come back, come back, look what we almost missed.' The other birds turned back and flew down when they heard the falcon's cries. The falcon wrapped her talons around the bracelet and fluttered her wings, trying to wrench it free. The bracelet was stuck fast between the rocks.

"'Why do you delay us?' asked the hoopoe. 'We have no time for baubles and bracelets. The king is waiting.' But the falcon was adamant.

"'It would be a crime to leave something so valuable lying on the ground,' she said. 'Why should we pass up a chance like this?' The falcon pulled and pulled at the bracelet until the other birds became uneasy and pressed on without her. The falcon was so consumed by her task that she barely noticed their absence. Finally, as the sun set, she realized she was alone and began to grow frightened.

"'What a fool I've been,' she lamented. 'For one bracelet, I missed my chance to meet the king of the birds. Oh, hoopoe! How sorry I am!' Just then, she saw a flash of red in the deepening gloom. It was the hoopoe, come back to fetch her companion. The falcon was so happy to see the hoopoe that she let go of the bracelet and pushed off into the air, beating her wings. In the commotion, the bracelet rolled free and tumbled down the rocks, ringing as it fell.

"'Look, falcon,' said the hoopoe. 'Your bracelet is free at last.' But the falcon shook her head. 'It was never mine,' she said. 'It was only weight, and I am glad not to carry it.' And on they flew."

"Are your stories always so moralizing?" murmured Fatima.

"No," said Vikram. He yawned and for a moment she saw the muzzle and lolling tongue of a dog. "But this isn't my story."

He ambled along the thick branch where Fatima was sitting and lay down across the tapering end, where it thinned into innumerable little leaf-clad fingers, draping his limbs on either side like an indolent leopard. Just past him, the topmost branches were split, revealing a fragment of sky. False dawn had turned it the color of smoke; only the brightest stars were still visible. Fatima watched them wink and grow indistinct as they faded into the light of the hastening sun. She felt alert and clearheaded, though disinclined to move.

"I'm awake," she said.

"You're asleep," said Vikram. "You're still asleep."

* * *

"Hsst! Fa!"

"See? She looks dead to me. Poke her with a stick to make sure."

"She's not *dead*, you animal. Fa! Wake up."

The cicadas were riotous, their heady thrum nearly drowning out the sound of voices. Fatima tried to rouse herself and succeeded only in twitching her eyelids. Her stomach was a pit of fetid water. Even the smallest movement brought up the taste of blood and flesh and a sour, boggy feeling: a bodily bad omen. Moaning, Fatima reached out and felt herself lifted in furred arms and then set down again. A matted mound of yellow grass as dry as paper came into focus beneath her feet.

"If you're going to be sick, don't do it here," came Hassan's voice, alarmed. Fatima forced herself to straighten, breathing slowly to keep her bowels in check. The sun was bright and hot: it was late morning.

"Why did you let me sleep so late?" she demanded. "I thought we were going to leave at dawn."

"We did leave at dawn," said Vikram, flashing his teeth. "I've been carrying you like a baby for most of the way. You slept like a baby, too, with your fingers curled up in my pelt to keep yourself from falling."

Fatima flushed and turned in an unsteady circle, attempting to orient herself. The tree that had sheltered them at night was nowhere to be seen. They had passed from the flatlands into the gentle hills that made up the southern reaches of the Vega. Fatima was standing on the edge of a loamy, terraced slope with rows of thick-bellied olive trees marching from end to end. A packed dirt path led down the hill and into a valley toward a stone house with no roof. The trees had not been pruned in several years and had a feral look about them: their leaves were parched and silver, but some of them had fruited in spite of their neglect, and clusters of small green pips were visible among the branches. Hassan had availed himself of this modest bounty and was seated between the roots of the largest tree with a pile of olives in his lap, his shoes off and overturned in the dust.

"They taste awful," he said cheerfully, spitting out a pit. "A raw olive is a different animal from a cured one, apparently. God bless the man who first taught the world how to cure olives. He and the man who invented cheese are two unsung pillars of civilization."

"They were probably women," muttered Fatima, fanning her face with the sleeve of her robe. "If they were men, we would remember their names."

"You're in a good mood this morning. Here, have an olive. It's no worse than what we ate last night, tastewise."

Fatima winced and shook her head. In front of her, Vikram was bounding along the dirt path down the hillside, his black hair trailing behind him like a tattered flag. In the strong light, he looked quite human: like a hermit perhaps, or a dervish, a man long alone in the wilderness, but a man nonetheless. When he reached the bottom of the hill, he made for a stone circle with slats of wood piled on top that sat a little distance from the empty house, ringed with clumps of grass that looked very green against the parched landscape that surrounded them.

"Come down," called Vikram. "I've found a well."

Hassan got to his feet with a groan and shuffled into his shoes. Fatima followed him, still dazed, her limbs heavy with the heat and the protests of her stomach. Vikram was pushing the slats of wood off the mouth of the well, singing wordlessly and clacking his teeth for percussion. The scent of sweet water wafted up from the exposed stone.

"Thank God," said Hassan fervently, falling to his knees. A copper kettle tied to a length of cord sweltered in the sun nearby;

he dropped it into the well, laughing in triumph when it landed with a faint splash some distance below.

"Let's live here," he said, drawing up the kettle hand over hand. "Now I know why heaven is said to be awash in pure water. I never want to drink out of an old sluggish river again. You should have seen what came out of me before you woke up, Fa. I didn't know I could produce matter of that color and quantity, of such—"

"Stop," begged Fatima, queasy again. "Stop talking."

Hassan shrugged. The kettle came up cold and dripping, beads of sweat forming on its battered surface as he drew it into the light. Putting it to his lips, Hassan drank noisily. When he was done, he wiped his sodden beard on his sleeve and passed the kettle to Fatima.

The water was cold enough to make her teeth ache, but very clear, and so sweet that she forgot herself for a moment and gave a little cry of pleasure. Vikram laughed at her. He stood on the lip of the well and surveyed their surroundings, glaring out at the quiet hills that tumbled south, rising suddenly at the horizon, like waves breaking on a seawall, to become green and violet mountains.

"If we make good time, we can reach the southern pass by nightfall," he said. "And strike the harbor road while it's dark."

"A road sounds nice," said Hassan in a hopeful voice. "I like roads. Better than scrambling over streambeds and cutting across other people's fields."

"You say so now, but you won't when the time comes," said Vikram with a smile that Fatima did not like. "That road is watched day and night by Castilian scouts, and there is no other way through the southern mountains—at least, none for human feet. The Vega may be abandoned, but the coastal towns are not, and they all belong to Spain now. The danger of the past two days has been slight compared with what lies ahead."

Hassan chewed on his beard.

"Give me my satchel," he said, gesturing at Vikram with one hand. Recognizing the glint in his eye, Fatima felt less sluggish and went to sit next to him, pressing her back against the warm stone lip of the well.

"Are you going to draw something?" she asked.

Hassan pulled a roll of paper from his satchel and spread it out across his knees. "There's never no other way," he murmured. "There are always other ways. If there are scouts who watch the harbor road, there are scouting paths that run alongside it. They won't expect us there, especially in the dark. It's better than nothing." He ran his fingers around the edge of the paper. Picking up a charcoal, he drew a meandering line. On either side of the line, he began to sketch what looked to Fatima like the ripples caused by throwing a stone into a quiet pool, yet instead of concentric circles, these were irregular shapes, bulging and shrinking at odd intervals.

"What are those?" she asked, not quite touching the paper with one finger.

"The southern mountains," said Hassan. His eyes had grown bright. "I'm drawing the elevation of the range that runs alongside the harbor road—which is this line, here. Each peak is highest where I've drawn the smallest shape. The widest shape is the base. The closer together the lines are, the steeper the slope. If I had more time, I would mix some colored inks and shade everything, so it would make more sense. But you can still grasp the abstract. Think of it like looking straight down at a mountain from overhead, as a bird does."

Fatima squinted at the map taking shape beneath Hassan's long fingers. After a moment, the nebulous shapes seemed to pop in front of her eyes, taking on depth, becoming a range of hills that rose and flattened at organic intervals.

"I've never seen a map like this before," she muttered.

"That's because no one else makes them," said Hassan with a little smile of pride. "Most mapmakers draw little ticks to show you where the hills are, but that tells you nothing except 'There is a hill here.' Anyone who wants to navigate between the hills must rely on the knowledge of someone who's already been there. If that person dies or forgets, the knowledge is lost. The map goes silent. This map cannot be silenced. If you learn how to read it, Fa, you can walk through those mountains to the south as sure-footedly as the best Castilian scout, all by yourself if you want to."

Fatima looked again at the map. Running between the feet of the mountains were narrow bands of white space—gullies perhaps, or little valleys, zigzagging toward the edge of the map haphazardly.

"Here," she said, tracing a path with her finger. "If I wanted to stay off the main road, this is where I would go."

"You see?" Hassan actually giggled. "There's always another way."

A shadow peered over their shoulders.

"Your way is clever," said Vikram, "but also slow. Many sharp drops and sharp rocks on which to break ankles. There's a reason your ancestors put the harbor road where they did. If I were you and I had Vikram along to rend and rip where necessary, I would take my chances on the road and reach the sea with all possible speed, rather than fumble through gullies and give my enemies time to turn every shipmaster in the harbor against me."

"Do you think they will?" asked Fatima, looking up at him. He was a dark blot against the sun. "Do you think we're that important?"

"I think you're that distinctive," said Vikram, leaping off the edge of the well and landing in a soft puff of dust. "All one would have to do is put out the word that a Circassian girl is making her way south with a red-haired scribe for a companion, and make it clear that anyone who helps them will run afoul of the Holy Office. How many travelers fit that description, do you suppose?"

Fatima looked down at her hands and said nothing.

"Besides," said Vikram in a quieter voice, "that woman—the golden-haired one—she has a vicious streak in her. Do you know she broke two of my ribs that night in the harem garden? *Crunch*, with that little white foot, right here." Vikram gestured to his side, where the broad chest of a man blended shade by shade into the dappled pelt of a beast. "It's difficult to hurt something like me. You couldn't manage it, Fatima, because you don't like to cause pain, even at the height of your fury. You could kick and kick without making a dent. No—to hurt me, you'd have to enjoy it."

Fatima didn't like to remember that evening. The thought of Luz made her chest tighten unexpectedly. She rose and shook the dust from her bloodied robe. A breeze had kicked up and was dancing down the valley, buffeting her face; it smelled of the sap and oil of the olive groves, the warm untended earth. A lone sheep-bell clanked tonelessly somewhere nearby, rattling with the breeze and then going silent when it died down, only to start up again when the air roused itself. Fatima followed the sound into the shadow of the abandoned house, now more a carapace of stone than anything resembling a dwelling: everything made of wood had been looted or burned, leaving the doorways empty and the windows unshuttered, the slanted roof open to the sky. Fatima ducked through the remains of the front door to stand inside.

The house was generous. It had been two full stories once and a stone staircase still ran halfway up one wall, ending at nothing. Fatima was standing in what must have been the kitchen. There was a blackened hearth in a tiled niche; a domed clay oven sat above it, unraked coals still inside. The floor was filthy, covered in a thin layer of dried mud and rushes and signs of animals bedding down at night. An animal smell lingered too. Near Fatima's foot was the unmistakable imprint of a man's boot, the toe pointing toward the center of the room like the tip of a spear: the smallest suggestion of violence.

A bell began to clank again, so close that Fatima jumped. The sound was coming from a far corner of the room, where, draped across the steps leading down to a weedy garden, lay the skeleton of a ram. Its skull, all jawbone and hollow eyes, was flung back, as if the beast had offered itself up for sacrifice. The bell Fatima had heard hung from the sinewy remains of its neck and swayed back and forth in an invisible current. Fatima stared at it, transfixed. How quickly the earth and air reclaimed the dead, stripping fur from flesh and flesh from bone, leaving behind only an outline, a tailor's pattern, pinned together with vertebrae. Fatima felt as though she was intruding on something sacred. It was as if a tailor was there in the room, unstitching the work of man, returning the house and the beasts to rubble and loam, and Fatima was not meant to see.

A sudden flash of red made her gasp. There was something moving behind the ram, extricating itself from the nest of bones in a rippling mass of fur. Fatima groped at her knife. The mass made a small chittering sound and sprouted a pair of tufted ears. It was a fox. Fatima sighed with relief and sat down hard on her tailbone, her legs weak and sweating.

"You scared me," she told the fox. It looked at her with round yellow eyes, baffled.

"I thought you were a jinn," she said. "Some horrible thing with too many teeth, like Vikram."

Indifferent, the fox flicked its tail at her. It slipped down the garden stairs on tiny black feet and disappeared into the weeds. Fatima took several long breaths, fanning her face with one hand.

"You shouldn't be here alone." Vikram appeared beside her as if summoned and sat on his haunches, his own yellow eyes following the trail the fox had left behind in the swaying grass. "It's not safe."

Fatima wiped her face on her sleeve.

"I like to be alone sometimes," she said. "This isn't an evil place. Evil things have been done here, that's all."

"You try very hard to be brave. Well and good. You can be as brave while walking as you can while sitting. The sun is high, it's time to go—and you've got to change first. If you're spotted in that butcher's apron, someone might think you've killed a man."

Fatima looked down at the blood-stiffened embroidery along the front of her robe. Beneath it, her skin felt tacky; she had not yet washed.

"Is the whole world like this?" she asked, half to herself. "Full of endings? Does anything begin anymore? Are there places where people laugh?"

"Why should it matter to you?" Vikram picked himself up and shook the dust from his pelt. "You don't laugh much."

"Sometimes I think I might like to." She watched as he ambled into the sunshine on all fours, growling incoherently.

"Vikram," she called after him. "I'm serious."

He turned and considered her.

"This isn't the end of the world, little Fatima," he said in a voice that was almost kind. "It's only the end of the world you know."

Boots scuffed toward the threshold of the house: Hassan stood in the ruined doorway, holding a sheet of paper above his head.

"Finished," he said.

Vikram curled his lip.

"I still say we follow the harbor road. Why must I be the civilized one? You'll add at least two days to our journey if you insist on taking this martyr's route."

"Better two days in the wilderness than the rest of our short lives in the hands of the Inquisition," snapped Hassan, waving his map like a flag. "Lady Aisha told us to stay off that road, and you yourself say it's always watched. Why can't you be sensible?"

Vikram paced back and forth across the threshold on his knuckles.

"Fatima wants to live," he said. "Let her decide. The map or the road, Fatima. Choose."

"So you can blame me when things go wrong? You're the ones who are bickering—you settle it. I want whatever route gets us to the harbor alive. I don't care about anything else."

"For God's sake, woman," barked Vikram, baring his teeth. "If you don't pick something, I'll eat you both and save us all the trouble."

Fatima looked from the dog-man to Hassan and bit her lip. Hassan was doing a sort of pirouette, drawing the map across his body like one of the coquettish boys who danced for money in the medina, his face expectant.

"The map," said Fatima.

Chapter 9

By nightfall, Fatima could no longer feel her feet. Long hours in large boots had left a mass of blisters on her heels and along the ball of each foot; long hours after that, the blisters had broken and bled. When she began to weep silently, Vikram had taken pity on her and carried her for a while, slung over his shoulder like a bear cub. Now she was walking again. Each step landed in her ankle, as though her feet had worn away entirely and she were walking on bone. The landscape that had looked so mild in the sunlight was alien in the dark, the soft hills swollen and pale as they listed south into the starlight. Beyond them, the Sierra Lújar rose in a jagged line, pierced here and there by campfires. At their lowest point, where the scrub-clad peaks dipped down to bow toward one another, was the southern pass, and strung along it, cloaked in the newborn darkness, lay the harbor road.

"We need to keep to the west," panted Hassan, squinting at his map in the dim light cast by Vikram's eyes. "See this flood basin?

We're going to pass by its southern tip presently. There's a little river that feeds into it, running out of the mountains—we'll follow it upstream, and then—oh God, give me a minute." He sat down on a flat boulder, or perhaps a remnant of a stone wall, half concealed by grass. "I need to catch my breath. The harbor road—here, look. It runs along the river valley of the Río Guadalfeo, which we'd be able to see by now if there were still good light. That empties into the sea at Salobreña. Any ship we might want to take will be docked at Husn Al Munakkab, just to the west. So the way we'll take is actually more direct, after a fashion."

"If you like sharp rocks and bandits," muttered Vikram, "then yes, very direct."

"Can't we stop here for the night?" pleaded Fatima, easing herself onto the boulder beside Hassan. "I can't walk another hour, and it sounds as if you mean to go two or three."

"This isn't a good stopping place," said Vikram. In the dark, he was nearly invisible; a pair of eyes above a crescent of teeth. "We need to get to higher ground and find a copse of trees or a rocky hillside."

Fatima curled her lip at him and reached down to work at the laces of her boots. Her feet stung as they slid free, peeling away from the damp leather only grudgingly. The shock of air on her raw flesh made her catch her breath.

"Is it bad?" asked Hassan, peeling back the hem of her robe with two fingers. "I hate blood. Or anything—pulpy. I have no courage at all."

"You did all right with that old Castilian," said Vikram. He squatted at Fatima's feet and took her left heel in his talons. "It was Fatima who nearly fainted."

"I was the one who killed him," said Fatima, incredulous.

"I beg your pardon, but you were the one who refused to kill him. Hassan, on the other hand, landed some very creditable kicks on the man."

"That was different," protested Hassan. "It was just instinct. I couldn't very well let him murder Fa while I stood there doing nothing."

"What do you suppose courage is, for God's sake? You're not a palace sycophant anymore, young Hassan. There's no need for any of this affected modesty. Blood doesn't bother you one bit. Be yourself, it's far less irritating." Vikram bent close to Fatima's foot and sniffed. "This isn't good."

"You wouldn't smell like a rose either if you were forced to walk all day in those boots," snapped Fatima.

"I don't care about the smell. You were right: you can't walk anymore tonight. We have to bandage these and find you some willow bark to chew on, otherwise you won't be walking tomorrow either."

Hassan went to kneel next to Vikram and peered at Fatima's feet. His eyes widened.

"Oh Fa," he whispered. "You must be in horrible pain."

Fatima was glad it had grown too dark for her to see what he was looking at. She lay back against the rapidly cooling stone and shut her eyes. Free and toes up, her feet were beginning to throb.

"Is this really the farthest you've ever walked?" asked Hassan, massaging her ankles. "When I came to apprentice at the Alhambra, I walked for four whole days with a pack that weighed half as much as I did. I still remember the way my knees felt at the end. The other boys were all from wealthier families—they bought rides to the capital with the cloth merchant caravans. They made fun of me for weeks."

"Hassan," said Fatima, trying not to betray her frustration, "I was born in the harem, in the yellow-and-white guest room that opens onto the shaded part of the courtyard. The farthest I've ever walked in my life was from my room to yours."

Hassan stared at her in disbelief. Then, impulsively, he leaned down and kissed the instep of her foot.

"Precious girl," he murmured. "Your poor feet."

"She'll survive," said Vikram with a long-suffering sigh. "Though I may not, at this rate. Up you go, Fatima. Put your arms around my neck. We'll make for the foot of that slope, there. Hassan—stay close to me and clear of the lights. The men at those campfires are not your friends."

As gamely as she could, Fatima laced her arms around the back of Vikram's neck, clinging to him as he hoisted her onto his back. At this angle, all his limbs seemed disproportionate; it was difficult to look at him without a stab of revulsion, of primitive fear. Fatima laid her head between his shoulders and closed her eyes again, remembering the palace dog and attempting to forget everything else.

"This way, then."

The lithe shoulders beneath Fatima's cheek swayed back and forth. She could hear Hassan traipsing along nearby, his breath labored. Night air had altered the scent of the hills: the sweetish perfume of carob and juniper replaced the yellow-green smell of grass; the breeze was full of pine sap. Opening one eye, she saw the ground to their left spill away into a rubbly depression, the stones marbled in the bluish light of the band of stars overhead. At the bottom was a shallow pool of black water.

"That's the flood basin," said Hassan. "We're doing all right. We're doing very well, actually."

Fatima felt Vikram grumble beneath her cheek, though he said nothing. The grasses thinned into rock and scrub as they moved toward higher ground. The mountains were opaque before them; the campfires Fatima had seen at a distance seemed to hang in the sky. She could hear laughter, faint but sharp, carried with the smell of woodsmoke.

"Men everywhere," muttered Vikram. "Men on the road, men in the foothills, men at our backs. What a pageant. This is the last favor I'll ever do for that woman."

"It's only a bit farther to this first gully." Hassan's face was ghostly in the dark. "It's quite steep. Maybe we can find an overhang or some such thing to shelter under."

"Make one," said Fatima. "A nice, dry place to rest. You can do that much, Hassan, I know you can."

Hassan mumbled something inaudible and scuffed at the ground with the toe of his boot. Nevertheless, he withdrew the map from his satchel, holding it up against Vikram's flank as they walked and scratching away at one corner with a nub of charcoal.

"That's not terribly comfortable," Vikram complained.

"Wait," said Hassan. "I'm almost done. There. Look at this, Fa."

Fatima unlinked one hand from around Vikram's shoulders and held up the altered map, turning it this way and that to catch what feeble light she could. On the northwestern edge of the map, near the mouth of a narrow valley between two steep slopes, there was now a series of closely concentric shapes, like a knot in the bark of a tree.

"A cave," said Fatima.

"Yes, a cave," said Hassan, dancing a little. "I do so like being useful."

"Let me see that." Vikram reached over his shoulder and snatched the paper out of Fatima's hands. He examined it for a long moment. "Remarkable," he said finally. "The wind has just changed key to accommodate your landscaping efforts. I can hear it whistling up ahead. Look."

Fatima followed his gaze up the embankment they were climbing. Beyond the pine trees, the ground rose sharply and narrowed to a peak. Another hill was visible just beyond it. The pairing was familiar: it was the entrance to the gully that led southwest on Hassan's map, and sure enough Fatima saw, tucked into the eastern flank of the nearest slope, a blot of darkness among the rocks.

"Your talent is a far finer thing than I had thought, Hassan of Granada," said Vikram. He sounded somewhat astonished. "It's one thing to alter the works of man, but quite another to alter those of nature. Tell me—when you were a child, did you confuse colors with sounds, or perhaps with numbers?"

"Yes," said Hassan, surprised. "And numbers had genders, too— they were male or female, and sometimes both, and sometimes a third sex without a name. Whenever I heard a loud sound, I saw a color or a pattern, as though a cloth had been laid over my eyes. It was abominably confusing."

"It would be," said Vikram in a distracted voice, studying the map again. "Yes. That's common enough with a gift such as this."

"What does that mean? What's common?"

Vikram handed the map back to Hassan and shifted Fatima on his back.

"All children of the *banu adam* are born with a bit of the First Speech," he said. "The language spoken by the angels and the beasts and the jinn before the birth of humankind. Incorruptible knowledge. Helps you see the intersections of things. You call it *fitrah* in your faith. In nearly all cases, it fades as the child grows up, but for a very few, it doesn't."

"Does that mean you know what it is?" asked Fatima, sitting up straighter. "Is there a name for what Hassan does?"

"Oh, undoubtedly. It's a miracle."

"Don't make fun of me," protested Hassan.

"Who's making fun of you? I'm as serious as I ever get."

"But Hassan isn't a holy man," said Fatima. The image of Hassan as a wandering ascetic, with a long beard and a short robe and a pious scowl, was so comical that she almost laughed.

"Neither are most miracle workers," said Vikram. "Most are ordinary men and women with all the usual flaws and hypocrisies. People would rather call them witches and burn them than acknowledge that miracles are bestowed upon the world with glorious, unfathomable generosity, because people are idiots."

Fatima studied Hassan's long fingers, occupied now in stowing the map in his satchel. They did not appear miraculous. Or if they did, so did everything else: the trees exhaling in the darkness, insensible of any danger Fatima might face; the halo of distant stars overhead, more insensible still. The matter that populated the world seemed bound together by nothing, yet it all persisted nonetheless: trees, stars, foxes, corpses, Castilians and Berbers, jinn and men and slaves. Fatima was hungry and dirty, but somewhere far behind her, Lady Aisha was clean and well fed, and perhaps thinking of her at that very moment, just as she was thinking of her old mistress. Perhaps the real miracle was that the world could support so much contradiction. Next to that, Hassan's talents seemed rather modest.

"A miracle," said Hassan from the darkness beside her, his voice small. "I never had the courage to think of it that way. People always thought it was funny that I still pray, in spite of being—well, being the way I am. The imam who gives the Friday sermon at the Alhambra told me I needn't bother. To my face, Fa! As if I had no right to pray, as if one must be perfect before one sits on a prayer mat. Yet I have always prayed. As a child, I asked for so many things. I would kneel and ask and ask and ask. It was the only time I ever felt as though someone heard me. I never got most of the things I prayed for. But I did get this."

He lapsed into silence. Fatima reached out and took his hand and held it up against the sky, and through his fingers saw the starlight winking. The cave Hassan had coaxed out of the rock looked small as they approached it, a simple confluence of sandstone blocks to which a few young pines were clinging: when Hassan stood upright, his head brushed the ceiling; and when Fatima climbed down from Vikram's back and limped toward him, she had to duck to fit inside. Nevertheless, it was dry and level and several strides long, tapering downward as it merged into the rubbly hillside. Fatima lowered herself to the ground with a moan, curling her knees up toward her body.

"Give me your feet, little sister," said Vikram. "And chew on this lovely thing I picked as we were walking." He pressed something flat and damp into Fatima's hand. It was a length of pale tree bark, its greenish underside glistening with sap. Fatima popped it into her mouth. A bitter, herbal flavor burst over her tongue. She chewed obediently, trying to ignore the stabs of pain as Vikram bent her foot from side to side.

"What a mess," he said. "Hassan—choose the least offensive of those gaudy sashes you've got in your sack and give it to me."

Fatima heard Hassan sigh as he riffled through the canvas bag.

"That's three robes and two sashes you owe me now," he told her.

"I saved your life," said Fatima.

"When we're stashed in a nice little cog on its way to Tunis or Timbuktu, with a hot plate of food and one snug berth apiece, I will thank you properly," said Hassan. "For now, I'll keep a tally of my clothes."

"You're so sweet," Fatima muttered. Hassan lay down next to her and flung his arm across his face, kicking off his own boots and wiggling his toes in the night air.

"I really am grateful," he said in a different voice. "It's an awful thing, you know, to be tolerated—everyone needs you, nobody wants you. There was a time when I thought the sultan—" He paused with the smallest catch in his voice. "He was always very pleasant to me, except for once or twice. He never seemed afraid or disgusted. I know he has to do what he thinks is right, but I never imagined that he—that I could be taken from my own room in the middle of the night, and he would say nothing. That I could mean so little in the end."

Fatima found Hassan's hand and stroked it, unsure of what to say. The willow bark was doing its work: the pain in her feet, though persistent, was no longer at the forefront of her mind. Vikram was a surprisingly delicate nurse, winding one half of Hassan's sash around her heel and tucking the end in with a gentleness that did not seem possible for a set of talons. Looking down, Fatima saw two neat bundles of blue cloth where her feet had been. The effect was somewhat ridiculous.

"Why do we have to run?" she burst out, suddenly exhausted. "We were on the bottom of the heap anyway. We haven't started any wars. Why should we be chased into the sea when we haven't done anything wrong?"

No one saw fit to answer her question. Hassan was rapidly falling asleep, his breathing softer and more regular. Vikram had arranged himself at Fatima's feet with his back pressed gently against her aching heels. Suffused with warmth, Fatima felt her body go heavy.

"I wish we were running toward something," she murmured, "instead of away."

"Would you like to hear more about the journey of the birds?" asked Vikram from the vicinity of her toes. "Something you haven't heard before?"

"You're offering to tell me a story?"

"Yes, I am. I feel you're about to do something stupid and I'm trying to delay you."

"Why can't you ever be nice?"

"I thought you were grown-up enough to prefer honest counsel. Do you want to hear the story or not?"

"Fine," said Fatima. "Tell me something I haven't heard before." A thought occurred to her. She propped herself up on her elbows, eyes widening.

"Vikram," she said. "Do you know how the poem ends? The real poem, the one Lady Aisha bought from the bookseller all those years ago?"

Vikram raised one eyebrow, or perhaps it was just a smoky crest of fur; the sleepier Fatima was, the more difficult she found it to distinguish between what he was and what he appeared to be.

"I do know how the poem ends," he said. "But *your* poem, the one you and Hassan have been telling to one another, has diverged from it so profoundly that it doesn't matter. There is no longer any real poem, or rather, one is now as real as the other."

"There is so a real poem," said Fatima, annoyed. "The real *Conference of the Birds* was written by someone, by a real person. He had certain intentions. I want to know what they were. He wrote the poem for a reason, and the reason matters."

"Does it?" Vikram stretched his toes, revealing a row of claws as black as obsidian. "Once a story leaves the hands of its author, it belongs to the reader. And the reader may see any number of things, conflicting things, contradictory things. The author goes silent. If what he *intended* mattered so very much, there would be no need for inquisitions and schisms and wars. But he is silent, silent. The author of the poem is silent, the author of the world is silent. We are left with no intentions but our own."

His voice, the least frightening part of him, as mirthful and resonant as a piece of music, sounded so unhappy that Fatima reached out instinctively to stroke his head. She had no notion of how she had blundered; the conversation had seemed safe enough. Yet Vikram was disinclined to tell her whatever it was he had intended to say, lapsing instead into purposeful silence.

"Tell me one thing, then," she pleaded. "Tell me about the king of the birds."

Vikram was silent a moment longer, and Fatima began to think he wouldn't answer her.

"The king of the birds is a *simorgh*," he said finally. "A phoenix."

"What does he look like?"

"What a silly question. What do I look like?"

"You look like a lot of things, depending on how I look at you."

"Well. Perhaps I'm not the only one."

Fatima was too tired to press him further. She turned on her side, nestling against Hassan's warmth, the skin on her neck prickling with eddies of air, warm and cool, warm and cool, as he breathed out and in again. She thought she might like to tell him that she loved him. It seemed a shame to wake him up, yet she did not often have such an uncomplicated impulse and could not let it pass.

"Hassan," she whispered, nudging him with her shrouded foot.

Hassan made a small, high sound, like a child, and did not stir.

*   *   *

Fatima woke again in the bluest part of the night. Habit roused her: in the Alhambra she nearly always awoke to the voice of the palace muezzin as he called for the daybreak prayer. His invitation, melodious though it might be, was heeded only by the most pious of the women, among whom Fatima did not number. Lady Aisha was different: her shrewdness was tempered in those lucid hours by a more spiritual impulse, which caused her to rise, cloak herself in a plain shawl, and go to the courtyard to kneel. For Fatima, it was simply an interruption: she would wake and yawn and sigh, and relieve herself in the chamber pot, returning to her bed in a half-conscious state of protest. Lady Aisha had once said, "You might join me one day," to which Fatima replied, "I might not," and there the conversation had ended. Yet it seemed the continual summonses of the muezzin had done their work: she was awake now, called by a voice she could no longer hear but still heeded.

Extracting herself from Hassan's limp arms, Fatima stood, hissing as she put weight on her feet. She was surprised to discover she could walk well enough if she wasn't too hasty about it: Vikram's bandages were wrapped so tightly that they diffused much of the pain. Vikram himself had disappeared. Stepping gingerly toward the mouth of the cave, Fatima retrieved her boots and levered her feet into them by careful degrees. They were snug now, but they would serve.

The birds were waking as she stepped out onto the mountainside. A little snow star nestled between the rocks just beyond the mouth of the cave, its pink blossoms incongruous in their bed of nettles. Farther downslope, dwarfish pines twisted out of the steep gradient and turned toward the sun at right angles, taking on a dizzy, scattered appearance, like a forest tipped on its side. Fatima squatted against one of them and pulled up her robe. She found herself looking downhill, past streams of gray rubble that merged and split like water as they descended toward the bottom of the ravine. There was movement below her: the glossy shoulders of a crow stretching its wings in the boughs of a woody rosemary. It croaked bitterly to itself, as though the riot of songbirds had disturbed its rest. Fatima laughed. The crow cocked its head and looked up at her. In a burst of black feathers, it leaped into the air, rising steadily until it cleared the pine tops, and then turned south, disappearing into a damp and still-dark sky.

Alone again, Fatima shook out her robe and began climbing back up the mountainside. Going up was more difficult than coming down: the angle hurt her feet and the rubble that had been so compliant while she was going downhill slid about when she put weight on it, giving her no purchase. It was noisy too. Cursing in a whisper, Fatima dug her fingers into the earth and pulled herself along, glad there was no one to witness her fumbling. After a few minutes of this, she cursed in earnest, and leaned against the roots of a dead tree to reorient herself.

She could not see the cave. The rocks, the bent trunks of the pine trees, all these looked familiar, but then again, they all looked alike. Turning in a half circle, Fatima couldn't determine where she had gone wrong. She thought she recognized a ledge of sandstone some distance above her, yet there was nothing below it but rocks and dirt. Fatima climbed a bit farther and tried not to whimper. Something pink trembled just beneath the hem of her robe: she teetered to avoid it, startled.

It was the snow star. Fatima's limbs went wooden.

"Hassan?" she called, as loudly as she dared. No one answered. The songbirds had fallen into a syncopated rhythm, each melody filling the silence left by the one that preceded it, making the air dense with sound. Fatima called for Vikram, willing him to frighten her, to pop out of the ether near her elbow as he seemed to like to do, but wherever he was, the opportunity did not tempt him. Fatima felt as though she were hovering over the crown of her own head, observing herself with the dispassion of an undertaker.

She had left without the map.

It had not occurred to her to do otherwise. The cave seemed profoundly unremarkable: chilly, shallow, perfumed by loam and the chalky scent of sandstone, as banal a place as Fatima had ever seen, except for the fact that it hadn't existed before she and Hassan set foot in it. It felt unfair: she had gone out unthinkingly, with every intention of returning. She had walked only a dozen paces downhill. Surely a little convergence of stone and earth, even one Hassan had created, could not be so far outside the ordinary scheme of things that it couldn't be found if sought. It was as if Fatima had been snubbed. For a moment she was envious of Hassan, not for his talents, but for the way the silent, visceral elements of the world seemed to love him and conspire on his behalf, to the exclusion of others.

Fatima turned in a circle, scanning each little undulation of rock for some sign. She found none, and began to make her way down the mountainside again, in what she hoped was a southerly direction. Light was beginning to break on the narrow valley below, illuminating tangles of gorse still pricked with yellow flowers. The wind carried hints of smoke; the campfires she had seen in the night would be out by now, leaving her with no way to guess where the men who had lit them were waiting. Fatima told herself she would not cry again: she hated crying; it gave her none of the relief it seemed to give other people. Instead, she balled her hands into fists, digging her nails into her palms until they smarted. This sensation, and the complicated nature of scrambling down a steep slope in bad light, occupied her thoughts so completely that she did not at first register the sound of singing that carried toward her from the valley.

The voices were gruff and happy and possibly a little drunk. It was only when she realized they were singing in Castilian that Fatima seized up where she stood, one swollen foot hanging in midair. Limping toward a fallen log, Fatima peered down at a small clearing on the valley floor, and saw a cluster of felt caps around the remains of a fire. A pair of broad-shouldered packhorses dozed nearby. There were cuirasses of battered steel plate piled beside the fire, attended by a boy, a squire or a servant perhaps, who appeared to be fiddling with the buckles while half asleep. These were soldiers, then, or mercenaries of some wealth. In the half dark, Fatima could not make out the colors of their doublets to determine where they owed their allegiance: all she could tell for certain was that they were directly in her path.

The rubble beneath Fatima's feet began to slide away. She crouched and pressed her back against the hillside, holding herself rigid. A trickle of rock clacked and tumbled down the meandering slope to rain on the edge of the clearing below, tickling the boughs of the pines that ringed the soldiers' camp. One of the men looked up and swatted his companion on the belly.

"*Creo que he oído algo.*"

"*Qué?*"

The first man whistled. The boy who had been fiddling with the stack of armor got to his feet and frowned up the hill, lifting

a pike in his small hands. Fatima closed her eyes and willed him
not to see her. She thought of the contours of Hassan's map and
tried to re-create them in her mind: the way the ravine turned west
at its narrowest point, the gentler slope of the hill on the far side.
Hassan himself had said that Fatima could navigate the mountain
passes on her own with a map such as his. These were not simply
tick marks on a piece of paper: they were hills with a definite
shape, if only she could remember. Perhaps if she could cross the
ravine in front of the soldiers, she could put the far hill, the one
with the more forgiving elevation, between them and herself. Barely
breathing, Fatima altered course, inching sideways along the hillside
instead of down, lowering each foot to the ground by increments.

"Start singing again," she whispered. "Sing your horrible songs."

The men stayed mute. Fatima could hear the clatter of steel
and wood, the squeal of a rudely awakened horse. In front of her,
the ground was dropping away: the ravine shrank to a treeless gap
wide enough for a single man on horseback, full of brittle shale,
the debris of old rockslides. Clinging to the branches of a young
pine, Fatima lowered herself into the gap, dropping the last several
feet to land hard on the shattered rocks below. The jolt made her
howl. Somewhere behind her, the men began to shout. Clawing
at the pliant earth, Fatima dragged herself up the far side of the
ravine, kicking up a hail of dirt and stone until she could taste both
when she breathed. She didn't dare look over her shoulder. Finally
she emerged onto turf and autumn weeds: the far hillside sloped
upward toward its mild zenith, treeless except for a few knots of
juniper. Fatima ran, her feet protesting, registering each footfall as
a dull throb in her heel. The voices behind her were growing closer.

"*¡Una mujer! ¡Veo a una mujer!*"

The air sang in Fatima's lungs. Panting, she crested the hill, cursing at the bushes that snagged her robe. Beyond the downward slope was another valley, much wider than the first and still concealed in gloom. It was papered with overgrowth, a thick, undifferentiated mass of brush and turning leaves that petered out into a colorless darkness. Fatima kept running, lifting the skirt of her robe to keep it from tearing in the dense brush. For a moment she felt giddy with triumph: the voices behind her were growing fainter and farther away and it seemed she might escape them entirely.

She was dismayed when she felt herself begin to fall. First there was packed earth beneath her feet and then there was air: she twisted, reaching for something to grab onto, and felt her fingers brush the woody bark of a tree. It was not brush and overgrowth she had seen from the hilltop but the canopy of a scrub forest. Fatima had thrown herself off a cliff.

Instinct overtook her. When she hit the ground, she was already curled into a ball, her legs tucked against her chest and her arms around her legs, her forehead pressed against her knees. The impact drove the breath from her body. For a moment, she thought she was drowning, and began to flail, reaching for a surface that did not exist, tearing up handfuls of loam and rock. Ground and sky switched places and then switched again. Fatima reached out a hand to stop herself. The world came to a halt and went silent.

Fatima could hear herself breathing. Faint, rosy outlines of clouds were visible overhead, and all the stars had gone save the herald of morning. She opened and closed her hands. There was a sharp pain in her left side when she breathed in. When she turned

her head, she saw white, chalky gravel bordered by pines, the de-
marcation between the two abrupt and purposeful. Turning on
her side, she lifted herself carefully to her knees, repeating in her
mind the little lullabies Lady Aisha had sung when she or one of
the other children scraped a knee or an elbow in the courtyard of
the harem. There was no one to kiss her now: she rocked back and
forth, singing to herself under her breath. Her head pounded in
time with her heart. It was several minutes before she felt ready to
sit up and examine her surroundings.

The white gravel scar was plane and level and wide enough to
admit several wagons abreast; it curved into the distance between
the rust-colored cliffs that flanked it on each side. Fatima got to her
feet and turned in an unsteady circle. The scar continued behind
her, leading briskly uphill, cutting a path through the scrub until
it vanished beyond her range of vision.

It was the road.

Chapter 10

It was empty: at such an early hour any sensible merchant or mercenary would still be breaking his fast and readying his horses. Fatima limped a few steps, testing herself. She wanted desperately to sit down, but there was nowhere to conceal herself: the road was hemmed in by cliffs with only a narrow ditch running along one side, a ditch where Fatima could see shattered wheel spokes and bundles of rags and animal bones, the refuse of human transit. An odd clarity overtook her. She limped to the edge of the road, slid down into the ditch among the discarded things, and drew her knife. The voices began again in the high ground. They were shouting, calling downhill toward someone she couldn't see, and then there were hoofbeats on the road behind her, where the ground rose.

She told herself not to look. The horses were armored or carried armored men: she could hear the chattering complaints of steel on steel. Someone ordered a halt and the clatter ceased. A single rider came forward, the dull iron of his mount's shod feet grating against the stone, and stopped near Fatima's head. She closed her eyes.

"Ho, old boy," came a woman's voice, as high and ringing as a girl's. The horse danced a few steps and chewed noisily on its bit. "That's enough now."

Fatima looked up and into Luz's face. The sight of her braided hair, the snowy crest of her collarbone above the bodice of her black gown, filled Fatima with a feeling she couldn't name and didn't like, something that wandered between fury and regret. Luz was not looking at her. She was staring down the road with a frown, her brows knit together, one hand soothing the neck of her coppery gelding. Fatima adjusted her grip on the knife. Its weight was familiar now; the heft of it calmed her. She couldn't kill a battalion of armed men with it, but she might kill one woman.

"Fatima," came Luz's voice softly. "Come out, come out."

Fatima froze in terror. Luz's gaze was fixed on the road. At first, Fatima thought it was a trick: Luz was taunting her now, forcing her to reveal herself. But Luz gave no sign of having seen her. She pulled one hand from its black calfskin glove and chewed restlessly at her thumbnail, as if she did not know she was being watched. Her skin glowed faintly as the dawn intensified, illuminating the flush of her bowed lip; yet there was something in her left eye, a splinter perhaps, or a fleck of soot from a campfire, that made Fatima recoil with a disgust she could hardly justify. An unhealthy air clung to Luz's black velvet shoulders like the residue of a long illness. Fatima's head throbbed. She was certain she had been spotted—by whom, she couldn't tell—and dug her fingers deeper into the yielding ground.

"Are they certain the girl came this way?" Luz called above her. "And that she was alone? No one else was with her?"

"No one else, my lady," came a man's voice.

"Strange," murmured Luz. She was silent for a moment. The throbbing in Fatima's head increased. She closed her eyes again.

"Bring the man who pursued her," called Luz, sighing in a weary way. "And bring my implements, please."

There was a rattle, a shuffle, the squeal of an offended horse, and several sets of footsteps approached.

"Here he is, my lady," said a rough voice. "One of the mercenaries who followed the girl over the hill."

Luz slid from her horse's back. There came a pretty sound, the clang of fine metal conversing with itself, like an anklet or a necklace unrolled from a velvet pouch, but the sight of it, whatever it was, made the mercenary whimper in fear.

"Please, my lady," he begged, "I told the truth, the absolute truth—I ran after her on foot through the gully on the far side of the ridge, and when she came out onto open ground, she jumped—jumped, as plain as could be, into the trees."

"Bind his hands, please," instructed Luz, her voice impossibly gentle.

"Please!" echoed the mercenary. "I'm telling you the truth!"

"You're lying," said Luz in the same gentle way. "Why would the girl jump? And even if she did—that drop is sharp and high. She would be injured, perhaps even dead if she fell the wrong way, yet I see no sign of her. And where are her companions? A man and a dog on foot with an injured girl—they couldn't get far, not in this terrain. Yet I see no sign of them either."

"Why would I lie?" countered the mercenary, fear making him ambitious. "I'd never laid eyes on her before this morning; I owe her nothing."

Metal rang merrily against metal again. The mercenary's breath went ragged.

"Perhaps you felt pity for her," said Luz. "A beautiful girl lost in the mountains—it would be only natural if you did."

"She was a slattern," spat the man. "Out on her own, hair loose, dressed in a fancy man's robe. Not a respectable lady like you, my lady. I could never feel pity for a girl like that. She was probably a Moor, even pale as she was. She had hair like a Moor's. They say they're all feebleminded, the ones that come from south of the Great Desert, no more than animals some of them—"

"That is a vicious lie," said Luz calmly. "There is an empire south of the Great Desert larger than any in Europe. The best doctors in the world are trained at its capital. All they lack is faith. If ignorant men like you would not stand in our way, sir, perhaps we could bring it to them." She drew away to where Fatima could no longer see her.

"Please," said the mercenary again, "please—" Metal clinked and sang and the mercenary shrieked in pain.

"Where did the girl go?" asked Luz. Her voice was soft, maternal.

"I told you, I've already told you—" The mercenary shrieked again. Fatima could smell his fear from where she sat: it congealed with the bittersweet resin of Luz's perfume to form something rank and almost solid. Fatima felt light-headed. She dug her fingers farther into the earth and pressed the back of her head into the dirt, telling herself to take small breaths, small breaths, though she longed to gasp and run.

She had a fleeting impulse to reveal herself and spare the mercenary further pain, though she knew he would hardly do the same for her if their places were reversed. Yet the guilt was there nonetheless: she would live and he would not, and though she preferred her own life above his, it hardly seemed fair that he should die for telling the truth.

"Where is the girl?" coaxed Luz. "This could be over in a moment. I'll bathe your wounds myself, with my own hands. Wouldn't you like that?"

"Yes," wept the mercenary. "Yes."

"Tell me, then."

"She jumped, may God be my witness—"

There came a sound Fatima would remember for the rest of her life: the dull pop of bone forcibly dislodged from its slick cradle. An irreparable sound. Fatima was only half aware when the mercenary tried to scream and found he couldn't. Stars rose and set in the sliver of sky beyond the ditch; the sun crossed rapidly before her eyes and was lacerated by clouds. She heard a muted exchange, an irritated sigh, and then the sound of horses turning, their iron-shod hooves grating like knives against the gravel road. The retinue moved off in the direction from which it had come, its clatter replaced by the little noises of the woods.

Dazed and thoughtless, Fatima got to her feet. There was no sign that Luz or her retinue had ever been there but the half-moon depressions of hooves in the packed gravel—that and a spatter of blood, small but ominous, pooling between the stones. She could think of nothing better to do under the circumstances than continue down the road. She climbed out of the ditch and limped away, following the trail of gravel as it spooled south between the sentinel cliffs. The sun had broken free of the mountains and hung low in the east, casting rosy shadows across Fatima's feet. That she was alive and upright struck her as extraordinary. She lingered on the gold-flecked dust that dripped from the pines, the clumps of green reeds that lined watery depressions in the earth, presaging the sea. How had the brutality she had witnessed occurred on this very same road? Every time she blinked she saw the little spot of blood and heard the thunder of the birds, and wondered how it could all be cut from the same eternal cloth as the sun, the grass, the unseen ocean.

Fatima was so lost in herself that she did not hear the return of hoofbeats at first. It was only a feeling of dread that made her stop and hold her breath. The road was flat there and the sun was high; there was no ditch in which to conceal herself; there were no shadows to protect her. She turned, preparing herself. A very lathered mare was cantering up the road from the north with her head high and her eyes rolling. A large dog, brindle-black, ran along beside her and nipped at her flank. And atop the horse, keeping his seat remarkably well, was Hassan.

Fatima's feet gave out; she collapsed onto her knees and then fell to her side, sobbing harder than she ever had in her life, as if her body was trying to expel something upon which she had choked.

Little idiot, came Vikram's voice in her head, *why are you lying here like a beached porpoise? I expected more backbone from you. Get up.* Fatima felt teeth grip the back of her robe. *Up, up.*

Fatima forced herself to her feet. She couldn't catch her breath. Hassan was reaching down: she took his arm, struggling to throw her leg over the mare's broad back as he hauled her up.

Run, pretty pony, hummed Vikram. *Run as fast as you can, or Vikram will start at your hocks and eat his way up.*

Squealing, the mare turned on her heel and bolted. The road became a shuddering line, the trees a blur on either side. Fatima wrapped her arms around Hassan's waist. With each hoofbeat, her teeth clacked in her jaw. She pressed her face into Hassan's back to make it stop. He smelled ripe, like sweat that had dried over dirt. She didn't mind: she took it in, scent and color and all the jumbled sensations that made up the mutable world.

I want to live, she thought. *It seems a terrible lot of trouble, but I want to live.*

I know, said Vikram. *You've developed a talent for it.*

Chapter 11

The mare ran until she couldn't. As the sun climbed higher, they passed slow-moving caravans on the right and left, their haggard custodians leading mules and oxen harnessed to canvas-covered wagons laden with cloth. They stared in disbelief as Vikram set about with his teeth, driving anything that breathed out of their path. No one tried to stop them; no one could. Fatima looked over her shoulder once or twice but could see no evidence of Luz and her men. They pressed on along the road, which widened and narrowed according to the terrain of the valley it followed, shrinking when the mountains on either side grew steep, widening when they flattened out into grassy high plains dotted with the dark green of wild olives. It was the ragged breathing of the mare that finally drew them off the road and into the dwindling hills.

"This poor beast is done for," said Hassan, his own breathing labored as he slid off the mare's back. The cicadas were deafening and seemed to be everywhere. Fatima allowed herself to be lifted down and immediately collapsed, clinging to the withered trunk of a juniper bush when her legs wouldn't hold her. The mare, too, fell to her knees, her flanks heaving. Bipedal again and barely winded, Vikram sat cross-legged on the ground and cradled the animal's boxy head in his lap, stroking its ears gently.

"She's run her last," he said. "She won't get up again. What selfless creatures horses are. Remember her in your prayers, dull and dumb as she is, for she has saved your lives."

The horse groaned and pressed its ears back along its neck. The sight of it was pitiful. Suddenly furious, Fatima lashed out at Vikram's woolly extremities, kicking him as hard as she could.

"You left me," she shouted. "You both left me. I called and you never answered. I wish I'd never set foot in that stupid cave—it was gone the moment I turned my back. I thought I was going to die—I nearly did. You *left* me."

"We looked for you," said Hassan, crestfallen, his face sallow. "We called too. I had the strangest feeling you were nearby, near enough to touch, even, but I couldn't see you. We stole this poor horse from a sleeping tinker farther up the road so that we could try to find you. And we did. Everything was all right in the end, wasn't it?"

Everything was so profoundly not all right that Fatima thought it best not to answer. She lay down in the stiff grass and drew her knees against her chest. She felt Hassan's fingers on her head, stroking the curve of her skull.

"I wouldn't leave you behind," he said, sounding hurt. "I didn't leave you behind. Please don't shout at me like that."

Fatima sniffled and reached back to intertwine her fingers with his.

"I'm sorry," she murmured. "I saw Luz on the road. Something was different about her—something was wrong, though I can't tell what. There was a man who chased me through the hills. She asked him about me, and when he couldn't answer, she—I was right there, under her feet almost. I should have been caught, I should have been dead."

Hassan squeezed her hand. The cicadas droned in her ear, their shrill song rising and falling in waves. She knew she should apologize to Vikram as well, but apologies were costly and she hadn't the stomach for another. When she looked up, she saw his face close to her own, framed by a dark mane, looking, for the moment at least, wry and real.

"Cousin," he said. "Haven't we been friends, in our own way, since you were a fat baby in swaddling clothes? Is this any way to treat such a friend, kicking him and cursing him?"

Fatima let her head fall forward and buried her face in Vikram's hair. The scent of it awoke old memories of the harem and its long afternoons, vague and shot through with sunlight.

"I get so angry," she said. It was as close to an atonement as she could manage.

"Anger is good," she heard him say. "Anger teaches you things. How to lead. How to make the decisions you'd rather not make. It protects you from fear and hesitation and the desire to turn back. Don't waste it on old Vikram, or on Hassan, who would die for you in a moment."

"I was taught to waste it," said Fatima. As soon as she said the words, she saw the truth of them. "On silly fights with Nessma and the other girls. Clothes and food and who'd gained weight and who'd seen the sultan that day. Lady Aisha encouraged it."

"Yes, you were taught to waste your anger. It's convenient for girls to be angry about nothing. Girls who are angry about something are dangerous. If you want to live, you must learn to use your anger for your own benefit, not the benefit of those who would turn it against you."

"I don't know how."

"You've already begun." Vikram rose to his feet and surveyed the landscape. "We need to keep moving. Over the top of that next hill is a sight that will make you smile. I'll carry you for a little while."

Fatima clung to Vikram's shoulders as he lifted her up. Beside her, Hassan stood with a groan.

"Are we going to leave this valiant creature unburied?" he asked, wincing as he looked at the silent mare.

"She doesn't care," said Vikram. "She's already grazing in fields of eternal grass. Rally yourself, young Hassan—we're nearly at the end of this little journey." With that, Vikram shifted Fatima on his back and set off through the brush, away from the road. Fatima felt herself nodding off, lulled by exhaustion and the hearthlike warmth of Vikram's body. A crow swooped low and threw its shadow over her neck, complaining hoarsely. Fatima convinced herself it was the same crow she had seen on the mountainside at daybreak, the one that had set off southward into the gloaming when she laughed at it.

"Lucky crow," she said. "At least the birds have a proper king, even if we don't."

"Ah, but the crow's part in that story is not a cheerful one," said Vikram. "Crows are clannish, disliked birds. None of their cousins will let them roost close by. The smallest songbird will chase down an entire murder of crows that settles too close to her nest. The crow who set off with the hoopoe to find the Bird King was flying into exile, and he knew it."

"What happened to him?"

"He chose the love of his king and of his friends over his own happiness."

"But doesn't love make a person happy?"

"Fatima was raised for the purpose of love. Fatima knows better than most whether love makes a person happy."

The horizon rocked back and forth in time with Vikram's steps. The afternoon light had grown red-orange and brought with it a wind that was light and cool. Fatima knew, somehow, that the summer had spent itself for good; there would be no more days of heavy heat.

"Love must make people happy sometimes," she murmured. "Otherwise, I don't see the point of it."

Vikram only chuckled and continued along his invisible path through the grass. Hassan was leaning on him now as well, one hand braced against the jinn's brindled back, his brown eyes glassy.

"I had a dream," he said faintly, wiping his brow, "in the cave last night. I heard you talking as I was nodding off to sleep, and then I dreamed of a great golden bird. I sat in the shade beneath its wings. There was a beach—all lovely pale sand and white cliffs going right down to the water. You were there, Fa. It was very pleasant. You've just reminded me of it."

Fatima tilted her face toward the sky and thought it was easy to be reminded of pleasant things in this place. The early evening was entering the peak of its violet beauty, heightening the contrast between the parched earth and the green-dark trees. Ahead of them was a sharp drop between two hills: the gap was spanned by the pocked remains of a Roman aqueduct, its stone columns weathered to a golden brown the same shade as the fading grass.

"How lovely," said Hassan. He jogged ahead, his satchel thumping against his back. "It's even taller than the one outside Granada," he called back to them. "What master builders the Romans were! You've never been on the high road into the North, Fa—wide enough to race horses on and as level as you like, and over a thousand years old. How the earth remembers!" He sat down on a flat rock with a sigh, craning his neck to take in the stone edifice above them. Vikram veered around him.

"Hold on," he instructed, and leaped up the rocky incline that hugged the aqueduct's right side, his talons crumbling the stone as he went. Fatima held her breath and shut her eyes. Her center of balance shifted wildly, leaving her dizzy even with her eyes shut, as though the world had spun off its axis. After several long minutes of this, Vikram came to a stop.

"You can open your eyes now," he said in a merry voice. Fatima opened one and then the other. They stood at the crest of the hill. Below the aqueduct, the ground wandered down into the winking lights of a small city, its red-brown tile roofs overhung with smoke; at its zenith was a dusty rise on which stood a Roman fortress. Beyond that, the earth stopped, replaced by a color Fatima had never seen. It was neither green nor blue but encompassed both of

these, like dark glass. It broke against the land in a line of white
froth, which pushed and pulled against a thin ribbon of sand in a
rhythm she could hear from where she stood. Fatima's throat closed.
Her robe furled around her ankles as if to draw her into the wind,
which rushed down the hillside toward the waves like an eager lover.

"That's the sea," she rasped.

Vikram sat on his haunches with a sigh. "Yes. That is the sea."

Fatima reached toward it with her hands. The color stretched
out toward a horizon that was perfectly flat, where it merged with
the setting sun.

"I want to touch it," she said. "It can't really be water. It must
be something else. I want to touch it."

Vikram only smiled and began to sing. Fatima stood where she
was and listened to the breathing of the waves. She could hear
Hassan struggling up the hillside toward them, exhaustion making
his gait halting and irregular. At the summit, he lowered himself
to the ground and reached up for Fatima's hand.

"We're alive," he marveled. "Three days on foot over bad terrain,
with worse food, and nearly murdered, and we are still alive. If only
Lady Aisha could see us now."

"I don't even care about that," said Fatima. "I don't want to look
at anything else except the sea, ever again. Let the Holy Office come."

"Let it not," sighed Hassan, leaning against her leg. He followed
her gaze over the firelit town and down to the open water. The roll
and hush of the waves below steadily filled the silence between them.
The line of sand thinned minute by minute as Fatima watched it,
and the slim hulls of beached fishing boats began to right themselves and float.

"The beach is disappearing," she said, alarmed. "It's filling up with water. Look."

"The tide is coming in," laughed Hassan. "It'll go out again before dawn."

"Why?"

"The moon pulls the water when it rises and sets."

"The moon?" Fatima looked over her shoulder and saw a waning crescent peek out from beyond the hilltops. "How is that possible?"

"Merciful God, I don't know. But the look on your face right now is so funny. Ask some more questions."

Fatima realized her mouth was hanging open and shut it. She lay down and looked at the first of the stars overhead. They glittered faintly, multiplying as the light faded. The air was full of salt and smoke. There seemed, for the first time since she had left the Alhambra, paths through the great world that were open to her.

"It's time to make a decision," came Vikram's voice in the twilight, gently. Fatima turned to look at him. His hair streamed down across his shoulders, lifting strand by strand in the light wind; his smile was, she thought, a little sad.

"Not now," she begged, propping herself up on one elbow. "I haven't had a rest since before dawn."

"You can't live on this hill. Down in the harbor there are ships. Each will run a different course, but you can only board one."

Fatima twisted Lady Aisha's ring on her finger. Now that she had the leisure to admit it to herself, she found she had thought no farther than this hill at the edge of the map that hung on the wall in the sultan's bedroom, beyond which was only blank paper and Hassan's crudely drawn sea serpent: perhaps she never believed they would survive long enough to decide what came next. They had fled to spite their masters but now they must live for something else. The *how* seemed as important as the *where*, but the where came first, and try as she might, Fatima could not imagine a place that felt safe.

"Should we cross the Strait, like everyone else?" she hazarded.

"You ask that as if there is a right and a wrong answer," said Vikram. He was looking at her in a way she found unsettling.

"I want to say something," announced Hassan, looking out toward the water. "Something mad."

Fatima recognized the vacant light that had entered Hassan's eyes and quaked inwardly.

"The thing I do with maps. I've always wondered whether it isn't some kind of intuition, better than what everyone else has, but the same sort of thing: whittling unconsciously through possibilities until I arrive at the sole possibility, the truth. Like being very, very good at guessing, so good that sometimes the angels indulge me and make my guess right even when it isn't—so that a cave appears in the rocks, or a tower in the palace, or a trapdoor in the floor of my room. That's what it feels like—like being spoiled by heaven as if I'm some willful but beloved child. Though I don't know why it should be so—I haven't been good, not really." He sniffed and rubbed his nose absently with the back of one hand. Fatima felt a swell of tenderness and pulled his hands away from his face, kissing one and then the other.

"You're wonderful," she pressed. "You don't lie or steal or gossip and when you've had a terrible day, you don't even take it out on your friends." She paused, her words hanging reproachfully in the back of her mouth. Everything seemed clearer to her on the hilltop: the horizon and the curve of the earth, and also her own faults, which seemed to multiply the farther she got from the life that had fostered them. "You've saved the lives of people who are afraid of you," she said in a softer voice. "More than once."

Hassan was shaking his head.

"It's not enough. Luz and her inquisitors are probably right: I should be put on the rack and made to atone or some such thing, for my impudence if nothing else."

"No one can choose who God loves, or change who God loves," said Vikram. "Not even the Inquisition."

Hassan looked back toward the water.

"I want to say something," he repeated. Fatima knew what it was, and her heart sank.

"I can get us to Qaf," he said. "I can get us to the isle of the Bird King. That's where we should go. That's where we'll be safe."

Fatima closed her eyes and attempted to muster her self-restraint.

"It's a game, Hassan," she said as gently as she could. "We were bored children shut up in a crumbling palace, so we made it up. Bit by bit. We made up a story."

"But that's just it," said Hassan, leaning toward her. "What if our stories are like my maps? What is a story but the map of an idea? There is a secret in the poem of Al Attar—we made it into a joke because joking felt better than despairing. But perhaps that *is* the secret. The Bird King is real, and we are his subjects."

"Hassan—"

"What other choice do we have?" Hassan's voice rose unsteadily.

Fatima pressed her hands to the sides of his face, smoothing away the mania that lodged in the creases around his eyes. She understood now: he was not quite mad, but he had chosen madness over despair. Yet if she followed him there, into madness, it meant she had despaired already.

"Don't look at me like that," he begged. "Please."

"All right, all right." She pulled away. The sea below her was unchanged, or rather, it was changing as it always had, exhaling against the brief shoreline, a white curl of froth the only bright color left in the waning day. She should have seen it. The way he had laughed at meeting Vikram, at the scout they had left dead beneath the willow tree on the Vega: the brittleness of it, his fine nervousness, like that of a racing horse. Of course he was going mad. He needed solid walls and certainty to counter the constant upheaval of his gift. If the world couldn't keep him safe, he would seek safety in the stories of their childhood. Her cheeks were wet: she dried them with her sleeve and tried to smile.

"I'm not mad," he said, reading her thoughts. "I'm as sane as I've ever been, though perhaps that's not saying much. I've just decided we weren't ever living in the world we thought we were. Everyone always looked at me and saw the odd one, the freak, the pervert. But maybe I wasn't any of those things. If we can drop through a door and land in the dark, in those tunnels beneath the palace, and see demons, and the palace dog was really a jinn after all, who's to say I wasn't the only person in that pile of stone who saw things clearly? Why did we tell each other those stories if not to escape? We were making a map, Fa. We can follow it out of this."

He made her want to believe, though she was no more convinced than she had been when he first suggested it. The thought of leaving entirely, leaving not just the siege, the war, the threat of capture, but the world itself, caught her powerfully, and she answered him before thinking.

"All right," she said. "We'll do as you like. We'll go to Qaf."

Hassan grinned. Fatima saw his fingers, bluish under the moon, twitch on the leather flap of his satchel.

"I've never tried to draw a sea chart," he said. "I've only been on a boat a handful of times, and never out of sight of land."

"You want to try," said Vikram, roused from silence. "Your fingers say so."

"But if I can't—" Hassan flexed his hands and began to crack each knuckle, one after another. "We'll die of thirst or drown or be killed by brigands or worse."

"You'll never be free of danger. But that's a choice you've already made. If you wanted certainty, you would never have left Granada." The jinn studied Hassan intently, as if to assess his fitness: if he thought Hassan mad, his face did not betray it. Yet he seemed to be waiting for something, and Fatima, now that she had made her decision, did not want to linger and hear a jinn talk her out of it.

"We're going," said Fatima. "Hassan, draw your map."

There was a small pause.

"I'll need some light," he said.

Fatima knelt next to him and put her arms around his neck.

"I love you madly," she whispered. "Even when we do get lost and drown or die of thirst or any of those other horrible things, I'll still love you madly."

Hassan kissed her shoulder.

"We won't get lost," he said.

* * *

Husn Al Munakkab was cloaked in a murky darkness that was half smoke, half fog. This was a blessing, or so Vikram said, for it made two silent travelers and a dog less remarkable as they slipped through streets of salted mud toward the harbor. Torches lined the main thoroughfares, where weary fishermen loaded the evening catch into barrels and onto wagons, assisted by equally weary boys who managed the tack of their mules and oxen. The side streets were dark, however, and it was along these that Vikram led them, skirting kitchen gardens and lines of washing hung out to dry and the constant punctuation of animal waste.

Fatima had taken another sash from Hassan's canvas sack and draped it over her head and shoulders, pulling one end over her face as a freewoman would do in the presence of men, leaving only her eyes exposed. Managing this was unexpectedly difficult. Lady Aisha had always made an art of it, holding her scarf across her cheekbone with three fingers, her wrist bent at an elegant angle. Fatima feared her own clumsy approximation would give her away. She felt shy in the unfamiliar garment, even fraudulent; she had to remind herself that she had the same right to wear it now as any freeborn girl. Yet there were no other women in evidence: she could hear women's voices singing or scolding children from inside the mud-plaster houses they passed, but the streets, it seemed, belonged to the realm of men.

Eager to appear irrelevant, Fatima kept her head down, watching the interwoven tread of Hassan's boots and Vikram's paws. She made a game of setting her feet precisely where Hassan's had been, filling his watery footprints with her own, exactly equal in size in her borrowed boots. They had been walking for at least a quarter of an hour when the footprints paused. Fatima looked up. A forest of masts was bobbing between the roofs of the houses up ahead. She almost gave a little cry of happiness, but Vikram nipped at her hand.

Quiet, he murmured from somewhere inside her skull. *There is a man behind us, and he stopped when we stopped. No, don't look. There may be more where he came from.*

Fatima pursed her lips to keep from making a sound. Beside her, Hassan was clutching a thin sheaf of paper to his chest as he walked, and seemed not to hear what Vikram had said to her. He had drawn the map while hunched over a stack of split wood behind a barn at the edge of town, beneath a greenish circle of lantern light. It was not like the other times Fatima had watched him work. He swayed back and forth like a woman in childbirth, muttering to himself and sometimes to Vikram, who had perched on a log beside him to hum and stroke his hair, like some demonic midwife. It had taken so long that Fatima became restless and wandered too far away, nearly getting lost on a cow path as the night darkened. Afterward, Hassan had been flushed and quiet. He showed the map to Fatima only once before clasping it to his chest: it was a beautiful thing, an astonishing thing, radiant with thumb lines originating at set intervals across an empty sea. To the east was the coastline from the map that hung on the wall of his palace workroom; to the west, where the sea serpent had been, was an island.

It was an odd shape, nearly rectangular, punctured by small harbors shaped like flowers. It had the effect of something man-made, something imaginary, and when Fatima looked at it, her resolve had wavered.

Yet she said nothing, and neither had Hassan. He looked defiant now, staring past Fatima at the row of masts before them. Only Vikram looked back, his canine tongue lolling between his teeth with a look of unmistakable irritation.

This will be more difficult than I had hoped, he said. *One, two, three—yes, four of them. You'll have to run for it.*

You're not coming with us? The thought came unbidden.

No, I'm not. I told Lady Aisha I would see you safely across the Vega, and I have. What happens now is your own affair.

*But—*instinctively, her hand went to the scruff of the dog's neck, which she had shaken and caressed so many times. *We can't just part like this. This is such a silly way to leave things. I'm afraid. Vikram—*

He shook her off and padded down the street in the direction they had come from. Fatima felt her heart begin to race.

Vikram!

Damn it all, don't you dare panic now. Go, run. Both of you.

Fatima let the scarf fall from her face and seized Hassan's free hand. He yelped as she pulled him along, splashing through a pool of foul-smelling water in her haste to move forward. A vile curse followed them, succeeded by the sickening hiss of a drawn sword. Unable to resist, Fatima looked back.

Four men in dark doublets and mud-spattered woolen hose circled uneasily around Vikram, who looked, in the darkness and at this distance, like little more than a shadow with teeth. One of the men feinted toward him with a dagger, only to be rewarded by a perfect semicircle of puncture marks on his arm. His scream was so high and terrified that Fatima felt momentarily light-headed. The scream brought shouts and whistles and still other men, who came rushing down an alleyway with their weapons already drawn.

"There! Toward the docks!" The one in front, his face masked beneath a steel half helm, pointed toward Fatima and Hassan with his pike. Beneath his cuirass, his doublet was red and black. Fatima's stomach dropped.

"She's here," she whispered. "Those are her men."

Hassan pushed her forward. The street behind them was dark where blood had soaked into the muddy ground. Vikram snapped and snarled at the men in red and black, but there were too many. Fatima saw the blade of a slender espadon flash in the torchlight and heard a wail that was neither human nor animal. She fell against Hassan, screaming. This was the wrong thing to do. The man with the espadon looked up and into her eyes and pointed toward her with a mail-clad finger. A moment later, the men in red and black closed in, and the shadow, or what was left of it, was entirely eclipsed.

"Let's go—please, Fa, *please*."

There was a sharp tug on her arm. Fatima didn't realize she had stopped, and stumbled onward, too dazed to speak. The tangle of houses and refuse and wash lines parted in front of them: the horizon opened, revealing a wooden wharf with a line of cogs and fishing vessels moored alongside it, bobbing up and down in the soft swells. Under the moon, the boats were only half real, the conveyances of ghosts, their softly clanking masts discolored in the faint light.

"Which one? Which one?" Hassan was turning in a circle, the map clutched in one hand. He laughed in a way that frightened Fatima. She was struck by the impossibility of their enterprise. Even

if they had time to search for one, no captain alive would agree
to sail west with only Hassan's map for reassurance—not for the
ring on Fatima's finger, nor for all the rings in Lady Aisha's jewel
box. Yet there was no way of escape now except by water. Fatima
took one breath, and then another. Wrapping her fingers around
Hassan's sleeve, she pulled him down the nearest gangway, a mere
plank of wood that shuddered under their combined weight, and
tumbled him onto the deck of a small one-masted cog. The deck
was pungent with the smell of tar and hemp. The cog was moored
to a post with a thick rope, tied with a knot so elaborate that Fatima
thought she might lose her wits entirely.

"Help me!" called Hassan. He had drawn his knife and was
sawing furiously at the rope, just beyond the deck rail. Fatima hurried to do likewise, fumbling as her dagger balked at such a menial
task, better suited to a sailor's knife or a pair of shears. There were
raised voices on the wharf. Fatima said another prayer, for herself,
for Vikram, and most of all for the rope, which unwound strand
by strand, complaining as it pulled against itself. Hooves clattered
against wood, too close. Fatima looked up as the last strand of
hemp snapped and the cog glided free, its sails belling eagerly in
the night wind.

Luz was sitting astride her copper gelding at the edge of the
wharf. For a moment, she was almost close enough to touch. She
said nothing, only looked at Fatima with a colorless expression, her
mouth set in a rigid line. Fatima looked back at her. She wanted
to speak but could find nothing to say that Luz did not already
know. The intimacy between hunter and prey had rendered speech
unnecessary. Luz raised one gloved hand. A salute, or a farewell,

or a warning; Fatima couldn't tell. She raised her own hand unconsciously. A smile formed on Luz's lips. Then the ashy fog that clung to the shoreline closed around her gelding's feet. The lights, the town, the Roman fortress on the rise above it, the aqueduct standing guard in the hills above that: all were muted in gray, and there was only Luz, clothed in a veil of smoke.

Chapter 12

Fatima sat down where she was. Waves lapped at the sides of the cog, which heaved in time with the rising water. Hassan took her hand. They leaned against one another, panting for breath, until Luz had vanished, her image swallowed by the nervous sea. The stars returned to their stations in the darkness overhead. Fatima realized she was still holding her dagger and slid it back into its sheath, flexing her cramped fingers.

"Vikram——" said Hassan anxiously.

"Don't." Fatima pressed her hands against her eyes and bit back a sob. "Don't."

"What are we supposed to do now?" demanded Hassan, loosing her hand. "Without Vikram, we're just two hapless idiots with a map. How do we steer this boat? How are we to provision ourselves?"

"Vikram's lying dead on the wharf where we left him and this is all you can think about? He never promised to hold our hands for the rest of our lives. He said he'd take us across the Vega and he did, and now—" Fatima broke off as her breath caught.

"He abandoned us," insisted Hassan. "We were meant to board a ship with a captain, a crew even, to buy passage as Lady Aisha said, not to *commandeer* a vessel like a couple of sad pirates."

"Buy passage? *Buy passage?* To an island nobody can get to without your map?"

"Yes! That ruby on your finger would've been enough to convince an unscrupulous captain, and there are more than a few of those in Husn Al Munakkab."

"This was *your* idea." Fatima slammed her fist against the deck for emphasis. She looked about her for something she could throw for yet greater emphasis, but found nothing useful: only the salt-bleached wood of the deck and a coil of rope listing against the stern castle behind her. Instead, she lay down where she was, curling into the railing of the deck, which lifted and dropped her in an easy rhythm. Sleep suggested itself. The deck was warm and level, a better and safer bed than any she had had in recent nights. Thinking too hard, about Vikram or anything else, seemed wildly irresponsible.

She sat up when she heard a door bang open and shut again.

Hassan seized her arm with a startled cry. On the narrow wooden steps leading down to the galley stood a young northern man in the white woolen habit and black cloak of a Dominican friar, his straw-colored hair tousled from sleep. He froze where he was, staring at Fatima and Hassan in blank disbelief. Though he was not a tall man, the breadth and heaviness of his shoulders gave him the appearance of one. He had a face like a butcher's cleaver: all thick, reddened angles beneath a prominent brow, yet his eyes were very blue and had a candid, appealing symmetry, rendering the sum of his parts less hostile than it might have been.

He frowned at them, fumbling in his corded belt for a weapon he did not seem to possess. For a long moment, no one spoke.

"Fa," whispered Hassan. "I think we've kidnapped a monk."

The monk looked from Fatima to Hassan with his lip curled.

"*Penaos oc'h deuet?*" His voice was low and grated on the ear. Hassan, in lieu of an answer, attempted to smile, and for a moment, Fatima thought everything might be all right. Then the monk seemed to coil up and threw himself across the width of the deck. He collided with Hassan, who shrieked, and both of them went down in a tangle of limbs. Fatima heard Hassan's head hit the salt-swollen planks beneath it. The sound froze in her guts.

"Stop!" She reached out and wrapped her hands around the first thing they encountered, the pointed end of the monk's long cowl, and pulled as hard as she could. The monk fell backward with a squawk. Hassan was looking upward into the phantom darkness without expression, his eyes fluttering. Fatima drew her knife.

"If you've hurt him, I'll kill you," she said between her teeth. Blue eyes stared up at her in astonishment. "Do you understand me? I'll kill you." The monk struggled to sit: she drew back her foot and kicked him in the jaw, harder than she meant to, and sent him reeling back again, spitting blood. He moaned once, steadying himself on his hands. Fatima knelt on the deck next to Hassan and stroked his face.

"Please say something," she whispered. He was gasping, his eyes wide and sightless.

"I see light," he said. "I see light, but not you."

Fatima put her cheek against his chest and closed her own eyes, battered by waves of hot and cold that seemed to break against her skin. It was impossible that Hassan should be hurt. Why had she come so far if not to avoid having to endure the world without Hassan in it? She thought of his narrow back as he hunched over his desk, his smile as he pretended not to notice her slip into his room and lift wedges of charcoal from the bowl beside him; he had been a boy, she barely more than an infant, and there had been a thousand other such moments, ordinary then but precious now, for they had been innocents together. She sat on her heels and howled, wondering if she could muster the courage to turn her knife on herself.

"Oh for the love of God—he'll be all right." The monk, smelling of wool and sweat, lowered himself to the deck beside her. He winced and rubbed his jaw. A line of blood was congealing across his clean-shaven cheek. "No reason to panic and carry on so. It's only a bump on the head." His Sabir was broad and accented, delivered with a singsong rhythm. "You can understand me when I speak like this, yes?"

Fatima forced herself to look up at him. There was no malice in his face, only a profound fatigue.

"Yes," she said.

The monk nodded.

"I've a tooth loose," he muttered, bending over Hassan. "You did me one better than I did this *blev'ruz*." He cupped Hassan's chin and turned his face one way and then the other. "You, friend. Does that hurt?"

"N-no."

"I took you for brigands. Now I see you're a couple of fops. You could have killed me twice over with those knives, as I've no weapon. But you can hardly even hold them properly." He opened and closed his mouth experimentally, leaning sideways to spit a driblet of blood on the deck. "Your lover will live, madam, but he'll shortly have a headache that'd make angels weep, infidel though he is."

"It's already here," groaned Hassan, pressing his hands against his eyes. "It feels like being punished for something I didn't do. I think I'd prefer death, all things considered."

The monk laughed hoarsely. It was a good, full sound; an immodest sound; the laugh of a man who was not often afraid. Fatima felt her shoulders uncurl.

"I'm Gwennec," said the monk. "Brother Gwennec, they call me. You'd best not move awhile, *blev'ruz*. If you think the pain's bad now, wait until you get up and the blood rushes out of your head." He looked as though he wanted to say something else, but his eyes traveled across the deck and out to the white-capped waves, and his smile fell.

"We're at *sea*," he said. The cog listed a little, as if to concur with him. Gwennec got to his feet, hitching up the skirt of his habit with one hand and nursing his jaw with the other. "Where is the harbor? Where is the lady Luz? What the hell have you done?"

Fatima groped for her knife again.

"I'm profoundly sorry to tell you this," said Hassan, flat on his back, "but we've stolen this boat and have no immediate plans to return it. You'll have to come with us, unless you're a very good swimmer."

Gwennec's face darkened until his complexion was a shade of red Fatima had never seen before. He paced up and down along the deck railing, massaging his jaw.

"Stolen the *boat*," he exploded. "Are you out of your minds? Which one of you is the crack sailor? Our delicate friend whom I laid out on the deck? Or you, madam? Where is your crew? Where are your supplies? Damn you both." He sat down with a groan. His face, Fatima noticed, was swelling where she had kicked it.

"We had no choice," she said, adjusting her grip on the dagger. "It was that or stay behind and be taken by the Holy Office, or go—" She almost said "back," and realized, with some surprise, that the thought was abhorrent to her. Luz seemed a lesser punishment than returning to captivity, though captivity was surely pleasanter than death by burning was likely to be. Yet the internal logic of the palace, with its precise gradients of worth and worthiness, had failed her beneath that lonely tree on the Vega, at the feet of the dead Castilian scout, and would never be real to her again.

"The Holy Office," muttered Gwennec. "I was wrong about you twice, and I was too kind in both instances. Here I thought, 'Ah, not brigands—running away, more like, perhaps their families wouldn't let them marry or some such thing.' But you're worse than runaways and worse than brigands. What could you have done that's so bad the Holy Office is after you?"

"I'm a sorcerer," said Hassan.

"Aye, I can see that. You've transported us into open water without a damned idea where we're pointed, all by cutting through a fucking rope. That's magic." Gwennec tucked the dirty hem of his habit into the cord at his waist, exposing a pair of shins covered in the same thick blond hair that populated his head, and divesting himself of his sandals, vaulted onto the mast to make for the rigging.

"You haven't even set the mainsail!" he called down. "That's why we're keeling! Were you aiming to swamp the boat and drown? Take that rope that's flapping about down there—yes, you, madam, since our friend is having a little rest."

Fatima sheathed her dagger and stumbled across the deck as the cog pitched, sending a spray of froth over the railing. There was, indeed, a rope trailing from one corner of the mainsail, slapping against the outer railing in a petulant rhythm. Though it was thicker than her wrist, Fatima wrapped it around both hands and braced her feet against the deck.

"My name is Fatima," she called up to the monk, who was holding himself aloft on a ratline with his toes and appeared to be cursing in his own language. "Not madam."

"I don't care," snapped Gwennec. "The less I know, the less I'll have to tell the inquisitors when they catch up with us, which they will. Christ Jesus, the beating I'll get! I was meant to be keeping watch over this damned boat while the others went ashore." He looped another, thinner rope around a beam partway up the mast, twisting it into a series of shapes which, when he pulled them, miraculously became a knot. The rope went taut and the mainsail belled out, carrying the little cog over a swell with such force that Fatima thought they might leave the water and take to the sky. Her own rope began to resist her violently. She dug her feet into the humid deck and pulled back with all her strength, certain, for one grave moment, that she was going to be slung overboard into the froth below.

Gwennec landed on the deck beside her with a thump and dried his hands on his habit.

"A good, following wind tonight," was all he said, relieving Fatima of the rope. He looped it around one shoulder and leaned into it like an ox in harness, gritting his teeth. The mainsail swung slowly around until the beam above their heads made a right angle with the mast. The cog settled into the wind almost meekly. With a weary sigh, Gwennec threw the rope around a large dowel set into the railing.

"Watch me," he said. "This is a reef knot. You'll need to know how to tie one, if you plan to make landfall in one piece." He took two loops of rope, one in each hand, and bent them over each other. "Left hand, right hand. See?"

Fatima did not, but nodded anyway.

"You seem more like a fisherman than a monk," she said. Gwennec shrugged, unoffended.

"You're correct, as it happens. I was a fisherman until I took vows. My family fishes cod off the Breton coast."

"Are you Breton?" called Hassan, sounding livelier. "So was my grandmother. She was captured from a trading ship that got caught up in some kind of naval encounter near the Strait. Her family never ransomed her, so my grandfather ransomed her as a dowry and married her. I'm one-quarter Breton."

"Well I'm four-quarters Breton," snapped Gwennec. "And if you think I'm going to clap you on the back and call you brother because your grandfather kidnapped one of my countrywomen, you'd best think again."

"There's no need to be ugly about it," said Hassan. He raised himself to his elbows with a groan. "I was only making conversation.

200

Am I supposed to act contrite over something that happened forty years before I was born?"

"Not contrite," Gwennec muttered, untucking his habit from his belt. "Only a little less glib."

The cog rose and dipped, gliding down the far side of the swell almost gently, as if to apologize for its earlier misbehavior. For a moment, Fatima saw a young, red-haired woman standing at the rail, wearing a dress too thin for strong weather. She wondered whether Hassan's grandmother had mourned in secret, whether she had looked upon her children with ambivalence, as offspring who were not quite hers, from whom her history had been erased. Was it possible to love children born of war? Fatima tried to remember her own mother's face and found she couldn't. Perhaps if she had birthed her child in her own land, among those she loved, she would have lived.

"My grandfather loved her, if that means anything," said Hassan in a different voice. "She used to sing to us in her own language. I've forgotten the words now. I was her favorite grandchild. Out of all of us, I was the only one who inherited her coloring."

Gwennec studied Hassan with a scowl. "You do have a Breizhiz look about you," he said. "Though only in the hair and complexion. Your features are Moorish." He spat a clot of blood onto the deck. Turning his back, he stumped up the short steps to the raised platform that made up the stern castle and ran his hands over the tiller, soothing it as he might a nervous horse. Satisfied with whatever the tiller had told him, he tugged on several of the slender ropes that ran from the top of the mast to the deck railing, testing each for tension. His hands, like his face, were red and wind-roughened, but

Fatima liked the way he used them: they were fluent, like Hassan's, though their language was wood and water instead of paper and ink. When they finally settled on the tiller again, the cog began to turn, gliding obediently where they told it to go.

"What are you doing?" cried Fatima, roused as if from sleep.

"Turning around," said Gwennec. "The wind will be against us, but if we tack a little, we should make it back to port in a few hours."

Fatima stared hard at Gwennec. He only spat again and wiped his mouth on his sleeve. Gathering her robe, Fatima ran up the steps to the stern castle and dug her nails into Gwennec's clever hands, wrenching them away from the tiller. Gwennec gave a hoarse cry and danced backward. Fatima put herself between him and the tiller, pressing her back into it until she felt the pressure in her spine.

"We're not going back," she said. Though she had spoken as calmly as she could, her voice shook. "She can't have him and neither can you. He's mine. He isn't a sorcerer. I'm not giving him up to die."

Gwennec's face rearranged itself, the lines and hard edges softening with incredulity. He looked her up and down.

"My God, but you're made of stern stuff," he said. "Somebody must have done you a terrible wrong if you've lost your natural fear of the sea."

Fatima looked over the railing at the nameless hues rising and falling around them, the green that was also gray, the deep wine color that hinted at an element finer than water, an echo of the fire the alchemists said burned undying at the center of the world. Every sinew in her body was taut; the profound anxiety of being so close to both escape and recapture left no room for any other emotion.

"I'd never seen the sea until earlier this evening," she said. "I don't know it well enough to fear it."

Gwennec was shaking his head, though whether in admiration or disgust, she couldn't tell.

"They say people in love do mad things," he said. "But this is madness of a purer sort than any I've ever seen."

It was the second time he had implied that Fatima and Hassan were lovers. Fatima glanced at Hassan, but he had closed his eyes again and was pinching the bridge of his nose, taking long, dramatic breaths to quell his headache.

"We're not in love," said Fatima.

"You must think I'm an idiot," said Gwennec. "I might be a monk, but I still know what two people in love look like."

"It isn't like that." Fatima felt her cheeks go hot. "We're not—we don't—Hassan doesn't—"

"In addition to being a sorcerer, I'm also a sodomite," supplied Hassan. "But let it be known that I am passionately in love with you, Fa. I'd offer to marry you if it were even remotely fair to either of us. Alas. The world doesn't supply happy endings to people like us."

Fatima looked at Gwennec and saw her own bafflement mirrored on his face. She wondered with fresh alarm whether Hassan might really be injured, and tripped back down the steps of the stern castle to kneel by his side. He looked up at her and cocked one eyebrow.

"This blond, hulking fellow, on the other hand, I would tumble in an instant," he said to her in Arabic. "If he could only be persuaded."

"Shush," said Fatima, looking over her shoulder. "What's wrong with you? Why are you saying these things? I'm worried you've cracked your skull. And anyway, he's celibate."

"It only adds to his appeal."

"You shouldn't have made that little speech." Fatima smoothed the front of his robe with hands that shook. "Northerners aren't friendly to men like you. Who knows what he might do now that you've told him?"

"North, south—it's all the same," muttered Hassan. "Even in the Alhambra, all it would have taken is for four pious men of sound mind to open my bedroom door at the wrong moment, and I would have been banished or executed. The only reason I still have all my limbs is that everyone was willing to pretend I'm something I'm not."

"They pretended because they loved you," said Fatima. She smoothed and smoothed, as if her hands could brush away whatever had possessed him.

"That's not love," said Hassan, shaking his head. "You were the only one there who loved me, Fa."

On impulse, Fatima bent and kissed him. She didn't want him, exactly, but the intensity of feeling that overwhelmed her suddenly had no other means of expression. His lips were warm and soft and dry and parted under her own without returning their pressure.

"Marry me anyway," she said, withdrawing only a little. "We like each other best of anyone. The other things don't matter."

The smile that rose to Hassan's mouth was too quick. It told her he had considered and rejected this possibility, perhaps many times over.

"They matter, sweet friend," he said. "They matter."

Gwennec thumped down the stairs from the stern castle and sat down hard on the last step, splaying his legs and leaning back on his elbows like a large child.

"You're a very strange pair," he said. "And not to be trusted with a ship." The wind was only skimming the mainsail now, and the ship rode over each swell at an angle, bringing the surface of the water up and down, up and down, as though the bow were a needle pulling through cloth. Fatima saw the lights of Husn Al Munakkab bobbing in the distance.

"Turn us back around," she said to Gwennec, her chest rising and falling with the water. "Or show me how."

Gwennec glanced out at the lights and rubbed his scalp vigorously with his fingertips, shedding dander on the shoulders of his black cloak.

"You don't really want that," he said. "There's barely any food to speak of on board. A couple of casks of water, another of wine, though that's not much good to you Mohammedans. Wherever it is you think you're going, you won't get there in this ship, not without resupplying." He looked around the deck and laughed harshly. "And not without someone who knows a thing or two about sailing."

"Did you say wine?" Hassan sat up and looked suddenly alert. "Do you think you could go and get me a ladleful, since we're having such a nice conversation?"

"You drink, then?"

"I do. I have. I've broken one of God's dictates. I might as well break several. It's a cycle, you see—I adore Him, I disobey Him, and I drink to make sense of it."

Gwennec looked hurt, as if Hassan had leveled a personal insult.

"I don't think that's so," he said. "God isn't like that. He knows we've all got things we can't do or can't stop. It doesn't follow that we're excused from those things we can do and can stop."

Hassan, wincing, propped himself against the deck rail with a dry smile.

"You really are a monk," he said. "Can I have some wine or not?"

Gwennec snorted and rose to his feet. Crossing the deck in a few long strides, he clattered down into the darkened hold, from whence came the sound of a barrel scraping across the floor. After a moment, he emerged again, balancing three dripping wooden cups dexterously between his fingers. Two cups were full of dark liquid, but the third was clear; this he set beside Fatima.

"Water for you, madam," he said. "Since you told me no different. Here, *blev'ruz*. Your liquor."

Hassan reached up and took the cup reverently between his hands. He drained it in a few gulps, smacking his lips with obvious relish.

"Bless you, Brother Gwennec," he said, wiping his mouth with the back of one hand. "My head feels better already."

Gwennec himself took only a small sip before grimacing and setting his cup on the ground.

"The salt air has tainted it," he said. "In Breizh, we drink ale and beer. Keeps better at sea. But southerners insist on the fancy stuff by land or water."

Fatima, forgetting herself, leaned over Gwennec's cup and sniffed: a vinegar smell, embroidered with a more compelling scent of fruit and earth, jutted into her nose. She leaned back, tears pricking her eyes.

"How do you drink this?" she asked from behind the sleeve of her robe. "It smells like something the washerwoman uses to make soap."

Hassan and Gwennec laughed. Hassan pushed his empty cup toward Gwennec and helped himself to the monk's full one, raising it in a halfhearted toast before draining it as he had his first. Gwennec smiled and let his head loll back against the railing. His skin, though coarse, was unlined; despite his skill in handling the ship and reckoning with God, he could not be older than Hassan, and might well be closer in age to Fatima herself. Fatima could see doubt flickering in his eyes: he had fought and laughed and reconciled with them, and this had upset the straightforward matter of turning them over to his masters. She told herself not to hope too much, though hope promptly suffused her limb by limb, making her heart thud against her ribs.

"Show me how to turn the ship," she said again, in a softer voice. Gwennec studied her for a moment. His gaze made her uneasy: it was frank, direct, without any of the cool hesitation of the men of the Alhambra, to whom she had been both an object of desire and a source of uneasiness.

"Where is it you mean to go?" asked Gwennec. Fatima leaned over and coaxed Hassan's satchel from behind his back. Unbuckling it, she withdrew the map, curling now from the damp and the heat of Hassan's body. She held it out toward Gwennec, only to be stricken with fear as he took it from her, worried for a moment that he would tear it up, or worse, that he would laugh.

Gwennec did neither. He adjusted himself so that the slender moon was at his back and frowned hard, attempting to read Hassan's complex web of intersecting rhumb lines in the weak light.

"This is a portolan chart," he said with some astonishment. "Where did you get this? Did you steal it?"

"I made it," said Hassan indignantly. "I'm a cartographer by trade."

"But you've used a thirty-two-point compass," pressed Gwennec. He put his thumb over one of the spindly roses that marked various points on the empty seascape, radiating lines across the page at measured intervals. "Only a master navigator would know how to use one of those. Yet you can't even point this little cog where you want it to go."

"I used no compass," said Hassan. "Only the skill of my fingers."

Gwennec considered this for a moment.

"You're a liar," he said finally. "Or you really are a sorcerer."

"I'm neither. I have one talent. This is it." The wine had softened Hassan: he gazed steadily back at Gwennec with the calm of a saint. Gwennec looked as though he wanted to argue, but thought better of it, and frowned at the map again. "Here's the Strait of Gibraltar," he murmured. "The Dark Sea. And this—" He brushed the oblong perimeter of the island with one flushed finger. "This is Antillia." He looked at Hassan and then at Fatima, visibly perplexed. "The Isle of Seven Cities. You're going to Antillia."

Fatima leaned forward and took Gwennec's musty woolen sleeve, as if to tether his words to her.

"You know this place?" she asked. "Have you been there? How far is it? How many days?"

Gwennec threw back his head and laughed.

"Every Breizhiz sailor knows it," he crowed. "And nobody's ever been there. It's a myth. No one's set foot in Antillia for six hundred years, if anyone ever set foot there at all."

Chapter 13

The sounds of the water and the quiet groaning of the ship went dull in Fatima's ears. She leaned against the rail and shut her eyes against the stars, lapsing into darkness. Gwennec's voice came from somewhere else: another ship, another sea.

"It's an old legend," he said. "I'm no poet, but I'll tell it as best I can. Long ago, when the Moors conquered Iberia, seven sainted bishops on seven ships fled into the Dark Sea with their flocks. They were from the old tribes—the Visigoths, the Vandals. Ancient folk whose tongues are all lost now. They sailed for many days and nights without sight of land. Then, when their supplies were almost gone and death seemed certain—"

"Ah," came Hassan's voice from the darkness. "Death always seems certain at this point in the story."

"When death seemed certain," continued Gwennec, "a child sighted land on the western horizon. They had discovered an island, rich with every conceivable kind of country—dense forests, watery plains, deserts as white as bone, hills under eternal snow. At the center was a lake, perfectly round and so clear you could see every fish that swam in it. They named the island Antillia, thanked God for His bounty, and determined to settle there, burning their ships to remove the temptation of return. Each bishop founded his own city—Aira, Antuab, Ansalli, Ansessali, Ansodi, Ansolli, and the largest, called Con. There they lived in prosperity, and there they remain, for all I know, since no one else has ever reached Antillia to tell of it."

The moon flickered behind Fatima's eyelids. It took the form of a bird, a gull, beating its crescent wings against the vastness of the sea.

"I don't understand," she said. "How can there be two such different stories about the same island?"

"Two stories?"

"Ours is about the king of the birds." She opened her eyes to make the moon stand still again. "Long ago, all the birds of the world began to forget their history and their language because they had been leaderless for so long. So a brave few sought out the king of the birds, a king in hiding—the wisest and greatest of all kings, living on the island of Qaf in the Dark Sea beneath the shadow of a great mountain. Waiting for those with the courage to seek him."

"Are these Muslim birds we're talking about?"

"I suppose so."

"Well, there's your answer then." She heard Gwennec shift his weight and drum his fingers against the wooden steps. "These are stories about two different kinds of defeat. Mine is about an empire that was conquered by force. Yours is about an empire that faded away. That's why yours is sadder. There's no real ending."

"But which one is true? Either the island is the realm of the Bird King, or it's the colony of your seven bishops. One or the other must be false."

"I don't particularly want to hand myself over to a bunch of bishops, or to their descendants," Hassan chimed in, waving his cup. "That's exactly the fate we were hoping to avoid when we embarked on this little misadventure."

Gwennec shook his head at them.

"Neither story is true," he said. "They're both made up. Made up! It's a pretty map, though. Thirty-two-point compass." He chuckled and squinted at it again. "True north and each and every rhumb line as fine as you like. A beautiful map."

"If I drew it, it's real," said Hassan. There was no malice or defensiveness in his voice, only soporific certainty. Gwennec laughed at him, his eyes disappearing into the thick slope of his brow.

"You've got a high opinion of yourself, *blev'ruz*," he said. "As I've told you, no one living has ever set foot on that island. It's a story they tell in church to seagoing people who need to believe there's something left once they've lost sight of land."

"No one has ever set foot in the Kingdom of Heaven and returned to tell of it either," said Hassan, setting his jaw. "Yet I'm certain you believe heaven is a real place, Brother Gwennec."

"That's different," said Gwennec curtly.

"How? How is it different?"

"Because heaven isn't some little sandspit off the coast of Spain," the monk snapped. "It's another realm entirely, one only those beloved by God will ever see."

"Yes." Hassan leaned forward to look into Gwennec's eyes, his cheeks mottled with high color. "That's it exactly. What if this island is just such a place? What if we are thus beloved by God?" In spite of the liquor, his posture was straight and purposeful; his face, though wine-flushed, was lucid.

"We?" Gwennec's mouth twitched, as if he couldn't decide whether or not to smile. "Christ Jesus. A redheaded Moor who likes it with men, and a fisherman who's only recently learned his letters, and—" He looked sideways at Fatima and a mild flush of embarrassment crept up his neck. "Forgive me, madam, but I can't tell at all who you might be or where you might come from. There's no one like you in my land."

Fatima looked up: the stars overhead formed a thick band, like a thread-of-gold sash holding up the garment of the sky. She didn't care to summarize herself. She was no longer a concubine to a king or a companion to queens and princes, yet there was no word for what she had become instead. Hassan, at least, had a skill and a title that persisted beyond the palace walls; Fatima had been taught to describe herself only in relation to the palace itself.

"I was born in Granada," she said finally. "And rose as high as a girl without rank could rise."

"And your people?"

"My mother was sold as a captive."

"Like this one's grandmother?" Gwennec's expression altered a little. "Then you're not a Moor. We're not enemies after all."

"I didn't know we were enemies before."

"Well." Gwennec sighed and followed her gaze upward. "There is a war, after all, and you did steal this boat."

Fatima looked back at the monk. He faded into the unlit ship, his cloak an uneven blot slightly darker than the deck around them.

"Are you one of them?" she asked, uneasy again. "One of Luz's people?"

"You mean the Holy Office?" Gwennec shook his head. "I haven't even taken my perpetual vows yet. I'm just a novice. I was sent down because I'm all right with boats and I don't speak enough Castilian to go bearing tales." Here he laughed. "They're regretting that decision now, I promise you! Oh to be back at Saint Padarn's! I should be waking for lauds and singing the antiphons while the dew settles on the hay crop out in the big field, yet here I am." He hummed under his breath in a voice that reminded Fatima of the sea itself, resonant and cold.

She stood and leaned against the railing, bending as far over the water below as she dared. It was nearly invisible now, more sound than substance: a rhythmic thud against the hull of the cog, a line of white foam where it broke over the prow. It had never occurred to Fatima that the stories she and Hassan told each other might also belong to someone else. Though Qaf was a myth, it must be real in the way she had envisioned it: the seat of a king who was good as she understood goodness. Now it was all thrown into doubt: other people longed for the same place, but in a different way, and in a hostile language. It seemed there was nothing that war could not touch.

"Fa." Hassan reached out his arms for her. Fatima curled against his side and rested her head on his collarbone, ignoring the sharp

pain that flickered between her eyes every time she blinked. Her
body's sole purpose now seemed to be to keep her awake and ready
for whatever minor disaster came next. She shuddered and pressed
her face into Hassan's robe.

"I'm right, Fa," he said in Arabic. "Don't listen to this celibate
Ulysses. My maps are never wrong. When I sat down to chart our
way, I was drawing a path to the isle of the Bird King. I'm certain
of it."

Fatima reached out and slid the map from between Gwennec's
fingers. Holding it up to the sliver of moon, she counted the strange
little inlets that punctured the perimeter of the island.

"One, two, three, four, five, six, seven," she said. "They're cities,
Hassan. Seven cities."

Hassan took the map from her. She felt him shiver beneath
her cheek. Then he laughed—a high laugh, like a madman's—and
clenched his hands as if to tear the map in half.

"No!" Fatima pulled it away from him with a wail and pressed
it against her chest. Brother Gwennec twitched, startled, and again
groped at his belt for a phantom weapon. Hassan's face was ghostly
and wild in the dark, his eyes like gray fragments of the invisible
water. Fatima backed away from him on her knees.

"Don't do that," she begged. "Not to your own beautiful map.
It's like hurting yourself."

Hassan shook his head violently. "It's no use," he said. "The
monk is right. We should turn back. At least our fate is certain in
that direction. We're fools, and we've been fools since we left the
Alhambra. I should never have let you come with me. You could be
safe at home right now, well fed and warm, in bed with the sultan,

everything as it was before, instead of sailing into nothing with me like a pair of children. Think of it—if you conceived tonight, you could be the mother of a king nine months from now. That's a better fate than most. I should have left you behind."

"You talk like a coward," she spat. "It wasn't your choice to make. It was mine. I chose to leave. I couldn't let you die. You're alive because of me, yet you talk about leaving me behind to breed heirs for a man who will be sultan of nothing as soon as he hands the keys of Granada to King Ferdinand."

Hassan laughed again. Fatima would rather have come to physical blows. She would rather he struck her so she could strike him back: it would be over then, and the sting would fade, and the marks would remind them that they were capable of hurting each other. She sat back on her heels and hugged herself, the map crinkling and bending across her chest.

"I, I, I, me," said Hassan. "It wasn't me you wanted so desperately to save, it was yourself. You can't bear to lose me because it would cause you pain. That's not the same as wanting to save my life. You do nothing for its own sake, Fa, you never have. You do what serves you best, and damn anything or anyone who contradicts you."

The words Fatima wanted to say would not come out. She stroked the map as if to comfort it, running her fingers along its crackling perimeter. She had never quite understood what was meant by heartbreak: when the sultan was cold to her or Lady Aisha was cruel, she would simply withdraw. What she felt now was something else, something so visceral that she found herself taking shallower breaths, until she was dizzy; Hassan, the person she knew and loved best, now sprawling wide-eyed against the rail before her, seemed as foreign as their kidnapped monk. Betrayal bloomed in her.

"I think our friend might be a little addled after all," murmured Brother Gwennec from somewhere behind her. She felt the pressure of his fingertips on her shoulder, lightly. "Look at his eye. The left one."

Fatima did as he bade her: Hassan's pupils were lopsided, the left far larger than the right.

"I shouldn't have given him that wine," said Gwennec. "He needs to be abed. Propped up, though, so the blood doesn't settle where it oughtn't to. You might as well sleep yourself, madam, as it's clear you've had none in some time. I'll keep watch a few hours."

The lights of Husn Al Munakkab were growing brighter. Fatima peeled the map from her body and held it up again, studying the punctured shore of the island floating in its net of rhumb lines. Perhaps it was the Qaf of the Bird King, perhaps the Antillia of Gwennec's seven bishops. Perhaps it was neither, and Hassan's miracle, confronted with her own overweening ambition, had deserted them. Yet the map remained: real enough to touch, full of possibilities that the way behind them lacked.

Fatima plucked at Gwennec's sleeve, knowing this was a kind of trespass, and was rewarded with a wary glance.

"Help me turn the boat," she said.

"No," said Gwennec.

"I won't sleep," she said. "I'll wait until you do, and then I'll throw you overboard. We'll be no worse off than we were before. So you choose. Help me turn the boat and you can be on your way when we dock to buy supplies. Or don't and I'll find a way to kill you." The words came easily to her.

Gwennec pulled his arm back, turning his wrist to loose the fabric from her grasp.

"You don't have it in you," he declared.

Fatima laughed in what she hoped was a careless way. "The last man who thought so is lying on the Vega with his guts out," she said. That she had stabbed him accidentally and lost her nerve seemed like an unnecessary level of detail with which to burden the monk. Gwennec looked her up and down, attempting to guess whether she was lying.

"You really mean to," he murmured.

"Yes," said Fatima.

Gwennec got to his feet with an oath.

"You can resupply at Marbella, let's say," he said. "That's as good a place as any for me to go ashore. From there, you pass through the Strait, assuming you're not taken by pirates or the inquisitors don't catch you first, and once you've cleared the Strait, on to the Dark Sea. Yes, Marbella will do nicely. There's a Franciscan priory nearby—I stayed there for a night on the way down. They'll take care of me. I'll tell them I was kidnapped, and I've got a swollen face to show for it." He thumped up the steps to the stern castle, folding the sleeves of his habit past his rough elbows. "Sleep a while, madam, while I get us under way. When you wake up, I'll show you how to manage this boat."

Fatima studied his face. There were weary creases around his mouth, and resignation in the bright, flat blue of his eyes. There was no love there, but no malice either.

218

"You're the one with the knife," he said drily. "I'm not even allowed to carry one, and I'm not likely to bludgeon you to death in your sleep with my sandal."

She had to smile at this.

"Very well," she said, and turned away toward the hold.

Chapter 14

Fatima slept without dreaming. The hold of the cog was outfitted with four narrow bunks set into the hull; a wooden screen separated this makeshift cabin from the aft portion of the hold, where the barrels of water and wine and one precious crate of hard cheese were lashed together. Gwennec half carried Hassan down the stairs and secured him in one of the bunks, rolling blankets and burlap behind him to keep his head elevated. Fatima collapsed into the opposite bunk without speaking and turned her face to the hull, listening, for no more than a few moments, or so it seemed, to the groans and sighs of wood and water before sleep took her.

When she woke again, there was sunlight streaming down the open staircase from the deck above, leaving a square of yellow on the sloping floor of the hold. A familiar shadow fell across it, its sloped shoulders rocking up and down with its strange gait. Vikram paced back and forth, his dark head awash in light.

"You're alive," she called to him, laughing, reaching out her hands. He turned and curled his lip at her.

"If you can call it that," he snapped. "I had a vision of my own death at that stinking, mud-caked wharf. It's all I can think about now. Mortality! If you'd listened to me and run when I told you, I might have been spared such awful knowledge, along with enough spear wounds to impress a messiah."

Fatima tried to make sense of this accusation. "How?" she asked after a pause. "How will you die?"

"In bed with a full-figured, golden-haired woman who will weep and rend her garments at my passing." Vikram sat down and began to chew on his talons, looking melancholy. "An enviable death. No less than I deserve."

"When?" pressed Fatima.

"Many hundreds of years from now, as far as I can tell, though visions aren't always precise about these things."

Fatima felt her shoulders drop. "That's a very, very long time away," she said, relieved.

"For you, perhaps. But I've lived five or six times that long already. It doesn't seem very far away to me." Vikram looked into the sunlight cascading down the staircase. "Listen: remember this part. I'm sending someone to you, someone I trust. I say *I* trust her, but you must not. Do you understand? She will help, but only so long as it pleases her to do so. You mustn't make her angry. And try not to fall in love with her. That's a doom I wouldn't wish on anyone."

"What are you talking about?"

"Are you thick? I've just explained it all. You should get up. That monk is too polite to come and wake you, and it's after midday."

"I'm already up," said Fatima.

"You're so funny," said Vikram.

*   *   *

Fatima opened her eyes. The hold murmured around her as the boat shifted from side to side, as if it, too, had been resting, and was stretching and rousing itself now in the bright sun. Across the narrow width of the hold, Hassan was still asleep, his breathing regular, his lips parted slightly. His color looked better. For a moment, Fatima was happy. The way they had left each other intruded on her thoughts slowly, like a child dragging its feet. Averting her eyes, Fatima kicked off the rough blanket under which she had slept and stumbled across the gently swaying floor to the stairs.

A rush of cold, wet air pummeled her as she emerged onto the deck. Above her head, Gwennec clung to the mast like a great black crow, his cloak and habit flapping about him. It was an unsuitable garment for ship work. Every few moments, he was forced to interrupt the complicated operation he was performing on the rigging to curse and push his skirt down over his legs, which, in contrast to his reddened face and hands, were blue-white, as if he had been stitched together from two entirely different skins. Fatima couldn't help herself: she laughed, leaning against the last stair for support. Gwennec twisted up his face at her, one hand raised to shield his eyes from the cloudless glare.

"Laugh now, madam," he said, "but you'll miss me when you've got to do all this by yourself."

Fatima let her gaze wander across the ship to the series of ropes that connected parts of the deck she couldn't identify to pieces of the sail and rigging that were likewise inscrutable. She adopted an aloof expression, determined not to let Gwennec see her uncertainty. He clambered down the mast and presented himself with a lopsided smile, shaking out his scapular.

"Let's start with pointing the boat the right way," he said. "There's a treasure on board you didn't know about. I've set it all up. Look." He led her up the steps to the stern castle. Fatima could see nothing but sail and water, a field of royal blue unfurling in every direction. A thin ribbon of land lay off their right flank, the sky above it discolored with smoke: this was the only sign of human life.

"A sane man would stick closer to shore than this," said Gwennec. "But you don't want to be spotted, so." He gestured toward the tiller. Beside it stood a little table, upon which lay Hassan's map, weighted by stones on three corners and by a small oil lamp on the fourth. Next to that sat an instrument Fatima had never seen before: a hemisphere of brass suspended between two slender halos of similar metal. The face of the hemisphere was a wind rose with arrows to mark each of the cardinal directions; smaller lines marked the degrees in between. The compass lay still between its twin satellites, which orbited around it slowly, keeping it flat as the ship rocked back and forth.

"What is it?" asked Fatima. She didn't dare touch the thing, which seemed to move through some delicate, internal volition, like a living being.

"It's a dry compass," said Brother Gwennec with a hint of pride in his voice. "Suspended in a pair of gimbals to keep the needle from grounding. It was a gift from the Portuguese to Queen Isabella, who lent it to the lady Luz for her journey. It's worth more than this boat and all our lives put together. She'll be wanting it back, I've no doubt."

"It's beautiful," said Fatima. More beautiful, perhaps, because it had been Luz's and now belonged to her.

"Aye," said Gwennec, who looked at her approvingly. "It's very beautiful. Better than the old water compasses—a child could make a water compass, but one big wave and the needle goes sloshing out on your shoes. And the dry ones as they use on land ground like hell aboard a ship for the same reason. Too much back-and-forth. This—" He reached out and tapped the edge of one gimbal; it responded silently, sending its sibling rotating in the opposite direction. "This is as pretty to me as a painting in a church or a sleeve of the best silk brocade. If a man can dream up a compass like this, we must not have forfeited God's grace just yet."

Fatima realized she was smiling at Gwennec and looked away. She heard him clear his throat.

"Anyway," he said. "Here's what you must know: you align the compass with the keel of the boat, as I've done. That way, when the ship turns, the wind rose'll tell you which direction the keel is pointed in. That's your heading. You must keep the joints of the gimbals oiled so that they have free motion, otherwise the needle inside the compass may ground, and then you're blind. And whatever you do, by God, don't get anything made of iron within five feet of this table. Now, your map." He smoothed the corners and traced the edge of the Iberian Peninsula with one finger. "These rhumb lines, here, are like a compass that doesn't move. You pick out where you are on the map as best you can with your dead reckoning, then you choose the rhumb line that most closely gets you where you want to go." He traced one, a long arc that began just inside the Strait of Jebel Tareq and continued toward the lone island that hung silently in the middle of the Dark Sea. "You turn the tiller until the keel of the boat lines up with that rhumb line. If we were here, say, which we're not, it'd be four degrees west-southwest. Then your job is to keep the boat on that heading with all the wind and the currents and the tides working against you." He grinned wolfishly. "That's the hard part."

Fatima swayed on her feet, looking from the tiller to the compass to the implacable water with a dismay she no longer bothered to conceal.

"It would take months to learn all this properly," she said. "Years."

"You haven't lied yet," laughed Gwennec. "We're a day out from Marbella, though, so we'll see what you and the *blev'ruz* can learn before nightfall tomorrow."

At the mention of Hassan, Fatima felt a little thrill of doubt. She looked over her shoulder at the empty stairwell leading down into the hold: no shadows interrupted the square of sunlight on the floor below. Hassan must still be asleep. She was surprised by how profoundly she did not want to see him.

"Do you think I'm selfish?" she asked.

Gwennec shifted on his feet.

"I don't know you at all, madam," he muttered. "And you nearly broke my jaw."

"I think—" Fatima stopped and searched for words in the water that foamed and clapped against the hull of the cog. "I think I'm much smaller than the things I set out to do, that's all. It's not selfishness. I spent all my life in the same place. You get no sense of proportion that way." Her eyes were watering; she wiped them with the back of her hand. Gwennec's face softened.

"You're very brave," he said. "That I do know. Brave to a fault."

"You know we're going to die," said Fatima, unwilling to be flattered.

Gwennec was quiet. Beyond him, the shoreline in the far distance had changed shape: a fat line, cliffs perhaps, marched along the horizon in a sweep of ocher and green.

"Yes, I know you're going to die, one way or the other," said Gwennec after a while. "I spent all night thinking about it. You're daft as a pair of barnacle geese, you and your friend. But you're not bad sorts. I could tell if you were. I don't know why the Holy Office wants you, but—" He stopped and scratched at the back of his flaming neck. "Sometimes these things get muddled."

"Muddled." Fatima laughed spitefully. "What a stupid word for the state we're in. A death sentence for something you didn't do isn't a *muddle*. It's a crime."

"Call it what you want," said Gwennec, looking away. "What I meant is I'm sorry for your trouble."

Fatima regretted hurting him. The day was so fine that they might have been on a pleasure outing: though the wind had already begun to chap her face, the air itself was delicious, a vapor of salt and pitch and warm wood. Black-headed gulls rode the breeze overhead. They complained at the lack of food scraps, diving toward the deck and then veering away again as if puzzled. A familiar gait trod up the steps from the hold, and Hassan, his hair askew, emerged on deck, wrinkling his face at the strong light.

"Afternoon," called Gwennec. "How's the head?"

Hassan made a noncommittal gesture. He took several deep breaths, holding the last for a long moment before letting it out again. Fatima tried to smile: he wouldn't look at her.

"Do you think you can take the tiller for a little?" Gwennec asked her in a low voice. "Watch the compass and keep us on this heading, just as I showed you."

Fatima straightened and nodded.

"Good." Gwennec hitched up his skirt and made his way down the stairs toward the main deck. "I'm going to teach our friend how to tie knots."

*   *   *

With only the sun to mark the passage of time, the afternoon passed slowly. Fatima watched Gwennec and Hassan squat near the mast with piles of rope between them: Gwennec would make coils and loops and pull them tight, then untie them again with a single tug, like a bazaar magician, and hand the rope over to Hassan for practice. Hassan was evidently enjoying himself. Fatima could hear him laugh as he produced a series of useless tangles, but she suspected this was a performance for Gwennec's benefit: Hassan learned everything quickly, and a knot, after all, was a map of sorts, a path that led into the heart of something and out again. Before long, he had mastered Gwennec's teachings well enough to follow him up the ratlines toward the top of the mast, where they were both obscured by sail, inaudible save for an occasional curse or howl when the cog pitched suddenly.

Fatima, for her part, watched the gimbals of the compass dance in their drunken, meditative way, completing a half rotation only to pause, seemingly think better of it, and slowly turn in the opposite direction. When they began to list off course, she put gentle pressure on the tiller, keeping the ship on a more or less westerly course to follow the distant shoreline. It was odd work, requiring a kind of detached focus that reminded her of sewing a hem or repairing a torn sleeve, each stitch, like each small correction at the tiller, closing the gap between two disconnected points.

Fatima fell easily into a stupor. She let her eyes rest on Hassan's map and saw the light change on the outline of the lake at the center, dappling its ink perimeter in gold and blue. Though she would never set foot in Qaf, or Antillia, or whatever it was, it pleased her to imagine it: to fill in the lines of Hassan's map with forests and fields and little streams, a sort of garden writ large. The king of the birds resided within it somewhere, at the foot of the great mountain, but he remained indistinct: the only *simorgh* Fatima had ever seen was in an illuminated book of Persian poetry, a beast in gold ink whose torso and head resembled an eagle's or a griffin's and whose tail was like a peacock's. The memory of that image made her wistful now, and filled her with a delicious, wasteful hope.

It was only when Gwennec stamped up to the stern castle with a wooden plate of bread and cheese that she realized she was hungry. Her mouth watered at the sight of food so plain and dry that she might once have refused it entirely; as it was, she took the plate without a word and dug her teeth into what was offered.

"Wait, wait," said Gwennec. "Soak it in a little water first, if you don't want your teeth broken." He pressed a wooden cup into her hand. Fatima sputtered out a mouthful of crumbs as arid as brick dust as he laughed.

"I'm going to sleep," he said, still grinning. "Much as it pains me to leave the two of you in charge of anything, I need a proper rest. Wake me at compline—that's like your night prayer, or close enough." He surveyed the deck, where Hassan was arranging the rope he had practiced with into neat coils, heaving each thick length over his shoulder with theatrical effort.

"He's as clever-handed as they come, our *blev'ruz*," said Gwennec. "He has a natural sense of where things ought to go. But he hasn't got brute strength and neither have you. You won't be able to reason your way out of a mess at sea, with who knows what following behind you. That's what should worry you." He sniffed, phlegm rumbling in his throat, and made his way down toward the hold, the top of his yellow head descending, or so it seemed, into the deck itself.

"You've been awfully nice to us," called Fatima, before he disappeared entirely. "You didn't have to be."

The head paused.

"I had a choice to make, and I made the choice I could live with," came Gwennec's voice. "That's all." She heard the thump of sandals being cast off, and then another that might have been a body landing in a berth, and then nothing. As if by silent agreement, the gulls overhead veered toward land, where a rust-colored river tumbled down over slabs of bare rock and ebbed by small degrees into the sea. The two waters did not mix. They battled one another in plumes of blue and red that extended into the open water, each color distinct, irreconcilable.

The clarity of the shoreline made Fatima twitch: she had allowed the cog to drift too close to land. Wiping sweat from her lip, she pressed on the tiller, watching the prow tip until it pointed southeast. Hassan dropped his coil of rope and stood to watch.

"You've overcorrected," he called, peering toward land.

Fatima clenched her jaw to keep from retorting. At some point, Hassan had pulled his hair back with a leather thong to keep it off his face; the sun had made his skin as pink as a *ferenji*'s. The effect was transformative: his jaw, newly exposed, was firmer; the lines of his face were more decided. He was increasingly unfamiliar. Fatima watched him, disquieted. They had revealed too much to one another. Fatima knew from experience that such a mistake was rarely reparable in full: she could remember lying in bed beside the sultan at fifteen, when the experience was still new enough to inspire giddiness, telling him how often she thought about him and how beautiful he was, and his laugh, forever stamped in her memory, reminding her that she was not his lover, nor were her confidences welcome. It had been the same with Luz, who had drawn her out only to extract what she wanted. Now it would be the same with Hassan. Intimacy invited ugliness; only girls like Nessma were silly enough to think otherwise. There was no point, really, in making such an effort to survive; great love, for which so much was sacrificed, curdled as quickly as the ordinary kind.

After critiquing Fatima's skill as a pilot, Hassan made no further attempt at conversation. He flitted into and out of her field of vision, disappearing into the rigging and reappearing near the prow, teaching himself to know the joints and sinews of the vessel. At one point he loosed a rope that caused the boom atop the mainsail to swing east and the keel to follow it in a big, swinging arc. Fatima thought of telling him he had *overcorrected*, but instead compensated silently on the tiller, returning the cog to its course while Hassan swore and tied the rope down again. By sunset they had achieved a wordless understanding of the way the work of one affected the other. It was only when pinpricks of fire lit up the shoreline in the growing dark that Hassan broke the silence.

"Is that Marbella, do you suppose?" he asked.

"I don't know," said Fatima. She glanced at their wake, as if the dimming outline of the coast behind them contained some clue. "Someone should go wake Gwennec."

Hassan, who had been leaning against the prow, pushed himself to his feet in a restless motion.

"What I don't understand is why they haven't followed us," he said. "It's been bothering me all day. Surely the Inquisition isn't put off by a little water. And they had more boats moored there at the harbor in Husn Al Munakkab. Bigger and faster ones, probably. They could have given chase. What are they waiting for?"

Fatima studied the fires along the shoreline. It must be a largish town, as there were many bright clusters of light; a few were suspended in the air, as if from the ramparts of watchtowers.

"Maybe they're waiting to see where we'll go," she said.

"You think they might be here at Marbella? You think it's a trap?"

Fatima shook her head. "It'd take them twice as long by land as it's taken us by water. Unless they managed to pass us by boat without being spotted, I don't see how they'd know."

"They could be trailing us, too far in our wake for us to see," pressed Hassan. "They could have sent a scout on ahead. A single rider with a change of horses could make that distance faster than we have."

"Yes, all right, there are half a dozen ways they could find out we're planning to dock at Marbella," snapped Fatima. "I just don't find any of them very likely."

The silence fell again.

"I'll go get our monk," Hassan muttered, disappearing below-decks. Several minutes later, Gwennec emerged, rubbing bloodshot eyes.

"You didn't sink the boat," he said, his voice hoarse with fatigue. "That's a good sign."

"Have we put it in the right place, though?" asked Hassan with forced cheerfulness. "That's the real test."

Gwennec leaned over the deck railing and studied the lights.

"Aye, I'd say you have," he said, sounding a bit surprised. "You haven't passed another port town like this one, have you?"

"No," said Fatima. "There's been nothing larger than a little smoke on the horizon until just now."

"Did you notice a river mouth, probably two or three hours back? Reddish water, lots of it."

"Yes," said Fatima, feeling more confident. "We passed it late in the afternoon."

"I'll be damned, then. This must be Marbella. I expected to wake up in North Africa or Italy or possibly dead. Well done, barnacle geese." He drummed his fingers on the railing in a cheerful rhythm.

"Save your praise," said Hassan. "There's still the small matter of docking and provisioning the ship and setting sail again without being caught."

"And paying for it," said Gwennec. "You haven't got any money, have you?"

Fatima pulled Lady Aisha's ring over her knuckle and held it up, admiring the many-faceted stone with a feeling of profound regret.

"Will this do?" she asked, handing it over with no small reluctance. Gwennec tested the band with his teeth and grunted.

"Handsomely," he said. "You'd eat like princes if you had time to kit yourselves out the proper way. As it is, you'll have to make do with whatever you can find fast at this hour."

The lights onshore were arranging themselves into straight lines, a few of which might be wharves reaching out like bright fingers into the bay. Fatima could smell smoke and charred meat.

"Pork," she said.

"Catholics," said Hassan. "All Catholics between us and the Strait now. The last scions of the Moorish empire stand here on this boat."

Fatima paced at the railing. Though the air was chilly, she felt moons of sweat cooling beneath her arms and in the hollow of her back.

"I can't go ashore," she said. "They'll know something's wrong if they see me. You'll have to go, Hassan. You look as if you could be Castilian."

Hassan stared at her incredulously. "I can barely speak the language. Your Castilian is twice as good as mine. I'll have to speak Sabir, and then they'll know at once what I am."

"Tell them you're Breton," said Gwennec drily. "That's only a three-quarters lie."

"You'll help, surely." Hassan put his hand on Gwennec's arm. "You know who to speak to and what to say. I don't even know what to ask for."

Gwennec looked away, rubbing his jaw.

"I'd rather not," he said. "I'd rather be done with this and part ways at the dock, if it's all the same to you. I've kept you from drowning—that's my right as a man in holy orders. I'm allowed to show compassion to the enemy. Any more than that and it starts to look like treason."

Hassan let his hand drop. Gwennec had used a Latin word, *hostis*, instead of the Frankish *enemi*, as if to take the sting out, or perhaps to make himself sound important, or because he was ignorant; Fatima couldn't tell which. She had almost forgotten what the monk was: he had become a part of the ship and the sea itself, as far removed from politics as a water spirit. But he was none of those things. He was a man, and he had a man's allegiances.

"That's fine," she said coolly. "Do what you want. Take your things and go, with the enemy's blessing."

Gwennec's face fell.

"I didn't mean it like that," he said. "Damn it all, this is my second language, and I barely speak my first one proper. Fa—"

"You don't call her that." Hassan, with great energy, was checking the ropes that secured the boom of the sail to the railing.

"But that's her name," said Gwennec.

"No, that's not her name. That's what I call her." He hurried toward the prow with his head bent. Gwennec stood for a moment without moving.

"We need to slow down," he said in a different voice. "I'll take the sail in. You keep us pointed at that string of lights." He clopped off toward the mast, his sandals flapping against the deck in a graceless rhythm. Fatima stiffened her back. The wind had slackened, but the tide was pulling them now, and the tiller jerked restlessly against her hands. She steadied it with some effort. The ship, at least, had a single purpose, loyal only to the one who stood at its helm.

They drew close enough to the wharves to hear voices. Smoke curdled the air, redolent of sheep's tallow. It made a dense haze around the torches that lined the mooring closest to them, creating the illusion of fog. Fatima was grateful for it. The cog was not large, and in clear weather, she would be plainly visible from the wharf: a girl in Arab dress in a place where she had no reason to be. As it was, Gwennec approached her with a wary look and his arms full of cloth: a cloak made of nubbly, poorly dyed wool and cut in a northern style, with a brass brooch at the neck.

"Put this on," he said. "There's one for the *blev'ruz* too. You shouldn't be seen in those clothes."

"Whose are they?" asked Fatima, plucking at the fabric.

"Mine," said Gwennec curtly. "Keep the hood close around your face."

The cog ghosted up alongside a stout wooden pier, its salt-cracked surface wavering in the torchlight. There was a man, or several men, standing a little farther along: Fatima heard a burst of laughter and the bright jingle of what might be a coin purse.

"That'll be the dockmaster," murmured Gwennec. "He'll want a fee for mooring your boat, and a name and a point of origin for his logs."

"What should we do?"

Gwennec thought for a moment and let out a sharp sigh.

"I'll take the *blev'ruz* with me and get him past the coin-jangler over there. You stay here with the boat. I'd say scream if there's trouble, but I don't know that it'd do much good." The monk looked hawkish in the firelight, his eyes shadowed beneath his brow, his face unreadable. Fatima knew she should say good-bye, or at least something that sounded final, yet all she could hear was *hostis, hostis*, and it stopped her.

"I wish we'd met some other way," said Gwennec, trying to smile.

Fatima looked away. "You're a monk from Brittany and I'm a freedwoman from Granada," she said. "This is the only way we could have met."

Gwennec sniffed and rubbed his nose with the back of one hand. The men on the pier were approaching, calling to them in Castilian, lowering a wooden plank against the lowest point of the deck railing. Gwennec flipped his cowl over his head and hurried down the steps of the stern castle, looking suddenly clerical. He pulled Hassan, incongruous in the borrowed cloak, with him, and then they were both gone, lost in the shadows of the men on the pier and the billowing smoke of their torches.

Fatima stood where she was, her hands on the tiller. Her cloak smelled of the man to whom it had belonged: wool that was more sheep than cloth, the sweat of physical labor, the sea, and beneath it all, a hint of precious resins, amber and oud and frankincense, the stamp of hours spent in prayer behind a censer. She pulled it around herself, rubbing her cheek against the folds of the hood. Perhaps the scent of Gwennec's prayers was worth something, and God, if God was listening, would look kindly on her by virtue of sheer proximity. Fatima hoped so, and waited.

The pier remained mostly empty. A few stray dogs, their ribs bulging, meandered up and down and sniffed for scraps; a man stumbled past and leaned against a piling to piss. Fatima didn't dare make a sound. The tiller grew slick beneath her hands: she dried them on her cloak and gripped the tiller again. It would make no difference: she would never be able to get the cog under way by herself, if it came to that, but standing at the helm gave her something to do besides worry.

She closed her eyes and thought again of the king. She saw, no longer a bird or a phoenix, but an outline of an unnamed creature that stood, dark and luminous at once, between her and the sun. It had no features, no limbs that she could see, yet it was feathered—crimson, green, blue, black pricked with starry gold, white tinged with copper and pink, like daybreak in winter. Fatima reached for it; it lay just beyond her grasp, and when she reached a little more, it moved a little farther beyond that. *Help me*, she begged. *Help me now.*

A thump woke her. The cog rocked back and forth indignantly. Another thump followed, then a third.

"Over there," came Hassan's voice in Castilian. He had affected a broad, halting accent—Gwennec's accent, Fatima realized, or rather a sloppy approximation. She laughed soundlessly in spite of herself. Two men in linen shirts and mud-spattered hose were rolling great barrels across the width of the ship, making for the entrance to the hold below.

"Put them against the hull with the others," instructed Hassan, waggling one finger in the appropriate direction.

"*Put them against the hull with the others*," repeated one of the men, his voice high and mincing. The other man snickered and elbowed him.

"Hush up, he may hear you."

"He doesn't hear, he's a Breton. Look at him, dumb as a post. Fish and beer and cow manure are all they know. Not proper Frenchmen, nor proper Celts—they barely understand each other, let alone—"

"Quiet, you idiot."

The men disappeared into the hold and reemerged without their cargo, slapping their dirty hands against their breeches. Hassan, who had heard quite well, deposited a number of coins in their outstretched hands without a word and waved them off.

"Salted beef, hard cheese, that awful crusty bread—but oranges and lemons, too, to prevent mouth-bleeding. Those cost some money." His head was level with the lip of the stern castle at her feet; she saw only a hood of nubbly blue. "We're to eat some fresh and dry the rest so they don't spoil, then soak them in water when we need them."

"How much do we have?" Fatima asked. "How many days of food?"

"Two or three weeks, I think," said Hassan. "If we haven't spotted this damned island by then, we might as well throw ourselves overboard in any case." He put back his hood. Fatima resisted the urge to stroke his coppery hair: the possibility that he would push her away was too terrible.

"It's nearly dawn," he said. "The tide will be going out soon."

"Then let's go." Fatima left the tiller and went down to the railing to untie the ropes that secured them to their mooring. Hassan climbed into the rigging with the hem of his robe between his teeth. The cog rocked back and forth like a horse that has seen the pasture gate, the sail dancing and shivering as Hassan pulled the boom up the length of the mast, hand over hand. Fatima returned to the helm. The light was turning blue, preluding dawn; at her fingertips, the map waited. She took a breath and looked out at the water, expecting to see the uninterrupted plane of turquoise that would lead them out of the Middle Sea, through the Strait.

Instead, she saw ships.

There were three of them, large carracks that loomed like a forest of masts and sails over their own little cog. They had arrayed themselves in a half circle at the mouth of the harbor, their broadsides toward the wharves, blocking the passage out. Their colors unfurled in the early dawn. With dread, Fatima watched them, though she knew already what she would see: the red-and-gold counter-quartered flags of Aragon and Castile. Fatima seized the rail of the stern castle, weak-kneed.

"Hassan!" she called, her voice high and shaking. Hassan dropped to the deck, landed wrong, and cursed, limping to the rail to look where she was pointing.

"God and His angels and all the prophets," he said, awestruck. "I was right, Fa. They've followed us."

"How?" For a moment, Fatima thought her disbelief might be enough to dispel the ships and send them back to wherever they had come from. "How, how?"

"Does it matter?" Hassan was pulling her away from the railing. Fatima followed vacantly, balancing step by step down the wobbly plank that bridged the gap between ship and pier, and found herself on dry land.

"What are you doing?" she asked, bewildered.

"What does it look like? We have to hide—we can lose them in town and wait until dark, then go—I don't know where—I'll make a new map—"

Fatima halted.

"We're not going anywhere," she said. "We're getting on that ship, Hassan, and we're leaving and never coming back again."

He laughed at her.

"You should never have listened to me. I've gone witless. We can't be children about this anymore. There is an *empire* out there, Fa. And it wants us dead, and we are not going to escape it in a tiny little cog, even if we had a king's ransom in terrible cheese and terrible salted beef." He spread his arms, a tall premonition in the tepid dawn, and gestured to the mud, the salt-warped wood, the indifferent sky. "This is it. This is all there is. There is no king of the birds."

Fatima sat down. The damp soaked through her cloak and into her robe, chilling her legs. He was saying only what she herself had thought half a hundred times since they left Husn Al Munakkab, yet it hurt to hear.

"You can't say that," she told him. "You made the map. I don't understand why you're like this, why what Gwennec said upset you so much. You believed it all until he told that silly story about the seven bishops—you made me want to believe it when I doubted. I don't understand."

Hassan grinned hysterically.

"I'll tell you," he said in a different voice. "It wasn't the story, it wasn't that. It was when you counted up those odd little inlets on the island. I knew it was over then."

Fatima pulled her knees up and hugged them in an effort to stay warm.

"It might not mean what Gwennec says it does," she countered, though softly. "They could be anything, those marks."

Hassan shook his head. "I know what it means. It means I can't run. The Inquisition and the Castilians—they're not just out there, they're in my head. Your head, too. They're inside the only thing that was ever really ours. Even our stories are not our stories. We tried to tell our own, Fa, and all we did was end up telling theirs."

Fatima reached for his hand. He took it and flung himself into the mud beside her. She wanted to disappear, to fuse with the familiar scent of his clothes, his hair. She searched her mind for some means of escape they hadn't yet considered and could think of nothing. Birds had wings, but they did not, and so they were left at the mercy of lesser kings. Fatima looked up at the sky and saw that the day would be cloudless: the sky was a smoky azure from horizon to horizon, tinged in the east by pink and gold. She looked down again when she heard the unmistakable sound of hoofbeats.

A row of horses in full regalia cantered down the furrowed high road that led toward the wharves, ridden by men wearing plate and helms and armed with a ludicrous show of weapons: pikes and heavy oak-shouldered arquebuses and even a few swords. Fatima struggled to her feet in her mud-sodden robe.

"All this for us?" she marveled. "For two people with only a couple of knives between them?"

"Let them overcompensate," said Hassan miserably. "Last time they tried this, we had Vikram. For all they know, we've got an army of jinn at our disposal. I'm a sorcerer, after all."

"How?" said Fatima again. "How could they know so precisely where—"

She stopped when Hassan gripped her arm in what felt like a spasm of pain. He was staring into the mass of horses and men at a dark, unarmored shape bobbing unsteadily atop a gray gelding. It was a monk's habit. As Fatima watched, the monk's cowl fell back, revealing a head of bright blond hair.

"Gwennec," she breathed.

"That lying pig-eater," said Hassan incredulously. "This is how they knew. He must have found a way to signal them from the boat while we were sleeping. That's why he was always scuttling up the mast and messing about with the ship's colors. He's betrayed us."

Chapter 15

The horses bore down on them so fast that Fatima could feel the rhythm of their hoofbeats in her feet, through the shuddering earth. She turned in a circle, looking for a path of escape: to her right, a cluster of low, plaster fishing huts streaked with lichen and moss; to her left, a row of merchant stalls and money-changing houses atop a stone seawall, flanked by weary-looking palm trees. Between the fishing huts, there were narrow alleys cluttered with remnants of old gear: moldy rope and buckets of lime and the half-finished errata of boat carpentry. These, perhaps, held promise. Fatima ran toward the closest opening, dragging Hassan behind her. They splashed through a puddle that was deeper than it looked and soaked themselves up to their calves, Hassan swearing loudly all the while. Then there was a sound, a hiss, and something rippled the surface of the water: it was a crossbow bolt, quivering where it had lodged in the mud. Fatima shrank back, panting.

"You can stop there," came an amused, accented baritone. "Unless you want a bolt in the back as well."

Fatima turned. She couldn't tell who had spoken: the voice had come from one of the innumerable steel helms, rendering the speaker as anonymous as a woman in a veil. The only bare head was Gwennec's. He was close enough now for Fatima to see his face: he looked stricken and pale, his usual ruddy color confined to a stripe of sunburn across his nose and cheeks. He stared at her with a trapped, wide-eyed expression that might have been guilt. Fatima felt a profound desire to spit in his face, but since he was mounted and she was on foot, the angle was inconvenient.

"Well," said the baritone. "This is a happy meeting." A stout man on a large, dappled charger removed his helm. The face beneath was familiar, sun-darkened and square: it was, Fatima realized with some surprise, the general who had come to the Alhambra with Luz under a flag of peace. He handed the reins of his horse to the man beside him and dismounted, landing in the mud with a solid, wet sound.

"Do you remember me, Fatima?" he asked. Fatima said nothing. He ambled toward her, smiling, as though they had met by chance on some pleasant outing. "No? You once served me bread with your dirty little foot." He balled one gauntleted hand into a fist.

"Fatima," came Gwennec's voice, trembling. "Fatima, listen to me—"

Fatima collapsed. For a moment, she couldn't catch her breath: it was only after she had air in her lungs that she felt the pain radiating out from her middle and realized the general had punched her in the gut. Pricks of light obscured her vision, and she heard, rather than saw, the sound of steel colliding with flesh, twice, while Hassan howled in agony.

"Send word to the baronesa," said the general, his feet squelching in the mud as he walked back toward his horse. "Tell her the situation is resolved. Take the girl back to my tent. On second thought—take the sorcerer too. Why not? Both of them, one after the other. We'll see who likes it better."

Fatima tasted blood in the back of her throat. Someone was dragging her to her feet: she resisted for only a moment before she began to wheeze again and the pain overtook her. She told herself she must find her footing and reached out with her toes, digging them into the mud to keep herself upright. The boat—their boat—rose and sank beyond the throng of men, tethered to the wharf only by the gangplank the dockmaster had left there, its sails struggling to catch the rising air. Fatima watched it with regret.

"It's not fair," she slurred, swaying into the steel-plated man who held her arm.

"No," came the general's voice, which sounded, at least to her, sympathetic. "It isn't fair. These things never are. But, my dear, this is the only possible outcome when a couple of unarmed civilians confront a superior force with heavy weaponry. You can count, can't you? This is about numbers. You should never have run in the first place. Not even your demon familiar can help you, unless he can conjure ten thousand men and arm them with pikes."

"He wasn't a demon," said Fatima, shaking.

"Of course you'd say so. You moon-worshipping sodomites are as backward about the unseen as you are about everything else." The general inhaled noisily and spat a gob of phlegm at her feet.

Before him was a row of tents forming a bivouack in the mud a short distance from the western edge of town, where the red-roofed houses gave way to pigsties and pastures. The largest, a circular tent of white canvas upon which the Castilian arms were painted, was open, the tent flap drawn back to reveal an interior as well appointed as a palace room: there were furs and a brazier with coals glowing inside, and a wooden table covered with charts and missives. To one side was a pallet on a low platform; it had been slept in recently, the blankets crumpled around the absent form of the sleeper. Seeing it, Fatima bent forward and gagged.

"You're making this too easy," said the general drily. He dismissed the man who held her arm, and taking her by the collar, shoved her through the open tent flap. She stumbled, landing on the carpet of furs inside. Behind her, she could hear the general begin to unbuckle his breastplate. A numbness crept up her legs, making them heavy, as if she had spent too long in a hot bath. She fought it, knowing it was surrender, her mind abandoning her body to save itself from what came next.

Fatima told herself she would not weep in front of this man. She flinched as his breastplate landed on the furs beside her: a well-made but battered cuirass, tattooed with an intricate design of flowering vines encircling the arms of his house. It had seen mauls and pike-staffs and probably more than one arquebus; it had known combat longer than Fatima had known life, yet here it was, on the ground, unnecessary for this particular act of violence. Fatima marveled vacantly at the discarded steel, at the quieter brutality that came on the heels of warfare, and wondered how many women had been dragged into how many tents, perhaps even this tent—how many men, even, for Hassan would not be spared.

"Why?" she asked her captor, shielding her eyes against the sun that streamed through the open tent flap. The question seemed to baffle him. He paused with his hand on his belt and twisted up his mouth.

"*Why?* Are you without shame?"

"I want to know."

The general laughed incredulously.

"This is what happens in war. Sometimes, even when the losing side is on its knees, it doesn't yet understand it's been defeated. So you take from it the only thing it has left to give. Then it understands." He kicked her knees apart and knelt between them. Behind him, past the tent flap, the morning had become intensely bright, the sky a peerless shade of blue: sunlight stung Fatima's eyes, breaking the stupor that had overtaken her. Without realizing what she was doing, she drew her knife, hidden beneath Gwennec's cloak, and pressed it against the general's throat as he leaned toward her. The edge was so fine that a thin seam of blood sprang up immediately on his stubbled neck, beading along the dagger like the embroidered hem of a sleeve. He cried out, struggling to back away, and toppled over, leaving Fatima with her knee on his chest and her fingers slick with his blood.

"Whore," he spat at her.

"If I'm a whore for resisting you," she said through her teeth, "what would I have been for giving in?"

"Whore," he said again. The sight of him belly-up, his belt undone, scrambling with his feet, filled Fatima with a tepid disgust.

Little men had waged this war. Together they could muster enough steel and gunpowder to be formidable, but singly they were soft, wretched things, squinting in the sun. Fatima levered herself to her feet and withdrew her knife, replacing it with the heel of her boot, which she pressed against the general's bleeding neck.

"You're not going to touch me again," she said. "You're not going to touch Hassan at all."

The general laughed at her.

"You think you can give me orders? You're dead as soon as I'm on my feet, and I'll do what I like with the sorcerer."

Fatima leaned harder on his neck.

"Get Luz," she told him. "Ask her what will happen if you hurt me."

The general had begun to wheeze with the effort of laughing. At some point he had lost a tooth to battle or bad food; a gap showed in his taut grin.

"You're a fool if you're more afraid of me than you are of her," he said.

"Get Luz," Fatima repeated. She removed her boot: the general climbed unsteadily to his feet, one hand on his neck, the other clutching his breeches, his face mirroring her own contempt. Yet he was wary now: she had invoked a name he did not dare contradict.

"Whore," he said a third time, and stepped out of the tent.

Fatima slid to her knees. She felt as though she were still at sea, unmoored and buffeted by surf, losing what little control she had possessed over her own trajectory. Why had she said Luz's name? Luz was worse than any general, for she could reproduce wide-eyed innocence so well that it was likely she had convinced herself of her own virtue.

Fatima wiped her dagger on the skirt of her robe, and despite the heat, hugged Gwennec's cloak about herself. The smell of incense comforted her. She sat, rigid, looking at the flap of the tent and the sun for what felt like hours, watching the light move across the ground and touch her feet and pass on. Her only visitor was a cat, a little black-and-gold tortoiseshell that danced into the tent as if there had never been war or death in the world and rubbed itself against Fatima's back. When it found no food about her, it left again, taking with it the last of the sunlight.

Torches were lit elsewhere. Fatima could hear men calling to one another across the encampment. There was woodsmoke and the scent of herbs and fat rendering in a pot nearby; Fatima felt her mouth water and remembered she had eaten nothing since the previous day. She strained to hear Hassan's voice, or to catch a glimpse of him through the tent flap, but she saw no sign of him. Fear came in waves: perhaps the general had made good on his threat and would deliver Hassan's head to her in a basket, as the Prophet Yahya's was given to Salome; or perhaps, having been thwarted in his own tent, he would take his anger out on Hassan in other ways.

With nothing else to do, Fatima prayed. She made ablutions in the dust, bargaining with the unseen to spare that beloved body, those beloved hands, that fine and vulnerable mind. She would give up many things in return: she would give up her own beauty, which had served others far better than it had served her. She would give up anything in return for some sign that Hassan was safe.

But no sign came. There was only a light bobbing toward her through the twilight, and when it paused at the threshold of the tent, Fatima saw that it was Luz, cloaked in black and carrying an oil lamp.

Fatima shrank from her instinctively. Luz entered without a word and set her lamp on the table near the center of the room, where it threw light on the peaked canvas overhead. She pulled a stool from where it sat near the table and settled herself upon it, tucking the skirts of her dress out of the way.

"You look thinner," she said to Fatima in her ringing voice.

Fatima swallowed and said nothing.

"You assaulted the general," said Luz, one eyebrow arching toward the feathery gold of her temple. "He wants to hang you."

"He assaulted me," protested Fatima. "I was only defending myself."

Luz smiled without humor.

"Your virtue is safe," she said. "I've seen to that."

Fatima knew she probably expected a show of gratitude but could not bring herself to thank Luz for something that should have been hers by right.

"And Hassan?" she ventured.

Luz didn't answer. She studied Fatima in the shallow lamplight with pursed lips. The spot in her left eye, the dark spot Fatima had seen from her hidden vantage point on the road south, was still there, gleaming beneath the blonde fringe of her lashes: not a speck of dust, then, but perhaps an injury, though what sort of injury, Fatima couldn't guess. Looking at it for too long made her uneasy, and she stared instead at her own feet.

A fat serving man in a stained tunic came panting through the door with a plate of food and set it on the ground near Fatima's hand. Fatima fell upon it like a hawk, scooping up hot fragments of leek and mutton and watery almond pottage with her fingers and licking each one clean.

"There's a spoon," said Luz drily. "If you want it. We don't normally eat so well, but today is the Feast of Saint Verena. She's said to watch over young girls on long journeys. She was born in Egypt and traveled all the way to Switzerland to evangelize the pagans there a thousand years ago. Perhaps it was she who saved you from being despoiled."

"I saved myself," muttered Fatima around a mouthful of leek.

"Well. You called for me, anyway, and I came." Luz smiled again. Her face and hands, the only parts of her visible in the dark, seemed to glow with an internal luminescence between the folds of her black gown, so that she appeared like the shrouded icon of some saint. Fatima withdrew instinctively, pulling her feet beneath the spattered hem of Gwennec's cloak.

"What happens now?" she asked.

Luz spread her hands.

"You tell me," she said. "We can have a short conversation in which you accept your Savior, the Son of God, and confess, in writing, the sins you have witnessed and participated in with the sorcerer Hassan ibn Haytham of Granada. Or we can have a longer conversation in which I extract those things from you piece by piece. It's entirely up to you."

The magnanimity in her voice, the little ironic thrum of laughter, turned the food to a solid, indigestible lump in Fatima's mouth.

If Luz had been slow-witted and humorless, or without affection, Fatima could have hated her, but Luz was none of those things, and it was this, the richness of her smile, the ample evidence of a tender heart and a lively mind, that made something in Fatima recoil with dread.

"The sultan will be furious when he finds out you're holding me here and letting your men lay their hands on me," Fatima hazarded.

Luz laughed.

"The sultan has repudiated you," she said. "You have no friends left, Fatima. Even the monk whose cloak you're wearing has learned better. Soon enough, Hassan will come to realize his own errors, and when he does, as I've promised you and I promise you now, he will be spared. So will you, if only you humble yourself and examine your heart."

Fatima examined her heart. Might she do as Luz asked? It was only a matter of words. She could, she thought, adopt an air of convincing sincerity. She was used to pretending. She could kneel and profess an alien faith and maybe even shed a few tears, and make up a story or two in which Hassan's powers were the gift of the Devil. But then there was the troublesome possibility that Hassan might tell different stories, or might, for all his nervous sensibilities, prove the stronger character in the end, and insist upon his own innocence, even in the face of death.

"Can I think about it?" she asked in a much smaller voice.

Luz's eyes went wide. She left her seat to kneel at Fatima's feet and take the younger woman's hands between her own, kissing the tips of her fingers.

"Of course you can think about it," she said. "You don't know how happy it makes me to hear you ask." She leaned closer, until Fatima could smell the oil of her hair and the honeyed scent of rose water rising from her bodice.

"Can I tell you a secret?" she whispered.

Fatima didn't dare reply.

"God speaks to me," said Luz. "He has favored me with His insight. I see things that are a vast distance away, in time and in space. I saw you on your stolen ship. I saw the place where you would dock. And I saw you before, on the road, when you hid in the ditch at my feet, but God told me it wasn't yet time. He told me that if I were patient, you would lead me back to the sorcerer Hassan. And it all happened, didn't it? It all happened just as the Lord showed me it would." Her breathing had grown rapid. Fatima tried to free her hands and found she could not. Luz's face was tense, elated, the chapped corners of her mouth pulled taut. As Fatima watched, the speck in her left eye began to wriggle.

"Let me go," she begged, but Luz seemed not to hear her. The speck squirmed, swimming against the white of Luz's eye, a feeble horror, a worm culled from some other earth. With all her strength, she wrenched her hands from Luz's grip and wiped them on her tunic.

"You're afraid," said Luz placidly. "Don't be. I've been praying for you, Fatima. And for Hassan, grievous though his sins may be. No one is beyond God's mercy. You need only repent. A new world is coming—I have seen that too. The banner of the Savior will fly over lands undreamed of by old men in their cassocks. Isabella of

Spain will reign over an empire so vast that the sun will rise on its easternmost shore before it sets on the westernmost mountain. The sins of the world will be cleansed with blood, as salvation was bought with the blood of the Son. You could share it with us, Fatima. You could stand by my side, by the side of my queen, and joy unending could be yours."

The speck had writhed its way across the surface of Luz's eye and lodged just beside her iris, a parasitic moon orbiting a convex host. Fatima's ears were ringing; the ground seemed to fade and run beneath her. She leaned heavily on her hands to steady herself.

"I thank you for your prayers," was all she could think to say. Luz smiled and rose to her feet.

"You'll be safe here," she said. "Eat and rest. I'll come and see you in the morning, after you've had some time alone." She hesitated at the tent flap and smiled again, and then was gone, succeeded by an eddy of cold air.

Fatima lay down on the furs that covered the floor of the tent and hugged her knees to her chest. Luz had left her lamp behind: it cast an uneven circle of light on the little table and the ground, and across Fatima's feet, leaving everything beyond it obscured. She heard a small noise, like a cry, from somewhere outside, and held her breath to listen, thinking it might be Hassan, but it did not come again, and she was left to imagine who or what had made it.

Through the tent flap, she watched a filament of stars progress across the sky and let herself fall into a stupor. She thought of Luz, whose hair was the color of the lamplight, and felt the imprint of her kisses upon her fingertips, and wondered whether she was wrong after all, and this was what goodness looked like. She spoke like goodness. It would be easy, thought Fatima, if Luz was right: if Luz was right, one need never bother about the wreckage left in the wake of these holy wars, about the lives lost and enslaved, for the wreckage was cleansed by the horrors visited upon it. She fell half asleep thinking about how easy it was. Yet against her lids, she saw the little speck, the worm, burrowing its way across Luz's field of vision, and knew, in a way she knew very little else, that whatever had spoken to her was not God.

*   *   *

Something warm and soft pressed against her and brought her back to consciousness. It rumbled happily, smelling of the pine woods: it was the tortoiseshell cat, the tiny queen that had been and gone in the afternoon, and it was blinking at her companionably in the dark. Fatima rolled onto her back and held out her hand: the cat rubbed its cheek against her fingers. But the little creature was after the remains of the meal Luz had brought her, and soon abandoned Fatima to lick mutton fat from the edge of the bowl. Fatima sat up to stretch her stiff legs. The cat twitched its tail and made small satisfied sounds as it ate, indifferent when she caressed it. It felt good to touch something so artlessly affectionate, something that neither promised nor demanded anything. Whether Fatima lived long enough to set foot outside the encampment or not, there would still be black-and-gold cats, and sparrows, and the matted grass she could feel beneath the furs that covered the ground, and though her time among them might be brief, the knowledge that these simple things would persist comforted her.

"Look at you, so small and neat. You're very pretty," she told the cat.

"So are you," said the cat, raising its head and licking its whiskers, "though my brother says you've heard it so often that the compliment annoys you."

Fatima fell backward onto her hands.

"You're not friendless," the cat continued. "The forces you see are working against you, but some you do not see are working on your behalf."

"The forces I see," repeated Fatima dully. The cat fluffed out its tail and shook its paws like a woman fussing with her skirts, and suddenly Fatima did see a woman, or the reflection of a woman, clothed in furs and in her own thick black-and-gold hair, which sparkled with fragments of ribbon and small jewels. She was angular, all sloping jaw and skewed brow, and her eyes were large and yellow in a face the color of temple smoke. On her feet were a pair of jeweled slippers sewn with thread-of-gold, like those a palace woman might wear.

"What are you?" Fatima whispered.

"You already know," said the woman.

Unthinking, Fatima reached out to touch the woman's hair, expecting to encounter only air and silence, but instead found her fingers tangled in warm, heavy tresses that gave off the scent of living wood. The woman closed her eyes and smiled with undisguised pleasure, offering the side of her neck for Fatima to stroke. In a stupor, Fatima let her fingers trail over the feverish skin, as soft as something newly born, and felt as though she had fallen backward, so that the woman and the world itself loomed over her.

"Are you frightened of me?" the woman asked. When Fatima didn't answer, she shifted, half shrugging, and Fatima's fingers slipped down a length of jeweled chaos to rest against the flat of her belly. Fatima was seized by something that was emphatically not fear, but frightened her nonetheless.

"I haven't decided yet," she said, her mouth dry.

The woman laughed and pulled away. Fatima felt her face go hot. She retreated again into Gwennec's cloak and palmed the grip of her knife.

"What do you want?" she demanded. Her voice sounded harsh and silly in her own ears, like that of a child pretending to be big. The woman must have thought so too, for she shook her head, making a dozen tiny bells dance and giggle in her hair.

"Why have you come?" asked Fatima in a humbler tone. "A week ago, I'd never met a jinn in my life, and now I can't seem to avoid you."

"You've met plenty of jinn," the woman replied, stretching her velvet limbs. "You've passed us in the twilight and in the empty places. If you didn't see us, it's because you lived between safe, well-lighted walls. Now that you're out in the dark, your fear makes you see more clearly." She smiled. The lamplight glinted on a double row of pointed teeth as bright and closely packed as shards of glass. Fatima fought the urge to run.

"But as for your questions," the woman continued, "my brother sent me. He says he told you to expect me, but that you might not remember."

Fatima searched her mind and could indeed remember nothing.

"Your brother," she repeated.

257

"You were dreaming," said the woman in a patient voice. Fatima sat up straighter.

"Vikram," she said. "I dreamed of Vikram on the ship."

"You didn't dream *of* him. You dreamed, and he visited your dreaming."

"Then he really is alive? Why didn't he come himself?"

"We don't heal as neatly as you do. He can't come to you in any form you could understand. If you saw him now, it would drive you mad. We're not meant to have these little conversations, your people and mine, sitting in the same room, in the same moment, and every time we do, it requires an effort of the will." The woman rose and drew Fatima to her feet also. "My name is Azalel," she whispered, her voice merry, leaning toward Fatima as if relaying a secret. "I've been all about the camp, looking and listening. Your ship is still in the harbor. Walk with me now and you might reach it. These men are used to looking at girls without seeing them. It would take very little to convince them you aren't important. It would take very little more to convince them you aren't even here."

Fatima looked out at the quiet camp, the ghostlike peaks of canvas where men were sleeping.

"I'd never make it," she said. "There are too many of them. And I wouldn't try, not without Hassan."

Azalel tilted her head, and Fatima once again saw the cat, its ears translucent with the light behind them.

"Why not? Isn't saving yourself better than saving no one at all? Your death won't prove a point—and even if it did, you won't be around to enjoy the satisfaction."

Fatima could smell newly fallen dew on the trampled grass, the bloom of sweet water over the tang of the sea.

"I'm tired of being told no," she muttered. "Especially tired of being told no by make-believe beasts who are supposed to say yes to things that wouldn't be possible otherwise. I won't leave without Hassan. I'm not trading one prison for another."

Azalel flopped on the furs and stuck out her lower lip.

"This isn't a proper adventure," she said. "My brother never told me you'd make speeches about prisons. I wouldn't have come if he had."

Fatima lay down also and let her arms fall outward. She remembered what Vikram had said about jinn not loving very much, or very often, and wondered what they felt instead.

"Vikram told me he had a sister," was all she said. "But he never mentioned your name."

Azalel turned on her back with a smile.

"Vikram only talks about nonsense. We've known each other so long that neither of us can remember what we are, so brother and sister is what we call each other. We lie together sometimes, so perhaps we're really something else. Who can tell? When you've been alive a very, very long time, you learn to forget certain things. There's a great deal in this world that one is better off not knowing."

Fatima turned on her side. Azalel's face was close to hers, and no longer so terrifying, or at the very least, less terrifying than the florid leer of the general that interposed itself over her vision at odd intervals, rendered unspeakable by its very ordinariness. A glass-toothed jinn was simply the most frightening thing she could think of: the general and, for that matter, Luz were something far worse.

"Do you really—you and Vikram—do you really lie together?" she found herself asking.

"Once in a while."

"How?"

"Would you like me to show you?"

"No! No. I only meant—" Fatima paused, frustrated at her own lack of subtlety, at the dissembling that seemed to come instinctively to everyone but herself. "Half the time you look one way, and half the time you look another way, and it made me wonder how you're born and how you die and how you do all the other things people do in between."

Azalel studied her with puzzled admiration.

"I see it now," she announced.

"See what?"

"Why he likes you." She sighed and gathered Fatima into the crescent of her body as though curling around a kitten. Fatima went limp, stupefied by the heat of Azalel's arms and not inclined to resist their invitation. If she wasn't going to run, she might as well rest: her rest had been stolen from her too often.

"The way we want," said Azalel, stroking her hair. "We do all those things the way we want."

Chapter 16

Fatima awoke when the lamp burned out. At the sudden intrusion of darkness, she sat up, as alert as if she had slept for days, and reached instinctively for her knife. Azalel was standing in the opening of the tent, her ivory claws illuminated by starlight.

"Hush," she whispered. "What do you hear?"

Fatima strained to listen.

"Nothing," she replied.

"Yes, yes, exactly. The night has been quiet. The men assigned to the last watch have fallen asleep around their campfire. You'll get no better chance than this."

Fatima wiped the sweat from her cheeks with the sleeve of her robe. Every garment she wore smelled ripe; she thought with regret of the hot bath and the rose water and the gowns and the praise that would be hers if she could only give Luz what she wanted.

"I'm ready," she said, grinding her teeth.

Azalel, bent in an odd shape, walked in a little circle on the pads of her fingers and rubbed herself against Fatima's legs.

"Are you sure we have to collect the mapmaker first?" she asked.

"Yes."

"Very well. It will end badly. What a pity Vikram isn't here! I don't make promises or sacrifices or grant wishes or any of those sorts of things. I'm the wrong kind of jinn for that. None of it interests me." She rumbled in irritation and slipped out of the tent into the moonless hour. Fatima hesitated on the threshold, her feet deep in the yielding furs, holding on to the dry warmth within a moment longer, and then followed Azalel out among the sleeping men.

Azalel walked silently between the white canvas tents, leaving no track in the dew.

Put your feet where I do, came her voice in Fatima's head. *One step at a time. I have turned you sideways so that the men see only what they expect. A camp girl, a serving woman, a fishwife on her way to the harbor . . .*

Fatima trained her eyes on Azalel's feet, the same color as the blue hour, their soles looking bloody with mud. The sight of them made Fatima giddy. The camp around her dimmed. She saw shadows, forms only slightly darker than the night itself, moving among the tents; when she looked at them, they paused to look back, staring across the distance between them through pinprick eyes.

Don't linger, said Azalel mildly. *Or my brothers and sisters might decide they like you too much to let you go.*

Where are we? asked Fatima.

Halfway, came the answer.

A shape, heavy and earthy, lumbered toward her, clothed in a spattered gray cloak and reeking of onions. Fatima watched it for several moments before she realized it was a man—a soldier, on his way to piss perhaps, or to begin preparations for breakfast, or returning from a night in a brothel. He was all out of proportion, his limbs long and hanging like those of an ape, yet he lacked the vitality of any living thing, so that he struck her the same way a boulder in a field might: he was a feature in a landscape, a heap of moving mud.

Is this what we look like? asked Fatima in horror. *Is this what we look like to you?*

The man paused, frowning, and turned in a half circle.

Move back, snapped Azalel. *You can't very well hide if you let him run smack into you.*

Fatima stumbled backward and let out a little shriek when her heel caught on a tent stake. There was a ringing hiss as the soldier drew his sword. Then a clawed hand clapped itself over Fatima's mouth and pulled her away, drawing her into an intangible fire, muffled and suspended above the ground, and held her there for a moment that stretched out so long that Fatima forgot to breathe, until the soldier muttered a prayer and spat a ball of phlegm at the grass, and continued on his way between the damp outworks of canvas and steel.

Fatima went slack with relief. She leaned into Azalel, held up by eddies of warmth like the air above hot coals.

Pretty child, said Azalel half pityingly, stroking her hair. *You want so much and are given so little. Forget your mapmaker and all the clay men like him. Come with me to the Empty Quarter. It's nearly as beautiful as you are—everything fashioned from quartz and song and light from the oldest stars. Come with me and I will teach you to drink fire. You need never lay eyes on anything made of mud ever again.*

So delicious was this offer that Fatima said yes, or thought yes, in an impulse over which she had no control, and felt Azalel dot her neck with delighted kisses, and saw the sky overhead grow bright, crowded with points of light on a canvas of pale violet. The tents of the men gave way to hills of white sand that billowed and glittered coldly in the starlight.

I promise you, said Azalel, *I will deny you nothing. I will be a better master than any you could have had on earth.*

At this, Fatima stood up, searching for the ground with her toes for several disorienting moments before she found it. She pulled away from Azalel, who was now little more than a pillar of flame, and blinked as hard as she could to replace the alien stars with the world that had preceded them. She felt wounded in a way she could hardly justify: the jinn had said herself that she had no honor, yet Fatima had taken her promises at their apparent worth.

"No one offers me peace or safety except to keep me as a possession," she said aloud. "No one reaches out to me except to take what little I have."

The pillar of flame gnashed its teeth. Fatima could see the tents of the camp again, and the muddy track that wound between them, and on unsteady feet, she began to walk away.

"Wait," called Azalel. "Stop—I'm sorry. It's only my nature. Please stop. If you're caught, my brother will be cross with me."

Fatima kept going. The mud sucked at her boots and made her wobble, and for a bare moment, she allowed herself to appreciate the ludicrousness of her position.

"Go away," she called without turning. The mud released her foot with a squelch.

"You're going to die," came Azalel's voice, rich with amusement.

"I'm going to get Hassan," said Fatima.

There was a sigh or a snarl and Azalel appeared beside her again. She lifted her arm and sheltered Fatima beneath it, letting her long sleeve fall between Fatima and the white tents, so that when Fatima looked to her left, she saw only the piercing starlight of the Empty Quarter.

"Quickly then," said Azalel. "Dawn is coming."

Fatima rushed along the muddy path as fast as her sodden boots would allow. The tents were all identical, anonymous; some had armor piled outside, or disorderly weapon racks, or empty plates of food, but there was no sign of Hassan, nor any way to determine where he might be held.

"Where would they keep him?" whispered Fatima.

"Perhaps he's over there," said Azalel, who sounded bored. "In the tent with the guards outside and a scribe's satchel lying in the mud."

Fatima stopped where she was and batted Azalel's sleeve out of her eyes. The starlight cleared: beyond it was another tent, larger than the others and set apart. Two men stood before it wearing half helms and holding pikestaffs, their heads nodding above their breastplates. In the mud at their feet, like the limp remains of a carcass on a butcher's floor, lay Hassan's leather carry case.

The sight of it filled Fatima with dread. She stuffed her knuckles into her mouth and bit down to keep from screaming. Not knowing what she did, she broke away from Azalel and began to run. The guard to the left of the tent flap, taller and heavier than the other, snapped awake, his head jerking up, his bloodshot eyes widening in disbelief. He lifted his pike.

There was a blur of black-and-gold and the jingling rebuke of small bells. The guard choked and stumbled, dark blood pouring from his neck, the scent of it so pungent that Fatima gagged. Dizzy, she reeled into the second man, who dropped as though felled by a lightning bolt, his throat open to the spine. Azalel stood over her kills impassively.

"Go," she said, her mouth full of blood.

Fatima went. She pushed through the tent flap into the gloomy interior, blinking impatiently until her night blindness passed.

"Hassan?" she called softly.

There was motion in the darkness. Hassan, kneeling, looked at her with vacant eyes, his skin a sickly yellow. For a moment, Fatima couldn't understand why he didn't get to his feet. Then she saw the cord snaking between his wrists and ankles. She fell to her own knees then. Outside, Azalel growled and paced on all fours.

"You'll bring the whole camp down on you if you don't hurry," she snapped.

Fatima ignored her. She tried to draw her knife to cut Hassan's bonds, but her hands shook too much to manage it. He looked through her without recognition, his body slack, his lips moving soundlessly.

"Say something," Fatima whispered. Hassan twitched. A wet feeling spread across Fatima's knee, drop by drop: she looked down and saw a dark stain on the lap of her robe. Panicked, she searched for the source of the blood, folding back tunic and undershirt and sash, but Hassan's clothes were clean, his face and arms unmarked. It was only when she looked down at his hands that she understood.

266

Tiny blades, as light and slim as bird feathers, had been shoved under the thumbnail and fingernails of Hassan's left hand, the hand with which he wrote and drew his maps. The bed of each nail was a dark crimson, the effect of it oddly beautiful, as though he had decorated himself with henna for a festival, filing his nails to sharp points. The ghosts of his pain slid through her own hands, making them throb in time to her heartbeat. She clenched and unclenched them.

"Hassan," she begged softly. "Please."

Hassan blinked and attempted to focus.

"I'm thirsty," he said. Fatima scrambled backward, searching in the dark; she encountered a small table and heard what might have been a wooden cup fall over and roll away. She grabbed at it, and at the pitcher that stood near it, and poured out a cupful of liquid she couldn't identify, pressing it to Hassan's chapped lips.

He drank in hurried swallows, moisture beading on the fringe of his beard.

"That's mead," he said in vague appreciation.

Fatima heard noise outside the tent: Azalel growled anxiously.

"My love," she said, "we have to go. I'm going to—I'm going to—" she looked down at his hands and began to cry.

"Let me," hissed Azalel, pushing past her. She squatted in front of Hassan and took his left hand between her talons.

"Look at her," Azalel instructed, jerking her chin at Fatima. Hassan, stricken, did as he was told.

"Fa," he whispered. "She's got blue skin. And very sharp teeth."

Azalel grinned. There was a small, terrible sound, like something sharp dragging against a wall, and one of the little blades fell ringing to the ground. Fatima fought the urge to gag. Hassan only moaned, rocking once on his knees.

"That's right," soothed Azalel. "Quiet and still and brave. They'll feel much better on the way out than they did on the way in." Another blade fell.

"Why did you let her do this to you? Why didn't you just tell her what she wanted to hear?" said Fatima through her teeth.

"Because it wasn't true," said Hassan, too loudly. He looked awake now, his eyes bright and wild. "Because I couldn't stand the little smile she had when she told me that I was loved, that she hated my sin, not me. I told her I've never seen the Devil. I told her I'm more certain of the truth and oneness of God than I am of my own miserable existence. And it made her angry." He gave a strangled shriek as the last of the blades fell to the ground. They made a bright pile there, blood gleaming upon polished metal. Fatima looked at them as the light danced. There was despair in them somehow: despair in the knowledge that man could make something so beautiful, so precisely conceived, for the purpose of inflicting pain.

"There was a spot," said Hassan. He was limp as Azalel took his wrists and cut the wire that bound them. "In her eye. Like a speck of dirt or a fleck of ash from a fire, only a thousand times more awful."

"I've seen it," said Fatima. "It's helping her, whatever it is. Telling her things. She thinks it's her own spotless merit." She got to her feet and forced herself to take deep breaths. She could smell salt as the air shifted to accommodate the rising sun: the tide would be going out soon.

"If we don't leave now, we'll never leave," she said.

"I don't think I can keep up, Fa," said Hassan. He sounded drunk, though whether it was from the pain or the mead, Fatima couldn't tell. "I don't have the energy for anything besides agony. I can't summon any more."

Fatima put her shoulder beneath his and helped him slowly to his feet.

"You're damn well going to try," she said.

* * *

It was nearly bright enough to read outside. Fatima watched as crisp avenues of light formed between the rows of tents, illuminating churned-up mud and the detritus of war. They would surely be seen: a redheaded, bleeding scribe and a girl as tall as a man could not escape notice, even with a jinn escort to shield them. So Fatima looked straight ahead, ignoring the shouts and curses that disturbed the limpid air as the men around them woke up. She could see their cog beyond the pigsties and washhouses and tents, its little sails askew and unkempt among the larger ships docked at the wharf.

"You can't be serious," said Hassan when he saw where she was looking. "Back to the ship? My God, Fatima—where do you suppose we're going?"

"To Qaf," said Fatima, clenching her jaw. "To the king of the birds."

"Don't you mean Antillia? Avalon? Shambhala? I wish to God I'd never made that map." Hassan was swaying as he walked and paused to suck on his bleeding fingers as though insensible of danger. Watching him, Fatima felt a thrum of real fear. Even if they escaped, they would not escape intact: the act of saving themselves would leave scars, had left scars. The greatest danger was not that they would be caught, but that Hassan's own life was less precious to him than it had been the previous morning.

"Hsst." Azalel halted in front of them and held out her arm. A row of men, all still half asleep, was coming toward them, each pair of legs moving in the same rhythm, so that the clack of armor echoed across the camp, giving an impression less of men than of some machine. Fatima pulled Hassan between two tents. Azalel followed, ushering them over tent pegs and ropes and glancing with deep disgust at the sun struggling to free itself from the mountains behind them.

"Too much daylight," she murmured to Fatima. "Soon I will be of no help to you."

"It doesn't matter. We're nearly there."

"Are we?"

Fatima stopped and stood straight. They were surrounded on all sides by identical canvas peaks. The pigsties and the muddy foreshore had disappeared, and the masts of the ships at the wharf along with them.

"Damn it all to hell," she breathed.

Azalel gave a little chiding sigh. She gathered herself, her bells and beads and swaths of velvet, into a pillar of delirium, retreating, or so it seemed to Fatima, behind some invisible screen, so that looking at her was like looking through a lattice at a world into which she couldn't venture.

"If you had listened to me, you could've been aboard your ship by now," she said. "Instead, you wasted time on this sentimental errand. What a shame! So pretty, so lovely . . ." She walked away through the maze of canvas, her feet suspended above the ground. Fatima stared after her in speechless fury.

"That ship can't be crewed by one person," she shouted.

Tittering bells answered her. Fatima wanted to throw something, to rend her clothes or pull her hair, but the light was emphatic now, and Hassan was standing beside her looking less and less inclined to move.

"Damn all the jinn," she moaned, grinding the heels of her palms against her eyes.

"That's not a wise thing to say," said Hassan.

Fatima cursed him silently and slipped her arm through his. She half pulled him along the narrow path between tents, choosing a direction at random, ignoring the muffled, surprised sounds of the men in their tents as they responded to her voice. Despair drove her as powerfully as hope once had: there was nothing to do, nothing at all, but continue.

"I hated you last night," Hassan said lightly. "While I was sitting there bleeding and going mad in the dark, I hated you."

"I don't care," said Fatima. The tents ended a short distance ahead; she could see color and sky but little else to tell her whether she was heading toward the harbor or away from it. Stumbling over tent stakes, she broke into a run, pulling Hassan behind her, ignoring the heady, persistent smell of his blood. She ran toward the sky, toward pale yellow and rose slashed by slate-blue streaks of cloud, and toward the morning star that hung above it all like an inferior sun, and collided, at the last moment, with Luz.

Fatima reeled backward and fell solidly at her feet. Luz didn't move. She was flanked by the general, silent, his neck bound in linen; four other men, almost boys, stood behind them in chest plates and broad-brimmed helms, their pikes glinting. Luz's face was rigid; her cheeks were glowing with high, offended color; she wore a sable-lined cloak over her dress; and her hair had been combed and pinned. She had, it seemed, slept well.

"I believed you," she said, looking down through her lashes at Fatima. "I sang psalms of praise last night because I thought you were ready. I imagined standing beside you at your baptism. I would have made a place at court for you and put eligible gentlemen in your path. But you've dashed all my hopes. Your pride and your insolence and your unnatural attachment to this sorcerer have veiled you from God." Luz looked past her at Hassan, her eyes blank and unmoving save for the parasite lodged beside her left pupil.

"You will tell your secrets," she said to him. "One way or another. Sorcery is like a fast-growing weed—even if you cut off the vine and the flower, the roots will continue to spread beneath the earth and spring up elsewhere, just like the tunnels on your maps. You received instruction from someone. Perhaps you have given instruction to others. You must tell me who and how, or you will lose your life and any chance you may still have to save your soul."

Hassan, who had been swaying and sucking at his bloody fingers, drew himself upright. He looked back at Luz with a rage that startled Fatima, transforming his face into something luminous and terrible, a star haloed in a thicket of red curls.

"I've already told you the truth," he said. "Many times over. I am as I am and there seems no point in pretending about anything, since I'm going to die anyway. I will tell you my sins. At eight, I stole figs from a neighbor's tree and lied about it. At fifteen, I slept with my fellow apprentice mapmaker, who went on to die of rot after he was sent to battle and wounded in the foot. It was then that I began to drink. I drink, I lie with men when I can manage it, yet I spend more time in prayer than you do, judging by the relentlessness with which you've pursued us. God knows all my faults, for I tell Him constantly. If you're going to kill me, do it now. I might be a courtier who slouches and spends too much on clothing and shrinks from pain, but I am not afraid of death. God knows what I am, and I am no sorcerer."

A baffled silence followed. Luz stared at Hassan, momentarily uncertain, her chest rising and falling within the confines of her bodice. Her face softened. Fatima had never known anyone to succeed in hating Hassan, and thought for one desperate moment that his artlessness might save them after all.

"Execute her," said Luz gently, her gaze opaque. "Take him back to his tent and bind him."

Fatima screamed. She lunged for Hassan but was caught by the hair with a gloved hand and dragged back. Hassan was shrieking her name, his composure gone, straining against the arms that held him; for a moment Fatima brushed his fingers with hers, but they were slick with blood, and she was parted from him with only a red smear on her fingertips.

The man holding her yanked her head forward, forcing her to stare at the ground. She saw the hooves of horses dancing nervously in the mud and heard men muttering to one another and palming their weapons, but all was eclipsed by the awful sound of Hassan's despair, a howl like the end of things, a sound that shattered Fatima's nerves.

"Fatima."

Her name came like a plea from somewhere behind her.

"Please—please just look at me."

It was Gwennec's voice. Fatima tilted her head as far as she could and caught sight of a black scapular.

"You," she snarled. The fist in her hair tightened and pulled her head around before she had a chance to compose an insult. She was stumbling past Gwennec's horse: she could see the monk's foot clad in its modest leather sandal, his heel as rough and brown as what shod it, and cracked in several places. He drew it back, and for a moment, Fatima thought he was going to kick her in the face as a parting insult.

Then he did kick, but not at her: his foot landed beneath the jaw of the man who held her, slipping inside the gap between his helm and his breastplate as deftly as a letter knife parting a wax seal. The man gurgled in protest, released Fatima's arm, and clawed at his throat.

"Run!" shrieked Gwennec, pulling at his horse's head. He was holding the reins in an awkward, clawed way, and Fatima saw, belatedly, that his hands were bound together with twine.

"Run!" he repeated. Fatima pelted away. Her insides burned. She could feel every contraction of her muscles as she ran, a screaming, labored push-pull beneath her skin. There was cursing and shouting behind her and a hand reached for her borrowed cloak, but the general's men, clad in armor that weighed half as much as Fatima herself, were slower than she was. Behind her, Gwennec's horse was squealing. Fatima saw a blur of copper and green and realized Hassan was following her, or trying to. By instinct, she had run toward the cog, though it was only when her feet hit the gangplank that she realized how foolish this was: the three ships at the mouth of the harbor hadn't moved. But she was propelled by sheer momentum now, tumbling onto the deck as Hassan collided with her, sending them both sprawling on their sides.

Over the rumbling of the tide and the clamor of horses and men, Fatima heard Gwennec cry out. There was a mechanical thud and a crack as an arquebus discharged: the tart smell of gunpowder filled the air. Fatima knew they should push off, tighten the sail, pull the tiller until it pointed away, but all she could see was a monk's habit surrounded by steel.

"Gwennec," she said, struggling to her feet.

"Leave him," called Hassan. Fatima pretended not to hear. She stood at the edge of the gangplank, watching as a soldier reached toward the reins of Gwennec's terrified gelding. Gwennec looked up and met Fatima's gaze. The distance was too great; the soldiers were too many and too well armed. A terrible resignation settled over his face. The reins slid uselessly through his bound hands and into those of the soldier, who yanked the horse's head down, dragging it to a halt.

Fatima unsheathed the dagger at her hip.

"What the hell are you doing?" screamed Hassan. Fatima breathed in and out, steadying her hand. On the third breath, she loosed the dagger. It flew end over end, glinting in the new sun like a fish leaping into the air, and clattered off the soldier's breastplate into the mud.

Fatima howled in frustration.

"Give me yours," she ordered Hassan.

"No!"

She reached for his sash.

"At least throw it properly this time," pleaded Hassan, sitting down where he was. "Hold it by the blade, Fa, not the hilt—the blade, the blade."

Fatima took the blade of the dagger between three fingers, trying hard not to cut herself. The impact of her first attempt had prompted the soldier to turn and look at her: his helm was tilted back, and she could see his lightly bearded face, his disjointed nose, broken in undiscoverable circumstances. He had a home; he had come from somewhere; someone had loved him. For a moment, she was moved: if not for all of this, all of the steel and the quartered arms, the borders drawn and redrawn on maps, they might be something else to one another. Perhaps not friends, but at least not enemies.

The soldier twitched. Fatima didn't realize she'd thrown Hassan's knife until she saw it lodged between his brows. He twitched again, grimacing reflexively, and collapsed into the mud.

Gwennec stared at her in disbelief. Then his gelding bolted and he lurched forward, clinging to its mane as it thundered away from the throng of soldiers. A second arquebus discharged, a third, a fourth. The railing closest to Fatima exploded into splinters. She skittered away, giddy and horrified, as Gwennec grabbed at the gelding's reins with both hands and forced it up the gangplank, which bounced and dipped under its weight. The horse leaped the last stride onto the deck. The force of its hooves dislodged the gangplank entirely and sent the narrow beam into the churning water below like a body thrown overboard. Free at last, the cog

began to spin, sail flapping, the tiller rotating in half circles under
pressure from the eager tide.

Fatima heard high, disbelieving laughter. Gwennec slid off the
gelding's saddle and looped his bound wrists over her head, pulling her into a clumsy embrace. He kissed her forehead, her eyelids,
the pulse at her temple. Fatima felt points of heat where his lips
had been that lingered after he withdrew them. Then he was gone:
Hassan was tearing the twine from his reddened wrists, and he
was running, throwing himself over the prow with his legs hooked
around the bowsprit, reaching down over his head to unfurl a second
sail, a spritsail, which Fatima had never noticed.

"Speed!" he shouted back at them. "Get on the damned tiller,
it's flapping like a drunkard!"

Fatima left Hassan to placate the hysterical gelding and sprinted
up to the stern castle. She threw her weight against the tiller, ignoring the surge of fire in her middle. Wind snapped into the mainsail
and the cog jerked forward as if stung by a whip.

"Point us between those two big carracks," called Gwennec,
hurrying back toward Fatima along the deck. "It's our best chance.
They'll not be able to turn as quick as the little caravel off our
right flank over there."

Fatima heaved the tiller to the left. The cog tilted and veered,
sending the horse into a frenzy: it reared, dragging Hassan with it.
Fatima watched the animal's panic unfold in silence. The sound of
the prow cutting through the surf muted everything else. Fatima
could see figures hurrying across the deck of the nearest carrack,
sunburned men, some armed and in hauberks, others in sailors' caps;
they swarmed toward the rail and into the rigging as if caught by

surprise. She narrowed her eyes at the gap between the two ships, through which the open sea was visible: it was wide enough to admit the cog, but only just, and they were closing in on it very fast.

"Make your peace with God," called Gwennec, sounding almost merry. A volley of noise cut through the roar of the surf: a dozen arquebuses, two dozen, half a hundred perhaps, fired at the cog from both sides. Shattered wood flew up from prow and railing and hull, sending a rain of splinters down on their heads. Fatima flinched, sheltering beneath the tiller.

"We're still too slow." Gwennec leaned over an uninjured portion of the railing to assess the damage. His hair was damp with salt spray and curled across his brow, making him look younger, almost like a boy. "If we don't get out of range of their guns, they'll put a hole in the hull and sink us right here. We've got to lose something."

"Not the horse!" shouted Hassan, who was standing with the poor animal's face pressed into the front of his robe.

"Then throw yourself overboard, you bony heathen! Christ Jesus!" Gwennec was gone again, shimmying up the mast until he reached the very top, where the boom of the mainsail met the mast and made a cross.

Fatima went cold. "What are you doing?" she called, convinced he was about to martyr himself. Gwennec didn't answer. Beside him, the Castilian flag flew stiff and proud, yard after yard of expensively dyed canvas and rampant lions pulling at the rope that secured it. Gwennec reached out and loosed one knot, then another. With a roar, he flung the colors away. The lessening of the drag against the mainsail was slight, but sufficient: the cog slipped between the two larger ships like a well-oiled bolt.

"Reload!" Fatima could hear someone overhead shouting in Castilian. "Reload!"

"They timed that last volley all wrong," said Gwennec gleefully. "They'll pay for it now. We'll be well past them by the time they've reloaded those great clanking things."

A canyon of interlocking pine planks enclosed them. The hulls of the two carracks sat many feet higher in the water than the little cog, and loomed overhead, echoing with the thwarted cries of soldiers. The sound of rushing water quieted. A bluish gloom fell over the deck of the smaller ship as the shadows of the carracks enveloped it.

"They'll crush us," came Hassan's voice, sounding thin and metallic.

"They won't," said Gwennec from his perch in the rigging. "They can't turn fast enough. Just wait."

Fatima waited. One lonely arquebus discharged from overhead, then another, but they were too late: as Fatima turned, she saw the railing of the stern castle clear the larger ships, releasing the little cog from their long shadows and into open water. Gwennec, invisible behind the mainsail, gave a wild yelp, and even the gelding seemed to understand its good fortune, for it threw up its shaggy head and whinnied.

A flutter of red caught Fatima's eye. The Castilian flag was still aloft in the air behind them, as if it had run after the cog to say farewell. As she watched, the wind folded it upon itself and cast it into the sea. The flag puckered, sinking under its own weight, until finally it was gone, and there was only water, green and wild, spilling toward the edge of the earth.

Chapter 17

"We can't feed it, *blev'ruz*. Surely even someone as daft as you can see that. The thing'll need pounds and pounds of—"

"There are carrots and apples in one of those barrels down below. We can spare some for the poor beast. We've got lemons and so forth for ourselves, when it comes to that."

"Lovely. Lovely! Do you have any idea how much a horse eats? And shits? We'll all starve together, the three of us and this damned nag as well. Who's to say you get to decide, anyhow? It was Fa's ring that bought the supplies."

"Hush, you'll wake her."

Fatima inhaled sharply and opened her eyes. Overhead, she saw the swaying ribs of the hull as they curved up to meet the deck. The sunlight that gilded the bottom of the stairs across the floor from her bunk was richly tinted. Sitting up, she was rewarded by a surge of nausea. The Middle Sea, so placid where it touched the eastward shores of Spain, had grown rougher as they approached the Strait. She felt, or thought she felt, the ship gather its strength, preparing itself for hostile, unknown water.

Fatima put her feet on the pitch-stained floor and shook her head to clear it. Hooves pawed at the deck overhead. Bracing herself against the ribs of the hull, Fatima made her way toward the stairs and up into what remained of the sunlight.

"There, see?" Hassan, his hair stiff with sweat and sea mist, stroked the gelding's dun-colored nose to soothe it. "You did wake her."

"You should have woken me hours ago," said Fatima, yawning. The sea came into focus around her: it had turned a milky green, thick with the sediment of rivers. Land reached out to encircle them on both sides. To her left, in the far distance, Fatima could see a range of blue-green mountains beneath a veil of cloud; to her right, much closer, an uneven row of arid cliffs, bone-white and barren of vegetation. Only the way forward was open. The Strait of Jebel Tareq led into the setting sun, between the parted hands of Europe and Africa. At its narrowest point, a mountain crowned with lights rose straight out of the sea, its appearance so solid and abrupt that it seemed conscious of itself, like a sentry lifting his lamp over the threshold of the world.

"What is that?" murmured Fatima.

"Jebel Tareq himself," said Hassan, coming to stand beside her. The gelding followed him anxiously. "Gibraltar, as the Christians call him."

"And he'll be watching," said Gwennec. "From that peak, the Spaniards can see anything that comes and goes in this waterway. There's a fortress up there where you see the lights, with walls ten feet thick and a ring of watchtowers. Always under guard, day and night."

Fatima leaned over the railing to get a better look. Behind her, the gelding snuffled at the pocket of Hassan's robe, hoping for an apple. It was an ugly beast, its fetlocks untrimmed, its coat a muddy roan: a packhorse, more than likely, before the Castilians had set Gwennec atop its back. Fatima craned her neck to study the monk. He was rubbing his wrists absently: the red marks had deepened to purple and blue.

"Tell me what happened," said Fatima in a quiet voice.

Gwennec flushed and looked away.

"I didn't—" His voice caught, and he made silent shapes with his mouth, as if trying to remember an unfamiliar word. "I think you ought to know that I tried to turn you in," he continued evenly, his eyes fixed on nothing. Fatima went hot and cold by turns. She could still feel the points of heat on her face where Gwennec had kissed her, but a chilly knot in her chest told her *hostis, hostis,* and she reminded herself that he had drawn a line between them.

"You said you'd go to the monastery," was all she offered, matching his tone.

"I never made it as far as the monastery. There were guards posted everywhere. But I never had a chance to give you up, because they already knew well enough where to expect you, as if they'd been here on this ship, listening at your elbow. They asked me who I was and where I'd been and it seemed foolish to lie. But I wouldn't tell them your plan. Where you were headed, the map, all of that. Didn't seem relevant, as you were sitting there in the harbor, nor was it my right to say anyhow. They didn't like that. They took me to a public house somewhere up the main road, where the general and the lady were waiting."

"The lady?" A chill rippled down Fatima's arms. "Do you mean Luz?"

"Who else? So kind, she seemed at first—I'd met her before, of course, aboard this very cog on the way down the coast, but she took no notice of me then. This time, though—" Gwennec shifted on his feet and flushed again, turning crimson from neck to scalp. "She knew all sorts of things about me. Asked after my father, my three sisters, wanted to know whether the youngest was married yet. Spoke about this year's catch, which was paltry compared with years past, and asked whether I thought the cod mightn't be thinning out along the Breton seabeds. Fishermen's talk. It was the oddest thing. She knew my father'd been furious when I told him I wanted to join the brothers at Saint Padarn's. Said she'd pray for me and for him, that his heart might soften and come to accept my vocation." Gwennec licked his chapped lips. "I asked her what she wanted. And what she wanted, apparently, was for me to tell her I'd seen our *blev'ruz* using his powers to commune with the Devil."

Hassan spat out a laugh, startling the horse.

"I told her I'd seen no such thing. I told her the truth—that Hassan seemed ordinary enough, a bit delicate maybe, but as smart as they make 'em, and as good-hearted. And as for Fatima here—" He smiled at her lopsidedly. "I told her that if ever there was anyone as could put the Devil in his place, it was Fatima."

Fatima could imagine it: she could see Luz sitting across from the baffled monk, smiling in her sympathetic way, her wintery eyes opaque, disguising whatever fury or fervor she might feel.

"Did you see it?" Fatima pressed. "The speck in her eye—her left eye."

"A speck?" Gwennec looked puzzled. "I can't say I remember any speck. Her eyes seemed regular enough to me. It's what comes out of her mouth that's so terrifying. Not even that—it's the fact that people listen to her. That's the most terrifying thing of all."

Fatima pressed her hands against her sides to warm them. When she blinked, she could see the speck struggling and wriggling in its bed of flesh, and she turned toward the sun to blot it out. It unnerved her that Gwennec couldn't see what she had seen. She thought for a moment that she might be mistaken, that in her terror she had imagined the parasite. Perhaps it had been only a fleck of ash or dirt after all. Yet Hassan had seen it too, and Hassan saw more than anyone else. Fatima wondered whether Gwennec simply hadn't noticed the speck, or had disregarded it, or whether something else yet more unsettling was at play. He had risked much to help them, but some part of him, the largest part, still belonged to the world Luz inhabited: perhaps he could see only what he had been taught to see.

"Something's wrong with her, anyway," said Fatima, half to herself. "Something awful."

Gwennec grunted in agreement, rubbing his wrists.

"But what happened then?" prompted Hassan.

"She bound me with her own little hands," said Gwennec, and laughed strangely, as though to mask pain. "I didn't move or protest. The general and the guards, none of 'em said anything. It was as if we were all transfixed. She said my faith was lacking and that I wasn't to be trusted. Said she was taking me under guard for my own good. Then the general ordered his men to ready themselves and mount, and they threw me onto the back of this nag here. The rest you already know."

The monk's rough, guileless face went still. He watched Fatima intently, as though awaiting her judgment. Fatima reached out to touch the bruising on his wrists. He let her. She could feel his expression change with the pressure of her fingertips, though she was looking at his wounds and not at his face, and she smiled, for he was a man after all. Gwennec shook himself and drew away. He pulled his cowl up against the persistent breeze and leaned against the railing to look past the stern at the lacy, white-foam wake they left behind them.

"Look there, Fa," he said, pointing. "That's what happens next."

Fatima looked where he pointed. Far behind them was a square of silver against the milky sea: the mainsail of a much larger ship. Atop its foremast, Fatima saw a glimmer of red.

"They're following us," she said flatly.

"Well of course they're following us," snapped Hassan. "They weren't about to shrug their shoulders and go home empty-handed."

"We've the benefit of a head start," said Gwennec. "But not for long. A smaller ship is easier to maneuver, but a ship under so much sail can make better time. They'll eat up the distance between us, bit by bit, especially since, no offense meant, they've a more experienced crew."

Fatima tensed and relaxed her fingers on the railing, judging the distance to the Castilian carrack. It was no use: her mind still reeled at so much space, at the absence of walls and doors.

"How long?" she asked. "How long until they catch up?"

Gwennec narrowed his eyes and thought for a moment.

"Two days at most," he said. "Maybe less."

Fatima turned and looked past the bow. They were drawing near the foot of the great mountain: she could see waves breaking white along its rocky shore. The pinnacle was so far above them that the lights of the fortress had vanished, obscured by the sheer mass of rock overhead. The sun had dropped below the horizon: looking ahead no longer hurt Fatima's eyes. The water was deceptively still, a pane of glass hinged to the sky. She felt warm breath on her hip: the gelding, still hungry, had abandoned Hassan to snuffle at her pockets. She stroked its musty-smelling head to calm herself.

"I thought horses were afraid of boats," she said, trying to sound jocular.

"They are," called Gwennec, who was leaning over the bow to check the spritsail below.

"This one is a brave fellow," said Hassan, patting its mottled flank. "Aren't you? A brave bitty pony."

Gwennec snorted. "It's not brave. It's just too stupid to realize it stands inches from a watery death."

"Poor Stupid. Don't listen to the monk. You saved his life and now he insults you. You can have his share of the apples. Come along now."

Hassan made for the hold. The gelding pricked up its shaggy ears and clopped after him like a large dog, filling the mouth of the stairwell with its head and shoulders as Hassan ducked below to uncrate their supplies. Fatima looked back over the bow. The spritsail belled and waned; the cog surged forward, leaving her weightless for a moment. She gasped, laughing, as it subsided gently into the water again.

"Do you ever get used to it?" she asked Gwennec. The monk straightened and ran a hand through his damp hair.

"I never did," he said. "I got to liking it, though." He followed her gaze out toward the remains of the sunset. They stood in silence for several minutes, watching the sky turn from copper to gray.

"Look," said Gwennec softly, nudging Fatima with his foot. Fatima blinked. There was a line in the water below, as clean and straight as if it had been cut with a knife by some unseen hand. On one side, the water was green and mild; on the other, it was a blunt, threatening color, a blue so cold and deep that Fatima's teeth ached when she looked at it. The seas met and parted without intermingling, a thin ribbon of foam between them the only sign of trespass. As she watched, the cog lifted a little and then settled, passing from one world into another.

"So that's that," she said wonderingly.

"That's that." Gwennec grinned. "And thus did the Lord part the waters."

"I never imagined it would be like this—one so distinct from the other. I thought water was water."

"The Dark Sea is sweeter than the Middle Sea. You can tell we're already riding lower than we were. The *blev'ruz*'s ears'll be popping down below."

"What's that word you keep calling him?" asked Fatima. "*Blev'ruz.*"

"What? Redhead, of course. What else would I call him?"

Fatima smiled and leaned over the rail again, watching the border of the two seas recede behind them.

"*Hostis*," said Fatima. "Even the seas are enemies."

"No." Gwennec shook his head, his ragged voice softening. "Not *hostis*. Not the seas, nor we. I should never have used that word. I meant *hospes*."

"A guest from a foreign land. Certainly you did."

"I did, I did." Gwennec smiled lopsidedly. "I meant *amicus*. I meant *intimus*." He paused, his color heightening. "I thought for sure you'd let me hang after what I'd done and the way we left things."

"Hassan wanted to leave you behind. But you looked too sad. I couldn't."

Gwennec's face immediately twisted itself into the expression that had prompted her sympathy.

"It's never going to be put right," he said. "It's all over and done with, my life is. My abbot, my cell, the view down to the hay fields—I'm never going to see those things again."

Fatima saw no reason to give him hope where none existed.

"I'm sorry," was all she could think to say.

"Don't you miss your home?" he pressed. "Won't you miss it?"

"No."

"Odd that you shouldn't miss a palace, yet I'm half dead with grief for a bare room in a monastery. I wonder what it means."

"It means you can't choose what makes you happy."

Gwennec gave a sharp little sigh, and for a moment, Fatima thought he might start crying. She gave in to an impulse and stroked his fingers, one after the other, each knuckle white and taut against the deck railing.

"Do you really believe in him?" asked Gwennec. There was a note of pain in his voice. "In your bird king? Is he worth all this?"

Fatima thought about it. She no longer knew what she believed, but she knew what she was, and this, oddly, amounted to the same thing. She knew now what parts of her persisted when the things that didn't matter were stripped away: the embroidered slippers, the quiet routines, the room in which she slept, her few possessions. Those were not her; they formed no integral part of her personality, though they had defined her for so many years. What remained was slight but strong, and what remained, believed.

"I don't know whether I believe in him or not," she said. "But I believe he is worth all this, yes."

Fatima thought Gwennec might mock her for giving such a strange answer, but instead he looked out of the corner of his eye with puzzled respect.

"That makes me feel a little better," he said, "though I don't see why it should." He had made no attempt to withdraw his hand as she stroked it, and now turned his palm up as if in supplication. His eyes, too, pleaded silently, like those of a man who is drowning. Fatima withdrew her fingers and wrapped them in the rough wool of his habit. She pulled him close, seeking his mouth with her own. He made a small sound, a whimper, as though from fear or need or both, and suddenly she felt his hands in her hair and on her face, as if he wanted to touch all of her at once.

She almost laughed: his ardor, so different from the sultan's, was at once clumsy and impossible to resist. Then his lips strayed from her mouth to her jaw, her throat; he whispered her name into the curve of her neck again and again as if in prayer. The laughter left her. There was too much cloth, yards of it, habit and robe and cloak and shift. Fatima pressed her hands against her face in frustration.

Gwennec cursed and tore something at the seams. Finally she felt the warmth of his skin against hers, the pressure of him, the counterpressure of the railing against the small of her back. A wail slid from her lips: she was hungrier than she thought.

"No?" panted Gwennec.

"Yes," she reassured him, "Yes, yes."

* * *

When she woke, she saw Hassan outlined in lantern light on the lip of the hold, his face unreadable. She jerked upright, unaware she had fallen asleep. Gwennec was out cold, his body curled protectively around hers, his habit bunched about his knees.

"It's your watch," said Hassan.

Fatima pulled herself to her feet. There was an ache, not unpleasant, in the tendons of her legs; a corresponding ache in her lower back. The deck was silent, dark except for the ring of light where Hassan stood. Even the horse was drowsing: a bulky lump wedged against the rail in the widest part of the ship. Fatima swayed toward the ring of light, rubbing her arms to warm them. The chill in the air had deepened. It was her shift that had torn: she could feel air on her sides, where her tunic was slit, sending gooseflesh up the ladder of her ribs.

"Hassan." She reached instinctively for his hand. He turned away.

"I need to sleep," he said. "I'm the only one who hasn't slept."

"Sleep, then." But they both remained where they were, saying nothing.

"I didn't mean—" began Fatima, "or at least, I didn't plan—"

"No, it's all right." Hassan sniffed and rubbed his nose. "Naturally it's you he wants. It's not as if I'm surprised. Only after that little speech you gave me when I said *I* wanted him, and you pretended to be shocked, I would have thought—no, I don't know what I would have thought." He sniffed again. "Never mind, it doesn't matter."

Fatima breathed on her hands to warm them and willed Hassan to look at her.

"Do you love him?" he asked.

It was this that stung.

"No," said Fatima flatly. "I barely know him. I've only ever loved one person."

Hassan finally met her eyes. His face was pinched, as if he was in pain.

"Sometimes I look at you and I think, 'There goes my heart, walking outside my body,'" he said. "And yet—oh, Fa. How can this end any way but in a mess? Where are the princes with their legendary swords and white steeds, who love where they ought and fight what they ought? Why is it only us, all muddled up?"

She reached out: she touched his brow, his cheekbone, the fringe of coppery lashes above each eye.

"You smell like him," said Hassan, brushing away her hand. "I'm going below."

"Take Gwennec with you," begged Fatima. Hassan glanced at the bundle of slumbering black wool and made a derisive noise.

"He seems fine where he is."

"It's freezing up here. Hassan, I'm serious—take him with you."

Hassan gave her a withering look out of the corner of his eye but did as she bade him, walking toward the monk and toeing him lightly in the side. Gwennec groaned.

"Let's go, my Breton brother," said Hassan. "She whose word is law says you're not to sleep out in the cold." He looped Gwennec's arm over his own shoulders and pulled him upright.

"Hassan," muttered Gwennec, stumbling beside him, "I've done something."

"Oh, I heard all about it. Come on."

Fatima watched them disappear into the hold, the blond head drooping against the reddish one. A light flared up from the stairwell and wavered a little before extinguishing itself: Hassan must have lit a lamp to make his way in the dark and then shuttered it. On deck, Stupid shifted in his sleep and whuffed through his stubbled nostrils. His breath hung in the air for a moment before dissipating. Fatima climbed to the stern castle and surveyed the quiet ship, feeling unwontedly satisfied. The cog was small and she had stolen it, but it felt like hers in a way nothing else ever had. Happiness, she decided, came only in pauses, neither regularly nor predictably. She breathed in and out, savoring the faint taste of salt and resin.

The tiller was warmer than the air and twitched as she pressed her hands against it. Fatima straightened and squinted at the compass. They had drifted northward a little: Fatima put her weight into the tiller and pushed until the compass needle swung west again. Hassan's map, weighted under stones, trembled in the lamplight. Hassan had added something while she slept: now there were faint, parallel dashes in the emptiness of the Dark Sea, pointing northwest. Tracing them with one finger, Fatima realized they must represent the prevailing current that had been pulling them gently northward. She marveled at the little charcoal ticks and at the fingers that had drawn them, rendering a great force into a small mark with such economy. And for this, Luz wanted Hassan dead.

Fatima turned and leaned out over the sternmost rail. In the pitch black, the carrack that followed behind them had been reduced to a flickering dot, like a star that had alighted on the water. Fatima suddenly felt as though she were somewhere else, somewhere familiar, observing a series of events that had already happened. Luz was aboard that ship, and was staring at her from across the mute water, just as she was staring back at Luz. The thought grew so emphatic that Fatima began to rub her eyes as if to clear them of sleep. Perhaps the carrack would turn back. The pursuers would abandon their intention when they realized their quarry meant to keep sailing west. Fatima repeated this to herself until she was calmer. She did not look at the lights of the carrack again.

Piloting a ship that jerked and shied like a living thing was enough to keep her occupied until the sky began to pale in the east. In the hours before dawn, she lost the moon, and everything outside the circle of lamplight on the table beside her fused with the darkness; she kept her eyes fixed on the needle of the compass and her hands wrapped around the tiller, and remained there, unmoving, until the muscles of her arms began to ache and the stars began to fade. She heard the sails flap and drag, beating themselves rhythmically against the mast, and knew the wind had changed, but she didn't dare leave the stern castle to examine them. Only when she heard a heavy tread in the hold below did she relax her fingers on the tiller and slump down to rest her head on her knees.

"We're losing the wind," came Gwennec's voice. Fatima heard him cross the deck and grunt as he pulled himself up the ratlines. She knew she should say something to him, something appropriately poignant, yet she was too tired to summon the words. She was nearly asleep when she felt him throw himself down beside her with a sigh.

"We need to set proper watches," he said. "Two awake, one asleep, eight hours on, four off, so that everyone overlaps. I wish I could tell how much distance that damned carrack made up overnight, but there's too much damned fog this morning to see a damned thing."

Fatima looked up: a weak, gray light had penetrated the gloom, revealing nothing. The air beyond the cog was wreathed in white. Gwennec's breath ascended around his chapped face in puffs of vapor, giving him a haloed appearance, like a weary seraph. He was looking at her uneasily, waiting for her to speak.

"What are the chances there'll be a baby?" he asked. His voice was low, as if he worried they might be overheard.

"Not good, I don't think," murmured Fatima, unwilling to admit the things she had done to prevent this possibility. In spite of all that had happened, he still felt unfamiliar; his gestures, his accent, the profound blue of his eyes, everything about him was too blunt. "I haven't—I've never—"

"You don't have to tell me anything you don't want to tell me," said Gwennec, sounding relieved. He found her hand and laced his fingers with hers. "Fa—"

"We don't need to have this part of the conversation," said Fatima, closing her eyes.

"I want to. Only to say—well, all right, have it your way. My heart belongs to someone else and so does yours. But we both know that already. So perhaps there's nothing to be said after all."

Fatima opened her eyes again.

"Who does yours belong to?" she asked sharply.

"Who do you think?" Gwennec gave her one of the lopsided smiles that were already beginning to irritate her. Fatima sat up straighter to get a better look at him. He seemed no different from how he had been the night before, only a little more rumpled, his cheeks golden with a day's growth of stubble.

"You can't mean—" She meant to say *God* but laughed instead.

"I can and I do." Gwennec looked into the fog, his face altering. "I eloped when I went to the abbey, more or less. There's a part of the Mass when the priest holds up the Host, like this"—he demonstrated, loosing her fingers to lift his rough hands—"and one Easter, as I was watching, I felt this—I don't know what it was. All I know is I couldn't stand it. It was as if all the beauty of the world was bound up in one gesture. I saw the body of God in the priest's hands. And that was that. I never went home again."

Fatima didn't know where to set her eyes. She felt faintly embarrassed, as though she had intruded on something private, next to which their night together seemed rather feeble. She had taken him for a fisherman who happened to become a monk; she saw now that she had reversed the order of things. A wariness crept over her, throwing suspicion on the little artless gestures and smiles that had made him so appealing.

"I don't see how you can believe what she believes and yet be so different," she muttered.

"She?"

"Luz."

"Ah." Gwennec gave a grunting laugh. "I think about this, when I'm alone. Luz isn't the worst. I've met others since I've been in the abbey who are—well, I shouldn't say, since they're trying to put themselves right. Some ideas are so beautiful that even evil people believe in them. I thought the abbey would be full of saintly folk, but it wasn't. Isn't. It used to depress me. But I've come to realize that I must share God with the things that God has set askew."

Fatima felt something harden in her chest. She drew away from him by inches until she could no longer feel the warmth of his body beside hers.

"Am I one of those things to you now? Something askew?"

"You?" Gwennec's eyes widened. "Because we had a tumble once, after you'd saved my life and we were all giddy to be alive? I'm as askew as you are, if that's true, and more so, seeing as you've broken no vows. Lord, Fa, if I told you what sins some men drag with them, even monks—especially monks, I sometimes think. We oughtn't to have done it and we won't do it again, but it was so lovely that I haven't even repented of it yet, because I'd be lying if I said I was filled with remorse. I'm waiting until I can muster some proper humility."

Fatima relaxed; the warmth returned, transmitted between their shoulders.

"I was worried you'd go funny afterward," she said.

"I don't go funny, generally speaking, though if I do, I'll warn you first." Gwennec grinned again and Fatima found she didn't mind it so much. Then he glanced back, over the sternmost railing, and the smile slid from his face.

"Fa," he said hoarsely.

Fatima scrambled to her feet. The mist was thinning: water was visible again, as calm and milky as a lake. Rising up from it was the darker outline of the carrack, close enough for them to count the muffled booms of each sail.

"Wake Hassan," shouted Gwennec, leaping down the steps to the main deck. "Get him up here!" He rushed past Stupid; spooked, the gelding squealed and clattered sideways. Fatima raced down one set of steps and then another, emerging into the murky half-night of the hold, where Hassan lay prone in a bunk, his long body still fitted around the emptiness where Gwennec had lain.

"Hassan," said Fatima, shaking him by the arm. "They've caught up."

Hassan's eyes flew open. Without a word, he rose and stumbled across the hold, smoothing his shaggy hair with one hand. Fatima followed him up to the deck. Gwennec had adjusted the sails: a brisk current of air pulled at their clothing and battered their faces when they emerged into daylight. The sun, formerly a colorless, half-hidden disk, was burning through the fog, throwing weak shadows below the sails and the agitated figures of Gwennec and the gelding.

"What happened?" shouted Hassan. Gwennec swung down from the ratlines and landed in front of him.

"We lost the wind last night," he said, pulling at a series of ropes that ran from the deck rail up to the mast. "Not Fatima's fault— she was at the helm, nothing she could have done. We needed two awake, and we had two asleep, like a pack of fools."

"Not Fatima's fault," muttered Hassan as the monk continued his inspection. "Nothing will ever be Fatima's fault again, I suspect."

Fatima looked around for something to fling at him but saw nothing suitable.

"Don't pretend you wouldn't have done exactly the same thing if he'd looked at you the right way," she spat.

"Ah, but he didn't look at me the right way, did he? Nor will he—nor will any of the men we meet from now on, if we live long enough for it to matter. They'll look at you."

They stared at each other for a long moment. Then the cog pitched abruptly, sending everything that was not bolted to the deck careening sideways. Fatima heard herself scream. She collided with Stupid and clung to his springy mane, but the gelding was no more sure-footed than herself, and soon they were both pinned against the rail. Water rose up before Fatima's eyes, eclipsing the sky and the horizon. With a groan, the cog rolled back. Fatima found herself looking straight up. Above the fog, the sky was an opaque, mineral blue: the color of early autumn. For a moment, everything was weightless. Then the cog came crashing down, sending up a curtain of spray on either side of the prow, soaking Fatima in frigid brine. Voices were calling her name. She reached out and felt Hassan's arms lift her away from the railing.

"I thought you'd fallen overboard," he said, terror bright in his voice. "Oh God! I thought you were dead."

Fatima pressed her face into the curve of his neck: Hassan, half sobbing, kissed her forehead, where her hairline mingled by feathered degrees into her brow. It was not exactly an apology, but Fatima pretended it was, and let herself sink against him as the cog heaved again.

"What *is* this?" she heard him shout.

"A rogue wave," came Gwennec's voice from atop the mast. "There may be more where that came from. The Dark Sea is nothing but fog and violence, damn it all, and this cog wasn't built for open water."

"And the carrack?"

"Still there, though we've a bit more room between us now. Christ Jesus, don't just stand there—someone get on the tiller before I lose my mind."

Fatima looked up and attempted to steady herself. The cog was still rolling, though the angle was no longer so acute. Stupid was on his knees against the rail, showing the whites of his eyes; foam spattered from his mouth. Something fluttered on the table beside the tiller: it was the map, still pinned by its quartet of stones, struggling like a bird caught in a hunter's trap.

"Hassan," said Fatima. "I have an idea."

Chapter 18

He didn't like to let go of her hand. Gwennec found him a crate to sit on near the little table on the stern castle, but it was Fatima he wanted beside him, his right hand clutching hers as he sketched with his left. She rose every so often to check their course, though the compass, and the gimbals in its orbit, went oddly still after Hassan began to alter the map. Fatima imagined the compass had been a living thing and was now dead: they had killed it, and the halos and half spheres of metal constituted a corpse.

The fantasy was so vivid that she found herself unwilling to look at the compass after a time, focusing instead on the movement of Hassan's fingers, the darkening circles beneath his eyes. He was working in ink now, not in charcoal: he had selected a blue bottle from the innards of his leather case and mixed powders and oils to create a color that reminded Fatima of the ship, a red-brown, water stained, earthy hue, each drop of which pulled them closer to the king of the birds.

"What's moving?" Gwennec asked at one point, hovering over Hassan's shoulder. "Us, or the island, or the sea?"

"Nothing is moving," murmured Hassan. "I'm just shortening the distance between us and what we want."

"You know the sun's gotten confused," pressed Gwennec. "I've been up the mast, watching it tick around in a circle. It's as if this cog is the still point at the top of the world, where they say there is no darkness."

"You're awfully calm about it," said Fatima.

"I don't know what else to be. I don't know what else to do. I've never seen anything like this."

Fatima untangled her fingers from Hassan's, kissing his head when he made a noise of protest. She straightened and stretched her back. The fog had returned; or rather, the horizon had vanished, and the carrack, if it still followed them, was hidden in a gray blur.

"I'm tired," she announced.

"Go sleep," said Gwennec. "I'll stay with him."

"I don't want you," muttered Hassan.

"You've not got much choice. It's me or Stupid, and Stupid shits every twenty minutes. I notice neither of you refined gentlefolk has bothered to clean up."

"You clean it up, since you're the least domesticated."

"Oh, I see how things lie. Shall I wipe your ass as well, while I'm about it?"

Fatima left them to bicker and went belowdecks. Her shoulders ached from being too long in one position: there was pressure in her temples that blinking did nothing to dispel. She crawled into the bunk where Hassan and Gwennec had slept and breathed their mingled scents. Before her eyes, the grain of the oak trees that had become the hull of the ship slid along from plank to plank, as solid as ever. Everything around her seemed too real: surely she was asleep, or she had gone overboard in the rogue wave, or she was back in the palace, dreaming, and had never left at all. Nothing real could follow from desires like hers. They were adrift in what was surely no longer the waking world; fate did not reward such recklessness. *If you climb too high,* Lady Aisha had once told her, *the angels will come down and ask you where you're going.* Yet the hull, as she touched it, was rough and sturdy and shifted almost imperceptibly beneath her fingers to accommodate the motion of the water. The ship was still real, still hers.

"Qaf," she whispered, tracing invisible letters on the hull. "Antillia." Perhaps the difference didn't matter; perhaps it was only the escape that mattered. And she had escaped: she was free, and though freedom was neither happiness nor safety, though it was in fact a crueler and lonelier thing than she could have imagined, it was real, just as the ship was real, and like the ship, it was hers.

She fell asleep with her finger pressed against the hull. A jostle and the scent and heaviness of a warm body half woke her sometime later—when exactly, she couldn't tell; the light had not changed when Hassan collapsed beside her with a sigh.

"Move over," came Gwennec's voice, whispering.

"Not big enough for three," muttered Hassan.

"Then turn sideways, you radish. I'm freezing out here. Move, move."

Fatima found herself pressed between Hassan and the slope of the hull.

"No one is sailing this ship," she murmured.

"Nothing to sail," said Gwennec. "No wind, no landmarks, compass dead."

"Is that it, then? We wait here to die?"

"No," came Hassan's voice. "I think we're close now. I think this is how it's meant to look. Hidden in the fog. That's what the story says."

Fatima was about to correct him—surely they had added that detail themselves—but stopped herself. She could no longer remember what they had read and what they had written. Sleep pulled at her again. Gwennec's breath was already deepening; beside her, she felt Hassan twitch in the violent prelude to dreams. She rested her cheek against his.

✳ ✳ ✳

She dreamed of a white shoreline. Hills of thick, pale grass, flattened by wind, leading down to the sand; small trees, their trunks like warped silver, hanging over the cresting hillsides, their branches straining backward, like the grass, as if a strong gale had swept over the whole of the landscape. The air was heavy with the smell of rain. Fatima sensed rather than saw the figure standing beside her, yet even before she turned to look, she knew what she would find.

The Bird King did not touch the ground. He hung in the air, held aloft by currents Fatima could not feel, silently beating his great wings. She could look at him only in pieces. He had no face, at least none in any sense that Fatima could describe, but he was clothed in feathers: crimson, blue, gray, glass-green, dark ocher. There were colors that were not colors but memories: the rosy-edged white of a winter sunrise and the mottled red and green of earth blending into water, and here and there a blue-black parted by gold like the quiet dawns in which Lady Aisha had touched her shoulder and asked if she would rise to pray.

He was too frightening to be truly beautiful. There was a remoteness about him, a terrible, unrelenting kind of mercy, the kind that could meet good and evil with equal tenderness. Yet Fatima reached for him with both her arms, saturated with relief and bawling like a child.

I'm here, she said. *I've come. I crossed the Dark Sea to find you, and now I'm here.*

The Bird King folded his wings around her shoulders. She expected him to speak, to communicate something infallible, a tidy ending for the story she and Hassan had begun, but he was silent. The landscape around them dimmed, and Fatima felt a little thrill of doubt. In that doubt, she saw Luz, or rather, the spot in Luz's eye, which seemed, in the jumbled logic of dreaming, to contain a vast stretch of time in which all the failures of men were chronicled. It pulled itself toward her, closing the rupture of moments and miles between them, until it was so close that it filled her sight.

Hurried footsteps thumped over her head; the space where Hassan and Gwennec had slept was cold. The ship had begun to pitch again. Across the hold, water rose and sank beyond the little row of portholes, each wave knife-edged, crowding against the white sky. Fatima clenched her teeth to fight the nausea that swelled in her gut each time the cog heaved upward. She made her way across the hold and up the steps, swaying like a drunkard, and looked past the stern at what she knew she would find there.

The outline of the carrack was sharp and solid in the pale nothing behind them. Shouts came from the deck. Fatima could see men pointing toward the cog; a dog's bark cracked through the chill air; a loud blast sounded on a horn.

"We failed," said Hassan, appearing beside her. "I failed." His skin looked sallow in the odd light, the skin beneath his eyes as dark as a bruise, as if the effort of altering the map had bled his strength. He looked at Fatima for absolution. "I thought surely they couldn't follow if I bent things a little. They don't have the map. But perhaps they have something better."

"Whatever they have, it isn't better," said Fatima. "It's something worse. Something awful can work as well as something wonderful. That doesn't make it better." She stroked his hand with its dirty, ink-stained bandages. "It was my idea, anyway. If anybody's failed, it's me."

Hassan looked at her in surprise.

"I'm not sure I know you at all anymore," he said. "That sounded almost like an apology."

The deck of the carrack seethed with activity. Within the scrum of men, clad in black, Fatima saw, or thought she saw, a woman with brassy hair. But the slender figure was quickly eclipsed by the lead hooks of arquebuses as they were propped upon the deck railing, the dull thunk of metal audible across the water. Fatima watched the guns and wondered whether she might still be asleep. That an idea of her own, an idea so clever, the only logical continuation of their excellent luck, might fail so profoundly, had rendered her dull, and she watched with indifference as the row of scarlet-clad fusiliers opposite her loaded shot into each arquebus. Then there was a sudden flare. The sound came a moment later, and a moment after that, a hot breeze stung her neck, too close.

"Get down!" screamed Gwennec. "You madwoman!"

Fatima threw herself onto the deck. Stupid, less easily reasoned with, was on his feet, lathered in sweat, galloping back and forth between the railings. The cog heaved and dipped over rolling water. Fatima braced herself against the rail and gritted her teeth.

"Another rogue wave?" she asked.

Gwennec looked into the surf.

"No," he said after a moment, "too regular. It's more like—like a tide coming in. Waves breaking somewhere close."

"Which means what?"

"Land. It means land."

Fatima stood, ignoring Gwennec as he shouted at her to keep down. She turned in a circle, looking for some sign, but there was only fog and the carrack and the fading echoes of voices.

"I don't see anything," she howled.

"You think I can explain this?" said Gwennec. "You think I can explain any of this? It looks like a tide breaking, that's all I know. So for the love of Christ, get down before an arquebus catches you straight in the neck."

Fatima shrank as another volley of lead popped and sang against the flank of the hull. There followed a moment of quiet as the smell of gunpowder dissipated. The cog began to list ominously.

"We're sinking," said Fatima.

"Well of course we're *sinking*," shouted Gwennec. "How much fire do you think a ship of this size can take? Someone has gotten off a lucky shot and punctured the hull below the waterline. It was only a matter of time."

The waves beyond the railing of the deck had become a steady, rolling surf, loud enough to muffle the groaning of the cog as it began to buckle. Fatima sat with her legs sprawled in front of her. An empty barrel bounced across the width of the deck and lodged against the lowest point of the rail, where salt spray was already licking at the deck. Fatima realized with dismay that Stupid was gone. The pitch of the waves, the listing of the ship had carried him overboard without a sound, one small life claimed by water. Hassan was kneeling where the horse had been, his robe pooling around him in the rising foam, communing in silence with what had been. Tears stung Fatima's eyes. She looked toward the carrack, which filled one half of the sky like a mountain under sail.

There was nothing left to do; or rather, there was only one thing left to do. Rising, she climbed the short steps to the stern castle and leaned into the tiller. It resisted her, and as she threw her weight against it, she heard a corresponding groan from deep within the ship. Slowly, the prow began to swing around, until the bowsprit pointed, needlelike, at the exposed hull of the carrack.

"What the hell are you doing?" called Gwennec.

"Take Hassan," replied Fatima. "I think that barrel stuck against the railing over there will float, don't you?"

"What do you mean? What are you saying?"

"If you get away, it's not suicide," she said, half to herself. "If we all die, it's just silliness and dramatics."

Gwennec looked from the tiller to the carrack and back again.

"You mean to ram them," he said incredulously. "You'll never get up enough speed, Fa. Not with us listing like this."

"I don't care. If one little hole can sink us, then one little hole can sink them. Now shut up and take Hassan and do as I say."

Gwennec slammed his closed fist against the step nearest him, then pulled his hand back and slammed it down again twice more.

"You're selfish," he spat. "Hassan was right. Everything must be done your way, on your say-so. I'll be damned before I cling to some barrel to save my own wretched life and let an unarmed girl go down with the ship."

"I'm selfish," muttered Fatima, pressing the bones of her hips into the sluggish tiller. "If I were a man, you'd call me a hero. Instead, you want to argue with me because I've reversed the order in which honor demands we must die."

"Oh *don't* be such an ass! I didn't say anything about honor! Only I can't stand the idea of you drowning, Fa, it's a horrible way to die. You're awake and in pain 'til the very end—"

Fatima turned to look at him. He was on his knees on the steps with his face turned up toward her, blond stubble obscuring his jaw, his eyes flat and blue and full of horror. She stooped and pressed one hand to his roughened cheek and bent to kiss his brow.

"Help me," she said. "Hassan has to live. If he dies, then I don't believe in anything. God loves him, if God loves anyone at all. He'll take care of Hassan, and if you're together, He'll take care of you too."

"Then you go with Hassan. It's you he needs, not me. I'll stay with the ship. I'm the only real sailor between us, anyhow. Don't ask me to leave you behind, Fa." His eyes flickered at hers, pleading.

Fatima saw that he would not be persuaded. She disengaged herself from the tiller and came down the steps, helping Hassan up
from where he knelt near the railing. The empty barrel was already
floating in the bed of foamy water that had swamped the lowest
part of the deck.

"What are you doing?" asked Hassan. "What are—where—"

Fatima ignored him. She darted up the stairs to the stern castle
and grabbed the map, bundling it into Hassan's carry case, which
swung by its strap from the table. Below her, Gwennec had taken
off his cord and lashed it around the thickest part of the barrel;
he took one of Hassan's hands and curled it around the slender
rope, as if teaching a child how to hold a spoon.

"You don't let go," he said. "No matter what, you hold on for
dear life, because that's what this is."

"Don't treat me like an idiot," Hassan snapped. "We're not
abandoning ship, surely. What's the point? We'll drown in any case."

"We are abandoning ship," said Gwennec. "All three of us. The
tide will take us to shore or to paradise, or to hell, but at least we'll
arrive together." His habit ballooned in the surf, not yet sodden
enough to sink. Quickly, while he wasn't looking, Fatima pulled at
one edge, wrapping it under the cord, against the water-fattened
wood of the barrel. Then she looped the strap of Hassan's carry
case over his shoulder and put her arms around his neck. She kissed
his cheeks and the bridge of his nose and rested there for a moment with her forehead pressed against his. The pain she had felt,
the small losses and slights, the lonely silences were all hallowed
by memory: they had led her to this choice, this end, in which she
might finally do something beautiful.

"I love you," she said, and shoved the barrel into the surf.

Gwennec yelped when he realized his habit had pulled him overboard. He called her name, but she had already turned away toward the stern. He began to shout, to curse, to weep, and then the sound of the surf overpowered all human noise. Fatima allowed herself to look back. She saw a red head and a yellow one borne up on the crest of a wave and carried toward some unseen shore where the insistent tide was breaking.

Fatima returned to the tiller: it swung stiffly, catching on something in the bowels of the ship. The bowsprit was pointing past the carrack now, as if flinching before a larger foe. Fatima bit her lip until she tasted blood and threw all her weight against the tiller. Wood screamed and splintered. The cog heaved, pointing out toward the carrack's rolling hull. Gwennec was right: she would never get up enough speed to damage the bigger vessel; at best, she would glance off the hull, at worst she might be pulled beneath it by the sheer force of the water rushing past.

Yet the carrack must sink. Love made some lives more precious than others. Fatima draped herself over the tiller and closed her eyes.

"Three people and a horse," she muttered. "That's all I wanted to save. And the horse is gone. And one person must make sure the other two get away safely. So two people. That doesn't seem like very much to ask." The sound of the surf intensified. It occurred to Fatima to be afraid. She clung to the tiller, telling herself she would not cry.

When the noise stopped, she lifted her head. Before her was a hill made of blue. White lace dappled its edges, and within it, as if under glass, she saw a frightened school of iron-colored fish and a long, furred tangle of water weeds. Atop the hill rode the carrack. It was leaning hard, falling on one side, and across the glassy water Fatima heard screaming. The sound of the surf returned. It built to a roar so loud that something popped in Fatima's ear, and suddenly the great swell of water fell in upon itself.

Fatima was flung across the deck and hit the far railing. The cog snapped as cleanly as kindling. Water surged into the open hull, flooding up the steps and around her knees. Above her, the carrack groaned. The mast splintered, bearing down on the wreckage of the cog in a mass of pulverized beams and canvas. The world reversed itself. The sky was made of wood and water, and below Fatima was only air. Then the sky collapsed.

Fatima was in the dark. There was no sound but streams of air struggling to reach the surface. It was blessedly cold. She felt a blade of bright pain travel across the length of her face, and then nothing: not the ominous nothing of the fog, but the end of a sentence, the little moment when a deed is finished and is succeeded by silence.

Chapter 19

Someone was humming.

Too wet down here, came a bright-dark voice. *Not enough air, or not enough for you, at any rate.*

A mouth closed over her own, gently.

Breathe, said the voice.

Fatima breathed. The mouth withdrew; she sputtered water.

All right, now stop breathing. Little idiot! Do I have to explain everything?

Fatima's lungs ached. She reached out blindly, clawing at the dark water.

More? You are a persistent creature.

Warmth encircled her; lips pressed against hers again, coaxing her mouth open. Fatima gasped and gasped, thirsty for air. She tasted salt and sulfur.

Vikram, she thought.

Who else would I be? Don't try to speak. In fact, don't open your eyes. The surface is still some distance away.

Fatima curled her limbs around the radiant heat and let it carry her upward. She only half believed the evidence of her senses, and felt at the edges of the darkness, searching for something familiar, encountering long hair, the ligament of a shoulder, a furred back.

In other circumstances, this would be an unspeakably pleasant reunion, came Vikram's voice drily.

I thought I was going to die, said Fatima.

You still could, if that's what you want. But it's unnecessary.

Light bloomed, slow but persistent, before her eyelids, and the feeling of weight above her lessened. Fatima opened her eyes. Above, a rosy sky glistened through a film of clear water; below, in the darker gradients, she saw shadows with long fins slipping through the gloom.

Sharks, she thought with alarm.

Worse, said Vikram cheerfully. *Sea folk. Nasty, smelly, half-intelligent things with glass teeth. If that one gets much closer, I'll eat it whole.*

There was a muffled squeal in the dark, and one of the shadows darted away.

That's right, you ugly eel-spawn. I'll strip out your fishy guts and suck them clean.

Fatima's head broke the surface. She pulled away from Vikram and arched her back, drawing air into her lungs so fast that they began to burn. A wave scooped her up and carried her forward, rolling her like a log. It deposited her on a slope of warm sand.

Fatima tried to move and couldn't. She heard Vikram emerge from the surf, muttering and shaking water from his pelt. She tried to focus on him and found she couldn't do that either: he was a mere suggestion of himself, a blot in her eyesight, like ink suspended in water.

"You're different," she croaked, her throat raw.

"I'm not," said Vikram indignantly. "I'm exactly the same. You're different. Or rather, you're seeing things differently."

"But you don't look anything like yourself. Not like a dog, or like a man, or—"

"I'm not any of those things. I never was. Those are corpses I carry around for convenience's sake. Every hunter has his camouflage."

Fatima repeated this to herself, testing it for some deeper meaning she was too exhausted to detect. She began to shiver violently. The coil of dark fire that was Vikram interposed itself between her and the velvet sky. Though he had no expression, she could tell he was uneasy.

"You're hurt," he said.

"I'm not," said Fatima. "I'm only a little tired."

"You're hurt, though." He bent down and Fatima felt pressure on her face. Then Vikram straightened and spat a stream of blood into the sand.

"What are you doing?" cried Fatima, shielding her face with her hands.

"Cleaning the wound and sealing it. I don't know whether there's anything here that could make you septic, but it's best not to take chances." He bent again, straightened, and spat more blood. Fatima closed her eyes.

"Where's here?" she murmured.

"Where do you think?"

Fatima's eyes flew open. The sky was a buttery yellow, fading along the edges into blue and pink; in places a few radiant stars

were visible. It might have been dawn or dusk or anything in between. Fatima was reminded of the long late afternoons of high
summer, when light left the sky with reluctance. She knew where
she was. She cried out and reached toward Vikram, impatient with
her own weakness.

"Take me to him," she begged.

"What, *now*? To the Bird King? You're hardly fit to walk."

"It doesn't matter." She wriggled her fingers, the only part of
her body still under full control. "He knows me and I know him."

"Yes, I expect you do. All right, little beast! You always get your
own way in the end. Hold on." Furred arms lifted her. Fatima found
she could still feel the delineation of Vikram's body, or corpse,
though it was no longer visible to her. She threaded her fingers
through his hair and held on as he carried her, like a cat with a
kitten, away from the beach.

Trees cut through Fatima's view of the sky. The sound of the surf
was replaced by the hiss and rustle of leaves and the steady drip of
dew, and high, curious animal sounds that Fatima could not identify.
The trees, too, were not any sort she had seen before, not elm or
cypress or oak or pine, but graceful, thin-limbed things with rough
silvery bark. Fatima let one arm drop to caress the ground. Mosses
slid beneath her fingers. She could hear running water, and soon
enough she touched it: a stream, bitingly cold, lined with smooth
stones. She lifted her hand again and sucked on her fingers, tasting
water that was sweet and rich with some tart mineral.

"It tastes like silver," Fatima murmured, half drunk.

"It tastes like rocks," said Vikram. "Like the quartz vein that
runs along the streambed, which you'd see if you looked down. This

island is halfway between your country and mine. Where you find quartz, you'll find the jinn."

"Why?"

"I don't know why. Why do the *banu adam* love gold? We were all made to covet one thing or another. Rest, if you can. You're hurt and there's still a bit of a walk ahead."

Fatima closed her eyes obediently, and for several minutes, Vikram's hunched, loping gait lulled her into a light sleep. But the air changed, growing steadily colder, and when she felt her breath begin to freeze on Vikram's fur, Fatima opened her eyes again.

The ground before her was covered in snow. The forest had given way to a sloping hillside fringed with winter grass. The air was soundless, hanging over the blue earth in one chilled breath, and leading away over the crest of the hill was a line of forked footprints made by a creature much larger than anything Fatima had ever laid eyes upon. She clung to Vikram in a panic.

"What made those?" she demanded, struggling to climb onto his back. Vikram shifted to accommodate her.

"If your people ever had a name for it, it's long been forgotten," he said. "But listen to me, little friend—stop clambering around and listen. You have only one natural enemy here, and that is fear. Nothing in this place can hurt you, no matter how large its footprints. But if you give in to your terror of the unseen, those very same things will devour you and leave not one bit of gristle behind."

Fatima pressed her face into Vikram's pelt and began to relax the muscles of her back, one after another. It was the effort itself that calmed her.

"You might eat me too," she muttered.

"I might, but I only eat when I'm hungry. You *banu adam* eat whenever the mood strikes you, whether you're hungry or not. Judge for yourself which impulse is more reliable."

"And the thing that made those tracks? When does it eat?"

"Whenever it senses opportunity. Ah, here we are. Look, Fatima. You're the first of your kind to lay eyes on this place in many hundreds of years."

Fatima lifted her head. Vikram had taken them to the summit of the snow-covered hill. They stood looking down its far slope, where the snow faded by gentle gradients into yellow sand. A series of mounded dunes led down into a shallow valley, at the bottom of which was a cluster of trees whose thick fronds threw shade over low, flowering bushes; all were suffused with ambient light, as if the sun shone on the little oasis from beneath. In the middle, ringed by the sharp-shadowed trees, was a small lake.

It was perfectly round, the lake was, and a shade of blue that was not reflected in the many-colored twilight of the sky above. Fatima was sure she had seen it before. But she had not: the lake was part of Gwennec's story, and she had committed its image to memory.

"Is this Antillia?" she asked, startled. "Are we not in Qaf after all?"

"Perhaps it's time to consider the possibility that it doesn't matter," said Vikram. "The place remains, regardless of what you want to call it. Go! Go down and see the king."

Fatima slid from his back. Her feet landed in a borderland between sand and snow, where the ground was frozen on top but warm underneath. She hurried down the face of the dune, her steps kicking up sheaves of fine sand until she was forced to slow down and shield her face. The haze before her settled. The lake came into view, nestled in its bed of palm trees. It was not so much a lake, she realized, as a pool or a spring: some ancient race had enclosed it with a low wall of limestone that might once have been white but was now water stained and spackled with lichen. Fatima rushed toward it and pressed herself against the warm stone, searching the curvature of the wall, the thicket of flower-strewn thornbushes, the face of the rosy limestone hill that emerged abruptly from the desert just beyond the oasis.

Nothing stirred except a little current of air through the dry fronds of the trees. Fatima heard Vikram pad toward her and come to a stop, sniffing the air.

"There's no one here," she protested.

"Certainly there is," he said. "We're here."

"But where is the *king*?"

"Where do you suppose? Look into the water."

Fatima looked down. The surface of the spring was preternaturally calm. Peering into it, she saw only herself. None of the copper and silver mirrors in the Alhambra had reflected images so precisely. She found herself surprised by the sight of her decisive jaw, the skeptical curve of her brow. They belonged to someone older and more intent than she had been when she last saw herself; someone who had gone without food and could take a life if the need arose. But her features were interrupted by something that had not been there before: a thin seam cut diagonally across her face from forehead to chin, traversing her nose at its widest point, less a wound than a fracture, like cracked glass. She touched her face, startled.

"I fixed what I could," said Vikram, sounding almost apologetic. "You're lucky you didn't lose an eye. But the line will always be there, I'm afraid. Will you mind? You look as though you might mind."

"I don't mind," said Fatima, running one finger along the seam. "I was only thinking that people have been telling me how beautiful I am for as long as I can remember, and I've always hated them for it. But they were right. I am beautiful."

Vikram threw his head back and laughed. The sound echoed off the chalky hill on the far side of the spring and bounced back again, doubling itself.

"Come along," he said. "Let's go back—it's too hot in this part of the island."

Fatima sat on the edge of the little wall and watched Vikram amble away.

"I want to see the Bird King," she called after him, feeling something had gone wrong.

"You've been looking at the Bird King for the last five minutes," said Vikram.

Fatima looked into the water again. Her own face stared back at her. All the moments that had come before, the things she had remembered and forgotten, arranged themselves into a straight line. She could look back along it to the yellow room in the palace where she had been born and see how they had each proceeded, one after the other, to the wild place in which she found herself, though she could not have imagined at the beginning where the end would be.

"I am the king of the birds," she whispered to herself.

"Yes, you are," came Vikram's voice. "Get up, Fatima. Rise, oh King of the Birds."

Chapter 20

Fatima took off her boots and left them by the lip of the spring, and walked back up the canted dunes in her bare feet.

"Why didn't you tell me?" she asked.

Vikram was hunched over beside her, a dark blur above the sand containing eyes and teeth and little else she could identify. Yet there was nothing about him that frightened her anymore: she knew, in some real sense, what he was, and more than that, she knew what they were to each other.

"There was nothing to tell," he said. "To find the Bird King, you needed to rid yourself of all the parts of you that were not the Bird King. I had nothing to do with it, and neither, for that matter, did anyone else. If you had made your choices differently, you might be in Morocco now, comforting a deposed sultan; or in Castile, crowning an empress; or in the Empty Quarter, sitting at my sister's feet. You could have clung to hope. Instead, you chose something more radical."

"What? What did I choose?"

"Faith." Vikram galloped ahead, racing toward the top of the dune, where a breeze that smelled of amber and oud-wood was lifting eddies of sand and mingling them with the snow that covered the far side of the slope. Fatima thought his choice of words odd—she had been filled with doubt every step of the way, and had, in fact, disbelieved in the Bird King at the very moments when it seemed most necessary to have faith. Yet she had continued anyway, and had somehow imparted faith to Hassan and Gwennec when theirs had waned, so perhaps it amounted to the same thing; perhaps after all it amounted to belief.

"Say I had chosen differently," pressed Fatima, struggling to keep up. "Say I had gone to Morocco. Who would be the Bird King now?"

Vikram danced on the knife-edge of the dune, a darkness that mingled all colors, and grinned down at her with disembodied fangs.

"You won't like the answer!" he sang. "It's a jinn answer. The Bird King would be the Bird King. The Bird King is, and has always been. The Bird King doesn't change."

Fatima made a face at him.

"You see? I told you you wouldn't like it. Come along, let's see to your subjects. They're all gathered on the beach not far from where I found you, waiting for someone with enough sense to tell them what to do." He tripped down the far side of the dune into the snow, where the light softened and grew richer, throwing rose and purple shadows into the gentle swells of the landscape and gilding the bare-branched trees. Fatima set her foot on the frozen earth and felt a small thrill of delight. She would not wear ill-fitting shoes again: she would feel heat and cold and earth against her bare skin, or she would have shoes made for her, tailored to her own feet and worn by no one else. She walked across the snow as lightly as Vikram, and laughed, propelled by joy so intense that it verged on something entirely different. When she caught up to him, she took him by the claw and danced in a circle, leaving a stuttering track on the white ground.

The island, as they made their way back toward the beach, never arranged itself into a memorable pattern. There was a forest, but not the forest she remembered passing through on the way to the spring at the center; in this forest, it was autumn, and great straight-limbed oaks shed their yellow leaves over the silent, trackless ground. Fatima saw a deer, or something like a deer, drinking from a stream: it paused and lifted its head when it heard them approach, revealing a dry little smile in a face that was almost human. It stared at Fatima with its luminous eyes, slit like those of a goat, holding her gaze not like a frightened animal, but like a traveler on a road, curious and cautious. Fatima froze where she stood.

"Fear only God," murmured Vikram, pulling her onward. "Not man, nor beast, nor jinn, nor death: fear only God and you will be safe."

Fatima forced herself to continue. As she walked, she repeated Vikram's words until her thoughts echoed the rhythm of her foot-fall: fear not, fear not, fear not. She watched her feet too, until the yellow leaves upon which she walked thinned into rippling grass and then abruptly to blocks of stone. Fatima looked up, startled. Before her rose the wall of a city, or what had once been a city: the wall had tumbled down in places, revealing an empty street paved with river rock and lined with dark-windowed houses, the style and character of which Fatima couldn't place. The city was not Moorish, certainly, and not Spanish either: the stout, square houses were made of rough-cut stones with no mortar between them, the windows tiny and vaulted, as if to defend the edifice against siege or bad weather. No, not Spanish, but human enough to stand at odds with the wild, unsettled land around it. Fatima reached out and touched the wall, and felt within it the rumble of a waxing tide.

"Are we close to the sea again?" she asked.

"Nearly. If you walk along this main road, you'll rapidly come to a cliff with a tidy little fortress perched over it, and below that, a sort of harbor, though no ships have docked there in centuries." Vikram climbed a pile of rubble and surveyed the vacant street, the color of his shadowy pelt mimicking that of the stone around him. Fatima struggled up the rubble behind him. The city, as she looked at it, began to feel familiar, like an image from a dream or the pressure of a memory. Inhaling sharply, Fatima realized where she had seen it before.

"The map," she said. "Hassan's map. Seven harbors. Seven cities for seven bishops—that's what Gwennec's story said."

"He was right enough," said Vikram, leaping from stone to stone until he stood in the street below. "Though 'city' is a generous term. Most of them are little more than a few houses clustered around a watchtower. This is the largest."

Fatima touched the wall again. The rumble of the invisible surf pulsed through her hand, as though the wall were breathing in a labored way, in and out.

"Con," she said. "This is Con."

Vikram smiled.

"The king knows her kingdom," he said, loping along the street. "Let's walk this way. There are steps cut into the cliff below the fortress, which will lead us down to the beach." He trotted off, casting no reflection on the polished stones. Fatima hurried to follow. The emptiness of the street was profound: nothing moved; no sound came from the crowded houses, the doors and shutters of which had long since rotted away; even Fatima's footsteps made no echo, as though the air itself consumed her passage.

"What happened here?" she asked. Without thinking, she dragged her fingers along the stone wall, as she had done in the corridors of the Alhambra, learning the vertical terrain of the place with the most fundamental of her senses. "What happened to the people who built this city?"

"Do you think I know everything? I imagine they died from a failure of imagination. They probably tried to build a road into that forest and never came out again. Or perhaps they left in their ships, intending to return, and couldn't find their way. This place—"Vikram paused and sniffed the air as if for answers. "No, it isn't a place at all. Only an idea with a location. Unless you're a jinn, or something else created in the First Age, you're not likely to visit it twice."

"Unless you're Hassan," corrected Fatima. "And you have a map."

"Unless you're a miracle worker with perfect faith," said Vikram drily. "He could go anywhere he liked and the unseen would gather to clear his path. But it was you who took the final steps, little friend, when there were no more maps to guide you."

Fatima pressed her palm against the doorway of a small house built into the hillside at a slant, the keystone at its peak suspended like a pendulum above the empty space where a door had once been: an invitation or a warning or something more indecipherable. Its hinges were still there, rusted but expectant, angled toward the darkness of the interior rooms.

"This feels like something Hassan could have made," she said, more to herself than to Vikram. "Like one of the rooms he used to make for me in the palace when I was bored. They were always empty. There was something—I don't know—muffled about them. But I always had the strongest feeling that other people had been there before. If there was a staircase, the steps were worn. If there was a windowpane, the latch was scuffed, as if it'd been lifted and locked a thousand times. But I never saw a single other person."

Vikram studied her face and made no reply. The thought of Hassan, the memory of his ink-stained fingers, landed in Fatima's chest and settled there, halting her where she stood and draining the glamor from the scene around her, a feeling disconcertingly like waking from a dream. Had Hassan and Gwennec reached the island, or had the wave that bore them away carried them somewhere else? Her kingdom, if such it was, was without meaning if Hassan had not survived to see it, and Gwennec, for whom her heart spared a small cry—if they were gone, then her victory had been bought at too high a price. The air felt suddenly close and oppressive, as if the silent city had been shut like a disused wardrobe until the moment Fatima set foot in it. She took great, hollow-feeling breaths that did nothing to relieve her. Fatima began to hurry along the street, craving sunlight. Vikram called out to her, but she ignored him, pelting across the rippled pavement toward the crest of the hill, past stone houses pressed tightly against each other, until she came to a squat little four-walled fortress, an ancient sort of keep, with only sky behind it.

She could see straight through the arched entryway and out the other side. A second arch, the twin of the entrance, revealed a hazy line of clouds and a fringe of sea grass that wandered indoors through the cracks in the paving stones. Between the two arches was a square, high-ceilinged room hardly as large as the courtyard of the harem in the Alhambra, bare of any decoration, a mere interruption between the city and the sea. Breathing raggedly, Fatima stumbled inside.

It was like standing inside a seashell: within the main hall, the thrum of the waves was constant and the light from the open archways lacquered the walls in yellow and pink. Fatima paused, swaying. To her right and left, stone stairways spiraled up toward an invisible second floor; in the middle of the hall was a recessed pit still blackened by the remains of ancient fires. But it was the sky and the grass that called her, and she ran past the fire pit through the archway on the far wall and stood on the extreme verge of a cliff.

Beneath her was a drop of several stories: the stone below was white and soft, limestone perhaps, and long ago some enterprising person had cut into it rough steps at amateurish intervals. Adorned here and there with more pale grass, the steps ended at a thin strip of beach where the outgoing tide sucked and worried at shoals of well-worn sand, and it was there that Fatima saw the monster.

She saw its feet first: they were forked and covered in a kind of yellowish scale and as long as Fatima was tall, and looking down at them, she knew at once that they had made the unearthly tracks she had seen in the snow. They were attached to well-muscled limbs that doubled back on themselves like the legs of a cat, but they were hairless and speckled, supporting a barrel chest the size of a small house. Ribs slid beneath the thin flesh, causing a crest of water-stained spines to sway along the creature's back; it was moving, weaving back and forth as a snake or a monitor might, its slender tail suspended above the sand behind it, its head bobbing in an awful rhythm. It was the face, though, that filled Fatima with horror: as with the deer, there was something human about it, about the eyes set forward in the skull and focused intently on a single point; the mouth full and small and ready to speak. It advanced along the wet sand, a survivor from a time when the sundering of something from nothing required an act of divine violence.

She knew it immediately. She had seen it night after night as she lay flat on her back, watched it swim through an ocean of ink on the far wall of the sultan's bedchamber: it was the sea serpent, Hassan's serpent, freed now from its paper confines, a thing too fearsome to be taken in with a single glance.

Screams broke Fatima's trance. There were other figures on the beach, she now saw: two in identical dark, spattered cloaks and two more in varied states of disarray; one, a child, appeared to be wearing nothing more than a nightdress. The cloaks, the same as the one Fatima herself wore, and the windblown, salt-lightened heads of red and blond hair above them, sent her to her knees and tore a noise from her throat that sounded as though it came from somewhere else.

The monster whipped its head toward her and looked up into her eyes. Terror racked Fatima's body like heat, pulling at her sinews, begging her to flee. It was a displacing, disorienting fear, one that upset the hierarchy of things. If the creature below her was made from the same matter as Fatima, it was possible that God was not entirely on her side; if the thing below her was real, then God was also on the side of the monsters. The world, in all its upheaval, was not partisan, and might raise her up only to strike her down with luminous indifference.

"I am the king of the birds," she whispered to herself. "I am the king of the birds."

The monster—the thing, the leviathan—twisted itself into a crouch and leaped, sinking its claws into the white cliff. Fatima heard something scrabbling across the paving stones of the hall behind her: Vikram, a smaller darkness, had caught up and was howling piteously, like a dog.

"I am the king of the birds," Fatima repeated. The leviathan pulled itself up toward her along the cliff face, sending fragments of chalk down on the sand below, its supple mouth pursed—not a nightmare, she thought absently, but a challenge, a reminder that the dominion of mortal men and women was circumscribed, even here at the end of the earth.

The leviathan hauled its heavy body onto the ledge of the cliff. It smelled of hot metal or of summer sun on bare earth, like Vikram, and Fatima wondered if it, too, was a jinn, something made of fire, more akin to the stars than to herself. It made no difference: she would die or she would live, but the thing would acknowledge her. She stood before it and dug her toes into the yielding chalk and lifted her chin.

"I am king here," she said, and though it sounded forced in her ears, her voice didn't waver. "And you will answer to me."

The creature tilted its head. Its lips parted in a slit, behind which was elemental darkness.

"I am king here," it said, mimicking her tone, her inflection. "And you will answer to me."

Fatima hesitated. Was it mocking or threatening her, or, like a parrot, could it only repeat the things it heard? In the moment it took her to consider, the monster lunged.

Fatima was thrown backward on the chalk cliff and felt her teeth rattle. Light blinded her. It didn't fade when she blinked, and she pressed her eyes with the palms of her hands, fearing that she had lost her sight. But the light intensified: it was amber and gold and almost thick, and warmed the cliff beneath Fatima's back. It was, she realized, the sun, which had declined far enough to shine straight through the entrance of the keep behind her and out the other side, striking the monster full in the face.

It winced and gave a choked cry. The pressure on Fatima's legs receded. She kicked blindly, hitting air at first and then something more solid. The monster grabbed uselessly at the grass and the brittle chalk and cried again and fell, and the piercing light fell likewise, its glory fleeting, eclipsed by the stone parapets of men.

✳　✳　✳

Fatima saw the shapes of birds. A hoopoe hovered over her, its red crest and barred wings in disarray; beside it, a crow hooded in black was making a rasping, mournful sound. A sparrow, too, flitted into and out of her vision and chirped and fussed, and a dark-headed heron snapped and spread its blue-and-white wings.

"Stay back," the heron commanded. "She hit her head on that ledge. The bones in her neck may slip if we move her."

"To hell with you," wailed the hoopoe. "Give her to me. Fa! Please open your eyes—"

The crow stroked her brow and muttered prayers beneath its breath.

"I told you I knew where we were!" chirped the sparrow. "It is the isle of Avalon! And this is the High King who can make light spring from the ground and drive out the serpents—"

"This is a girl, though, not a king."

"A queen, then."

"No," muttered Fatima, alarmed at this suggestion. She thought of Lady Aisha, who ruled from inside a courtyard; and farther away, Luz's queen, whose lands were vast but who was outranked by her sullen husband. "Queen is a terrible job. Don't want that job. Want to be king."

"Bless me, she speaks!"

Fatima opened her eyes. The face of a man interposed itself between her and the milky evening: a blue-black face, marked with a triple chevron of thin scars that spanned the breadth of his forehead and met between his brows. It was a long, settled face, the jaw deliberate, the eyes large and watchful: the sort of face that bore age gracefully, leaving Fatima with no indication of how old the man might be aside from a certain gray cast about his temples. He was studying her face with evident surprise, touching the seam across the bridge of her nose with practiced fingers.

"You're quite human," he said. "When I saw you on the cliff, I could have sworn you were something else."

Fatima sat up too suddenly. The sky reeled: the scarred man clucked his tongue and steadied her head between his hands.

"That was foolish," he said. "What if one of your small bones had slipped out of place? You might never walk again."

Fatima sank back, but did not quite lie flat, for in the next instant, Hassan had his arms around her and Gwennec was planting stubbled kisses on her cheek.

"Thank God," cried Hassan, half sobbing. "I told you, Gwen, I told you I'd know if she were dead. I knew it wasn't so, I knew it in my soul—"

There was a little shriek. The scarred man rose to his feet and groped for a piece of driftwood, and a moment later, a shadow landed in a spray of sand and thrust itself in Fatima's face.

"Have you gone entirely mad?" roared Vikram. "Do you realize what that thing could have done to you?"

"Who's this now?" piped the sparrow's voice. "Why's it shouting at the king? What is it, anyway?"

"I'm the king's fairy godmother," snapped Vikram. He prodded Fatima, lifting and dropping her arms and legs until, apparently satisfied with the state of her health, he subsided into the sand with a long-suffering groan. Fatima struggled to sit unaided, blinking until the beach, the sky, the faces gathered around her came into clearer focus.

The sparrow's voice came, not from a child as she had first thought, but from a woman of very small stature; she was not in a nightdress after all, but in a man's linen undershirt, which fell nearly to her ankles. Her face, like Gwennec's, was ruddy and lined from the sun, and her hair was as straight and straw-like, but nut-brown whereas Gwennec's was blond. Her limbs, though short, were well muscled and bore the emblems of hard work: chapped hands and sinews that stood out across her wrists and forearms. Standing behind her, the scarred man seemed almost a giant, his white robe and blue linen coat catching the air and floating around him like the flag of some unknown country.

"Who are they?" asked Fatima, her voice cracking.

"The tall one is Deng," said Gwennec. "The not-so-tall one is Mary. They're all right."

"But where did they come from?" pressed Fatima, feeling suddenly wary.

"We were shipwrecked," said Mary, whose smile was unaccountably cheerful. "On the boat from Calais. A straight shot across the Channel, it was supposed to be. But there was a storm, a big storm, and then a calm that was even more terrible, and no land in sight. People began to talk. Someone said the ship was bewitched, and since Deng is very black and I am very small, they figured it must have been one or the other of us as cursed the ship. So we set off, just us two, in a shore boat in the dead of night. Deng had some fancy notion of navigating by the stars, but we got turned around anyway, and ended up here."

"And not before we were half dead from rowing," said Deng in a dry voice, tossing aside the stick he had picked up to threaten Vikram. "I still have the blisters to prove it. I'm used to cutting out cataracts, not pulling oars."

Fatima, still only half awake, looked from his hands to his face and back again.

"Are you a doctor?" she asked dully.

"Yes, I'm a doctor." Deng paused and burst into on odd laugh. "I'm a very, very good doctor. I don't say so to brag—only it's strange that I should be here in this unnamed place and not treating kings and delivering princes. I didn't think people like me were destined for journeys like this. Then again, I never thought I'd be accused of witchcraft by toothless old sailors, either." He patted his hands on his robe to knock the sand off and sat down facing the waves, laughing again.

"You can still be doctor to a king," said Mary, her smile unbothered. "We've got a king right here."

"Stop it," snapped Deng.

"No, I mean it. You might've been snatched from a life of renown, but for those of us as were laundresses, this beach isn't so unpleasant. I suppose I can wash clothes just as well on Avalon as I could in Cornwall." Mary flung her hair over her shoulder and walked down the beach with a stiff, uneven gait. Just beyond her, huddled against a sun-bleached log, was a rough sort of encampment: a series of damp canvas sacks, their contents spilling out onto the sand, and the fragmented remains of a campfire in a shallow pit.

"If I'd a needle and thread," called Mary, pulling garments out of one of the canvas sacks, seemingly at random, "I could even sew myself some proper clothes instead of wandering about in your unmentionables, Deng."

"We lost her pack when the boat capsized," muttered Deng, rubbing his eyes. "I grabbed my own kit without thinking, but not hers. Now she won't let me forget it."

Hassan laughed, his voice high and light. Fatima turned to look at him: his eyes looked very wide, as they always did when he was flirting. Stung, Fatima tried to rise. Hassan pulled her back again.

"Don't," he whispered into her hair. "Not for another minute yet. I'm still not sure you're real."

The invitation was irresistible. Fatima closed her eyes and buried her face in the front of his shirt, smelling salt and the dense, acrid sweetness of old sweat. She thought of the night she had come to his room in the Alhambra and told him to flee, and how much younger they had both seemed then, though it hadn't been so long ago—the miles and not the days had aged them. How very small had been the chance of survival. To be here, with all the empty space of the map between them and the Holy Office, seemed less a victory than a gift. Fatima breathed the milky air and realized her face was wet.

"Here." Gwennec's rough hand grazed her cheek; he settled something across her brow. "A king needs a crown." He laughed in his hoarse way. Fatima reached up and touched a circlet of sea grass crudely woven with small yellow flowers.

"Hail Fatima," said Gwennec, rising and shaking the sand from his habit. "King of the Birds. You idiots were right after all—you were right about everything, only not in the way you thought." The air was growing cooler; much of the light had left the sky. Fatima stood, one hand on her prickly crown, and surveyed the empty beach. The others watched her, waiting, just as Vikram had said, for someone to tell them what to do.

"We'll need a fire," she said.

"I'll get one started," said Mary, moving toward the little encampment. "We collected a good bit of driftwood this morning."

"No," said Fatima, surprised only for a moment by how readily they all responded to her suggestion. "Not here. We're a royal household now. We sleep in the palace."

*　*　*

Gwennec helped Deng carry the bags up the stone steps to the clifftop. Fatima followed with Hassan, their arms full of skeletal driftwood, rendered so leached and dry by salt and wind that it weighed almost nothing. Vikram offered no help: he scaled the cliff face, complaining under his breath, and disappeared over the top before the rest were halfway up the slanting staircase. Mary came last, for the short, rough steps hit nearly at her knees. Fatima knew better than to offer help, but slowed her pace and paused every so often, as if to catch her breath, when Mary fell behind.

"You needn't wait," Mary panted. "I'll get there eventually. Faugh! I'll never set foot on that beach again, that's for certain."

"We'll find another way down tomorrow," said Fatima. "The elevation wasn't nearly so steep where I washed ashore." She scanned the horizon: the little strip of beach bent away and disappeared into the deep blue of the harbor, then reappeared again in a distant haze against a fringe of trees. She wondered whether the perimeter of the island was fixed, or whether, like the interior, it rearranged itself according to some unknowable law, or no law at all.

"Do you suppose that serpent'll come back?" asked Mary, following Fatima's gaze. "I don't like to think of it running loose somewhere nearby. I've never been so terrified in all my life. It was like one of those evil tales mothers tell children to keep them close by."

"Evil?" Fatima stopped and frowned. "Is that what it was?"

"What else might it have been?"

Fatima considered: she saw again the creature's eyes, the unmistakable contempt, the malice, but these things, though dangerous, were not evil in themselves. Vikram had the same look often enough. It was less frightening, Fatima supposed, to be confronted by something that was honest about its capacity for violence than to dread the smiles and false assurances of something that believed in its own goodness even as it murdered and mutilated.

"I think it was testing us," she said, shifting the load of driftwood in her arms. "I think—I think the people who were here before, the ones who built the cities, didn't understand this place, or at least, didn't try hard enough to understand it."

Mary leaned against a dusty outcrop, her brown hair plastered against her forehead.

"Do you understand it, then?" she asked.

Fatima hesitated. The wind was picking up and pressed her robe around her knees; Mary, clad only in Deng's shirt, started to shiver.

"I won't say I understand it," she said finally. "But I think—I believe it understands us."

Mary smiled at this. She looped one hand through Fatima's elbow and leaned on her as they started up the steps again. The pressure of her hand, though slight, filled Fatima with silent pleasure. She slowed her steps, shifting the bulk of the firewood again, and led the way up the last few steps to the clifftop and the wall of the little keep, which the last blush of twilight had set afire.

Chapter 21

Fatima awoke the next morning to the scent of frying fish. She didn't move: her neck was stiff from her fall the day before and from her night's sleep on the bare stone of the main hall, where she had lain down, without seeking anything to pillow her head, as soon as the fire was lit. It was deliciously warm. Gwennec had scraped the crusted soot from the fire pit at the center of the room and bored them all with detailed instructions about the best way to build a fire in such a structure; it involved wadding up kindling and arranging the wood to face in a certain direction. Fatima had fallen asleep by the time he finished, suffused by the heat that crept toward her across the ancient flagstones, waking only when Hassan lay down beside her and Gwennec claimed the spot between her and the fire. Then she slept again, more soundly than she had since she was a child, her fingers wound in the tapered end of Gwennec's cowl, breathing to the concussive rhythm of the waves on the beach below.

Gwennec was up now: Fatima could see him bending over the fire with his sleeves rolled up, tending to a bowl that sat among the coals. Deng stood beside him. They both smelled of dew and open air and seemed very awake given that the light filling the room was still a solemn blue. On the other side of the fire, Mary lay snoring in a pile of canvas sacks with her feet curled up. Hassan was nowhere to be seen.

"Where is he?" asked Fatima, her voice throaty with sleep. She sat up slowly and stretched her neck.

"Where's who?" asked Deng.

"He's upstairs," said Gwennec, "opening and closing doors. Come and have some fish."

Fatima sidled toward the fire, wincing as she unbent her cramped limbs. The bowl Gwennec was tending contained a row of smelts with blackened skins. Without further invitation, Fatima plucked one up by its tail and began sucking the meat from the bones.

"Deng and I have been up since first light," said Gwennec cheerfully. "I made a sort of net from an old scarf I found, and Deng made a very excellent fishing spear out of some green wood, and we went down to the harbor to see what might come up out of the deep water at dawn. We did all right. I caught a lot of smelts, and Deng hooked his spear into a little cave between two rocks and got an octopus. An *octopus*. That's lunch."

Mary sat up in her berth of canvas and rubbed her eyes, sniffing appreciatively.

"Is that a proper meal I smell? I haven't had hot food since—how long has it been, Deng?"

"Since France," said Deng drily. "I ate a meat pie straight out of the oven from a bakeshop near the wharf in Calais. It was good, too. I don't know what you'd have had, Mary. I don't remember seeing you at all until the ship was becalmed and the madness broke out."

"Most people find it easier not to see me until they have to," said Mary with her broad smile. "How funny that we should be such good friends now, yet not have known each other at all just a few short weeks ago! There's nothing like being threatened with death to make you feel close to someone. I saw you well enough, though, Deng, from the very beginning."

"I'm hard to miss at this latitude."

"That's the truth! I'd never seen anyone like you before. There were others aboard the ship who were frightened by those scars, but I thought they were very jaunty, and I said so whenever anybody got sniffy about it."

Deng touched the carved chevrons that arced across his forehead and smiled wryly. Fatima, unthinking, mirrored his gesture, touching the seam that ran across her own face, and felt, for the first time, something like regret.

"May I?" asked Deng in a softer voice, reaching toward her. Fatima stiffened instinctively. But something about Deng's expression, an alloy of sympathy and brisk interest, made her stop and take his hand and rest it upon her cheek. His fingers were still and weightless.

"This is new," he said in surprise, pressing gently at the edge of the seam. "It's closed so neatly that I thought it must be older. Someone very skilled at treating wounds must have dressed this for you."

"It was Vikram," said Fatima. She frowned, looking up without moving her face. "Vikram isn't here. Was he here?"

"The awful naked man with too many teeth? I didn't notice him leave," said Gwennec, stirring coals with a fat stick of driftwood.

"That's how he is," murmured Fatima, closing her eyes as Deng felt along the length of the scar. "You don't notice when he's gone, but when he's here, you can't notice anything else." The pressure of Deng's fingers was hypnotic. Fatima had never been touched this way, as a patient under the care of a doctor; as a body cherished for itself and not for the tasks it performed for others. She was almost disappointed when he pulled away, and thought fleetingly of inventing some unspecific pain for him to address, forgetting and then remembering the very real pain that still throbbed dully in her feet and her neck.

"You were gently raised," said Deng, sitting back on his heels. "I can tell by the softness of your hands and the pallor of your face. But not a noblewoman, I think."

"I was a concubine," said Fatima.

"Ah," said Deng. It was not the same *ah* that had always accompanied this revelation in the past: when Deng said it, it was wry and resigned and made Fatima smile.

"And now you're a king," he said.

"And now I'm a king," said Fatima. "And you're a doctor from France."

"I'm a doctor from Timbuktu," Deng corrected, "in the empire of the Songhai, where the great library is kept. I was trained at the university there. I was only in France by accident—I was on my way to England to treat the son of a wealthy man. The boy had childhood cataracts. No one in his own country could treat him without blinding him. I was to be paid a very handsome sum of money if I could manage it. Instead, here I am." He touched her face again at the spot where the seam met her jaw in a sore, raised point. "This little bit pulls against your jaw when you turn your head—that's why it's not closing up. I have some salve that will help. It's healing beautifully otherwise. But how did you come by such an injury?"

Fatima thought of the great wave and of the sea inverted overhead.

"Our boat was smashed," she said. "I thought I was drowning. There were spars of wood everywhere in the water—one of them must have cut me."

"We saw the two ships go under," said Gwennec. He wiped sweat from his forehead, leaving a streak of white ash. "Hassan and I did, clinging to that damned barrel. They were shattered, both of them, masts in splinters, like wood being mashed up for paper. I'd never seen such a wreck. I thought for sure you must have died instantly. But Hassan wouldn't listen to a word of it—just swore at me for even suggesting such a thing. And he was right, because nothing works as it should where the two of you are concerned." He snorted and began poking the fire again. Fatima felt a little chill flow across her shoulders like an eddy of air from an open door.

"Do you think—do you suppose anyone else might have survived?" she asked the black cowl bent over before her.

"No—I'd say not," said Gwennec, knitting his heavy brows. "The Castilian boat was up and sideways on that rogue wave. Anyone on board would've been knocked clean off the deck and then pulverized. Ugly death. Though I'd have reckoned the same thing had happened to you, and here you are."

Fatima was unsatisfied by this yet could not say why. She heard movement overhead: Hassan was walking along the second floor and could be heard moving heavy objects and giving cries of surprise or approbation. Presently, several wadded bundles of cloth were flung down into the main hall from the vicinity of the stairs, landing in clouds of dust.

"Look what I've found!" called Hassan. "There's a big wooden wardrobe up here that looks as though it hasn't been opened in a million years. That's thread-of-gold embroidery I just threw at you. My eyes almost fell out of my head just looking at it. It's got to be worth a fortune."

Fatima picked up one of the bundles and shook it out, coughing as a plume of dust enveloped her. Hassan was right: she was holding a sort of cloak or overdress of fine wool dyed a deep blue-purple, upon which had been embroidered repeating patterns of vines and flowers in gold wire so delicate that it almost disappeared in places, giving the garment the look of a landscape receding away from the viewer. Not even Lady Aisha had ever owned anything so extraordinary. Beside her, Mary was unfolding a second bundle, a quilted winter cloak dyed a lighter blue and trimmed in gray fur, with stars and clouds billowing across its width.

"The color hurts my eyes!" she exclaimed, wiping them a little giddily. "I've never seen such fabric. This was the lifework of some master tailor. Tell him not to throw anything else—don't throw them, please! You'll warp the wirework! I'll come collect the rest just as soon as I can face more stairs." She got to her feet and began to refold the cloaks, patting them and reassuring them as she did so.

"Soap," she said, more to herself than anyone else. "Today, I'll make soap, and get some white ash from the fire to clean the things as can't be washed. Shears and thread! If they left their best clothes behind, they must have left their tools somewhere . . ." She wandered toward the stairs, skirting the fire, and nearly collided with Hassan, whose entire torso was concealed by the pile of clothing he carried. There was a great exchange of shrieks as the two of them went through each of Hassan's finds, holding up lush, faded velvets, stiff folds of raw silk, leathers grown rigid with age, and argued animatedly over the best way each might be revived or refurbished.

"I'm going to collect more firewood," said Gwennec. He stooped and dropped a kiss on Fatima's forehead. The pressure was at once tender and remote: he had repented after all. "You might walk around and see if there's a likely stream nearby and haul some water, if that's something kings do. We've a cistern just outside, but it's empty. You fill the first pool and drink from the second one once the water filters through. Don't reverse it, or we'll all get sick." With that, the monk trundled out the eastern archway toward the stone steps.

Fatima rose and stretched and made her way across the hall in the opposite direction. She was certain the sultan had never hauled a bucket of water in his life and thought vaguely about what precedent she might be setting, but she was thirsty, and moreover, the others were too. Outside the western archway, where the keep met the cobbled streets of the city on its northern side, there was a round stone building, quite low, with a vaulted roof, and when she entered through a small door, she came to a silent, windowless room. It had a prayerful quality, yet contained nothing aside from two empty pools carved into the limestone, one set slightly lower than the other.

"They're older than me, these pools," said Vikram, gliding out of the shadows that clung to the edges of the room. "Or very nearly."

"Where have you been?" Fatima demanded. "You sneaked away without saying good-bye."

"I prefer empty places. Yours was filling up quite quickly. But when I do leave, it will be in the same way, so don't expect a grand, tearful exit." He loped across the floor toward the square of light where the door was. "There are buckets over here."

Fatima collected them: they were ancient and cracked in places, and she wondered dubiously whether they would hold any water at all. Nevertheless, she wrapped her fingers around the stiff rope handles and carried them out the door into the sunlight. Vikram followed her down the narrow main street with its silent press of houses and out through the walls, passing from the angular, tree-less outworks of human endeavor into the flower-strewn meadow beyond.

Looking past it, Fatima expected to see the forest she had wandered through the day before. She did not. Instead, she was confronted by the sloping outline of a hill covered in heather and moss, its top oddly flattened, a little stream with ferns tumbling down one flank to pool in the meadow below.

"But this is unmanageable!" said Fatima, setting her buckets down. "If the island rearranges itself every time we turn our backs, how are we to find our way between one place and another?"

Vikram galloped toward the pool, which was hung about with mist from the falling water, and threw himself in with a yelp.

"You're thinking about it all wrong," he called across the meadow. "You don't find anything here. The things you want find you. You set off with the intention of fetching water for the cistern, and here is this lovely waterfall a few steps from the city gates. Fill your buckets! You'll be at this all day if you want that cistern full."

Torn between offense and curiosity, Fatima hoisted the buckets and picked her way among clumps of goldenrod and violets and orange poppies toward the pool. It had no defined edge; water seeped out among the flowers and made them seem to float, their vibrant faces doubled on the surface of the pool. Fatima waded in and filled her buckets to the brim, watching Vikram, who seemed, with the little waterfall leaping behind him, like the reflection of something that wasn't there.

"Are you happy?" the reflection asked her. Startled, Fatima looked at him, and then at the floating flowers, and over her shoulder at the gray walls of the city, and above them, the milky sky.

"I'm afraid of being happy," she confessed.

"You mustn't be. Joy is one of the most powerful weapons your race possesses."

"Joy I feel," said Fatima, closing her eyes against the bright air. "Joy comes in moments. Happiness is supposed to last. Whenever I feel it, I'm afraid something will take it away, and it won't come back again."

"Little old woman! You're wise, and wisdom often makes people unhappy. But you're more afraid of happiness than you were of the leviathan you met on that cliff. Have you already forgotten what I told you when I pulled you out of the sea? You must be without fear: of the leviathan and of yourself." He hauled himself out of the pool and shook, sending a halo of droplets into the air. Fatima shouldered the heavy buckets and began to make her way back through the flowers unsteadily.

"Strange," she said, listening to the receding sound of water. "I'm meant to be the king of the birds, yet I haven't seen a single bird since I came here."

"Don't be dense. You've seen birds aplenty—the two you brought with you and another two who washed ashore as soon as the way was open. And more will come besides."

Fatima stopped where she was.

"What do you mean more will come?" she called. But Vikram did not seem to hear. He scampered ahead, keeping to the grassy track she had made on her way out. Fatima opened her mouth to call again and then thought better of it. The scent of the flowers was so thick and sweet that worry was impossible. Fatima shouldered her buckets, but she did not hurry. Vikram was a dark smudge against the verdant field, like a devil in heaven, cavorting among hillocks of grass. The air, thick as it was, carried with it the sound of familiar laughter from the city walls. Fatima felt a heaviness settle in her limbs, not unpleasantly; it pressed down on her with the sun like a blanket of light, inviting repose. Fatima let her shoulders go slack. At the end of the track of dew and crushed grass, Hassan stood in the empty city gateway, laughing, clad in green velvet, and Gwennec, who had summited the walls, waved to her with flowers in his hair.

✳ ✳ ✳

Their days quickly took shape and assumed a pattern. Fatima rose first, when the sun had barely colored the eastern windows of the keep, and remade the fire. Quite alone, she climbed to the second floor and exited through a door that opened onto the perimeter wall, then wound her way between the battlements and walked the length of the city until she reached the city gate. The meadow was nearly always just outside, but what lay beyond it changed day by day: sometimes it was a forest of autumn birches, sometimes a grassy plain, once the blue unyielding ledge of a glacier shouldering its way through the landscape toward the sea. Once, the meadow stretched so far toward the horizon that Fatima caught a glimmer of the spring at the center of the island and the mountain that rose above it. There was always water close by, a lake or a stream or a bank of melting snow, and if the cistern looked low, Fatima would spend the rest of the day filling it again. She found herself working harder than she ever had at the Alhambra, but minding it less: she worked to feed and water herself and her friends, and looked with pride upon the calluses that quickly covered her hands.

The others each took up the tasks to which they found themselves best suited. Within days, Mary had cataloged all the linen in the keep, and a week after that, she presented Fatima and the others with new tunics and gowns and hose cut from remnants of the embroidered velvets and silks. She commissioned Gwennec to build her two great wooden tubs from the old boards and disused doors that he had found about the city and then installed them in an outbuilding adjacent to the cistern, with a fire to heat the water. Here they washed their clothes when these were dirty and themselves too, bathing with soap Mary made from ash and salt and rendered fish fat, using handfuls of violets and flowering linden collected from the meadow to disguise the smell. Deng and Hassan fished and foraged; Deng taught them all the names of the medicinal plants and roots he collected on his walks, and what to avoid and what to eat, and hung bunches of herbs from a beam along the north side of the main hall to dry.

Gwennec, for his part, rummaged until he found a hammer and saw and began to collect all the nails he could find that had not rusted through. He built the two tubs for the laundry and a third, smaller one for Fatima after she confessed to missing the baths in the Alhambra: this he set in the eastern archway of the main hall, so that Fatima could bathe with a view of the sea. He built a lap desk for Hassan with pigeonholes for his quills and charcoals and bottles of ink, and Hassan, who had no land left to map, began to map faces instead. Sketches appeared around the hall, propped against columns or tucked next to sleeping mats like the gifts of a bashful child: Mary sewing, her head thrown back in laughter or song; Gwennec with the sleeves of his habit rolled up as he wove a reed basket; Fatima bathing in the empty archway, her head turned toward the sea.

When they were not at work, they wandered together along the coast, taking with them lunches of dried fish and acorn flour cakes baked in the embers of the cooking fire. Hassan always brought his map. Water-stained though it was, he rolled it up in its carrying case with a few charcoals and quills, hoping to add to it, but the interior of the island remained as opaque to him as it did to the others: he would stand on a bluff or a ledge he had bloodied his knees to reach and pause for a moment and then invariably begin to laugh.

"It's like drinking too much wine," he said on one such expedition. "I look west and see a forest. Then I turn and get a headache. Then I look back and the forest is a desert, or marshland covered in fog. My fingers are blind. I don't think the island wants to be mapped."

"Then don't try," Fatima had replied, feeling nervous. "Vikram says it's not a proper place at all, only an idea with a location. Perhaps we shouldn't upset it. Or—I don't know. Misconstrue it."

"You're starting to sound like him. Full of convenient little notions." But Hassan had acquiesced, and though he still brought the map with him on their walks, he no longer took it out every time they paused to rest, and once in a while, when the landscape faded or shifted, Fatima caught him smiling a little bitterly at it, communing with the only place that would not bend to his fingers and yet had saved his life.

The coastline, at least, remained as Hassan had drawn it: an hour's walk south along the beach brought them around the first of the tiny harbors to the second of the seven cities, which was, as Vikram had said, little more than a short, square tower with several houses crowded around its feet, their wooden roofs fallen in and desiccated. As they turned northward again, the beach widened, bordered by dunes rather than chalk cliffs; two subsequent towers were visible together, set on the westward side of the island, gazing toward one another from across a green lagoon. Continuing northward along the beach for another hour brought them to another tower, which leaned precariously toward the sea on a poor foundation and had mostly tumbled down. Then came a jagged loop around the northernmost point of the island, where the beach was reduced to a thread of sand so narrow that it was necessary to walk single file past a lonely outpost that loomed on fangs of slate over their heads. The final city was only half built: a square hole in the ground lined with stone blocks, abandoned so hastily that chisels and mallets and plumb lines lay discarded inside, all of which Gwennec happily appropriated and carried back to Con in the folds of his habit.

All told, it took less than a day to walk the entire shoreline of the island and arrive back where they began: if they left Con shortly after dawn and rested on the beach for an hour at midday, they would arrive back at twilight, while there was still some light left in the sky.

At night, they sang. It was in singing that they realized they had no common language: Hassan wondered aloud how Mary had come to know songs in Arabic, and she told him, baffled, that she was singing in the language of her own damp corner of Cornwall. Deng lapsed into his mother tongue without thinking as he taught them rounds learned in childhood on the red plains below the Nile, yet Fatima understood him just the same; Gwennec tried Latin and then Breton and sounded as he always had.

Fatima, tentatively, began to re-create a melody she had last heard when she was barely old enough to stand, a song learned at Lady Aisha's feet, when Vikram was still just a dog she could look in the eye when he was crouched on all fours. The memory, never more than an impression, became vivid now, the words to the song second nature. It was about a tree whose roots curled among the bones of the ancestors buried there: when Fatima sang it again now, she had to excuse herself and went out to the steps cut into the chalk cliff and wept.

She sat longer than she meant to, long enough for all the light to vanish from the sky and a white band of stars to appear overhead. Someone had banked the fire. When she made her way back inside toward her sleeping mat, she discovered that the place next to hers was empty. Hassan had moved away from the fire, into a darker corner of the hall, and Deng was slumbering next to him, under the same blanket.

Fatima sat awake a while longer and watched Hassan breathing. He slept with his lips slightly parted, the rise and fall of his chest mimicking the waves on the beach below. The firelight picked up the copper in his hair and beard and brightened them to a giddy hue, a red as vivid as autumn bracken. Only when he stirred and murmured did Fatima look away. The embers of the fire pulsed and flickered, their colors fading: she stared into them, past them, letting her eyes lose focus, watching blue slide into orange and red, unable to determine the precise instant at which one became the next.

*　*　*

The others began to arrive the next morning. On the first day, the tide brought in a tiny rowboat containing a lone Romani woman, a basket of chickens, and one half-drowned rooster. The woman's name was Sona: she had a mass of white hair as curly as Fatima's own and blue lines tattooed on her chin, beneath the fullest part of her lip. She had fled in the little boat, stolen from a fisherman's pier, when her family's caravan was attacked by Ottoman soldiers while they summered on the shore of the Black Sea. A few days later, the jagged remains of a raft, barely more than a few planks of water-gray wood lashed together, were spotted offshore: four boys were huddled upon it, their identical auburn heads pressed together, their skin blue. The eldest was named Asher and he was twelve years old: he volunteered this much, and no more, when he and his brothers had been fed, given dry clothes, and warmed before a fire. The youngest was no more than five and did not speak at all but stared up at Fatima with wide brown eyes from which childhood had been wiped clean.

It continued this way, the boats arriving in a stuttered succession, filled with the last hopes of people for whom the sea offered, if nothing else, a quieter and more dignified death than the land would have given them. They arrived surprised to find themselves among the living. The wariness took days to fade, sometimes longer; it took the first undercooked fish or poorly chosen mushroom, something that sent them retching into the bushes, to remind them they still had bodies. After that, they would begin to smile. Sona, when the glassiness left her eyes, set about establishing her chickens in the small abandoned green at the center of the city, building them a coop made from scrap wood: in a week, there were eggs as a change from the monotony of fish meals. Not long afterward, Asher and his brothers began to speak in full sentences and to apply themselves to small tasks without being asked: collecting soiled linen for Mary's washhouse, whittling stakes to make a fence around the poultry run, dispersing into the empty houses to salvage nails when Gwennec's supply ran out. If they were encouraged to play—Hassan made them toy knights and horses from river clay and almost begged them to leave off the little round of chores they had invented for themselves—they would only grimace and slip away or shake their heads with unnerving emphasis. They would live, they would smile again, but they would not laugh, and no amount of pleading by adults would make them into children.

Other things arrived as well. It was always during the fragile hour between sunset and full dark, the time between prayers, when the colors of the sky were haunted: shadows came, cast by nothing and speaking in whispers; slender trees that walked and did not speak at all; and things that looked like cats or jackals but went on two legs instead of four. One evening brought a fat, jolly creature that stood no taller than Fatima's knee and looked, to her eyes at least, like a frog that had undergone several additional metamorphoses on its journey from tadpolehood; if it wanted to talk to someone, it would climb onto the nearest rock or hillock or stair to look its companion in the eye and then hold forth at length, with extraordinary vocabulary, about the weather or the tides or any other subject that happened to catch its interest.

They emerged, it seemed, from the air itself, fleeing from shores unknown to the island's earthly inhabitants, and took up residence alongside their human neighbors in the empty houses and sheds that lined the cobbled main street of the city. The street was full of sound now at all hours of the day, full of jokes and arguments and the protests of Sona's rooster; and sometimes, when unknowable conditions were met, some of the jinn could be persuaded to sing. Fatima took to sitting in the western arch of the keep at twilight, warming her feet on the stone steps still radiating the heat of the day, and listening to the noises that persisted after the light had died. They suffused the extraordinary landscape with what was small and tender and banal: the anxious muttering of hens settling down to roost, the sound of washing water poured into basins, the gentle unmelodic snores of those who slept. Civilization was, Fatima realized, something very simple; it was the right of these small rituals to perpetuate themselves in peace. As king, she did very little but witness it. There were no lands to conquer, no riches to hoard, no rivals to dispatch; there were only water buckets to carry and boats to meet on the beach. The others called her *the king* when they were alone and *Fatima* when she was with them, for so she was: king of all and master of none.

Chapter 22

Hassan and Gwennec had taken to rising together before dawn so that Gwennec could pray lauds and Hassan could pray fajr, and afterward they could both join Fatima as she walked the walls of the city: it was on one of these occasions that they spotted a horse on the beach.

"Is that what I think it is?" said Hassan, peering over the ramparts that ran along the roof of the keep toward the brownish object treading through the sand below. "A *horse?* Have there been any boats?"

"Not for days," said Fatima. She stood on tiptoe and looked where Hassan was pointing. The horse was moving slowly, staggering like a drunkard, its track a jagged line along the beach behind it. It was wearing a rope halter but bore no other sign of human ownership; its shaggy mane and tail streamed water, as though it had only just emerged from the surf, a nautical oddity, divorced from any craft that might reasonably carry it.

Fatima watched the sun illuminate a familiarly dappled shoulder and went still. Without speaking, she turned and hurried back into the keep, running lightly down the curved stone staircase that led to the main hall on the first floor and exiting through the eastward archway. The day was gray and windy: wet air slapped against her face as she made her way down the cliff steps and finally stumbled onto the beach. The horse pricked its ears at her approach and stopped, raising its boxy head. Fatima halted likewise and caught her breath.

It was Stupid. Foam dripped from the stout gelding's mouth, and he was breathing heavily but seemed otherwise unharmed. He bobbed his head when he recognized Fatima, shuffling toward her to press his nose against her chest. Fatima stroked the animal's wet flank. A numbness crept up from her fingertips, which registered the warmth and damp of the horse's coat only remotely.

Muffled shouts reached her over the rolling of the surf. Hassan and Gwennec skittered to a stop just short of her, incredulous and laughing.

"It *is* Stupid!" crowed Hassan. "I told you, Gwen! What other horse have you ever met with a face like a brick? What a good boy"—here he reached out to rub water from the creature's mane—"What a *good* boy."

"Hassan," said Fatima, preparing herself to ask the question whose answer she dreaded. "How long have we been here?"

"Weeks," said Hassan.

"Months, surely," said Gwennec. "Four months, I think."

"That long? No—I say ten weeks at most."

"It's been four months," insisted Gwennec. "I keep track because I know how long it takes me to build things. A big tub for the washhouse takes three days, including salvaging wood and nails, and so on. It's been four months." He paused. "At least, I think it has."

Fatima shook her head. Her mouth was dry, despite the constant press of wet air, and she licked her lips.

"Stupid couldn't have survived nearly that long in the water," she said. "How long can a horse keep itself afloat by swimming? A day? Less? Look at him, look at how he's breathing, look at the way he recognized us—it's as if he only just went overboard."

Hassan's face, every inch of which had grown freckled from long hours in the sun, fell into an expression of dismay.

"What are you saying?" he asked in a very different voice.

"I'm not sure," said Fatima. Driven by something she could not describe, she continued down the beach, walking at first, and then, when she caught sight of a black lump rolling in the surf at the waterline, breaking into a run.

The lump was a bundle of sodden velvet, a black dress collapsing under its own weight, and inside, like a corpse washed and shrouded for burial, was Luz.

* * *

Fatima stopped so fast that her momentum nearly carried her over. For a few moments she wasn't sure whether Luz was alive or dead, but then she heard a little moan, as low and grating as an animal's, and Luz, shaking, propped herself up on her hands. Her hair hung over her face and trailed onto the sand, the blonde waves stained green with seawater. A stream of bright blood leached toward the surf from a wound Fatima could not see.

Luz began to cough. The sound of it made Fatima's stomach turn: it was deep and full, a grotesque, efficient spate of productivity, and with it, Luz brought up shards of wood and glass. Fatima found her legs would no longer hold her and dropped to her knees. It was as if Luz had swallowed the wreckage of her ship: she was returning it to the sea splinter by splinter, upholding some unspeakable bargain, her own body a borrowed vessel embalming the dismembered wood and metal in a rush of blood. Fatima watched, stupefied. The sea pulled everything toward itself in its insensible rhythm. In no more than a minute all was gone, wood and blood and metal, and Luz lay silent on the beach.

It was in this state that Gwennec and Hassan found them. They hovered behind Fatima's shoulder and stared, their mouths identically slack. Fatima realized she should offer some explanation, or at least some description, but words had deserted her and instead she reached for Hassan's hand. She had resisted touching him, or even looking at him more than was necessary, since he had moved his sleeping mat away from the fire; she sensed that this hurt him, though she would not allow herself to meet his eyes long enough to confirm it. Now she needed to remind herself that he was solid, that the island was solid, that there had been victory and peace, for if this was true, the crumpled figure on the beach was not, as she feared, the end of everything.

Hassan gripped her hand with a little cry that told her he had missed her. Sensing she would not have another chance, Fatima turned to look at him and say the things she should have said weeks ago, when a cleaner understanding was possible. Love was awful; this she had always known, but it was other things as well. It was real enough to thwart empires, to summon land out of the barren sea, even when the sentiment of it was entirely used up, even when the pleasure of it was gone, even when it was no longer a feeling at all, but a purpose. And she still loved him.

But she said nothing, for Gwennec shouldered past her with a howl, drew his foot back, and kicked Luz in the stomach with such force that Fatima could feel the impact in the sand.

Luz convulsed, coughing more blood. Gwennec raised his fists and brought them down on her slack body over and over again, the sound of it terrifying, at once too muffled and too loud. Hassan let go of Fatima's hand to wrap his arms around the monk, straining to pull him away.

"What's wrong with you?" he bellowed, half lifting the shorter man off the bloodied sand. "Damn it, Gwen, what are you doing?"

Gwennec struggled in Hassan's arms, sobbing.

"She's killed the things I love," he quavered, lunging again toward Luz. "She and her *Holy Office*. A holy office! They mutilate and terrify and shame and say they do it out of love. But they've killed love. They will burn down the Church itself so they can rule over the ashes. I will never see my abbey again, I will never see the Sacrament in my life, I will die unshriven, but that's not enough—no, like a pestilence, she raises herself from the dead so she can poison more lives, even in this place at the end of the very earth." He lunged again, but Hassan's arms, no longer those of a hunched scribe, held him fast; defeated, he collapsed against Hassan's shoulder and went slack, giving himself to his grief.

"It's all right, you silly boy," murmured Hassan, speaking, or so it seemed, into the monk's matted hair. "You think Luz has decided to be a particularly awful sort of person, and if you kill her, the evil will go away. But it's not like that. Plenty of ordinary, peaceful men and women think someone like me ought to be murdered, even if they'd never dream of doing it themselves. Get enough of them together and the Inquisition will spring into existence all by itself, as if called from the very air." He stroked Gwennec's hair, untangling one of the many knots that had formed in it, and looked over his head at Fatima with an expression she couldn't read. "But she's alone here. Just a half-dead inquisitor, cut off from all that ordinary evil. We have the king of the birds. She can't hurt us."

The confidence with which Hassan made this pronouncement caused Fatima to startle and stare at him, certain he wasn't serious. She had no power: she had done nothing but look into a pool of water. If she had stared down a leviathan, it was only because the sun had intervened; if she had opened the way to the island, it was only by throwing a mapmaker overboard. It seemed to her that she had acted in the only way she could have: there was nothing kingly about that. The others looked to her for leadership because they needed it. It did not follow that Fatima could wage a war, or keep a peace that did not want to be kept.

Luz stirred at their feet. A hand as bloodless as the chalk cliffs reached out to touch the instep of Fatima's foot. Fatima didn't dare move. With effort, Luz raised her hand a little more and clutched the sodden hem of Fatima's robe, the robe Mary had made for her from the purple brocade: a royal robe, she had called it. Fatima wanted to turn away, to leave Luz there on the beach where she would certainly die. She deserved as much. She would do nothing but disrupt the quiet order of things in Con, the little rituals that shaped their days; even when she was cut off from the source of her power, her faith was the sort that loomed over the lives of others. Yet the hand that clung to Fatima's robe was clenched like a child's.

Fatima snarled in frustration. Bending down, she put her hands beneath Luz's elbows and sat her up. It was only then that she saw her face, and her eyes. Her mouth was raw and cracked, as well it might be after expelling the better part of a wooden ship, but it was her eye, her left eye, that made Fatima sway on the balls of her feet. The spot was gone. There was a fine wound, a thread, running along the white of Luz's eye toward her pupil, as if the spot had been torn out by force. The wound was red and sunken and the effect was singular: it looked as though Luz's eye had very nearly been cut in half, slashed, like the mark a merchant might leave on old goods condemned to the scrap heap.

"Kill her," begged Gwennec, rocking in Hassan's arms. "Leave her for the sea. Don't bring her back to Con with us. She can't build anything, Fatima, she only knows how to tear down the things her betters have made."

Fatima wanted nothing more than to do as Gwennec asked, but Luz's hand was still wrapped in her skirt. She sat down on the sand next to the white-faced inquisitor and looked out toward the sea. Waves rose and fell, littered with the debris of Luz's ship, casting the spars up and down, up and down, as they bore them back into the east. Then a little movement, running counter to the motion of the water, made Fatima sit up straighter. It came again, bulging along the crest of a wave and subsiding into a foamy wake. Fatima stood. The spars gathered themselves together, pulling up foam and oily water and the dark ebbing liquids of Luz's own body, and rose up to crouch on the surface of the sea.

No one spoke. Fatima could hear the ragged pull of Gwennec's breath and the high keening of Hassan's; and her own breath, deeper, thundering along her limbs and returning again to her chest. The vision rose farther out of the water, twisting around itself like the coils of a serpent. The motion was familiar in a way that the vision itself was not, and in a moment, Fatima knew, though she could not exactly say how, what was gathering itself before her eyes.

"Hassan," she whispered.

"I see it," came Hassan's voice, strained and high. "The—the thing we set loose in the dark beneath the Alhambra. It's here. It's followed us."

Fatima felt a stab of guilt. It was her anger, in the end, that had freed the coiled horror in the water: anger she had turned on Hassan instead of toward some useful end.

"It was I," she said. "I set it loose, not you. Never you, love."

Hassan's fingers found hers and intertwined themselves against her palm. The thing in the water was looking at her, through her, though it had no eyes; she felt its gaze in her spine, as though it was peeling away each layer of her to appraise what lay at her core.

"Look, Luz," Fatima whispered. "There is the voice you thought was God."

Luz raised her head and looked silently, her eyes deadened and unreadable. Vikram had warned them that the thing would attach itself to someone, but in the panic of her flight, Fatima had never imagined it would settle in the very person pursuing her. A mote

362

in the eye of the Deceiver, he had called it, yet Fatima had failed to recognize it for what it was. It had seemed so small. Now it unfurled, surging upward until it loomed over the beach, eclipsing the pale sun. Fatima didn't move, couldn't move; her feet were sunk in the wet sand, the earth itself shrinking from the abscess of bile and wood that crouched upon the waves.

She could only stand, so she stood. She planted her feet between her friends and the wretched Luz and the thing in the water, and waited. The vision rushed toward her. She could feel the salt spray on her face and smell it, mingled with the copper of blood and some other unwholesome scent, like a boneyard. At the last moment, when she was sure it would engulf them all, it suddenly collapsed, subsiding once again into wood and water to be pulled apart by the sea.

Fatima swayed where she was, afraid she might cry, feeling unwontedly lonely, less like a king than like a child in borrowed clothes who was about to be found out.

"Is it gone?" quavered Hassan.

"Gone?" Fatima looked around herself without seeing. "It was never gone to begin with. It's been with us the entire way. Of course it isn't gone."

Luz, childlike herself, tugged at Fatima's sodden hem. Reaching out, she began to write in the sand with one finger, laboring over each letter until the message was whole.

More will come, it said.

Chapter 23

By the time they reached Con, the first of the Castilian ships had already been sighted from the city walls. The little frog-man, who liked to make himself important, had been standing watch ever since the king had left the keep, and bellowed an alarm from his half-inflated throat when a sail appeared on the horizon.

"A ship, a ship," he croaked, leaping down from the wall to spread the news. "Where is the king? Make ready our armaments and our supplies, for who is to say whether this vessel carries friend or foe? Have we no archers, no infantry? Like Darius and Alexander, we shall put all our strongest men on our left flank, for if it comes to open battle, the lines will drift—"

Fatima was, at that moment, near the top of the chalk stairs to the keep, with Luz leaning heavily on her arm. She could have seen the sail herself if she had looked over her shoulder, but her focus was on the inquisitor, who stared vacantly at the steps before her as if she did not perceive them. It was all Fatima could do to keep her from swaying too far in one direction and falling to her death, for neither Gwennec nor Hassan offered help. Instead, they led the horse, coaxing it when it balked at the narrow stairs, for the only other route from the beach to the keep took the better part of two hours to traverse. She could feel them both staring at her as they climbed, their sandaled feet scuffing reproachfully on each step.

"I should let you fall," she murmured to Luz. "I should let you be dashed to pieces against the sand. It would make those two happy. It would make me happy too, for that matter."

Luz made a rough, strangled noise; it was the only sound she appeared capable of producing. As the eastern arch of the keep came into view, Fatima had a profound urge to do exactly as she threatened. The sun had burned through some of the mist and lit the remaining clouds to a troubled, golden hue; here and there rays of light struck the gray stone, making it seem as though the world had been reduced to two rich but indeterminate shades of metal. She could see her bath, the wooden tub Gwennec had made with his own hands, sitting at an angle in the archway, a wadded scrap of velvet hanging over one edge to pillow her head. She did not want to bring Luz into this place.

Deng stuck his head around the archway as Fatima mounted the last stair and released Luz to sit on the verge of the white cliff.

"Hello, is that a horse? Where have you been? Our friendly frog has raised the entire city, claiming there are ships on the—" He stopped when he saw Luz. His face settled into an expression Fatima had come to know well: a fixed, bright focus, through which one could sense him assessing the vast catalog of his knowledge.

He swept his robe out of the way with a practiced hand and knelt at Luz's side. Looking at him made Fatima momentarily queasy: it was lovely to watch him, to see the economy of movement in his physician's hands, and she knew Hassan had marked this and that it had stirred in him a desire and a kinship she couldn't match. Hassan himself was at Luz's side a moment later. He brushed past Fatima to squat beside Deng, stroking the older man's wrist with the back of his fingers in wordless greeting. Fatima watched this tableau, the two men bent solicitously over Luz's slack body, and found herself blinking back tears.

"You were right, Gwennec," she said. "I should have left her on the beach."

Gwennec only grunted and led Stupid into the keep, where the gelding's hooves rattled against the flagstones and made him skitter.

"I'm taking Stupid to the common to graze," he said. "He can fight with the chickens for the best spot. If we're under siege by the time I get back, it won't be my fault." He pulled up his cowl, obscuring his face, and strode across the short length of the keep to the western archway, Stupid trailing behind him.

Noise came from the city below. Fatima could hear the frog-man bellowing and human voices answering him and the rattle of the crude spears they used to hunt small game. Remembering Deng's remark about the ships, she hurried back to the eastern archway of the keep in alarm. Luz was sitting up with Deng's hands to steady her. The horizon was still and bright, a milky silver under the tentative sun, and there, due east, half hidden by the curvature of the earth, were the topsails of two massive ships.

"How many?" Fatima demanded, turning on Luz. "How many are there? Just those two? Or are there more following behind?"

Luz opened her mouth to speak, but only a rasp emerged. Grimacing, she reached out to write in the chalk, digging her nail into the yielding stone.

We were three set out from Andalusia, she wrote.

"Counting yours?" pressed Fatima. "The one that was destroyed in the great wave along with mine? How long were you adrift before you washed up on our beach?"

Luz looked up at her helplessly.

"I can barely feel her pulse," said Deng, baffled. "You're being awfully hard on her. We all got here the same way, we were all half dead when we arrived, and we've always fed and clothed—"

"This is the woman who wanted Hassan stretched on a rack," snapped Fatima. "And those two ships on the horizon carry men who'd like to put him there still." She gathered up her still-damp skirts and walked away before Deng could respond. She had no desire to witness his dilemma. Mary, trailed by the frog-man and the small coterie of variously shaped jinn who seemed to think she was delightful, was coming toward her through the western arch of the keep, red-faced, her hair plastered against her temples.

"My king," she panted, "there's been news."

"I've heard," said Fatima, pulling back her own hair and binding it with a leather thong. "If you expect me to say something inspiring about banding together against a much larger foe, I haven't thought of anything memorable yet."

"It isn't that," said Mary. "Only Rufus—he's the Venetian man-at-arms who arrived last week—he was out hunting in that savanna that appeared outside the gate this morning, and took a few hares, and saw the tracks of the leviathan and decided to trail it to its den, or wherever it might lodge." She paused for breath.

"That was foolish," muttered Fatima, parting her hair to braid it. "He might have been killed."

"He might've been, but instead he followed the tracks to a sort of hollow, he called it, full of bones. Bones, and this." Here she held up a battered length of leather, cracked and soiled and very obviously a boot.

Fatima took it from her silently. The leather was water-stained and the crest of each fold was bleached from long exposure to sun and air. She studied it, bending it this way and that in her hands until the creases thinned and buckled, and instructed herself not to panic.

"What does it mean?" pressed Mary. One of the jinn, a tiny thing that, when visible, took a batlike form, had climbed up on her shoulder and sat gazing at Fatima with an identical expression of pleading and desperation. Fatima turned away and gritted her teeth. They all looked at her that way eventually, when they were frightened enough, and it never failed to make her angry.

"I asked for this," she said aloud to herself. "When the sultan asked me what I wanted, I told him I wanted this. And now here I am."

"When God really wants to test you, He gives you exactly what you desire," muttered the returning Gwennec, slapping dirt off his hands. He smelled of horse. "At the end of the story of Job, he gets all his wealth back again, and God leaves. Remember that."

"Are you going to help, or just dispense these little pearls of wisdom?" snapped Fatima.

"I haven't decided yet." Gwennec sniffed conspicuously and made off in the direction of the washhouse.

Fatima looked again at the weathered boot in her hand. She knew what it meant but didn't dare say to Mary or the jinn, who were still looking at her with expectant upturned faces. Instead, she told them what she had discovered on the beach.

"Time isn't passing properly here the way it is in the rest of the world," she said. "Luz and the horse—they went into the water at the same time Gwennec and Hassan and I did. Weeks have gone by here, or months even, but only moments have passed in the world we left."

Mary considered this for a minute and then lifted her chin.

"That's not so bad," she said stoutly. "Is it? It's the sort of thing you expect from an enchanted island. Avalon was said to be the same way, in the mists, with the High King waiting as young as ever."

"It's not that simple." Hassan appeared behind Fatima's shoulder and took the boot from her, turning it in his hands. "Time doesn't *pass*, at least not in the sense you mean. It just is. All of it, all at once. The past, the present, the future. Fate exists within time, but the master of fate exists outside it." He hesitated and gave Fatima another unfathomable look.

"What?" she said.

"There's a fellow here," said Hassan quietly, addressing the boot. "A Jew from Córdoba. He says the Spanish have issued a proclamation ordering all Jews out of Iberia. His family boarded a ferry to Morocco that overturned in bad weather. That's how he got here."

Fatima felt sweat break out on her upper lip and dashed it away with the back of her hand.

"And?"

"When we left, you and I, I mean, King Ferdinand and Queen Isabella had issued no such proclamation. The man says—Fa, he says he left Spain two years after the fall of Granada."

Humidity had saturated Fatima's brocade robe: she longed to take it off and send everyone away and bathe with her familiar view of the sea, lead-colored now under the mottled clouds.

"You're very calm about this," she said.

"I ought to be. I brought us here. We're no longer a *where*, so we're no longer a *when* either. Time is moving as it always has in proportion to those who perceive it. Nothing is wrong." He smiled crookedly. Days spent walking and working under the sun had burnished him until his skin was nearly the same red-brown as his hair; he stood square, his courtly slouch gone. Vikram was right: Hassan, in his own odd way, had always been the braver one, if for no other reason than that his very existence was a sort of trespass. Now, here, he had become an immutable version of himself, who knew by instinct what others could only guess.

"Why are you telling me this?" Fatima asked him.

"So you won't be afraid," said Hassan, smiling again, a pleading smile. "You've done so well, and I haven't told you, because it's been—" He stopped and caught his breath. "You haven't asked about Deng and me, but I can tell you've—I didn't expect you to be jealous, is what I mean. We've been friends for so long, and I've had lovers now and again when I could manage it discreetly, which surely you must have known, and you've never been jealous before, so—"

"It was different before," said Fatima, louder than she intended. She didn't want to have this particular argument in front of other people, but it seemed impossible to stop. "This was meant to be about you and me. Not about other people. You and me and to hell with the rest of the world—let them find their own way if they can."

"Well it damn well is about other people now, isn't it?" Hassan gestured angrily at Mary and the little jinn, who were pretending not to listen. "And it has been for some time. There are all the people who only came here because we opened the way, and all the jinn, and there's our Gwen, who doesn't even want to be here—and all of them, *all of them*, look to you for guidance. And right now they're terrified because there are two Castilian warships on the horizon and we've got no weapons aside from a few handmade spears and some cutlery."

"Rufus has a crossbow," said Mary helpfully. "Though only a few bolts to go with it."

"We are not without means," said the little jinn on Mary's shoulder, its voice no deeper than a cricket's. "If need be, we will fight alongside our cousins."

Fatima regarded the tiny creature with skepticism: it looked as though it would be overmatched by a determined squirrel. Nevertheless, there was no help she could afford to turn away.

"Gather everyone on the green," she said, lifting her chin. "And every stick and stone heavy enough to be called a weapon."

* * *

It was all managed soon enough. There was pitifully little to manage at all: twenty able human beings, not counting Asher and his brothers, who were too young to be asked to fight; and nearly as many jinn, though not all came when called and others were difficult

371

to perceive in the best of circumstances. They stood in the tiny green and arrayed themselves for war as best they could, amid the squabbling chickens, who resented the incursion into their pasture. Stupid, who regarded both chickens and spears with suspicion, watched them from a patch of clover, his mouth green with grazing. The sight of it was more pastoral than martial. Among them, only Rufus, a broad, well-muscled man who sweat profusely, had ever been in battle, though many could hunt and fish well enough to aim a spear. It was just as it had been in the Alhambra during the long siege: the walls and cliffs would keep them safe for a time, but when those were breached, by men or by hunger, no one inside stood a chance.

"We must find a way to close up the gate," said Fatima, standing before them. The wet wind took her words and muddled them, making her sound even younger than she was. "Whatever door was there rotted away long ago. Carts, crates, old boards—we must block the entryway as best we can. Then we stand on the walls and make life difficult for them when they try to breach the gate. They may decide it's not worth their trouble if their own supplies are low, which they must be after this long at sea. It's the best we can do."

"The walls are thick, but they're not high," said Rufus, leaning on his spear. The crossbow Mary had spoken of so glowingly was slung over one shoulder, pointing at the ground, shiny from overuse. "It wouldn't take more than a few siege ladders to put men on top and avoid the gatehouse entirely."

"They will have walked uphill for two hours by the time they get here," said Fatima, concealing her irritation at having been contradicted. "They won't go up the stone stairs from the beach—they'd need to go single file and we could pick them off one by one from the clifftop. Which means they'll have to go all the way around the harbor. And they don't know the paths as we do—they may get lost or turned around in the forest. They won't be in any state to put up siege ladders."

"Some of us will hide along the paths," said one of the jinn, a slim, glistening thing like a blue candle flame who seemed to speak with two voices at once. "We might kill a few, and we will certainly frighten the rest."

"Perhaps the island will help us," said Sona. Her big eyes glistened with fear or desperation. She was cradling Asher's youngest brother against her shoulder: the child would nap only when someone held him. Fatima didn't want to dash her hopes, but she needed every person sharp and ready, and hope did not make a person sharp.

"The island doesn't help," she said, thinking of the worn boot. "The island just is. We have only ourselves to rely on."

"Then we will make our stand," said the frog-man, belling out his throat pouch. "We may be few, but we are defending our home. There are forces at work in the world hidden even from the jinn, and they will be on our side."

* * *

The sun was low before work on the gate was finished. The empty houses that had not yet been pillaged for every nail and scrap of wood were picked over until nothing of use remained; the resulting barricade, a mess of stacked boards and crates packed with earth and stones to make them heavier, filled the empty gate nearly to its peaked arch. When everyone was covered in dirt and splinters and starting to snap at everyone else, Fatima dismissed them all to the washhouse, and though she was as sore and dirty as any of them, took herself back up the hill to the palace to see whether Luz was still alive.

She found the inquisitor laid out upon a pallet near the fire, asleep, dressed in a linen nightdress that looked very much like Fatima's. Her own black gown was drying in a patch of fading sunlight. Fatima pursed her lips. Deng was squatting over his mortar and pestle on the far side of the fire pit, frowning in concentration.

"I'm making a poultice for her eye," he said before Fatima had a chance to ask. "I've never seen a wound like that before. I'm not certain she'll keep her sight."

"She was possessed," said Fatima, unblinking. "Are there herbs for that?"

Deng looked up at her. He seemed tired: the grooves around his mouth were finely drawn.

"I treat the patient," he said. "I'm a doctor, not an exorcist."

Fatima swallowed the retort that sprang immediately to her lips. Walking past Deng, she stood in the eastern arch of the keep and peered toward the horizon, squinting in the rosy dusk. The two ships were larger now, their fat prows fully visible: they might make landfall by morning.

"We'll need an archer here," she said to no one in particular. "In case they get ambitious about those stairs."

"Where would you like me?" asked Deng.

"Exactly where you are," said Fatima, turning toward him again. "You'll have many more patients before this is over."

"Exactly where I am?" Deng stood, wiping his hands on a clean scrap of linen. A green smell emanated from him when he moved: the tang of willow bark and sweet rushes and camphor.

"He speaks of nothing but you," Deng said in a quieter voice. "No—that's not quite true. He speaks of many things, but you are part of each of them. Of the palace and his apprenticeship there, and your sultan, and the stories you told each other as children. I don't mean to step between you. Only—he would be happier, he would allow himself to feel more happiness, if the hold you have on one another were a little less."

Fatima felt heat rise in her face until it seemed as though even her scalp was blushing.

"I wouldn't have said anything," Deng continued, "but we're never alone, you and I, and we may all die in the morning." He let the scrap of linen fall and smiled wanly. "War! War and more war, even here. Destroying a body is far easier than fixing one, yet there are two dozen of you to do the destroying, and only one of me to do the fixing."

He was trying to end the conversation. Fatima, who had contributed little to it, turned away and hurried out of the keep through the western arch and down into the city to count spears and set a watch.

Chapter 24

No one slept. The inevitability of the ships, the ambiguity of time, the ripe humidity that had settled over the coast all conspired to keep man and beast and jinn awake: they huddled in twos and threes on the green or practiced with their spears by firelight to keep themselves occupied. Fatima sat on the cliff under the moonlight with a pile of stones beside her, teaching herself to use a leather sling; Rufus's crossbow was too heavy for her and Rufus himself was needed at the gate. There were no other archers among them. It was calming to load stones into the leather pouch and think of nothing but swinging her arm and loosing the pouch at the correct moment to send her burden whistling into darkness. She aimed at a flowering vine that clung to a step halfway down the cliff, its white blossoms ghostly in the night air. For some time all her shots missed, but as the night drew on they began to land on the step, and then to hit the vine itself. It was only when a shadow slid across the cliff, darker than the nighttime, that she put her sling down and stood.

"Vikram," she called. Her voice echoed off the limestone. The shadow stopped and turned.

"You're leaving," said Fatima accusingly. "You're sneaking away."

"I told you I would," said Vikram, his voice small.

"But we're going into battle." Fatima sat down again, feeling undone. "We need everyone. Even the frog-man and the little jinn the size of a soup bowl are fighting. And you're the—" Her breath caught in her throat.

The shadow sighed and ambled up the steps toward her, resolving, at the last moment, into something like the dog-man she had first met, something with a recognizable configuration of arms and legs, or legs and legs, though not in any order in which either a dog or a man might possess them. Fatima reached out to touch him and felt him lean into her hand.

"You're not meant to rely on me," said Vikram almost gently. "It's not good for you. It isn't good for me either. The rules by which the world was made don't allow for it."

"I don't care," said Fatima, "I want you here. I don't care about whatever silly rules you think you have to follow. You're terribly orthodox for a jinn. I am king, and I say you stay."

A grin appeared in the darkness. Vikram leaned forward and pressed a kiss against her forehead: it left no mark but burned even after he pulled away.

"You won't win by throwing rocks with that little sling," he said, gliding down the stone steps. "But you already know that, just as you already know why the leviathan hoards bones and boots. You never needed me, little friend; I don't make the wheels of fate, I just oil them a bit, and that only when it suits me." He began to hum his odd melody, the outline of his limbs evaporating little by little until it was possible to see the horizon through his body. "Besides, I don't fancy being trapped here when you close the way again."

"What does that mean?" called Fatima. She stood. "Vikram! What does it mean? Can you see the future?"

"Not exactly," came his voice, faintly. "Though I can see you well enough."

Fatima called again and received no answer. Only the horizon remained. The Castilian ships were so close that the crosses made by their masts and booms punctured the harbor on either side. Fatima heard, or thought she heard, voices calling across the dim water. She gathered up her skirts, observing absently that brocade was a poor fabric for warfare, and rushed inside the keep, where Deng was changing the poultice on Luz's eye.

"They're here," she said.

Deng folded a piece of linen with slow, precise movements, so that it was perfectly square, and placed it just below Luz's brow bone. She looked up at him, her visible eye drunk with pain or fatigue but struggling to focus, as if Deng, frowning above her, was the whole of the universe.

"It's all right," Deng said to her. "We're not going anywhere, you and I. Let them fight—we'll be quite comfortable just as we are. Would you like more water?"

Luz shook her head almost imperceptibly. Fatima watched them together, tethered by the particular tenderness of patient and physician, and thought that there was goodness in the world of a sort she couldn't fathom.

"He was the only person I ever chose," she blurted, confessing. "Everyone else was forced on me, one way or another. I don't want him to be unhappy. It's just that he was my only friend."

Deng looked up at her, his face impassive.

"He's not your only friend anymore, Fatima," he said, and turned back to his patient. There was noise from the western archway: shouts and one halfhearted attempt at a battle cry. Fatima palmed her sling. Mary came running into the main hall, barefoot but wearing a clever leather vest, a sort of hauberk, which she appeared to have made from pieces of a disused saddle; her familiar followed behind her, flapping its tiny wings in the encroaching dawn. Fatima wanted to laugh.

"We've got no chance whatsoever," said Gwennec, coming to stand beside her.

"None," she agreed. The monk grinned without humor. He was still wearing his habit and had made no attempt to array himself for war: standing among the rest of them, dressed either in makeshift armor or in the fanciful garments Mary had created, he looked like a visitor from some other, starker reality. Fatima felt silly beside him. They had been playing at kingdoms, at kings and courtiers, and now their play would come to a swift and ludicrous end.

"They would probably take you back," she hazarded. "Especially if you went now. There's no reason you should have to die for all this. You're a cleric. They can't blame you for what's happened."

Gwennec stared at her as if she had spoken in tongues.

"How could you possibly say such a thing?" he said. "How could you say that to me, after everything we've been and done?"

Fatima was immediately sorry. She did not have time to apologize, however, for as soon as she reached for the monk's threadbare sleeve, a sound she had never heard before lit up her ears, growing louder and louder until it became a mechanical scream and buried itself in the cliff beneath her feet. The keep shuddered. White dust bloomed in the air: chalk pulverized finer than snow.

"What was that?" shouted Fatima, her ears ringing.

"That's a cannon," called Rufus. "That's a bloody big cannon."

"On a *ship*?"

"On a ship, and probably not the only one."

Another shriek and tremor punctuated his words. Someone screamed. Out of the corner of her eye, Fatima saw Deng move to shield Luz from the white dust, covering her with a fold of his robe.

"They mean to win this battle without ever setting foot on land," said Fatima to the drifting powder.

"I wouldn't go that far," said Hassan, sweeping through the main hall to stand on the cliff. "Here comes a longboat."

Fatima pushed through the crowd that had gathered around her, her fingers sliding past leather and velvet and the slick poreless exterior of a jinn, all covered in the same white dust, as though prepared for some unknown sacrament. Outside, the air was clearer, the new sun baleful and hot in a sky from which the clouds and haze of yesterday had disappeared. Hassan was right: a dark shape was cutting through the water toward the beach, propelled by the amphibian dip and pause of oars. Wood scraped against sand and echoed between the punctured cliffs.

In the hall, the anxious press of men and women and children and jinn was silent. Fatima saw Asher's youngest brother standing at her knee. His hair was white with chalk, transforming him into an old man with an old man's heavy gaze. Fatima stroked his shoulder. He turned without speaking and pressed his wan face into her hip.

A braying squeal broke the silence. Fatima flinched as batlike wings brushed her face and Mary's jinn swept through the eastern archway and down the face of the cliff. It soared along the stone stairs, gathering speed as it dropped, then veered across the thin strip of beach toward the men in the longboat, who fell back, frightened, tumbling across each other onto the sand like poorly made toys, only to be engulfed by the tiny jinn, which was suddenly all mouth, and gone as quickly as if they had never arrived at all.

The empty longboat rocked gently on its keel and settled sidewise into the sand with a thud.

In the keep, there was a stricken pause. Then the noise began, howls and yelps of bewildered celebration, and Fatima found herself carried toward the stair by a fevered wave of bodies.

"Stop!" she called, but it was too late: the thrill of their advantage was upon them, and they rushed down the chalk steps toward the beach. Another scream filled the air; the cliff shook. Fatima heard the shrill creak of stone splitting behind her. There was another scream, a human scream, and a body fell past her too quickly to be identified. Sweat poured down her back. She tried to turn but found herself half lifted by the pressure of limbs and forced onward. Panic overcame her, a visceral panic that made her want to claw at the faces around her, faces she knew and cherished that were now simply objects in her path. She fought it, planting her heels in the yielding chalk.

"Stop!" she called again.

"Can't—no—not here," came a voice, possibly Gwennec's. "We've got to get below that cannon fire now, go, go—"

Fatima felt sand beneath her feet. She tumbled onto the beach, landing on her shoulder, and found herself staring at a thin spatter of blood, almost discreet, smelling faintly of bile: Mary's familiar buzzed overhead like a distended horsefly, its belly stretched tight and shining. On her back, Fatima saw an inverted tide through which another longboat was cutting toward them, upside down, the men already drawing their rapiers. Her own forces' good luck would not last through a second onslaught. She rolled onto her knees and spat sand from her mouth. A spear flew overhead: a fishing spear, one of the greenwood sort that Deng had taught them to make, barely hardy enough to kill its intended prey, let alone a man in armor. Yet it did fly, glancing off a polished hauberk and landing uselessly in the surf.

The second longboat scraped up on the sand. There was a wild cry and a man flew past her toward it, brandishing a club: it found purchase beneath the jaw of a soldier standing in the bow, who fell with barely a cry. The others were quicker. The man with the club— Bruno, Udolfo; Fatima could not remember his name—went down under the hilt of a rapier and did not rise again. Fatima fumbled for her sling. She watched her first stone fly with dispassion, as though someone else had loosed it, and was almost surprised when it caught one of the soldiers beneath his curved half helm. He reeled backward with a shriek, one hand to his face. Fatima loosed another stone and then another, but these missed their mark and went soaring wildly past the boat into the ill-defined gloss where the sun met the sea.

She was almost certain it was Gwennec who shoved her, for she saw his sandal as she went down. She swore at him as she fell, but he didn't hear her: his face was panicked and unseeing. Around him were identical faces, bodies pressed too close, a certain noiselessness, features not of battle but of chaos. Fatima curled up and protected her face with her hands. Through her fingers, through the forest of limbs and sand, she saw the water, and in the water, the coils of the mote.

Fatima held her breath. The mote rose from the froth, gathering about itself its shreds of wood and viscera, and though it had no features aside from the legless spiral of matter upon which it sat, it turned and looked at her.

Who is your master?

Fatima screamed, writhing to free herself from the miasma of limbs and metal, pressing her hands over her ears to block out the voice between them.

Who is your master? the voice repeated.

An opening appeared in front of her. Fatima lunged for it, scrambling to her feet. As she rose, she felt something fall from her sash: it was the boot her hunter had found in the den of the leviathan.

Who is your master?

She snatched it from the sand and ran, unthinking, across the beach, gasping for air amid the powdered chalk and the sulfuric scent of cannon fire. It was only when she was well away that she turned and looked back.

The horror sat atop the waves, many times the size of the Spanish carrack, slowly unfolding itself coil by coil. Though it lay very close to the beach, the men in the longboats never glanced at it, and instead looked past it, or through it, at the meager force confronting them upon the sand.

"They don't see it," said Fatima to herself. "They can't see it." A cannonball smashed into the cliff above her head. One or two of the ancient steps had come away, leaving gaps in the staircase that led to the clifftop, not too wide for someone as tall as Fatima or Hassan to jump across, but much too wide for Mary or for Asher's young brothers. The possibility of retreat was no longer certain. Fatima looked down at the boot in her hand. It could not end here, it must not end here, yet no other end was evident. They would end as the bishops had; they would end as boots, as a city hastily abandoned, tools left where they lay, for there was some secret to surviving a happy ending that they did not possess.

Something flickered overhead, a shadow that momentarily interrupted the sun. Fatima looked up. The leviathan, the dragon as Mary called it, was crouched on the clifftop, looking down at the battle below. The noise must have roused it, or perhaps the scent of blood. Fatima could see Deng standing in the arch of the keep and watching it in his imperturbable way. Luz was upright now, hanging behind him in Fatima's bleached shift, her hair a snarl of gold around her shoulders.

Fatima looked again at the boot and found it didn't move her. She left it in the sand and pelted toward the chalk stairs, taking them two at a time, heedless of the cannonballs that shrieked and shuddered around her. The leviathan swiveled its head. Its eyes fixed on hers and a smile bloomed on its supple mouth, unsheathing the rows of teeth. Fatima stopped on a step that ended at nothing, at a powdery crater where the next step had been, and wheeled her arms to keep the momentum from pulling her over. The leviathan slid down the cliff toward her. She could hear her own breath whistling in her throat and ignored it, looking into the face of the dragon, into the greenish, human eyes, until it was so close that she could smell the reptilian sweetness of its hide.

It was death; Fatima knew this, but if she could occupy the leviathan, Hassan and Gwennec and Mary and all the others, her friends, might have a little more time.

The beast blinked. Its eyes were still and glassy, like the surface of the spring at the center of the island. Fatima looked into them, expecting to see herself. But the reflection of the sun on the water below was too bright, and she saw instead a diffuse radiance, a light in which more light was enthroned, blotting out mere images.

"I'm sorry," she said to it.

The leviathan opened its mouth.

"Gwennec said something," said Fatima. "He said we have to learn to live with the things that God has set askew. I thought that meant that we had to learn to live with things like you, but I think perhaps it means that you must learn to live with things like us."

The breath of the beast was so hot that Fatima felt her hair lift and float around her. Down on the beach there were shouts, a scorched smell, and the dull sound of wood splintering on metal. She was shaking, not from fear but from the sheer pressure of time, the moments passing there on the white steps while death waited.

The expression on the leviathan's face had changed: it stared at her no less intensely, but with as much curiosity as malice.

"You are the Bird King," she said to it. "I am the Bird King. Hassan is. Even Luz. We all are, none of us are. Nothing is so frightening or evil that it doesn't come from the same thing that made the stars."

The beast roared and lunged. Fatima closed her eyes.

"We are the king of the birds," she whispered. But the end didn't come; instead, it leaped past her down the cliff, its claws puncturing the chalk, and hurled itself into the coils of the mote.

Fatima stood and watched it, dazed. It was only the howl of the mote, the demon, if such it was: a sound that seemed to draw all the air with it, that propelled her to move. She turned and ran, tripping over her sand-caked robe in her haste to rush down the stairs. The leviathan was tearing at the translucent coils that rolled across the water, rending shadow from blood and splinters, its own oily hide raked by jagged spars that heaved in the surf. The mote screamed again. It had an angry cry, vicious, as high and shrill as the cannon that was still firing from the deck of the Spanish carrack. Then, suddenly, it rose up, becoming a spiral, then a line, and then a mote again, a speck of sooty dust, to be carried away by the wind.

The leviathan threw back its head and bellowed in triumph. Those left alive on the beach scattered before it, the soldiers throwing themselves into the surf wearing their heavy armor, panic making them heedless of the weight they carried. With a hiss, the leviathan galloped over them into the water, crumpling breastplates beneath its forked feet. The cannon sounded; a ball flew toward the creature and missed. Out of the waves it leaped, slamming into the broadside of the carrack, which rocked and threw a sheet of foam high into the air. The cannon smashed through the railing of the deck and slipped into the sea, a weapon no longer; its iron barrel, still hot, disappeared in a eulogy of steam.

Chapter 25

The beach went quiet. Fatima sat down where she was, soaked in seawater and blood—someone's—and her own sweat. The churned-up sand came into focus only slowly: she saw figures lying prone in dark pools and twisted, unmoving shadows that could only be the bodies of jinn. Fatima pushed herself to her feet and began to walk, though where or for what purpose, she did not know. The ordinary sounds of the tide and the wind through the beach grass returned to fill the stifled air. Then came other sounds: a cry, a frantic inquiry. Hassan's voice.

Fatima broke into a run. Hassan was kneeling beside a cascade of white rock near the far foot of the cliff, where the sheer wall reached into the sea and left only a thin strip of sand to walk upon. He was hunched over a body. Fatima saw a rough, tanned foot shod in a sandal, the dirtied folds of a white habit, a black scapular. It seemed as though the air around her turned dense, slowing her steps:

she found she could no longer run, and approached the sandaled foot with a heavy tread.

Gwennec's head was pillowed on Hassan's lap. His face was greenish, all its high color gone; his breath rattled in his throat. His eyes, though, were the eyes she remembered, and they settled on her face, blinking up at her as she came into view.

"Caught a spear in the side," he croaked. His fingers twitched. Fatima knelt next to Hassan and pulled back the monk's scapular: underneath, on his left side, a stain like a poppy bloomed, brighter than it had reason to be. Grief assaulted her, grief and guilt, and she felt her face begin to burn.

"Oh my darling," she quavered, "I'm sorry, I'm so sorry. I said such an awful thing to you earlier and I don't even know why. I know you wouldn't have left us, I know you didn't want to, but I thought I was being—I don't know, I don't know. Generous."

"Cold," said Gwennec, and grinned. Then his face changed, tightened, and he gave a stuttering gasp. "I need a priest."

"You've only got us heathens," said Hassan, stroking the monk's hair with a hand that shook. "Which is why you're not to die, Gwen. You're to live. Perhaps if we never manage to fetch a priest, you'll live forever. Look! Deng is coming. I see him on the stairs. He's even brought a plank with him to bridge the gap where the cannons blew a step away. What a clever fellow. He'll make it all right, you'll see."

Gwennec laughed soundlessly. He reached up with two fingers, his hand marbled in blood and dirt, and touched Hassan's beard.

"My friend," he said, "my brother. Still an innocent, even after all this."

"Don't patronize me," said Hassan, his voice breaking. "I can't stand to hear you all solemn just now. You can't leave us, Gwen. Who will patch the roofs and tubs and doors, and who else is such a good fisherman?"

"There are others who can do all that," said Gwennec. "Fa—"
Fatima took his free hand and kissed it.

"When you bury me, someone must read the Rite of Committal," he said, panting between his words. "Someone on the island will know it, someone—one of the Italians—"

Fatima did not see fit to tell him that half of the men and women he had greeted in the morning were dead. She had not counted the human corpses but guessed there to be between ten and a dozen—a third of the island's visible inhabitants—and perhaps half as many jinn. Farther away, the leviathan was lolling in the surf, sloughing spars of wood and spearheads from its hide. The day had turned bright and clear; the wind carried the scent of wildflowers and mingled it with the salt of the sea.

"Everything will be done exactly as you say," she said to Gwennec. Her lips lingered on his coarse palm. "I swear on anything." She felt a hand on her shoulder and looked up to see Deng standing over her. Without speaking, he squatted down and tossed a satchel into the sand beside him. Opening it, he produced a slim knife and cut a slit in the side of Gwennec's habit, where the poppy bloomed.

"Well?" demanded Hassan, watching as Deng frowned and probed the wound gently. Gwennec whimpered.

"Well?" said Hassan again, louder this time. "You're hurting him."

Deng sighed and rocked back on his heels, his fingers glistening with blood.

"I can give him something to ease the pain," he said. "He should be kept warm and given water until he stops asking for it. There's no point in moving him now."

Hassan stared at his lover. His own hands were painted an emphatic red, along with the skirt of his robe and the sand beneath him, but he seemed not to realize how much blood it all amounted to, or what it meant.

"Can't you do anything at all?" he said. "What good is all your exquisite learning if the only thing you can say is *keep him warm?*"

"Curse you all, don't fight on my account," muttered Gwennec. "I'll not be held responsible. Only don't go anywhere, any of you, and keep petting my hair or whatever silly thing it was that you were doing, it feels nice—" He broke off and closed his eyes, as if the effort of keeping them open pained him. Fatima lay down on the sand and whispered in his ear, proclaiming things that startled her even as she said them: she loved him, she would miss him all her life, she couldn't bear it, she loved him. And though saying so shocked her, she knew it to be true. One could love many people. The heart was not a divided thing. Though part of hers would walk abroad into the unseen with Gwennec, it would not die. She nestled her face against his white wool shoulder and wept, as much for the things she now knew as for the man lying still and quiet beside her.

She couldn't tell how much time had passed when she heard unsteady footsteps coming toward her across the beach. Luz was still wearing Fatima's nightdress and had wrapped herself in a blanket, her hair loose, her mouth a raw wound. For one delirious moment, Fatima imagined she was the angel of death and half rose to send her away; it was only when Gwennec moaned that she sat again.

"Shall I go?" asked Luz. Her voice was unearthly, so ragged that it registered as neither male nor female in Fatima's ear. She looked shrunken and hollow. Yet Fatima could not pity her.

"Yes, go," she said, lying down again beside Gwennec.

"No, stay," whispered Gwennec. "Hear my confession."

Luz hesitated.

"I'm no priest," she said.

"Not asking you to absolve me. Only to listen."

Luz looked at Fatima warily. Fatima realized she would have to give up her place in order for Luz to hear the monk's fading voice and was seized by a sudden, visceral sense of betrayal. Yet she bit her tongue and stood, moving aside as Luz sank to her knees and bent her ear toward Gwennec's lips. She would never know what Gwennec said, but she saw Luz smile suddenly and then press her hand to her mouth, her eyes full of tears.

The light had yellowed and dimmed as the sun grew heavy, softening the awful cast on Gwennec's face until he looked like an effigy of himself; his eyelids translucent, his mouth set in a soft line that was not quite a smile. Fatima kissed his forehead and one sunburned ear and the unsettled frontier between his brow and hair. He did not stir.

"It's over," said Deng gently.

Hassan continued to stroke the monk's hair as though he had not heard.

"There are graves to dig," pressed Deng. "Our duties to our friends don't end in death."

Hassan began to weep like a child, his blood-caked hands still entangled in Gwennec's bright hair. Fatima took an unsteady breath.

"Who is left to read his funeral prayers?" she asked.

"I will," said Luz, "if you can bear to hear me speak."

Thanking her was out of the question. Fatima stood without bothering to conceal the tears that marked her cheeks, and forced herself to look out across the beach. Mary was there, the clever armor she had made for herself overturned in the sand like an abandoned shell. The boys were with her, Asher and his three brothers, covering the bodies that lay upon the beach in linen, the auburn of their hair lost in the glow of the sun. And there was the beast coming out of the surf, its hide streaming, gilded by the afternoon and not quite tame: it walked past Mary and the boys without looking at them and stretched itself along the base of the cliff, basking in what heat the day had left.

Fatima pulled her hair back in a leather thong and prepared to be the king once more. Her breath would come only in gasps, long stuttering things that burned her throat, but she took them, one after another, agreeing with each one to live a while longer. She made her way across the beach toward the stairs, looking only once at the leviathan, which raised its head as she passed, and blinked its eyes, and smiled.

Chapter 26

They buried the dead in the center of the island the following morning, beside the palm-encircled spring, where the shadow of the mountain of Qaf would lie over them. It was the only place, Fatima reasoned, that would stand still long enough for a proper burial; the only place where they could return to mourn and to sweep the graves. She did not speak, though the others looked to her to say something final and profound: the sight of so many shrouded bodies stopped her. They buried the Spanish soldiers alongside their friends, for doing otherwise seemed ominous. Luz recited the funeral prayers in her broken voice, and Hassan said the janazah, and afterward they covered the bodies in sandy earth, smoothing the graves until the only evidence that remained of death was a few dark smudges on the ground. Asher and his brothers grew bored and collected palm fronds from the blue shadows beneath the trees, swatting halfheartedly at pale butterflies that sunned themselves at the edge of the spring.

"Will there be no peace for us?" Mary asked when it was all over. "Even here? We won't survive another attack. It were only thanks to you and that beast that we survived this one. How shall we manage?"

Fatima looked around herself at the faces assembled under the palm trees and beside the spring, slack with the heat of midday and the effort of digging so many graves. A numbness had returned: the fear of living that had marked them all as they arrived half drowned on the shores of the island. Fatima sighed, shutting her eyes; the afternoon was cloudless and windless.

"Vikram said something before he left," she said. "Something about leaving before the way was shut. I didn't understand, but I think perhaps I should."

Hassan, his face wary, came toward her, wiping his hands; he had made his ablutions in the spring, and his arms and face glistened. He was wearing a clean robe that was too wide at the shoulders: Fatima realized, with a pang, that it was one of Deng's.

"I think I may have a notion," he said quietly. "But it isn't one you'll like."

Fatima reached out and touched his damp fingers. The nails on his left hand had grown back evenly; the only evidence that remained of the horror inflicted upon them was slight variations in the color of the skin beneath, where brown gave way to scarred pink and blue, as though the inks he used to draw had made their way into his bloodstream. He took her hand and pulled her to himself. Fatima breathed the scent of his hair and neck and let her head fall against his shoulder.

"I've missed you," she confessed to the folds of his collar.

"I never left," said Hassan. "My love, my love. Listen—it was my map that brought us here, so I think—I'm fairly certain—it was my map that brought the Spanish here too."

Fatima lifted her head to look at him.

"So we destroy it," she said. "We tear it up. Just as I used to do with the maps you made for me at the Alhambra—I would tear them up, and the rooms you had made for me would disappear."

There was a pause in which Hassan looked steadily into her face with an expression she found unsettling.

"We tear it up," he said finally. "But it mustn't be done here, on the island itself."

"What do you mean? Why not?"

"Because we don't want to destroy the territory. Only the way."

"But—" Fatima searched his face, which had hardened with resolve in a way that filled her with dismay.

"No," she said firmly. "You're not leaving. You're not, Hassan. You're needed here."

"I'm not needed anywhere. I have done one wonderful thing—I've brought us here. And now I can do one more wonderful thing to keep us safe. That's two more wonderful things than most people get to do in their lifetimes."

Fatima's eyes filled with tears. "You're meant to live," she said. "Why did we leave the palace in the first place? I could have stayed. I could have gone on to Morocco and borne the sultan's children and died a rich old woman, just as you said. But I didn't, because I love you more than I love any of those things."

"Fa—"

"*I will go.*"

The low hum of conversation around the pool ceased, and a dozen pairs of eyes looked up at her.

"I will go," Fatima repeated, standing straighter. "I will take one of the longboats out with the tide, into the mist, and destroy the map there."

"But you're the king," protested Mary, rising from where she sat on the lip of the pool.

"I'm not," said Fatima. "Or I am, but so are you. And Hassan, and all of us, and none of us. The Bird King is not a person, the Bird King is—" She broke off, lacking the vocabulary to continue. The sun shone on the surface of the pool, which reflected nothing but a bright glare. It was not the darkness that would annihilate all things in the end; it was the light.

"You can't go!" cried Mary, looking around herself for support. "Despite all your fine philosophy. We couldn't get on without you. None of us are angry enough to keep living, not in so strange and wild a place."

Fatima could think of nothing to say. Deng, who had been tidying the earth mounded over each of the graves, wiped his hands on the hem of his coat and caught Fatima's eye warily.

"If destroying the map would hide this island from the Spanish, presumably it will also hide it from anyone else with a mind to find it," he said in a quiet voice, tilting his head toward Asher and his brothers, who were running back and forth nearby, chasing one another with palm fronds. "No more boats. No one else saved from the sea."

Fatima wrapped her arms around herself and wished powerfully for Gwennec, willing the island to send him back. She wanted to lift

her eyes and see him walk out from between the shadowed dunes
with his lopsided smile, his sunburned brow, and say, as he always
did, the right things.

"We can't save everyone," she whispered.

"We can save many more than we have. Many more."

She turned to face him. Sweat stood out on his brow from heat
and effort; he was, as they all were, leaner now than he had been when
they arrived on the island, the lines of his jaw were more pronounced,
and the sinews of his forearms were visible. He pleaded with her
silently, anxious grooves drawn around his downturned mouth.

"Say we save a hundred more," said Fatima. "Or a thousand or
two thousand? What good will it do if the Spanish come back and
we lose them all to cannons and pikes? How many more graves
must we dig?"

Deng sighed and turned to look over the dunes at the line of
the sky.

"We will fade here," he said. "Out of time and memory. We will
leave nothing, no legacy. There will be no record of what we have
built. What is a kingdom if no one remembers it?"

Asher's middle brother shrieked and darted away from the hiss
of a palm frond, dancing on his toes and grinning through the
gaps in his baby teeth.

"It must be enough," said Fatima. "This must be enough. This,
us, each other. It matters that we lived."

"You really mean to go, then."

Fatima wiped her eyes. Asher's youngest brother came and
pressed himself against her legs in silent protest. She bent and
kissed the top of his curly head, still lush with the scent of infancy.

Her heart ached as much now that it was full as it had when it was empty, but the ache was sweeter, and would, she thought, carry her through her fear of death.

"A king must not ask anything of her subjects that she wouldn't do herself," she said. "I must go."

There was a sigh behind her. Luz stood, less pallid now after hours standing in the sun, and cleared her throat.

"Enough of this," she rasped. "The ground is already choked with martyrs. I will go."

Fatima spat out a laugh.

"Please," pressed Luz. "I can't stay here. It would be unbearable. You don't trust me enough to let me stay."

"I don't trust you enough to let you leave," said Fatima. Luz laughed soundlessly and turned away. The air picked up strands of her hair, the same color as the sand, and played with them, lifting them lightly with the sleeves and hem of her borrowed dress, so that she seemed to float, half dead already.

"Why would you do this for us?" Fatima asked in a different voice. "What about your queen and your empire and all the rest?"

Luz was silent for a moment, looking at her own feet.

"I will never see that empire," she said. "I thought I was saved. But I was looking for proof. That isn't faith. I thought Hassan disproved everything I believed was true. I needed to destroy him so I could believe again. Instead—" She paused, following Deng's gaze out toward the far horizon. "Let me have this one thing. Let me choose the way it ends."

They prepared the longboat as if for a lengthy voyage. Mary folded blankets and cloaks and bundled them into the keel; there was a packet of dried fish wrapped in palm leaves and a basket of berries the boys had picked, and several jugs of water. Luz protested that there was no need for them to waste their supplies, yet it was too terrible to acknowledge she would not use them, so they packed the boat full. It was early evening before they were finished. The day had remained cloudless: each gradient of color was visible across the sky, blue and yellow and rose, as perfect and distinct as the first moment color was born. Fatima could not take her eyes off the sky. She did not help load the boat but stood beside it, her foot on the keel, keeping it still in the restless water. Luz, overtired, sat on the sand and watched her.

"Are you afraid?" Fatima asked the sky.

"I don't think so," said Luz after considering for a moment. "I'm not certain of anything now. I don't love God as much as Hassan does, nor any living person as much as you love Hassan. I'm only biding time." She smiled a little bitterly and rubbed her eyes. "It's all right, Fatima. You needn't waste your energy hating me. There's very little left to hate. There's very little left at all."

Fatima examined the pale inquisitor. In the brilliant light, she looked almost translucent, as though the sun passed through her without interruption.

"Thank you," she forced herself to say. Luz shook her head.

"I should thank you," she said. "I'm only safeguarding your life. You're safeguarding my afterlife."

Fatima smiled in spite of herself. The tide had crested and begun to go out, pulling at the boat that leaned against her foot. She reached out and helped Luz to her feet. The map was folded inside a pouch that hung at her sash; she took it out and pressed it into Luz's hands. Luz unfolded it, tracing the rhumb lines, the outline of the coast she would never see again.

"It's beautiful," she said. "Like everything he does." She drew a shuddering breath. "Will you help me into the boat?"

Fatima pulled the prow onto the beach to steady it. She put her shoulder beneath Luz's and half lifted her over the edge of the boat, surprised by how little the older woman seemed to weigh, by how cold she felt. When Luz had settled onto a plank seat at the stern, Fatima pulled out one of Mary's cloaks and wrapped her in it, fastening it beneath her chin. Luz smiled.

"Good-bye, King of the Birds," she said. "I don't suppose we'll meet again."

"Perhaps in your afterlife," said Fatima. "If there's room."

Luz laughed at this. She folded the map and tucked it under the cloak, into the bodice of her gown. "I'm ready," she said.

Fatima put her shoulder against the stern of the boat and pushed. The water slid past her ankles, lifting the prow over an eddy of foam, and in an instant the boat weighed nearly nothing, and belonged to another realm. Fatima pushed until the water reached her waist and then fell back, shivering in her sodden robe, and stumbled onto the beach. The tide pulled the boat into itself and hid it from view. Taking up her heavy skirts, Fatima jogged across the sand toward the chalk steps; the leviathan was sleeping in the newborn shadows, its ribs rising and falling with the waves.

Fatima mounted the stairs. She could see the boat again, farther out, its sole passenger visible only as a dark blot in the stern. A pale arm was raised. Fatima raised hers in return, waving until the current carried the image from view. Then she let her arm fall and continued up the stairs toward the clifftop, balancing over the plank Deng had laid between the missing steps. She could hear Hassan and Mary arguing good-naturedly over dinner; Asher calling to one of his brothers. The wind dropped upon her from above, warm with the scent of a cooking fire, carrying with it the laughter of children.

Acknowledgments

With thanks to Warren Frazier for his unwavering faith in this book, Amy Hundley and Dhyana Taylor for their editorial insight, and Professor S.J. Pearce for her profound historical acumen.